The Kinsman's Tree

BOOK ONE IN THE KINSMAN'S TREE SERIES

The Kinsman's Tree

TIMOTHY MICHAEL HURST

The Kinsman's Tree

ISBN-13: 978-1-5215466-5-9

Dedication & Appreciation

To the one, true Kinsman—without whom this book would not have been possible.

To my lovely wife, Brandi—Thank you for your priceless support and feedback. There isn't anyone else I'd rather have alongside for this amazing journey.

To my mother and father—Thank you for teaching me to dream and for helping me find the wings to take flight in pursuit of them.

To my children—Thank you for your encouragement. I hope each of you find inspiration in the leap of faith your mother and I took in setting out on this adventure and that you find the confidence in God to set out on your own.

To my greater family in Christ—Thank you for all your prayers and encouragement in helping us arrive at the end of this project.

Glossary

General Terms

The Eben'kayah (EH-ben KAI-yah)—A group of mysterious Etom who meet beneath the olive tree in Endego
Endego (EN-de-goh)—Nida and Nat's home town
Etom (EH-tom)—A race of small, semi-insectoid creatures
Etma (ET-ma)—A female Etom
Etém (eh-TEM)—A male Etom
Gentletém (gent-leh-TEM)—An etém of noble, chivalrous qualities
Malakím (ma-la-KEEM)—The radiant servants of Lord Elyon
Shedím (shed-EEM)—Fallen, rebel Malakím

The Etom

Agatous—The Chief Counciletma of the Eben'kayah
Alcarid (AL-ca-reed)—A senior Counciletém of the Eben'kayah
Dempsey—A young etém highly involved with the Eben'kayah
Jaarl (YARL)—Nida's husband and Nat's father, now given up for lost
Kehren—The etma headmistress of Nat's school
Nat—An etém; Nida's son
Nida (NEE-da)—An etma; Nat's mother
Pikrïa (PIK-ree-ah)—Nida's Great Aunt, a wealthy and solitary etma concerned with status
Rae—An etma; Nat's best friend
Rosco—Nat's antagonist at school
Shoym—An enigmatic and kindly gentletém
Talcalum (TAL-ka-lum)—A senior Counciletém of the Eben'kayah
Tram—Rae's father, a wealthy merchant

The Supernatural

Astéri (as-TER-ee)—A messenger of Lord Elyon
Elyon (el-EE-awn)—The Creator of the universe and so much more
Helél (heh-LEL)—The villainous leader of the Shedím

Glossary (cont.)

The Humans

Belláphorus (bel-LAF-or-us)—A close comrade of Mūk-Mudón
Cloust—A close comrade of Mūk-Mudón
Imafel (EE-ma-fel)—A close comrade of Mūk-Mudón
Kessel (KESS-el)—The first Man, his name meaning 'fool'
Mūk-Mudón (MOOK muh-DAWN)—An ambitious, dashing Warlord
Parác (pa-RAC)—Mūk-Mudón's greatest rival
Pethiy (PETH-ee)—The first Woman, her name meaning 'gullible'

Prologue

Beneath the notice of Man and Beast, lived the lowly Etom. Diminutive creatures not much larger than a beetle, they bore a passing resemblance to Man in that they had arms, hands, and fingers, and stood on two legs at a mere three inches tall.

They were a hairless species, and their skin most closely resembled that of a grubworm. It was smooth, reflective, and ribbed at the joints, and was resilient like rubber, lending Etom some protection from the elements and from predators. Their skin also might range widely in color, particularly from region to region.

Though they had no hair, their heads were yet adorned with fleshy stalks, called zalzal, that varied drastically in size and shape from Etom to Etom. Much as a Man might arrange or fashion the hair on his head, the Etom did likewise, cutting their zalzal if they became cumbersome or unkempt, though not to the quick, as it was painful, or even harmful to do so.

They had two eyes and a nose nothing more than a superficial rise centered on their faces with two shallow slits for nostrils. Unlike the ears of Man, which stood out from the side of his head, an Etom's hearing organs were imbedded membranes on either side of the head like a frog's. Though they referred to themselves collectively as Etom, the males they called etém, and the females, etma.

The Etom dwelt in various environs, though their preference was for nooks, crannies, tall grasses, and hollows offering some protection from wind and weather that might demolish their tiny homes. On the grassy central plains, one such village spread under a grove of mostly weeping willows. It was in this village, called Endego, that one etma, Nida, awaited the birth of her first child.

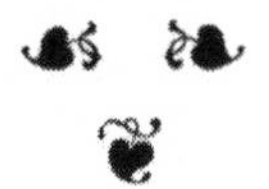

The Etom of Endego subsisted on what they could grow, scavenge, or hunt among the underbrush or low branches of trees. Trade and commerce likewise flourished among their kind. It had been while scavenging amongst the tall grasses outside the grove that Nida's husband Jaarl went missing, leaving her to hatch their egg and fend for the family by herself. Beneath Endego's singular and squat rubber tree, stood their humble home, a round, sandswept hovel with a domed, straw roof. Inside, a plentiful and bustling extended family chattered in anticipation as they crowded around the nest that stood in their midst.

From the ground up, the expectant parents had together formed the cradle out of clay, molding a stout pillar to the height of a low table in the center of their home. Across the column, they had laid sticks radiating from its center, to afterwards cover with yet more clay, forming a shallow depression atop the base. Though excited to welcome her child into the world, Nida found the nest a bittersweet reminder of her husband Jaarl's recent disappearance.

While she had yet to fully reconcile her grief at Jaarl's absence, the joy of her child's impending birth won the day. Looking to the depression where their egg nestled, Nida reached forth timid fingers to caress its surface, marveling again at its texture, at once akin to both paper and rubber. The life inside, responding to the warmth of her hand, knocked sharply against the very spot she touched, and rocked the egg slightly within the hollow.

The rounded edge of the nest and swaddling clothes laid around it kept the egg from accidentally rolling off onto the floor, but Nida still gave a startled and excited cry at the impact, a smile on her face. Such pounding and pressing from inside an egg were typical, and the pupa would continue to do so with increased frequency until it had broken through to emerge. It wouldn't be long now.

As all watched in breathless quiet, a faint glow grew inside the egg, growing brighter each time the egg shook. Evidence of the pupa's efforts came ever more rapidly, and each hopeful attendee anticipated the arrival of their clan's new member any moment now. The shaking continued for a time until, suddenly, unexpectedly, the egg fell still, and the light within grew dim.

Nida's heart plunged with dread as she imagined the worst of all possibilities. What could possibly be wrong? She resisted the urge to tear open the egg, knowing that to do so before her pupa was ready would render her child weak and susceptible to the debilitating Blight.

Instead, she cried out in her soul to the Creator, Lord Elyon, pleading for some small mercy, some grace for the moment in form of protection for her unhatched child. A deathly hush fell over the small crowd.

Those gathered perceived the answer to her whispered prayers, as almost too quietly to notice, a lilting chorus echoed forth from a mote of light on the wall. In size and brilliance, it grew, stirring the stale, crowded air within. The twinkling, shining light, now an orb the size of an Etom's head, refreshed them as it turned the sour odor of the cramped dwelling into a lovely fragrance befitting the most Heavenly garden. The wind grew from breeze to gust, and from gust to gale as the chorus rose, a swell of strength and beauty in song, scarcely fathomable.

The forceful wind parted the crowd, who turned from their places around the nested orb to face the spectacle. With minimal effort, one might escape its beauty, which rivaled enchantment, though for the wonder of it, not many might choose to do so. The wind and wordless song fell silent. Light alone now rose slowly along the curved wall to traverse the ceiling over the quiescent cradle.

In her awe, Nida had momentarily forgotten her still and darkling egg, and now recalled the tragedy with a sharp gasp. She turned to behold the wonder of the moment had touched none more deeply than her pupa, for there he was, a beautiful youngling of their tribe, his face turned up into the radiant marvel. The earlier gust had blasted the shivering husk of egg onto the floor, and the grublet stood, his smoothly ribbed, pale-blue skin now revealed as he lifted his face into the golden light that streaked over him.

While it was not uncommon that an Etom newborn might stand at birth, sight did not come to them until several weeks thereafter. A scaly, protective growth, usually lost as the child's sight strengthened, still covered the eyes of Nida's son. Yet how was it that he followed the light in its course until, directly over top him, it stopped?

So still he stood atop the cradle, inconceivably small with face upturned and stubby arms uplifted in the shower of twinkling golden rays! Newborn tears welled from beneath the scales on his eyes to fall streaming down his face. Loosely, the scales slipped from his eyes, and tumbled down to reveal beautiful golden eyes that blinked wetly in the radiance.

He smiled toothlessly, rose on his toes, and stretched himself upward, reaching into the light. As if something now lay in his hands, he drew them downward, cupping them close to his chest. In a momentary rush of wind, the light hastily withdrew, the starlit globe shrinking until it disappeared altogether, and all stood dim by comparison in the warmly-lit hovel.

Not all were pleased in the afterglow of the blessed event. While the rest of the family closed around the mother, reaching for the child—perhaps to touch, perchance to hold—Nida's withered Great Aunt, Pikrïa, skulked in the shadows. The moment the egg had darkened, a fierce and wicked triumph had likewise dimmed her countenance, but none present had attended it. She had disapproved of Jaarl and Nida's union from the beginning. The joining of her kin with unworthy stock and the incessant prattling on about "true love" had sickened her with disgust.

Pikrïa had taken particular notice of Nida's desperation, and in her shrunken soul knew the moment Nida had cried out to her precious "Maker," although she'd made no sound. She had reveled in Nida's despair, for she had warned her. Yes, quite thoroughly she'd provided her dire forecast: The humble craftsman could never provide and couldn't possibly satisfy the cultured needs of his bride. Even his children would prove as disappointing as the pittance gathered from his meager trade. More so, now he was absent.

The old monger prided herself on two things: her wealth and how relentlessly *right*, how studiously *correct* she was. Now, watching the tears pool in the corners of Nida's eyes, the hopeful mother's hands clutching for her faltering egg, only to droop in hopelessness, had Pikrïa ever been more deliciously *right?*

No, she had thought, *never.* A grim smile had opened on her wrinkled, scabrous face like baked earth cracking under sweltering sun. That was when disaster struck.

The simpering fools had turned to stare mindlessly at the wall when a horrid odor had struck Pikrïa, watering her eyes and wrinkling her nose—no, her entire face, if that were possible.

She had turned away to draw out her kerchief and dry her stinging eyes. In that moment, while turned away, everything had changed: There he stood, confirming for all that her noble line was joined inseparably with this common rabble, the solitary heir apparent to her family's house.

On top of that, the gathered family gawked with maddening delight, while she marveled at the slack-jawed expressions present even on the faces of noble-born kin.

Have they never witnessed a hatching before?

Her mouth pursed tightly as if collapsing upon itself, an implosion of bitterness and ill will buckling under all its bearer's schemes. She may have suffered a momentary setback, but she would certainly ensure the young family's lonely misery, as surely as they had caused her own.

Nida gathered up her smiling newborn to display him to the family and noticed from afar Great Aunt Pikrïa's displeasure. Filled with care for the aging Etom, she recalled the etma she once knew from her youth, before all joy had fled her, displaced by greed, worrisome suspicion, and . . . something else.

As Nida distractedly circulated through the room toward Pikrïa, excited relatives barred her approach, merrily interjecting themselves and their merry congratulations between the two. Before Nida could reach her, Pikrïa departed the home, still frowning her disapproval as she swept through the door and out into the darkening dusk of the village, leaving the new mother to stare after her with concern. Nida looked down at her son and kissed him on the brow between his bright and questing eyes, and in that moment, she named him.

"Nat," she spoke with gentle care, and lay her worries for Pikrïa aside.

Lovingly, she embraced her son, and turned back into the happy fold that filled her home. Difficult as raising Nat alone might be, at least she would have her family's support. Or so she had supposed.

In the days following Nat's birth, Great Aunt Pikrïa did grievous harm to the fledgling family, wielding her considerable wealth and influence to quash the unusual tales now circulating through Endego. The lowborn heir to Pikrïa's fortune posed a threat to the family's status, and thus, his very existence offended her, as did the peculiar circumstances of his hatching. Pikrïa coaxed, bribed, intimidated, and bullied each Etom who was present at the birth until they denounced its telling.

Soon blank stares and denials met Nida when she mentioned the strange circumstances surrounding her son's birth. Pikrïa had succeeded in suppressing the truth. Callous disbelief soon replaced the joyous wonderment once present among those who, at its occurrence, had celebrated Nat's delivery. One by one, all who had witnessed her son's arrival turned away, abandoning her to raise her son in complete solitude.

Nida and Nat were alone.

For Nida, Nat's first few years of life proved to be both the most challenging and most rewarding. Forced at times to forage outside the village for their survival, Nida would lash Nat to her back with broad blades of grass and set out in search of food. Nat's harness crossed about his body, yet left limbs free to splay and hands to grasp with merry curiosity as they trekked across the grassland wilds that encircled their grove. Many times, Nida would return home and unstrap her son only to find some delectable morsel for their supper clutched against her sleeping son's cheek. He was a treasure, and his presence a sanctuary from the constricting coils of lonely grief and longing she endured in Jaarl's absence.

The years passed, and Nat grew as healthy as any Etom mother might hope. At times Nida might observe him cocking his head to one side as if listening intently while he peered up through the leaves of their tree into the intermittent flashes of sunlight that slipped past the branches. Then he would return to his play, face serenely shining, as it so often did. Against the poverty and loneliness of the widow's lot, Nat's joy gave Nida strength, proving that happiness was possible, even as they wore little more than rags, ate little more than scraps, and slept on little more than dirt.

Chapter One

The Dawn of Life and Understanding

THE BEGINNING

The land of Gan was beautiful and prosperous, a green place filled with living things. Creatures of all kinds had lived in happiness for untold ages under the wise rule of the just and mighty King Elyon. The King was something of a mystery, and none knew whence He came. The eldest of creatures, those first born under the King's rule, remembered that He had always *been.* With newborn senses, they watched Him form all that followed, and rightly attributed the creation of their land to Him.

Though Gan was not large, its citizens enjoyed peace and freedom unrivaled in any other kingdom. The world outside their happy land was chaotic and dangerous, yet none from those troubled lands could infiltrate the walls of Gan while the mysterious Malakím stood guard.

Fierce and radiant protectors, the Malakím with piercing eyes perceived threats from afar. Drawn swords sparking bright as lightning, they swept from atop the walls on wide, resplendent wings to confront the enemies of Gan. None but the King knew the origins of the Malakím, and while they sought no glory for themselves, many among Gan's citizens counted them as heroes.

Among the Malakím, Nasi and Helél were most noteworthy. The stalwart Captain over all the Malakím, Nasi was mighty in battle and a skilled commander. Helél was chief in the King's court, with a brilliant form counted beautiful even among the Malakím. More impressive than his appearance was his voice, for from his mouth alone proceeded a chorus to rival the choirs of Heaven. At every sunset, his voice echoed sweetly across the land, exhorting all to praise the King as pleasant night fell.

In addition to the Malakím, the mighty wall that encircled the lush, fruitful land of Gan ensured its security. Lord Elyon had shaped His kingdom as a large circle, forming the towering wall, unbroken by gates to ring its borders. Just within its northern edge, a smaller wall surrounded the palace, which glittered high upon a grassy hill. Just inside the palace gates, which opened south into the kingdom, stood the gleaming Tree Ha Kayim, its white bark shining with alternating gold and silver light.

Dwelling in such abiding security and the overwhelming abundance of the King's blessing, the kingdom of Gan knew nothing of death or illness, but for a solitary exception. The stream of purest, living waters spread beneath the roots of the Tree Ha Kayim to water its counterpart to the south, the Tree Ha Datovara, which bore a mesmerizing fruit of vibrant, shifting color. From the Tree Ha Datovara, King Elyon forbade anyone to eat, stating that one who did so would surely die. In perfect contentment with the abundant life that King Elyon provided, none of Gan's creatures dared approach the Tree to pluck its fruit. No, not one.

It seemed the golden, peaceful age of Gan would continue forever under the favor of the immortal King Elyon, who blessed all within His borders with life and peace. But it was not always to be so, for strange, whispered rumors of discontent and anxious, looming shadows disturbed Gan's peace. The citizens of the land heard murmurs of a rebellion, and Helél's sweet melodies fell silent in the night.

Not long thereafter, a thunderous shout broke the midnight tranquility, shaking the land. Creatures great and small hurried from their homes, fearing for the first time some unknown and unexpected disaster might befall them. A comet of brilliant, colorful light flashed across the sky, streaking from the palace and over Gan's wall to land with bright burst and deafening crash.

A great horn sounded from the King's palace, and Nasi appeared over its gates holding his great flashing blade aloft to rally the Malakím. A great many allies gathered around him, suspended aloft on lucent wings as a starry crown about the palace. Opposite them arose a smaller group, the darkening stars of mutinous Malakím, and the potent friction of coming battle manifested as lightning flashed across the sky.

King Elyon spoke power from the heights of His palatial terrace, His light and that of His troops brightening to blinding brilliance while their opponents dimmed. Nasi sounded the charge with a shout, and the King's Malakím, shining, rushed across the sky, the wind rising at their backs to propel them forward with ever greater speed. The enemy forces appeared at first to stand ready to resist the surging wave of blazing light that sped toward them. Nevertheless, their fading line quaked, trembling before the advancing brilliance, and the battle became a rout as the rebels fled in terror with glory in pursuit.

From below, wide eyes watched the sunlight brightness of King Elyon shine forth from His Malakím to drive out the insurgent dark. The conquered sped as shooting stars over the walls, their glory dwindling to darkness dark as they passed beyond the borders, where a haunting, beautiful melody mustered them outside the wall.

A disconcerting comprehension grew among the creatures of Gan within: Helél and certain of the Malakím had attempted to take the kingdom by force. The first brilliant streak to crash outside the wall had without a doubt been Helél, ousted from the court by force of Elyon's command. The remaining traitors now regrouped around him following their retreat in cowardice. Never had Gan known betrayal, and the knowledge that traitors now lurked outside shook the subjects of the King.

The days following were full of uncertainty, though the peace and prosperity of King Elyon's reign continued. Ever aware of the wicked, rebellious Malakím outside their walls, the citizens of Gan came to call them by another name, the Shedím.

The creatures of the kingdom saw the remaining Malakím less often now, for fewer of them remained to stand watch over the land. Joyous, sweet music streamed from the palace every evening as ever it had, but Helél's voice was now absent from the song.

Instead, from beyond the Tree Ha Datovara, Helél and his Shedím in bitter counterpoint sang often a shadowy, seductive song bidding those within to join them outside. Though none desired to join Helél in his accursed song, all felt its draw, which crept in among hidden thoughts and secret desires. Like tendrils of a crooked vine it snaked among the heart's chambers to seize on what it might and drag its hapless victim away into the darkness.

Always, the song of the Shedím challenged the King's goodness and authority, whether with clever argument, open contempt, or backhanded ambiguity. Thankfully, Gan's peace and the goodness of its Ruler strengthened its people, who enjoyed all that He offered, and who recognized that the life and abundance of the land flowed from their King's provision. With the passage of time, the Shedím troubled the land less and less often, becoming a near-forgotten memory tucked away in deep mental recesses that most chose too happily to ignore.

The youngest of all His creations King Elyon had graced with a form to mirror His, and had shaped them both, Man and Woman, to walk upright on two legs as He did. To these the King had given stewardship over Gan and had bestowed upon the last of His creations the power of Speech.

It was a bounteous gift indeed, for whatsoever the Man and Woman chose to name a thing became known to all creatures, appearing in their minds unbidden. Speech flourished slowly at first, flowing as it did from the everyday efforts of the Man and Woman to name each animal, plant, and object they encountered in their curious questing.

Over time, the pair progressed to naming the natural activities of Gan, then abstract notions as well. The effect on the budding land was quite marvellous, for throughout it, crude and solitary words began to punctuate the creatures' gestures and motions. Primal monosyllabism soon gave way to the lilting rhythm of sophisticated syntax in excited exclamations, serious statements, and quizzical questions.

Conversation in short order developed into a rich tradition throughout Gan, and intense discussion into a spectator sport. A certain understanding, too, developed even among the voiceless green and growing things, mute though they remained, and they came to offer up their fruits with extended vine, stem, and branch to Man and Beast as they passed.

As the ages passed in the nurture of their land, the Man and Woman together plumbed the depths of intellect and philosophy with the innocent naivety of children, for while their age in years grew, children is what they yet remained in their hearts. For those untold years, they were satisfied, and grew wiser, free of care under Elyon's nurture.

Now, the King enjoyed long strolls in the cool of the morning with the Man and Woman, and on such occasions permitted them to ask whatsoever they desired. Often what they learned from the King became the centerpiece of conversation throughout land for many days following. From their discussions with the King, the two learned how He had created all of Gan, the world outside, and the whole of the universe, invisible or otherwise.

In the power of Creation, He instructed the Man and Woman, once more uniquely blessing them so that they might share their gift with the rest of the realm. Formed by novice hands, their first Creations were crude and elementary, plain figures and sculptures presented in tribute to the King, who was visibly pleased.

Over time, they developed greater command over the elements to shape and transform obedient earth into graceful spires with a sweeping gesture, calling up flowered vines to wreathe the spires in braided adornment with a playful twiddle of upturned fingers.

In one instance, the Woman was instructing a flight of birds in a chorus, conducting their flowing dance across the sky as they rose and fell with the tune. Meanwhile, the Man spun lacy wings like a dragonfly's over a frame of crystallized grass, calling willing spiders and silkworms to cover it in their gossamer strands. After, he hung the wings from the arched branch of a tree he had petitioned for assistance. Their design became apparent when the wind passed through them, creating a pleasing melody as they fluttered in the breeze.

The whistled note caught the Woman's attention, and with interest she came to see what the Man had fashioned. Joining in the project while the Man created several such arches at regular intervals along a winding path, the Woman called forth from the earth beautiful and fragrant flowering plants to line the path on either side. Together thus, they created a musical garden to play various tunes, depending on the present course of the wind.

The King and creatures of Gan enjoyed many such creations, and several creatures came to specialize in their own artful works as they observed those of the Man and Woman. It seemed to please the King and effect His purpose that through the gifts given Mankind, the whole of Gan achieved inspired order: birds in their woven nests, bees in their honeyed combs, beavers in their bracken dams, and spiders in their dewy webs, to name a few. Life in Gan flowed and hummed in a single, synchronous rhythm, orchestrated in harmonious movement that Elyon conducted as if the Man were one hand held aloft in steady tempo, and the Woman the other, gracefully shaping the color and texture of the symphony.

Alongside His other bountiful gifts to them, Elyon imparted to Mankind a vast capacity for knowledge, a great vessel seeking to be filled. Perhaps it was due to this capacity that they thirsted so deeply for knowledge. Thus, it was in this parched plot of their heart that the first seeds of discontent took root. For in every matter, King Elyon moved them to understand, often provoking them to discovery in shocking, delightful ways. In every matter but one, that is.

Regarding the fruit of the Tree Ha Datovara, King Elyon would only state that whoever consumed it would die. When they questioned Him what death was, He would liken it to sleep, to the setting sun, and to the exile of Helél and the Shedím from Gan. Death was the consequence for choosing to betray King Elyon and become His enemy. For the time being, the Man and Woman enjoyed the King's company each day. Nevertheless, His silence on the Tree Ha Datovara piqued the thirsting of their inquisitive minds.

Chapter Two

The Blighted Past

The sages and scribes record an impoverished history following the Sunder, in which the Man and Woman betrayed the trust of Lord Elyon by eating the forbidden fruit of the Tree Ha Datovara. In exile, they departed the shattered safety of Gan through the shambles of its walls, to establish a tribe of nomads, wandering from one sparse, yet fruitful plot to the next.

Though the Man and Woman while stewards of Gan had carried names, they lay long forgotten in the past. History instead remembers them by different names: The Man, Kessel, and the Woman, Pethiy. Their progeny mingled with those who dwelt outside, marrying, raising children, and dying in old age among the people of the wasteland.

Curiously, both Kessel and Pethiy lived long lives many times the normal lifespan of those outside, as did their children, and their children's children, for many generations until the blood of their line dwindled among their descendants. It was as if the vitality of their homeland yet dwelt within them, made finite after their disconnection from King Elyon and the Tree Ha Kayim.

The land, too, bore marks of vibrant growth in the many places Kessel and Pethiy sought in their wanderings. The streams of the Tree Ha Kayim, in a final gush, had broken forth from the boundaries of Gan, their waters spreading abundance as they passed through earth, rock, and sea to rest in distant reaches of the world.

Clear, pure waters reflected the peaks surrounding chilly mountain lakes, nourishing trees to grow straighter, broader, and taller than elsewhere. A wondrous, verdant oasis provided refreshment in the desert where before there had been none, Man and Beast alike flocking to its waters for refuge from the scorching heat. Emerald river deltas poured into the sea, nurturing aquatic creatures to immense size and unmatched savor, while the adjacent land grew crops both plentiful and delicious. Invigorating waters also passed below ground, invisibly seeping throughout the land to provide wellsprings in dry and salted plains, making life possible in the barren wilderness.

However, the destruction of Gan's walls had also unleashed upon the world Kessel and Pethiy's horrific legacy. What they unwittingly loosed became a certain and inevitable fact of life and death: The Stain. The blistering winds outside carried it far and wide upon noxious dust and sand, infecting everything.

The Stain upset Nature's peaceful balance and made enemies of those who had once lived in harmony. Not only did the wicked taint produce hostility and aggression, but it also twisted the unchecked power of Creation to equip living things with the means to act upon it. At Creation, Lord Elyon had provided all living things with the natural tools necessary for their purposed work. The Stain perverted use of these tools toward violence and rewarded those it most deeply saturated with thickest bristle, keenest vision, sharpest fang, and deadliest venom.

These were the most dangerous of Men and Beasts, and as each wielded their weapons to their own advantage and the harm of others, their Stain grew deeper still, spreading across skin, fur, and spine. The Stain etched the worst of these in patterns strange and arcane, as if branding upon its host in blackest of magic a claim for each vile act. These who had without reservation given over their bodies to The Stain became known as the Marked, each mark speaking a warning for others to steer clear.

Those most willing to enjoy the cruel pleasures of their dark gifts were granted an advantage over those less so inclined. However, their dependence on these gifts had severe consequences: The more they indulged their violent greed for pleasure, the more their indulgence demanded in satisfaction. Indeed, the twisted joy of each wicked act faded more quickly each time, driving them to commit more and more heinous deeds for diminishing rewards.

The Marked discovered that The Stain developed into something else altogether. The place The Stain had most deeply saturated their bodies darkened to an inky, liquid black. Over top the tender sore, skin grew paper-thin and transparent until it split, spilling wearily the black and noxious Stain, which dried into a scabrous, sickly crust the color of rust.

That which the callous growth covered, it numbed, and the affected area died bit by bit each day until it became useless. Such growths covered eyes, destroying sight, or a hand, destroying its use. A Beast's whiskers might grow hard, and heavy until they clacked lifelessly together below its snout. The creature, hampered and unable to maintain its balance or avoid colliding with its surroundings, was rendered senseless in a manner Men might only imagine.

In the worst of cases, the foul growth sealed mouth and nostril, petrified the joints, or drove inward through the chest, causing death upon touching the vitals. These noxious growths came to be called The Blight, and none escaped it, even among those who abstained from open wickedness and violence. Each harbored a secret Stain that over a lifetime bloomed into warted wound to sap what vitality might remain in ripe old age. Neither for The Blight, nor for the wretched Stain was any cure to be found, and each new generation was fated to pass it to the next.

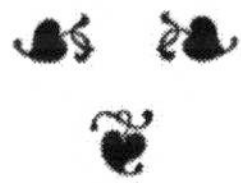

Yet the line of Kessel and Pethiy did not forget the promise of King Elyon at His departure to somehow right the wrong of their forebears through their own Seed. In the long and blighted years, they did not fail to share the history of their great folly as a warning and of the King's loving promise as a wellspring of hope. For in the cursed ages that followed, suffering was great and hope scarcer than the scattered abundance of the Tree Ha Kayim's waters.

For many long centuries, the world remained in chaos, and Man and Beast learned to gather in community for mutual benefit and protection. Although in roving bands the Marked came to steal from them, kill them, and destroy the life they worked together to build, communities persisted, growing in size and strength until better able to defend from hateful aggression.

It was these villages, towns, and cities that came to resemble the harmony, peace, and abundance of Gan before its fall, and for a time, they prospered. In time the Marked, too, discovered the benefits of setting aside their enmity to join forces with one another. For those who lived in peace, it did not bode well that the Marked formed such alliances, for their raiding parties soon became armies capable of overwhelming the defenses of their chosen victims.

Chapter Three

Warlords

ADVENT OF THE IMPERIAL AGE

Swallowing the land and resources around them, the roaming armies grew. Through battle, the victors engulfed defeated foes to grow larger still. The leaders of these armies became known as Warlords, and for many years, battles between them raged across the land. One Warlord fell to another, until two great armies remained, ruled by the Warlord of the West, Mūk-Mudón, and the Warlord of the East, Parác.

The two Warlords met in battle on the great and ancient plain of Za'aq Ha Dam, Mūk-Mudón to the west, and Parác to the east. Their contest would determine who would rule as chief among all Warlords. Thus, they gathered, arrayed in grizzled, ironclad splendor, and flanked by the grim countenances of hardened warriors and the flat, deadly stares of bloodthirsty beasts.

Though the army of Parác outnumbered the other by a large margin, Mūk-Mudón had the reputation of superior strategist and as wielder of strange, if not dubious, abilities. The armies faced off, Parác's somewhat disorganized line spreading wide in either direction to stretch over twice the breadth of Mūk-Mudón's. Both deployed archers, javelin-casters, cavalry, and infantry, Parác in much higher numbers than Mūk-Mudón, and it was upon his superior numbers that Parác tended to rely.

Mūk-Mudón, on the other hand, preferred a more agile force, able to adapt to the changing demands of the battlefield. Projecting sham impatience, he baited Parác's boar cavalry by sending his swiftest mounted forces around the far edge of a nearby mire in feigned attempt to flank Parác.

Parác's armored swine stormed into the mire, which Mūk-Mudón's forces had concealed with dead leaves and fallen branches under cover of moonless night before the battle. With Parác's main charging force sinking in the cloying earth of the mire, the armored spearmen of Mūk-Mudón advanced. Steadily they drove at the heart of Parác's assembly, whence the Eastern Warlord issued orders to regroup his battalions.

Meanwhile, Mūk-Mudón commanded unmounted beasts, those both swift of foot and sharp of claw, to beleaguer Parác's front line, which was already in some disarray. Mūk-Mudón also released his flying scouts, birds of prey all, to dart at the faces of the enemy, turning the disorder of Parác's front line into outright chaos.

Down upon the immobile boars and their riders, Mūk-Mudón's javelin throwers and archers rained sharp missiles, piercing most and pinning many to the slippery clay, grown more so with the blood spilt upon it. Mūk-Mudón watched on in grim satisfaction. He had disciplined his forces to maintain an eerie silence in battle. Only the orders of various unit commanders directing their troops issued forth from his army—and these spoke in code to prevent their enemies overhearing and predicting their movements.

It was in this deathly quiet that the frustrated grunts of swine struggling in the mire became terrified squeals carrying across the battlefield to their comrades' ears. The pained clamor of the wounded boar cavalry had devastating effect on Parác's troops. None were more affected than those on the front line already defending themselves from the swift beasts and fluttering birds that tore at them from all directions.

Parác's vanguard endured unrelenting strain to remain vigilant among the harrying attacks, the wall of spears closing in, and the bloodcurdling cries of comrades, which combined to ripen their panic. As panic reached maturity, the front line fell back in terror, and ran straight into their confederates. Some impaled themselves against their comrade's weapons, and those arrayed behind them stumbled under the unexpected crush of the retreating line.

Their panic would have become a rout if not for Parác's royal guard. Expert combatants all and clad in red, the guard marched out along the line to either side of their lord, unfurling bullroarers as they went. The guard barked at those nearby to give them space and began swinging their instruments overhead in circles wide and swift.

Among the tramping cadence of the marching armies, the low and ominous buzz of the swinging bullroarers captured the attention of Parác's panicked troops at the vanguard. The sound halted their retreat as they apprehended the whirring rally cry to turn and press the attack. With dawning dread, they likewise recognized its warning: They were well aware that the royal guard would execute any soldier falling back in the formation.

If there were not yet sufficient incentive for the vanguard to turn and fight, add to that the knowledge that their allies behind would sooner trample them in the advance than face the royal guard. The choice remained: turn and face their enemies in honorable service of their Warlord, or in disgrace fall, slain by their own.

Shaking off fear in a display of berserk and reckless determination, Parác's vanguard turned almost as one. In their sudden reversal, they spit several of their flying foes, and slashed at shoulder and flank of many a racing beast, hobbling a number of them. Prepared for this turn of events as well, Mūk-Mudón called off his marauding beasts and birds of prey, their purpose served for the time being.

From battle's start, both armies had at their fore shielded lines of spearmen. As the front line advanced, the spearmen interlocked tall shields before them to guard against the thrusting spears of the opposing force while the line behind them raised their shields overhead against volleys of piercing artillery.

A proven strategy in breaking a shield wall was to send mounted cavalry with lances charging into the line just before the armies met. With his cavalry now disabled, Parác no longer had the option of sounding such a charge. Also, his measures to prevent a mass retreat had forced his front line into a frenzied and disorganized charge that almost assuredly would fail.

Parác called out orders for the second line to form the shield wall, and for his archers and javelin throwers to send a volley to meet Mūk-Mudón's forces at the same time as his vanguard's desperate assault. The volley would strengthen the charge's flaccid impact, and who knew? Perhaps the missiles would catch some unawares.

Parác's crazed troops met Mūk-Mudón's disciplined hedge of spears to dash themselves in feeble failure by the hundreds against the orderly formation, which, undeterred, continued to advance. Parác viewed it all in smug callousness, aware that he had many thousands still to spend on victory. And amidst the persistent buzz of bullroarers, the opposing armies drew ever nearer.

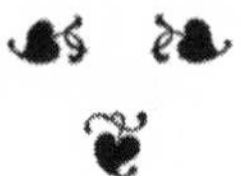

Mūk-Mudón was aware that the Eastern Forces could envelop his entire army, which would spell the West's certain defeat. In anticipation, he had prepared yet another surprise for Parác. Earlier, while sending his cavalry to draw Parác's boars into the mire, he had also sent a force of 50 war-elephants around the far side of his horsemen, in effect hiding them behind the cavalry's dusty, thunderous movement.

He had ordered his cavalry to carry the elephant's dismantled turrets, the additional weight serving a dual purpose of slowing their feigned charge to maintain their pace as a screen between Parác's army and the slower elephants. Before the cavalry had returned to rejoin the main force, the elephants had lain down on their sides with feet pointing across the mire toward Parác's forces. From a distance, they appeared as nothing more than several low and irregular grey humps on the far side of the mire, perhaps stones. In the meantime, the elephant drivers, or mahouts, had without delay pieced their turrets together on the elephants' far side, working quietly and staying low as they saddled the creatures.

Enlisting several dozen pair of lemurs, Mūk-Mudón had sent them scurrying along behind the cavalry and elephants, each pair carrying a wide plank. While the Mahouts were preparing the elephants, the lemurs had begun carrying the wide planks onto the mire with steps low and light, in silence building a narrow bridge for the elephants to cross the squishy clay.

Parác's forces had given no indication they detected Mūk-Mudón's plan. In stealthy perfection, it seemed Mūk-Mudón's plan had worked, and now it was almost time to spring the trap. The elephants lay at the ready across the mire to his army's north, his cavalry had now circled back around to wait in reserve to the south, and the swift beasts and birds of prey had retired behind the central formation to recuperate. All was in position. Mūk-Mudón commanded his army to halt.

In some confusion, Parác stared across the much-diminished gap at the Western Forces, now fallen still and silent. His massive, straggling line continued forward in disjointed movement, with commanders of the wings to the north and south prepared to swing forward from either side to envelop Mūk-Mudón's forces at his command.

Sudden, deep drums erupted—BOOM! BOOM!—from behind Mūk-Mudón's line, while in concert his army began to stomp, shout, and beat their shields in time with the drums' slow rhythm: BOOM! BOOM! Even cavalry and beast beat earth with hoof and paw, the overall effect shaking the battlefield. All Parác's army stared, half in perplexity at the spectacle, half in preparation for attack. Their attention fixed forward, they did not notice the war elephants to their right stomping—BOOM! BOOM!—across the mire.

From raised daises borne on oxen yoked in tandem, Mūk-Mudón's drummers kept their gaze on the elephants streaming over the mire, concerned only with keeping time with the great beasts to cover the clamor of their crossing. A rare, ingenuous laugh escaped Mūk-Mudón, and his attendants cast startled, side-long glances at him.

Upon reflection, Mūk-Mudón considered this was likely the noisiest and cheapest ambush on this scale in the history of warfare. Noisiest for obvious reasons, and cheapest since he paid his lemurs and elephants in peanuts. In peanuts! He let out another chuckle, this time louder and clearer, which garnered bemused glances from nearby attendees and generals.

The Warlord was in a wondrous mood today, and his cheery disposition inspired those around him. To them, he seemed almost a god, having proven himself more than worthy as a leader and commander-in-chief to even the most hardened and skeptical. He had taken in nearly all his most trusted commanders and generals after defeating their lords, and all respected him for his abilities and charismatic leadership. They believed in him, else they would not stand beside him now in battle, outnumbered 60 to 1.

Chapter Four

Provision

YEAR 26 OF THE IMPERIAL AGE

In Nida's mind, the five years since Nat's birth blurred into a single blessed, purposeful, arduous undertaking. In addition to the innumerable tasks involved in tending their home, she grew, crafted and sold her wares in the market. Love made her strong, and the joy she saw in her son helped her press forward without pity for herself.

And thus, the day arrived that Nat would join the other young Etom in the Bunker, as Endego's called their schoolhouse. Glancing in the mirror, Nida smiled at a reflection that had begun to wear with care and age. She was of average height and build for an Etom female yet bore striking coloration for their region. Her skin was fuchsia with a narrow black stripe running down the center of her body, and two black dots beneath her eyes. She kept her zalzal relatively short, not quite reaching her shoulders. The same fuchsia color as her skin, their tips darkened to black as they tapered at the ends.

Her son, Nat, though not so conspicuous as she, was an uncommon blue color that fluctuated between sky blue and cerulean, depending on his mood. If allowed to grow too long, Nat's thick zalzal were an unruly mess. They sprouted straight up from his head to twist and turn every which way as they lengthened. When he was yet a grublet Nida, had decided to crop his zalzal short. The longer they were, the worse they looked, and their resultant knotting had proven terribly painful for him. These days, Nida clipped them every week to maintain a precision flattop of thick stalks atop his great, round head.

A great and vacant grey tortoise shell served as entrance to the Bunker and lay half-buried in the earth beneath a sturdy oak, which the Etom of Endego felt sufficiently sheltered their young ones to leave them there for school. Pride and concern etching her face, Nida released Nat into the school. A bustling gaggle of youngsters meandered into the shell whence a wizened head had once protruded. Among his classmates' earthy skin tones, Nat's pale blue skin stood out until he disappeared into the Bunker's interior shadow, and Nida turned to the business of her day.

Feeling bare without her son in tow, Nida left Nat in the care of others on his first day of school, and, as was her custom, proceeded to market. While she walked, Nida pondered the familiar, weathered woven sling in which she bundled her goods for sale. Truth be told, the sling began its life as one of Nat's larger swaddling blankets and was the very blanket on which he had hatched.

It was a simple matter to wrap her things in it, as she typically did, and tie the ends together to throw over her shoulder. Its age was showing, the original brilliance of the colorful pattern now long faded, and every fiber worn to an inexplicable, yet resilient softness. She so enjoyed the sling's comfort and dependable familiarity that it had become dear to her.

"Loved," she spoke aloud, and startled from reflection by her own voice, she looked about, self-conscious, to see if anyone had taken notice.

Well-Loved, she thought. *Lovely, even.*

It was strange to consider that an object had given and received such use and care that she might call it thus, but there it was. In this blanket, she had first laid her son down to sleep, wrapping him to lay snug at her side in the darkening eve. With it, she had covered him where he lay, fallen fast asleep on the floor where he played, and with it had buffed him dry following innumerable midday baths.

After wash, it had hung in the breeze and sunshine on the line outside to be taken down and sullied again in useful care, the process oft-repeated until Nat had outgrown it altogether. Even then, its use had not expired, but instead, repurposed as a purse of sorts, it provided a different kind of nurture in bringing their goods for sale at market to feed and clothe the young family. Nida, now approaching market, chuckled quietly to herself, and wondered if she might soon begin to wear out like Nat's blanket.

Oh well, she thought, caressing the sling, *I suppose I would do well to be as well-loved as this old thing.*

Long ago she had claimed a place in the makeshift market, albeit one of the least desirable locations, tucked away as it was in an out of sight corner. What had begun as a few scavenged, knobby poles overlaid with

Lost in Thought

broad leaves from their rubber tree and lashed together with long grass had developed into a beautiful, tapestried tent.

After her first structure had almost toppled over onto her and her customers on a few especially breezy occasions, Nida had scraped together enough to purchase some proper lumber for her booth and had planted its posts several feet down in the earth for stability. Over time, she swapped the leaves for thick canvas overhead, then used rubber from their tree to waterproof it. Afterward, she had set about the painstaking process of creating the needlework tapestries that now hung about the booth as its walls.

A beaded curtain of sorts covered the front entrance, and she pulled one side open from the center to lash it to the frame, then repeated the process on the other. The "beads" of the curtain were an eclectic collection of items, most of which she and Nat had scavenged over the years, though she had purchased a bauble here and there to complement and complete the strands.

Bits of shell, glass, stone, polished wood, bone and carapace hung in the strings, seeming out of place on their own, yet somehow altogether they composed a decorative and inviting storefront for Nida's booth. Much like the beaded curtain across the front of her shop, Nida's wares, too, were somewhat eclectic.

Nida had begun her business selling anything of interest that she and Nat came across while foraging outside the grove. If she and her son couldn't put it to good use, she would put it up for sale at market.

More than all the scraps we scavenged, Nida recalled, *Elyon provided all we could have asked or imagined.* A plain and thick black curtain hung just behind the beaded one to protect the booth's interior from the elements. As she pulled it aside to enter her shop, she likewise parted the veil of history, and entered into memory.

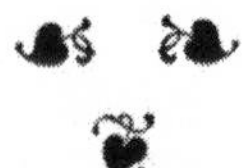

In Nat's second year, Nida had planted a food garden at home, starting with some tomato varietals, mixed greens and herbs. Given their own small size, the Etom grew small tomatoes, called among Men "cherry tomatoes" that to the Etom were about the size of a melon. Nida planted round, red ones, and yellow, pear-shaped ones, both popular and delicately sweet.

Without explanation, her first tomato crop had produced a great deal of fruit, so many that she was forced to sell them at the market to prevent them spoiling on the vine. Indeed, she and Nat had yet to partake of them before she took them to market and was thus surprised when the first few to sample the tomatoes exclaimed that they were quite possibly the best they had ever tasted, drawing immediate attention from other customers at the market.

Nida sold her entire stock within minutes, ending her day prematurely with plaintive explanations to the disappointed crowd that she had run out, and would return the next day with more. Racing home that day, Nat strapped to her back and a small fortune tucked away in her robes, Nida in tears thanked the Creator for the blessing, so joyful was she at His provision.

The next morning, she arrived quite early, dragging as many tomatoes as she could fit on a makeshift travois to encounter an impatient throng blocking her way to the booth. Excited patrons, either returning happy after enjoying the tomatoes the day before, or eagerly awaiting their first taste, gathered in front of her store.

Nida hadn't seen any sense in plunging through the crowd to reach her booth and set out the fruit to be immediately snatched up. Rather, she resigned herself to sell the tomatoes from her travois. There, on the dusty lane running through the market, she again sold out her stock, leaving still more disappointed customers when she ran out.

Not willing to lose the opportunity, she asked momentary patience from the remaining customers, and sped home to refill the travois again. Six loads of tomatoes she took to market that day, leaving her quite exhausted, but very pleased with the money she had brought in.

With a large quantity of tomatoes still ripening on the vines at home, and yet more customers requesting her tomatoes, Nida realized she would soon wear herself out running back and forth with the travois every day. With her earnings that day, she purchased a large, wooden, wheeled cart, and hired a great, trundling beetle named Raaj to pull her cart to and from market each morning until the first frost hit and the tomatoes were no more.

Her tomatoes an obvious hit with the townspeople, Nida was so occupied keeping up with the demand that she had scarcely given thought to what she might sell when cold weather arrived. Truth be told, she needn't have worried. She and Nat, her almost silent, but sometimes prattling partner, had earned a hefty sum with their first bumper crop of tomatoes, and could afford to rest while they enjoyed the fruits of their labor.

For the first time since Nat's birth, she felt at ease, and hoped he felt the same, hard as it was to tell if ever he felt otherwise, his broad smile a near-constant fixture on his bright-eyed face. They settled in for winter with plenty of food in the pantry and plenty of wood for the fire, contented with the warmth their small hearth afforded against the coming winter.

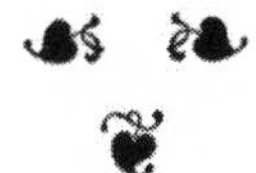

Through the winter, she satisfied herself with knitting a cap or scarf for Nat here and there between work on tapestries. With her summer earnings, she purchased yarns and threads of any color she desired, and her hangings, already known for their intricacy and quality, benefited with the additional of finer materials, coming alive with the introduction of abundant color.

Her first few tapestries recreated those tales of Gan she had heard since her youth, and, among other subjects featured the Tree Ha Kayim, its lush, verdant garden, and its mighty ring wall. She brought the tapestries down to market expecting to hang them as the walls of her booth, simply to provide eye-catching, decorative protection from the elements. The first few hours in her day about market she spent tidying, sorting, and preparing her goods for any customers who might chance by now tomato season was over. While thus occupied, a sharp gasp from over her shoulder startled her into whirling around to see whose arrival had escaped her notice.

An elderly, well-dressed genletém with skin the color of ash stood before her tapestry of the Tree Ha Kayim. He had a small Stain over his nose, and his mouth hung agape as he studiously perused the image.

Shaking his head from side to side as he admired Nida's wall, he muttered in apparent conversation with himself, "Such fine work. I've never seen its equal."

Nida, hesitant to interrupt his musings, nonetheless stepped into his view to ask, "Do you like it, then?"

He started in surprise, and turned his gaze on her, a smile on his face and his eyes twinkling with wonder.

Are those tears in his eyes? Nida considered, perplexed, before she regained herself to return to the business at hand.

The genletém, quite wealthy judging by his vestige and appointments, extended a hand in greeting, and introduced himself, "Hello! My name is Shoym. Do you know by chance who created these masterpieces? I've never seen their like!"

She took his hand, and he responded, clasping it in his warm hands as she answered, flattered by his excitement, "Why, sir! I'm the one who knit them. Do you have any interest in buying one?"

"Yes! Indeed, I do!" he responded with excitement. "Would you take 700 grains for this one here? I've never seen the beauty of the Tree Ha Kayim captured thus. As if it stands here before us. The only thing more amazing might be an image of King Elyon himself! You wouldn't, by chance, have one of Him as well?"

Nida blushed, and looked down at the floor, "Sir, I'm not sure He would quite like that. *I* couldn't do Him justice. Though isn't it true that we can yet see Him in all that's around us, and that He was never more clearly visible than in the Tree Ha Kayim and the land of Gan?"

"You're quite right, my dear," he replied. "Quite right! What was I thinking? You've given us all a window into that beautiful land of yore, and that is blessing enough. Almost brought tears to my eyes!"

So, I didn't imagine them, she thought, bewildered. She'd not seen anyone react to the tales of Gan like this elderly genletém since, well, since . . .

No. I can't think about that right now, she thought as her own tears began, scarcely under control but for the welcome distraction of the task at hand.

Returning her attention to her boisterous client, Nida set a price of 600 grains, uncertain as she was in valuing her own work, and not willing to take advantage of her new client's enthusiasm. It was clear he was pleased at the discount, and appraised her thoughtfully, a look of sincere appreciation in his shining eyes.

He gathered his prize under his arm, now rolled and wrapped in brown paper, and rough twine holding it together.

Turning back as he departed, he struck the beaded curtain with a tinkle and spoke over his shoulder, "I will certainly refer my acquaintances to you. I expect you are willing to accept commissions for custom work?"

Nida's eyes widened as she took an excited step forward, her mouth opening as she attempted to locate words of gratitude. He was already gone, however, hurrying away through the crowded marketplace.

Over the following weeks, Nida received several more such well-to-do clients, some somber, some gleeful, but all with the same familiar and breathless wonderment at her work, and all with the same twinkling gaze, their eyes wet with unshed tears. Each requested a custom work drawing on the folklore of Gan, and each paid up front, and handsomely at that.

With the glut of requests coming in, Nida explained with apologies that it may be a while fulfilling each order. Not one of her new clients showed the least impatience, instead they reassured her, aware it would be worth the wait, and that she should take time to produce each tapestry with the greatest care.

At first, Nida couldn't identify what was different about these who held such deep desire for the images of Gan, but after a while it became clear what was unique about them. These Etom *believed*. They didn't just fancy the stories of Gan as folk lore, they believed every word of the tales.

Nida had known someone who believed like these Etom did–her own husband, Jaarl, now long lost to her and her son. In wistful recollection, Nida eyes teared up as she remembered him, eyes shining, as, animated, he would recount the tales of Elyon, the Malakím, and the long, glorious days of Gan. Ever the more practical of the two, Nida had envied his exhilaration, even as he inspired her imagination to envision the tales, and it was such visions she recollected in creating her hangings now.

Word spread, and other clients besides these, these *believers,* came to recognize Nida's talents. Orders of a more generic species were born: perhaps a sunset, a family portrait, or landscape. Nida was scarcely able to recall them all, and asked clients to begin leaving written requests for their orders. She was content to receive payment at the time of completion so long as she had enough money for food and materials.

Thus, at times, she might find a small scroll of parchment attached to the stall with another order, and she'd happily add it her stack. Busy as Nida was, she and Nat passed the cold months in and out of the market collecting orders and materials to bring back to their home. With diligence, she worked to complete the requests, her young helper Nat at the ready to fetch whatever she might need. Rare was his success at bringing what she asked for, but so pleased was he to help that she enjoyed asking him anyway.

Chapter Five

Roots

12 YEARS PRIOR TO THE IMPERIAL AGE

Mūk-Mudón, besting his previous Warlord in typical gallant and charismatic style, ascended to the title of Warlord over a small camp at the young age of 18 years. In his early days as Warlord, he would break away from his forces with a small hunting party comprised exclusively of his most cherished friends as often as respite from his ambitious campaigns would permit. Mūk-Mudón valued the companionship and focused effort in tracking their prey, which coupled to invigorate and refresh the youthful leader.

The added benefit of being alone with friends was the ability to enjoy one another's company without the pretense of rank. Out on the hunt, they knew one another again: Belláphorus, the eldest and brawniest of them all, Imafel, swift and witty, Cloust, the moony philosopher, and Mūk-Mudón, the scrappy runt and youngest of the quartet.

Though he was now their Warlord and leader, the others looked out for Mūk-Mudón as a younger brother. And, seizing the opportunity a hunting trip presented, the older "brothers" would without a doubt dole out to him a ration of grief.

Belláphorus, in particular enjoyed sneaking up behind Mūk-Mudón to pinch his still baby-fat cheeks, squealing in delight, "Baby Mooks! Baby Mooks!" Though strictly reserved for their hunting expeditions, the nickname was an institution to be trotted out early and often while afield. After some years, the others reduced it to "Mooks" for their convenience, though certainly not for Mūk-Mudón's, who openly loathed (and secretly *loved*) the moniker.

After his ascension to Warlord, the familiarity was a homecoming, for it seemed the gulf between Mūk-Mudón and his friends grew every day, leaving him instead with the lonely ache of high destiny within. Perhaps if he had known how great the distance between them would grow, he might have satisfied himself with the lower climes of fate, but it was not to be so. For now, however, Mūk-Mudón contented himself with his present company as they set out once more to hunt, recalling their meetings in different times and places . . .

Belláphorus he met at a parley of war-camps when he was a mere ten years old. Belláphorus at thirteen years of age was close to six-foot-tall already, and loomed over Mūk-Mudón, a small boy for his age. A swell of red hair swept up and back from Belláphorus' milky forehead over a menacing brow, punctuated beneath with striking pale blue eyes. Despite his otherwise intimidating appearance, Belláphorus' rosy, freckled cheeks and cherub's mouth sapped some of his fearsomeness.

After their fathers introduced the boys to one another, they strode away to join the convocation, leaving them alone. As soon as their fathers were out of sight, Belláphorus stepped in close to Mūk-Mudón, staring down as his hulking frame overshadowed the smaller boy.

It would be dishonest to say that Belláphorus intended to befriend the tanned and baby-faced younger boy, whose curly blonde locks bounced a bit as they girlishly framed his face. For his part, Mūk-Mudón, unblinking and expressionless, stared up at Belláphorus as he spied the short, ornate dagger Mūk-Mudón wore chained about his neck. The knife was a treasure, bejeweled and sheathed in gold, and Belláphorus decided he would very much like to have it.

Mūk-Mudón, comprehending the focus of Belláphorus' gaze, read the bigger boy's movements as he stepped forward to snatch the dagger. The younger boy ducked under Belláphorus' grasp, diving over the older boy's bent knee. One hand trailing behind him, Mūk-Mudón hooked the inside of Belláphorus' thigh just above the knee, and pulled his upper body in close, causing his legs to whip in a tight arc as he planted his other hand just above Belláphorus' ankle. Finishing his mid-air rotation, Mūk-Mudón now fell downward, while in one fluid motion he pulled down on Belláphorus' thigh with one hand and pressed forward and up on the larger boy's ankle with the other.

All this took place in an instant, Mūk-Mudón wrenching Belláphorus' leg far outside his center of gravity. Forced to take his weight off the foot that Mūk-Mudón had captured, Belláphorus fall hard on his back behind his opponent.

Mūk-Mudón rolled with Belláphorus and continued to apply firm pressure against the ankle in one hand while pulling on the thigh in the other to torque Belláphorus' hip. Belláphorus screeched in pain, and his voice cracked as he begged for mercy. Mūk-Mudón relented, thrusting Belláphorus' leg away as he rolled lightly to the side and stood up. Turning to look at Belláphorus, who still groaned in pain, Mūk-Mudón offered a warm smile and a hand to help the bigger boy up. A look of mild surprise on his face, Belláphorus hesitated at the gesture before he took Mūk-Mudón's hand, and stood up, favoring his tender leg.

They became fast friends that day under the shade of a stitched leather canopy, chatting over cool, spiced ciders, and watched the roving war-camp's denizens pass by. Once Belláphorus was able to walk unhindered again, they spent the day exploring, playing the rough games that rough war-boys play, and dreaming together of days swiftly approaching that they would take up arms as warriors.

In their early days as friends, two things became apparent. First, Belláphorus soon learned that Mūk-Mudón was no ordinary boy, for he possessed an extraordinary, pure courage unlike anything the older boy had ever seen. Growing up in an active war-camp, Belláphorus had discerned what passed for courage was often disciplined suppression of fear or overblown anger. What he witnessed in his confrontation with Mūk-Mudón, and as the hours passed, was a simple absence of fear in the younger boy.

Second, Mūk-Mudón wielded insightful cunning to arrive at astounding solutions. Coupled with his fearlessness and apparent lack of concern for his own safety, his ingenuity often revealed itself in daring ways. Mūk-Mudón often hurtled himself not into, but through danger, considering it a calculated risk to achieve his goals. Truth be told, Belláphorus came to find the disarming boy with curly golden locks a bit. . .frightening.

Though still young, they pair had learned early the politics of war-camps and understood the value of aligning themselves with resourceful and powerful people. Belláphorus at once identified Mūk-Mudón as a singular ally, and protectiveness replaced his earlier aggression. Mūk-Mudón was exceptional, and Belláphorus predicted they might accomplish extraordinary things together.

It should be noted that thereafter the two never discussed their tussle, and Belláphorus never tried to lay a hand on Mūk-Mudón in anger again. Nevertheless, when Belláphorus' cheek-pinching and teasing was getting out of hand, Mūk-Mudón would admonish his hulking friend with a single shouted word, "Bella!" at which Belláphorus would immediately stop and blush a deep red, even to the present day.

Several years later, wandering the bazaar of the sprawling desert city Terábnis, Mūk-Mudón and Belláphorus encountered Imafel when they chanced upon a contest that interested Mūk-Mudón in an instant. At either end of a narrow rectangular pen stood two contenders: one a balding warrior, scarred all about and with a heavy Stain under his right eye, the other a slim and dark turbaned young man with sharp cheekbones and piercing black eyes.

Gracing the younger man's upper lip was a thin and wispy black moustache, which he often petted with an index finger, a superior look on his slender face. His turban, shirt, and trousers were of ragged muslin, greyed and tattered from the desert's blazing sun and blowing sand. He wore a vest and sash of emerald green, and he'd rolled his baggy trousers, cinching them at his knees.

At first glance, it seemed both contestants stood on short wooden platforms a few inches tall, but Belláphorus and Mūk-Mudón soon noticed the contestants stood ankle-deep inside curious low boxes. The men's legs seemed to sprout from the ankle stocks over the box, which prevented them from moving by design. The youth stood coolly, the gentle breeze teasing his moustache as he stared across the pitch at his opponent, who grimaced in concentration while beading sweat ran down the furrows of his brow in great drops.

Mūk-Mudón loved games, and those that combined daring, skill, and chance above all. This contest from the first had piqued his curiosity. The contenders stood about 15 yards apart with a small square table positioned waist-high right in front of each man. Inserted into slots in the table were six knives, by all appearances identical, the grips of which stuck straight up from the table, arranged in the shape of a triangle. Before the match, the judge positioned the knives at random in the table, and each player was allowed to select one of the blades at the beginning of each round. Three circular targets, each painted with a bull's eye, hung from separate ropes in a row inches above their heads, and behind them set a high wall of gashed wooden planks to prevent errant blades from striking any passersby.

Mūk-Mudón and Belláphorus watched as the grizzled warrior plucked a knife with dainty, careful precision and the youngster swiped his up without a look. The object of the game was to strike the targets hanging over the opponent's head. First to hit all three, or to accumulate the highest score before the end of the match, won.

The adversaries shifted in preparation. The youth cocked his elbow high, holding the knife by his ear and gripping the blade between his thumb and forefinger, while his opponent mirrored the pose. At the judge's signal, a noisy, clashing cymbal, the two contestants threw their blades.

The younger man threw with a fluid grace, and his knife seemed certain to strike his target. Meanwhile, the older man, with a grunt, clumsily heaved his blade. As the younger man's knife flew through the air on approach to its target, it began to fly apart, and in the end even the blade disintegrated in flight. Meanwhile, the other man's knife spun on an ugly trajectory, yet scarcely missed one of his opponent's targets, ending the first round with neither contestant scoring.

Mūk-Mudón turned aside to ask another of the spectators, a bug-eyed, toothless old man with jug ears, what had happened to the young man's knife. The old gentleman turned his gaze on Mūk-Mudón to explain what happened, his lazy left eye meanwhile drifting up and to the left. He corrected his vision, briskly pounding his left temple with the palm of his hand, which restored to him a temporary, steady focus.

Mūk-Mudón struggled through the comical distraction while Belláphorus nudged him, snickering behind his hand. Their new friend informed them that three of the contestants' six knives were cursed with ruin and would disintegrate mid-flight. Neither contestant could tell which ones were cursed, as they were otherwise identical in every way.

The young man's knife had disintegrated, but he still had three good knives in his table while the aging warrior had wasted a good blade on a bad throw. Given this fact, and the skill with which the youth had thrown his knife, Mūk-Mudón considered the younger man now had a clear advantage, so long as he was able to pull a knife that was true in the next round.

The young man's severe features betrayed no frustration as he closed his eyes and drew in a deep breath through his nostrils. With force, he exhaled from the mouth, his tragedy of a moustache stirring limply. The warrior barked in frustration, sweat pouring in ever greater profusion from his brow, to drip into his eyes. Sweeping the sweat aside with a gnarled and bristled forearm, he blinked a few times to clear his eyes, then picked another knife from the table, and readied himself as his opponent did likewise.

The brittle clash of the judge's cymbal clamored once more, prompting each to throw his knife. Again, the youth threw with a liquid ease, this time burying his knife in his opponent's right-most target, while the other man's knife turned to dust as it flew.

Rolling his eyes in frustration, the older man uttered a number of choice and unsavory words, which the noise of the thankful audience drowned out. *Children* were in attendance, after all. Hanging his head, he braced his body in tense anticipation, but of what, Mūk-Mudón had yet to divine.

The cool youth's knife remained stuck in the stricken target, which yet swung and spun. It stilled, and shifted slowly downward, the knife's added weight triggering a long-handled hammer-like device suspended over the older man's head. It swung down to strike the side of the box with a loud CRACK! Mūk-Mudón in perplexity watched the older man as he groaned in agony, his distressed body shaking, and his eyes glazing over.

"Migas," Mūk-Mudón's new friend said with a cheery, toothless smile, and pointed at the low box the contenders stood in.

Recognizing the high stakes of the game, Mūk-Mudón grew doubly intrigued. His eyes narrowed in concentration as the players faced off for the third round, the slim youth again selecting his blade. In the meantime, his opponent was in bad shape, and swayed back and forth on his feet, a slack expression on his face.

Whatever these 'migas' were, their venom seemed quite potent. The old soldier fumbled at the knives on the table, almost knocking several to the dusty ground before securing one in his grasp. As the hilt of a sword he held the knife in awkward grip, then realized he needed to throw this knife too, and turned it around to grasp the blade.

Both men cocked their arms to throw, and waited, the older man in drunken sway. The crash of the cymbal broke over the silent crowd, and the contestants threw their knives. The younger threw with familiar ease, while the older pitched forward, almost falling over as his knife flew wild. He passed near his young opponent, who, without flinching, dipped to the right. The knife flew past to stick in the planks behind him, where noisily it vibrated from side to side.

With smooth silence, the young man's knife had sunk into the center target over his opponent's head. He allowed himself a slight smirk, which the other man noticed, and lifted his wild-eyed gaze up to the blade piercing the target directly overhead.

The old warrior had enough. He cried his forfeit of the contest, begging the attendants to hurry and free him from the box before the hammer fell, all the while with eyes pinned to the descending target.

The attendants raced to open the stocks, the target hitching ever lower at the end of its rope. Frantically, they opened them, and the man stumbled forth on feet red and swollen. He managed a few shaky steps before he fell, sprawling on his face, where he remained until the attendants carried him to a cot under a nearby canopy.

Mūk-Mudón's attention, however, remained affixed to the open low box, from which emitted an angry buzzing, like a bee's hive, but darker, fiercer. An excited, burgundy mass swirled within the box until with censers the attendants administered a drooping, muddy smoke over the box. The migas grew still and quiet before the attendants covered the box in practiced fluidity, though this time with a solid lid. The judge collected the winnings, and hurled a hefty purse to the smug youth, who yet stood within his box.

With a slow and dramatic turn meant to catch the eyes of the crowd, the judge looked into each face, and called, "Who now is brave enough to challenge our champion, Imafel?!?"

Without hesitation, Mūk-Mudón's hand shot into the air, even as Belláphorus covered his face with his in resignation. It was hard looking out for this kid.

Mūk-Mudón strode up to the judge for instruction in keen awareness of Belláphorus' glare.

He glanced over his shoulder to catch Belláphorus as he mimicked slashing his throat and mouthed in silence, *I'm gonna kill you.*

The judge informed Mūk-Mudón there was a minimum entry fee that would also serve as his ante. Mūk-Mudón smirked as he reached into the leather pouch hanging from his belt and produced a thick, gold coin stamped with the likeness of some dreadful idol.

Handing the coin over to judge, Mūk-Mudón offered, "This should just about cover it."

The judge's eyes grew wide at the sight of the coin, which was easily worth a hundred times the ante. Belláphorus gritted his teeth as he watched Mūk-Mudón place the sizable bet.

Mūk-Mudón always bet big on himself, a natural consequence of the unnatural self-assurance that was both the kid's most infuriating and endearing quality. In any case, there was no sense worrying any further about it. The judge would rather separate Mūk-Mudón's head from his shoulders than part with the coin now. Not that Belláphorus would bother trying to stop Mūk-Mudón once he made up his mind anyhow.

Mūk-Mudón faced his starting position, where the attendants busied themselves over the box. The attendants signaled for him to remove his sandals, which he stooped to loosen, taking the time to observe the migas as he did. They were like ants in appearance, although burgundy in color, and much, much larger, each one about the size of a man's great toe and equipped with massive sawtooth mandibles.

They appeared quite docile now, milling about the box in quiescence. But Mūk-Mudón recalled how drastically their sting had affected the loser of the prior match. He eyed them with curiosity yet did not hesitate to slip his feet gently into the box, taking care not to disturb them as he did. He shifted his feet, sliding them with care across the sand inside the box to permit the stocks to close around his ankles.

He felt the momentary press of panic as the stocks closed, preventing him immediate escape from the migas. Self-possessed Mūk-Mudón reminded himself that the game was a contest of not only skill and chance, but of brinksmanship and fortitude. The loser might just as easily lose his nerve as flub a throw of the knife or have bad luck in selection of his blades.

Well, losing consciousness may be yet another option, he pondered, chuckling to himself.

The judge reset the blades in their positions in each table, and the opponents surveyed one another across the pitch, the sunny, golden-haired youth on one side, and the cool, dark youth on the other. Mūk-Mudón raised his hand in salute, smiling, and Imafel cocked his head to one side in incredulity.

He offered a wan and bemused smile in return, thinking, *Doesn't this fool understand the torture I'm about to put him through?*

Mūk-Mudón deliberated airily over his selection of knife, then glanced away to reach for a blade in blind comedy. Imafel, a vain individual, was perturbed at Mūk-Mudón's apparent lack of concern for his self-image. However slight, Mūk-Mudón's antics were a distraction to Imafel, causing him to almost miss his grip when he swiped for his knife with perhaps too little care.

Instead of cleanly catching the grip, Imafel somehow flipped the blade into the air before his face. Recovering without hesitation, he snatched the blade as it spun in the air before him. Imafel felt a hot, invisible flush arise beneath his deep coffee complexion. He lowered his trembling hands, inhaled deeply through his nostrils, and exhaled, his wispy moustache rippling on his breath. He repeated this a few times until his breathing grew smooth and controlled, then moved into throwing position. Pleased to finally begin, Mūk-Mudón mirrored him, and both awaited the starting signal.

At the clash of the cymbal, both threw their knives. The two throws were so alike in speed and trajectory that, zipping past one another, they cut the air over the center of the pitch in an "X," the crowd exclaiming their amazement at the sight. Mūk-Mudón's knife, however, began to fall apart as it approached the target, though the speed and accuracy of the throw was such that bits of his knife yet gently stirred the target.

The more fortunate Imafel's knife remained whole and sunk deep into Mūk-Mudón's target on the right, the tip of the blade piercing the target to show through the back. The force of Imafel's knife sent the target whipping at the end of its tether, and Mūk-Mudón sighed in disappointment, and awaited the sting of the migas.

On a peripheral level, Mūk-Mudón understood that the anticipation of the painful bite was meant to shake his resolve. Nevertheless, he was too excited to experience their sting to back down now. From the start, he'd had every expectation that he might have to endure the venom and had found the effects on the prior contest's loser interesting, to say the least.

Observing from the sidelines how much Mūk-Mudón was enjoying this, Belláphorus rolled his eyes, and shook his head, throwing his hands in the air as he turned away from Mūk-Mudón.

Placing his hands on his hips maternally, he spun back around to point a finger at Mūk-Mudón, "I'm not carrying you around on my back all day! Not again!"

Without turning to look his friend, Mūk-Mudón waved, a silly grin on his face. Imafel with chagrin recognized that this opponent wasn't shaken in the slightest at the prospect of the migas' sting. He glanced over at the large red-head on the sidelines, and smirked, happy to see another shared his vexation.

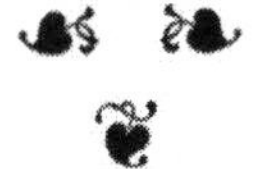

All this passed in the few short moments as the target stilled. Overhead, counterweights ratcheted, and the hammer fell. Mūk-Mudón closed his eyes, ignored the gasps of the crowd, and fell deep into his own awareness. From the outside, it might have appeared that Mūk-Mudón sought to escape impending pain when, in truth, he shuttered all other senses to focus on the agony.

The hammer banged into the right side of the box, and again the migas stirred, buzzing angrily inside. Mūk-Mudón felt the first set of mandibles sink into the flesh atop his foot, then pain exploded across his perception, splashing searing, white light against the inside of his eyelids. He resisted the urge to withdraw from the torment, and instead bent all his will on exploring the plentiful misery to discover its roots within flesh and nerves, mind and heart.

Long ago, Mūk-Mudón had decided that pain itself was not an obstacle. Rather, *fear* was the barrier to victory, cowering in consequence of pain, harm, and humiliation. This was a challenge he intended to overcome. For long moments, he endured silently with legs trembling and tears streaming down his face. After long moments, the waves of torment ceased to beat upon the shore of his awareness, and he opened his eyes to discover the world quite a different place.

Mūk-Mudón blinked once, and then again, attempting to clear his vision, which the migas' poison distorted. While the center of his focus remained for the most part clear, the edges of his vision swam and drifted, clouded in a yellowing haze.

It was distracting, and somewhat disorienting, but not insurmountable. With effort, he made out the knives before him, Imafel across from him, and the targets overhead his opponent. Shifting his focus, however, revealed more difficulties, and his focus drifted loosely past his intended target, requiring he correct his focus again, yet gently so as not to scoot past that which he wished to see.

It was a tedious effort, and one in which he would have failed if not for his prodigious willpower. Once he had affixed his focus to a target, it proved difficult to keep there, as at random his gaze might meander. After his eyes wandered a few times, the image of the old spectator striking the side of his head sprung to Mūk-Mudón's mind. He chuckled, again unsettling Imafel, who had yet to see an adversary laugh after feeling the migas' sting.

Mimicking the old man, Mūk-Mudón batted the side of his head with a palm and found it quite effective in correcting his vision. Pondering the codger's lazy eye, Mūk-Mudón wondered migas were responsible for the fellow's stymied vision. No matter. Right now, Mūk-Mudón intended to win this contest, if only to prove to himself he could, and so reached for one of the knives before him.

It was then that he discovered just how much it seemed the venom had sapped his physical strength. His right hand felt slow and heavy in reaching for one of the knives and put him off balance such that he almost fell over, and doubled instead at the waist, the ankle stocks helping to prop him up.

Strange. . .how slowly his hand extended. An interesting thought occurred to him, and he decided on a quick experiment. The crowd murmured in perplexity and impatience at the golden-haired youth's odd behavior while Belláphorus watched his friend with eager anticipation. Mūk-Mudón would succeed brilliantly, to everyone's surprise but his. Belláphorus had seen Mūk-Mudón work through a hundred such seemingly hopeless situations, each time winning through in unexpected, audacious fashion.

Mūk-Mudón felt inside his pouch for another coin. It didn't matter what kind. As quickly as he was able, he retrieved one, focused on it best he could, and dropped it. The coin, ever so slow and heavy, tumbled to the ground, where Mūk-Mudón observed the ponderous splash of sand around the coin where it struck. Uttering another chuckle, this one louder, Mūk-Mudón returned his attention back to the game, more confident than ever in his victory.

Imafel, on the other hand, was frustrated with his opponent's behavior. Having claimed victory over a number of opponents in this game, he had never seen one recover composure under the migas' venom as the strange young man before him had. It was quite common for a contestant to yield after the migas' first sting. Imafel counted on it, just as he counted on an opponents' lack of skill throwing a blade. This boy had surprised him with his cheery tenacity, and his obvious abilities in the warrior's arts. Even now, the curly-headed, blonde stranger was pulling another blade from the table. Obliged to do the same according to the customs of the contest, Imafel selected his knife, though less eagerly than before, and readied himself.

The two young men stood poised once more to throw their blades and awaited the clash of the judge's signal. With eyes closed, Mūk-Mudón prepared his mind to recognize the cymbal, which would likely sound strange under the decelerating influence of the venom. The leading edge of the cymbal's crash cut across his awareness, a slow, metallic, rasp, Mūk-Mudón hesitating to make certain of what he heard. He opened his eyes, pounding his left hand against the side of his head as he did, and found himself able to fix his gaze easily on the targets over Imafel.

Now, Mūk-Mudón had chuckled earlier when he discovered the unique advantage the venom had handed him: his mind now perceived an immense slowing of the passage of time, maximizing the potential for supreme control over his movements. Though he might not elect to experience the tiresome pain again, he found his state of mind intriguing after he had fought through to the internal clarity beyond the pain. In one sense, the deceleration made coordination of his body near to impossible. It was just too much sensory information to manage, each part of the body clamoring for attention over long, droning milliseconds.

Before the judge's signal, Mūk-Mudón had already bent his knees and set his hips low for balance in hopes that gravity would lock his lower extremities in place. He then blocked out awareness of all but his cocked arm, his fingers, which gripped the knife loosely, and the cymbal, of course. The cymbal! He had almost lost himself in labyrinthine thought but recovered himself at the swelling crescendo. Mūk-Mudón began his throw, loosening each joint in his right arm in perfect alignment, the shoulder, the elbow, the wrist, the hand and fingers all whipping fluidly under easy control, to release the knife.

At the signal, the target centered over Imafel had exploded, showering him in its remnants as, wide-eyed and still holding his blade, he looked up to discover the rope that once held the target dangling empty. In the planks behind him, Mūk-Mudón's knife stuck up to the grip. The ratcheting sound of the hammering mechanism brought Imafel's focus back to the game, and he without delay raised his hand to concede the match, dropping his knife in the sand.

Imafel had never felt the migas' sting, and he didn't intend to do so today. He was too vain to suffer the indignity of walking about on great, puffy feet that marked the disgrace of defeat. The attendants hurried to release him from the stocks, which he stepped from in relief as the hammer fell, then crossed the pitch to where the victor stood slumped over, his head down and arms hanging limply.

At the precise moment of the signal, Mūk-Mudón had loosed his throw in an imperceptible blur, the knife hurtling with such force it stuck in the wall beyond the target. Though he had felt he moved through some thick fluid such as honey, in reality his movements had taken on extraordinary speed.

The attendants gathered around him with their censers to calm the migas, and began removing the stocks while Belláphorus strode over, shaking his head. Imafel and Belláphorus arrived at the same moment to find the attendants hesitant to open the stocks. The two looked at each other, both hearing a low buzz, and became alarmed, believing it to be the frenzied migas.

As Belláphorus turned to bark at the attendants to hurry and release Mūk-Mudón, he noticed one of them motioning with forefinger over his lips "shhh." With a momentary, quizzical glance between Imafel and Belláphorus, friendship took root, and they recognized the sound for what it was: snoring!

Mūk-Mudón, exhausted from the ordeal, had fallen asleep on his feet, and even as Belláphorus supported him and the attendants released the stocks, his lower body was locked in some inexplicable paralysis. Careful not to disturb the migas, Belláphorus lifted his dear, statuesque friend over his shoulder to carry him. With a free hand and open reproach, he snatched the winner's purse from the judge on the way to the recovery area. Bemused, Imafel watched Belláphorus carry his friend away, and decided to follow, hailing him as he approached.

Imafel proved to be a worthy resource in matters regarding Terábnis and the surrounding lands. After all, he was one of the Hadza tribe, the hunter denizens of the outlying lush grasslands and windswept dunes. The Ward of Teráb had issued the Hadza a dispensation of the land surrounding the teeming city, and the tribe also enjoyed the benefits of the river around which the city had been built. In return, the Hadza, sharp of eye and swift of foot, provided a layer of protection and an early-warning system against any opportunistic Warlord who dared encroach.

After their match, Imafel felt it appropriate to offer them hospitality of the Hadza so Mūk-Mudón might recover. After all, Imafel was in part to blame for the young man's still-swollen feet. Out of the city and over sandy drifts south of the city Imafel led Belláphorus, who still carried on his back his now-conscious and talkative friend. The moon hung low and full over the over silvered sand, casting over them its blue-white light as Imafel told them of the Hadza and the land to which they were joined. Mūk-Mudón and Belláphorus soon gathered from their conversation that Imafel carried a fierce loyalty to tribe, family, and friends.

Imafel held their rapt attention as he spoke in curious, rhythmic, rapid-fire phrases about his closest friend, a war orphan who eight years ago wandered into their camp, delirious and with little more than a name in possession. It was clear Imafel admired his friend, who had learned the ways of the Hadza, though not raised in them, which was no small feat. Though none of the Hadza, nor the boy himself were certain of his age, he had seemed about Imafel's age at the time he had joined them, and the two had soon discovered the common ground upon which to found a friendship.

As they crested the top of a drift, Imafel exclaimed softly, "Ah! See! There he is now!" Beneath a slender tree atop a nearby mound stood a lanky robed figure, his head inclined toward the sky and covered in a turban. They approached him, and Belláphorus and Mūk-Mudón noted his absent expression as he gaped vacantly at the looming moon. In his left hand was a long, slender bow, and in his right, he clutched three arrows.

When they were a few yards away, the figure suddenly stepped back into shooting position, holding the bow sideways, and drawing all three arrows across the string in a flurry of flowing robes. He paused a moment to change the position of his bow in subtle tracking of some imperceptible target and inhaled sharply before letting loose his shot.

Mūk-Mudón, ignoring the pain in his feet, tapped Belláphorus to let him down, and the three strode to the top of the mound in time to hear a distant squawking while three feathery shadows fell to the ground a good eighty yards out.

Belláphorus and Mūk-Mudón gawked, and the spindly youth turned around as if he knew they had been there the entire time. His pale and doughy face broke into a great, friendly grin as he offered his long, alabaster hand in greeting, "Hello! I'm Cloust! Nice to meet you!" Blinking hard at the extended hand, Mūk-Mudón reached out, and shook it.

Chapter Six

The Rubber Tree

YEAR 26 OF THE IMPERIAL AGE

Nida spent the morning in recollection, the memories playing against the backdrop of her routine tasks until customers began to trickle in. A young mother with a wee etma not yet old enough for school was departing when the mother noticed her toddler without permission had procured one of the toy balls Nida sold in her stall. Chiding the child, she ordered her to return it. Nida knelt down, beckoning the preschooler roll it her way. As the tiny etma crouched with slow deliberation in preparation to roll the ball, Nida recalled playing with Nat at the same age, the memories rolling toward her as the brightly-colored ball did likewise.

Spring arrived, the first green blade poking up from the thawing ground as if waving a banner of exultation at the arrival of the season. Nida set about the business of planting what she was able in the still-cool earth, hoping for an early harvest. She and Nat had fared very well over the winter, far better than she had expected, and she invested now in the seeds of more exotic fare as she recalled the tomatoes from the year before. Of course, she planted tomatoes again, adding now to her garden small chilies, mint, spearmint, and, farther from the house, morning glory, clover and honeysuckle.

Mid-spring, once planting was completed, she turned her mind to their rubber tree, since its secretion, called latex, was useful in numerous ways. However, collecting more than a small amount was challenging, and required some serious planning and work. Unwilling to leave Nat unattended below, Nida decided to carry him on her back while climbing up to the first branch, which was high overhead. Etom were naturally strong climbers, but even so, to climb carrying a child was difficult, and due to the small stature of their kind, the distance to the first branch was considerable.

The harness of grass blades she had one used to secure Nat to her back after he was born had evolved into a woven harness fit with adjustable straps and buckles designed to better contain Nat as he had grown stronger, and, well, wigglier. Undaunted, Nida strapped him on her back, fastened a long rope around her waist, tucked a machéte at her side, and then began her ascent.

After about an hour of hard climbing, Nida reached the branch, and took a moment to rest atop it before drawing the blade at her side. She stuck the blade in the bark, the tree's white milky liquid swelling around it to drip slowly down the trunk, and revealing what they had ascended for, though in far greater quantity.

Untying the rope from around her waist, she cut a segment maybe four times the length of her body, one end of which she secured around the branch, then removed Nat from her back. Taking the loose end of the length of rope, she looped it through the straps of his harness, then passed it around his chest, and back through the straps to tie it off, creating a swing for him. With care, she lowered him down from the branch to where he dangled, happy as he swung and spun about.

She removed her blade from the tree and wiped the milky goo from it before returning it to her side, slipping it through her belt now the rope was out of the way. The remainder of the rope she tied around the branch as close to the trunk as she was able. Afterward, she passed it under one leg, then over and behind the opposite shoulder to grasp the dangling end in her hands in preparation to rappel down the tree's trunk. Nida stepped backwards down the side of the branch, pausing a second to glance over at her son, who smiled at her before returning to whatever inscrutable game it was that he played swinging far above their home below.

Nida turned, stepping out toward the trunk while pushing off the branch with her other foot, and releasing the tension on the rope to drop down gently against the trunk. Starting several body lengths beneath the branch, she began cutting straight down the trunk with the machete, difficult work but for the sharp edge of the blade in hand. She lowered herself a bit at a time, tying the rope off to itself as needed to free up both hands in difficult spots. Continuing down the trunk, Nida stopped her descent before the tree began to broaden at its base.

She put her blade away, and ascended on the rope, a much easier climb than her first, but taxing nonetheless. She stopped her ascent at the top of her cut beneath the branch, and carefully picked her way around the trunk to the left, cutting upward at a gentle slope as she went until she had described a spiral about halfway around the tree.

Aiming for the base of the tree, she rappelled, swinging around the trunk back to her right, and loosening the rope more than intended. Combined with her lateral movement, the sudden drop took breath away. Extending her feet to brake herself, she skipped and skidded to a halt a short way around the trunk, eyes wide with shock and exhilaration, and breathing heavily before an astonished grin spread across her face.

Her eyes still shining, Nida's grin turned mischievous. She gritted her teeth and took a few steps back to the left, her back toward the ground. Pausing for an instant to take a deep breath, she turned sideways, facing down and to the right while coiled in a low crouch. Springing forward, Nida released slack from the rope, and sprinted down the side of the tree in large bounds, with loud whoops of joy. It was thrilling to leapfrog a knothole or somersault away from the tree to continue her wild high-speed dash down the tree.

She arrived back at the base of the tree in a matter of seconds, opting to touch down altogether on the ground for a moment to rest, her body trembling with excitement. She swore she heard Nat high overhead cheering her plunge down the tree. She looked up and found him animated and turning about in his harness while he waved for her attention.

She waved in response and gathered herself again. From the base of her first, vertical laceration, she began another spiral cut around the tree to the left, roughly parallel to the one at the top. Nida swung back to the right, and from her starting position beneath the branch, she again climbed the rope to where Nat awaited her. When she reached the branch, she retrieved Nat to share a bite of lunch with her.

While they ate, Nida marveled at her son, who didn't seem the slightest bit afraid on their adventure, and who didn't stir from the place she had set him for their meal. Though for safety she kept him strapped into his harness and tied to the tree, it made *her* nervous to have him up here with her.

They enjoyed their lunch before she carefully lowered him again, promising to hurry so they could head home and take a bath before supper.

"Baaah!" he shouted, throwing back his head with a smile and clapping his hands.

Nat liked baths.

Nida smiled at him, and prepared herself to climb again, heading off the side of the branch, and traversing sideways to the upper end of her first spiral cut. From it, she cut straight down, aiming for the end of her other coiling cut near the base. It was by no means perfect, and she ended a bit to the side of the lower laceration, but she quickly rectified the problem, extending each cut until the two intersected.

Nida scurried up to insert her knife at the upper left corner where the vertical cut met the angled cut, prying the bark open to separate the top layer from the tree. With her blade, she peeled a long sheet of curling bark all the way down to the bottom of the lacerations at the base of the tree, exposing a wide spiral of the tree's tender flesh where the latex-producing vessels resided. From the lowest point of the open swath, she extended the first vertical cut beneath the branch nearly to the ground. Afterward, she gouged a semicircle deep into the bark at the bottom of the cut, then shaped a short spout out of the peeled bark, whittling it down to insert into the curved gouge.

While back on the ground, Nida let go the rope and pulled a wash bin over to the tree, placing it beneath the crude spout. Taking up the rope again, she ascended to the lower corner of the open swath, walking to the left along the narrow, coiling shelf created now the bark was gone. Holding the rope tight in one hand, she cut the tree's open flesh a bit deeper as she passed.

Milky latex slowly began to flow down the slanted track she had created until pouring off the spout into the wash bin below. Cutting the length of the spiral's lower edge until she reached its end, looked back to Nida see the tree was soon producing quite a bit of the latex. Taking care to avoid the sticky flow, she walked back to the right until she was back beneath their branch, then climbed up to retrieve Nat. She strapped him on her back and left the length of rope for his swing attached for another time.

Excited at her success in tapping the rubber tree, and grateful that no climbing remained for the day, Nida rappelled straight down trunk in large, gleeful bounds. Nat laughed wildly with each sudden, swinging drop until they arrived, safe on the ground.

Nida unstrapped Nat and removed him from the harness to join her at the wash bin, which was close to full of yellowish-white goo. Looking around, Nida went to grab an empty rain barrel and replaced the wash bin under the languid, off-white stream. Already, the flow had slowed so much that Nida was not concerned it might overflow the barrel before it stopped. She remembered hearing from a friend at the market, Granna, that the first few day's batches wouldn't be much good and turned to dispose of the latex in the wash bin.

"Baaaah!!!" Nat exclaimed from inside the wash bin, where he sat, contented, fully clothed, and covered to his neck in latex. Nida's mouth fell open, unsure whether she should scold the child or join him in his play. Seeing how jubilant he was in his bath, Nida could no longer suppress the smile she felt in her heart.

She went to him, and joined him in exploring the strange liquid, which had already begun to rubberize around the edges of the tub where it dried. They played with the latex, dipping a hand into it and letting the sticky liquid dry on their skin before peeling off the rubbery, glove-like second skin the drying latex created. As Nida recalled from her earlier conversations with Granna, the first several batches of latex from a fresh tapping were of poor quality, and the dried latex soon became brittle, then crumbled. No matter. Nida knew the latex needed to be tempered in various ways to be of proper use, which she would do once the quality improved with successive harvests, regardless.

Nida pulled a protesting Nat from his "bath," and drew another, this one of water. Thankfully, Jaarl had diverted a small channel from the nearby stream when they had built their home, so it was a simple matter to fill Nat's bath using a bucket. After undressing Nat, Nida put him in

Nat Takes a "Baaaah!!!"

the tub and found it easy to remove the sticky goo with some soap and water.

She pulled him out of the water and wrapped him in his favorite blanket to warm and dry him, then threw his clothes into the bath water. Without much effort, the latex detached from the clothes, though it had soaked into the weave of the garments. Nat didn't have many clothes, and Nida hoped that the latex wouldn't have discolored them once they had dried. In the deepening twilight, she hung his things to dry on the line outside and turned to the task of preparing their supper. Nat shuffled in behind her, wrapped in his blanket as they went into the house, the smoke of their stove chuffing homily from their chimney as Nida stoked the fire.

The next day, Nida found harvesting much easier now she had tapped the tree. Using the rope she had attached on her first ascent, she climbed the tree over the next three days to peel the rubbery, dried latex from the cut in the tree's trunk, and made a shallow incision where the cut lay to start the latex flowing again.

At the base of the tree, she busied herself catching the liquid latex in the barrel below, discarding it immediately, and taking extra care not to leave Nat unattended with it lest he take another bath in the sticky stuff.

The day after Nat had dipped himself in it, much of the latex flaked from his garments once it had dried. Nida had shaken the garments, and rubber bits flew from them, leaving nary a trace of it. Though she was pleased that the latex had come out of the fabric, the scenario set Nida's mind abuzz with fresh ideas how she might use it.

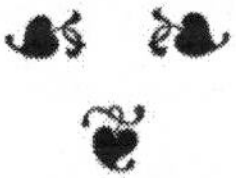

On the fifth day of harvesting, the latex flowed a purer, whiter color than that from days before, signaling its readiness for use. Instead of discarding the latex, this time Nida covered the barrels in which she had collected it to keep it from drying out prematurely. She then carted the latex over near the house, where she had set up a low work table, and had placed a few utensils and a bucket upon it.

Taking a large metal ladle, she filled the bucket with latex from a barrel. Nat, on his tip-toes, and hands gripping the table for balance, peered over the edge with only his wide, golden eyes and the top of his smooth, pale-blue head visible as he watched his mother. Nida, determined to put the latex to use, but unsure just how, experimented with the latex in the bucket.

First, she took a small spoon and placed some latex in her mouth. Its flavor was bland, and the flexible, gummy gob soon turned into firm, beady masses. She was certain from her conversations with Granna that the latex wasn't poisonous, and the taste wasn't bad, but its gritty texture in her mouth was so phenomenally unpleasant, that she spat the pea-like, hardened latex out of her mouth rapid-fire, the projectiles ricocheting off the table in Nat's general direction. He squealed with delight as he ducked under the table to avoid the barrage. Some excitement at last!

Nida, cocking her head in thought, tried to recall all that she'd learned, remembering that Granna said the latex would need either heat or combination with another ingredient to become useful.

"That's it!" Nida exclaimed, grabbing a knife from the table, which she held point-down, of course, as she hurried across the yard to the flower garden.

"I knew I planted these for a reason!" she said to herself, gripping a large stem of the morning glory vine, and cutting it free from the rest of the plant.

She wasn't a fan of the fast-growing vine, given its propensity to take over portions of the garden, and had sewn it sparingly far away from the food garden for this very use. Haphazardly dragging the severed length of vine behind her, Nida arrived at the table, and put her knife down. Holding the cut end of the vine over the latex in the bucket, she massaged it with both hands, squeezing a few large drops of pungent juice into the latex, and stirring the mixture with brisk strokes until the juice had disappeared altogether into the blend.

Bracing herself, she took another spoonful of the blended latex, which this time remained gummy, though it was a bit thicker than it had been before. Nida chewed on it for a few moments, the sensation not unpleasant, before it began to break down again into firm, lumpy masses. Grabbing the metal ladle again, she dipped it into the mixture until almost full, then walked it into the house, her hand beneath it to catch any drips.

Once inside, she poured it into a small pot on the stove and stirred it with a long-handled spoon while it heated. When it had noticeably thickened, she removed the pot from the heat, and took it outside. She gathered a spoonful from the pot, blowing on it until she believed it had cooled enough to try again. She placed the spoon of latex in her mouth, discovering solid mass too dense to chew. She spat it out and considered where she might have made a mistake.

Nida shook the hardened rubber wad from the pot, and Nat followed its fitful bounces along the ground with his eyes. Nida went straight to the barrel of pure latex and ladled several scoops into the pot. She took it inside to the stove, once more heating and stirring the latex until it began to thicken.

Returning outside, she took a spoon of the heated, pure latex, blowing to cool it before she tasted it. This time, she encountered a smooth, chewy texture that did not lose its flexibility, even after several minutes of chewing.

"Fantastic!" she shouted with enthusiasm, her lips smacking around the mouthful of gum.

"'Tastic!" Nat parroted, unsure why his mother was so excited, but happy to join in her celebration.

Not satisfied with the blandness of her chewing gum, Nida went for mint, spearmint, and a chili from her garden, and from her kitchen gathered a clay jar of honey and two wooden bowl. In the bowl, Nida pressed the mint and spearmint with a pestle, then poured some of the honey over the herbs, creating a sweet, minty concentrate. Next, she cut open the chili, scraping the flesh and seeds into another bowl, and repeating the same process she had used on the herbs, added honey to make a sweet and spicy concoction.

Nida filled another pot with the pure latex from her barrel, several ladles worth, and took it inside to her stove, where she stood several minutes stirring until the latex thickened. She left it over heat a moment longer to thicken it a bit more than her unflavored batch.

Nat in tow, she hurried outside once more to her bowls, pouring about half into the minty blend, and stirring it to ensure she produced an even mixture. She then let it rest and turned to the repeat the process with the chili blend.

Nida was happy she had left the latex on the stove a moment longer to further thicken it, as the honey thinned once the hot latex touched it, which thinned the final mixture as well. She knew each blend would firm up as they cooled but had wanted to make certain the gum would still be as pleasantly chewy as her unflavored batch had been. She lifted Nat to look over the bowls of latex as they cooled, and he sniffed the air, the appetizing scent rising on the air and his hungry drool falling to the table.

After a few minutes, Nida couldn't restrain herself any longer. She took a small spoonful of the mint gum, which was still quite soft, blew on it, then tested the temperature and texture with her finger, finding it now much cooler and more resilient. She looked at Nat, winked, then put the spoon in her mouth, hoping for the best. Sweet and refreshing flavor filled her mouth as she happily chewed the gum. Desiring to share her discovery with Nat, she took another spoonful from the minty bowl, blowing on it until she thought it cool enough for him, then offered it to him on the spoon.

Nat looked down at the gum, cross-eyed, and wrinkling his nose before he chomped down on the proffered spoon, surprising a laugh from Nida, who exclaimed "Don't eat the spoon, Nat! Just the gum!" as she attempted to extricate the spoon from between Nat's teeth.

One hand braced against her son's great blue forehead, Nida managed with the other to rescue the spoon from his mouth. Meanwhile, he began to chew the gum with great gusto, opening his mouth wide as he loudly champed the tasty treat. It was obvious Nat also enjoyed the gum. Nida watched him for a second, his enjoyment evident from his greedy mastication. He paused with mouth and eyes closed, his head at a slight upward tilt, and swallowed the gum with a loud gulp.

"Noooo!" shrieked Nida, unsure how his small body might process the gum, or if it would at all.

Nat, eyes wide at his mother's shriek, froze in place, looking sidelong at her, unsure what to do. Flummoxed at what she might do with her son now he'd swallowed the gum, which doubtless wasn't for eating, she decided she just needed to keep an eye on him.

Hopefully, nothing harmful would befall him, but there wasn't anything she could do about it anyhow. She decided not to worry about it and left her concerns in Lord Elyon's hands.

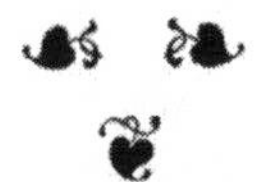

They finished up outside before lunch by spreading the gum flat across a rubber tree leaf to cool, keeping the batches separate, of course. Nida cleaned up her utensils and took them to soak in a dish tub while they ate.

They enjoyed a lunch at their leisure, Nida content with the result of the morning's experiments. She could sell the chewing gum at market and had a plethora of other uses in mind for the latex besides gum. Nat seemed his usual self as he ate, so Nida was no longer much concerned that he had swallowed the gum. She would keep it in mind as they went about their day, but for now, she was too excited figuring out what else she might do with the latex to stress about it.

Gathering the now-clean utensils from the countertop where they dried, Nida took Nat back outside to her workspace, where he occupied himself by playing with the oblong rubbery wad she had knocked from the pot before discovering how to temper the gum. He would throw the wad and then chase its unpredictable bounces around the yard.

Entertainment for hours, Nida thought, a dry smile on her lips before she turned back to her work.

Nida busied herself cutting the chewing gum, now solid and dry, into long strips, which she halved, and folded over to make paired sets of "gum-sticks." After making all the gum into sets, she cut the leaf down into strips of appropriate size to wrap the gum, tying a string around each wrapped packet to hold it together. Her mind wandered contentedly while she performed the menial task until Nat's play in the yard inspired a new idea she thought might work.

After finishing up with the chewing gum, she tucked it away in the house, and gathered more morning glory. Again, she squeezed the juice into the latex, which she had poured in a much larger pot. Stirring it all together as she walked to the house, Nida carried the pot back to the stove to heat the mixture. She waited for it to thicken as she stirred, unsure just how thick she should let it become before pouring it.

In the end, Nida erred on the side of caution, allowing it to just begin thickening before removing it from heat. She plucked two identical, round wooden bowls from the cupboard on her way out the door to the worktable, where she set them down, and filled them to the brim with the latex. Keeping a close eye on the latex in the bowls while she continued to stir the pot, she noted a slight discoloration along the edges of the bowls, where the latex had begun to solidify as it cooled. She inserted her knife between the bowl's edge and the rubber, to confirm it had indeed solidified along the edge. Working around each bowl's perimeter with the knife, Nida loosened the rubber from the bowls as it cooled, pushing the knife deeper with each pass around.

Seeing that the rubber "shell" around the cooling latex in the bowls had thickened, Nida jabbed the "skin" that had formed atop the bowls of latex, the viscous liquid oozing from the perforations. She then took a large dab of the still-soft latex from the pot and spread it over top one of the bowls to comingle with latex that oozed out. She took the other bowl and carefully turned it over, setting it atop the first, and pressing down on the bottom of the upside-down bowl to secure a complete seal between the two.

Nida watched the edges where the bowls met for any latex that might come oozing out, prepared to cut it away with her knife before it solidified. After a few moments, she saw that none was forthcoming and relaxed before delicately turning the whole arrangement over.

Tapping on the bottom of the bowl with the back of her knife's blade beforehand, Nida lifted the top bowl away with both hands, uncovering a solid, smooth, round mass resting in the lower bowl. Taking the bowl in her right hand, she carefully passed the round, rubber ball into her left hand, and checked the seam where the two halves joined for signs of separation. It appeared that the centers of each half had been just soft enough when joined that the latex inside each half had met and bonded together, forming a cohesive core that still needed to cool some before it was ready.

So intent was her focus on the ball she created, Nida had forgotten about Nat.

From behind her she heard a quizzical "'Dis?"

With the ball in her hands, Nida turned toward her son, whose mouth formed a persistent "O," as he gazed in wonder at the ball in her hands. Then, rather disappointed, he looked down at the irregular rubber lump in his own, which he threw down to the ground before pointing at the ball in Nida's hands.

"'Dis!" he said again, with a forceful scowl.

Nida chuckled at his brazen behavior, shocked that her laid-back son was suddenly so assertive.

She insisted, "Nat, please be patient for a few minutes while the ball cools. Then you can play with it. I'll *want* you to play with it then."

She couldn't think of a better way to test the ball's resilience than handing it over to her son. Still scowling, and with lower lip protruding, Nat looked down at the ground in apparent meditation, before he took a deep breath, chest rising and shoulders shrugging as it filled him.

Looking up at Nida with an understanding look that almost brought her to tears, he said, "Otay, Mama." Eyes wide, he pointed again at the ball, "Baw?"

Nida responded, "Yes, son. This is a ball, and it's close to ready for you. Would you like to come look? Just don't touch, please." His usual, brilliant smile breaking across his face, Nat toddled forward to examine Nida's experiment alongside her.

The ball had cooled to a light and dirty yellow-orange, and since the bowls were a tad taller than they were wide, the imperfect mold had formed a somewhat oblong ball. Chips and other irregularities inside the bowls had also left their marks on the ball, leaving random dimples here and bubbles there.

Though the ball was far from perfectly circular or unblemished, Nida was nonetheless proud of what she had made, and thanked her

Creator for providing the determination, intelligence, and resources to make it. Along with the chewing gum, the ball represented yet more opportunity for her and her son, another wall erected around their fortress of hope against the onslaught of poverty, despair, and loneliness that had threatened from the moment Nat was born.

Giving the ball a gentle squeeze, Nida determined it was ready for a true test. Stepping back several steps from her son, she signaled for him to put his hands out and receive the first toss. Nida's throw was true, but she underestimated just how springy the ball was. The ball bounced off Nat's forearms into his unblinking, smiling face.

Nida expected perhaps some tears, but Nat instead giggled with glee, and took no notice of the impact to his face, but rather embraced himself in delayed reaction as he tried to capture the ball. Hysterical, Nat chased the ball, finally snatching it up with the clumsy, deliberate care common to the young and disproportionate.

Nida urged her son to toss it back, smiling brightly now herself until she noticed the impish gleam in Nat's eye. With a jealous, sideways look, he clutched the ball, hiding it behind him. Bemused, Nida planted hands on her hips, her mouth falling open in disbelief at her son's nerve.

Nida took a few steps toward Nat, threatening him in jest. Her threats fell silent when he bolted away, shrieking joyfully as he held the ball overhead in triumph. Nida gave chase, sprinting after him to catch him up in the air. They both fell to the heathy earth, laughing breathily from the exertion.

They played past sunset without a care, their frolicsome shouts and exclamations echoing about their garden beneath the rubber tree. Finally, they turned in for a hearty meal, and fell afterwards into a deep and restful sleep, exhausted.

The din of activity outside Nida's stall drew her back to the present. Although lost in recollection, she had yet managed to complete her morning routine, and had successfully prepared for the day's business, so familiar she was with it. In the afterglow of pleasant memory, Nida conducted her affairs, the day flying by in a happy haze until the hour arrived for her to close shop and walk her son home from the Bunker.

The first day of school! she thought, with glee. Excited to hear about Nat's day, Nida tidied the shop and secured the entrance before bustling off to meet him.

Chapter Seven

A Fated Hunt

9 YEARS PRIOR TO THE IMPERIAL AGE

In his third year as Warlord, Mūk-Mudón's campaigns brought their army west into a wild and wooded land. As they were often in distant and unfamiliar lands, hunting expeditions also provided an opportunity to explore and to discover exotic creatures.

After subduing the local Warlord and some roving bandits, Mūk-Mudón, as was his tradition, struck out on a hunt with his companions, Belláphorus, Imafel, and Cloust. Past fragrant, flowered meadows, through crisp, clear brooks, and over jagged, unyielding stone they traveled for two days, tracking an elusive mob of what they believed to be deer, for they had yet to lay their eyes on them.

Though their days were full of intense effort spent seeking their prey, their nights on were a time of recreation, mischief, and storytelling. It was on the second night of their hunt, the voices of his companions carrying into the wilderness around their camp, that Mūk-Mudón slipped away, strangely drawn into the wood.

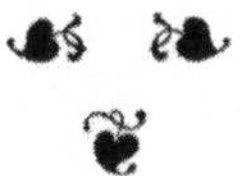

At first, he thought he just imagined a lilting tune drifting along the breeze but followed in the direction he believed held its source. As he did, the song became louder, and grew clearer until he was able to ascertain its increasing complexity as new instruments joined in, and then a voice singing unintelligible, yet somehow wonderful words. He quickened his pace, desiring to understand the song's substance, and meanwhile noticed a brightening of the forest around him. It was as if the moon shone full, though the New Moon was just past.

Mūk-Mudón broke into a clearing to discover a shining, brilliant creature hovering several feet above a nearby low and rocky rise. Though in appearance much like a Man from head to waist, the creature held himself aloft on two of six large, glittering wings while covering his lower body with another pair. The third set of wings waved gracefully through the air, casting the same silver light that emanated from his body, their movement producing the mesmerizing symphony that drew Mūk-Mudón there.

He had never witnessed such a spectacle, and though the creature appeared male, his face was the most beautiful that Mūk-Mudón had ever seen. The strange being yet remained with face lifted to the sky, and with eyes closed, seemed to take no notice of his guest.

Suddenly, and with eyes still closed, the wingéd one flew straight at Mūk-Mudón, then swung his head to face him. Mūk-Mudón fell back, startled, as the creature approached. Fluttering to a stop, he languidly opened his eyes, levelling a half-lidded, ruby gaze on Mūk-Mudón. Straightening one of his curious, waving wings, he extended it toward Mūk-Mudón in a delightful shower of light and sound.

"What is it you most desire?" he asked Mūk-Mudón in pleasant polyphony.

Without hesitation, for he had most desired the same thing from an early age, Mūk-Mudón answered, "The power to rule!"

"Oh? Is that all?" the creature answered. "It appears you rule many already..." the creature's voice trailed off in disinterested reverberation.

"No!" shouted Mūk-Mudón, "I mean to rule it all!"

"Ah! Now that's a bit more interesting," the being answered with approval. "How do you intend to manage that? And why?"

Passion in his voice, Mūk-Mudón answered, "The chaos of this world. The disorder. It's all just such an infernal mess of violence and murder. And everyone just does what he or she pleases. I want to put it all in order and give everyone a purpose. I intend to become Warlord over all Warlords and unite everyone to put this world aright."

The wingéd creature spoke again, "Indeed. A noble goal. I have decided to help you. You will indeed come to rule this world, and I will ensure you do. Here! Pluck one of my feathers. You will know what to do with it when the time comes. As a sign to you that what I've told you is true, you alone of your party will find and slay prey on the morrow."

Mūk-Mudón reached forward to grasp a feather from the extended wing, finding it silky and ethereal. He tugged gently on the wing. Cool sparks flew before his eyes and tinkling chimes struck his ears as the feather loosened from the wing. Gripping the feather in his hand, he fell back, the sparks blooming and blinding him, while in his mind, the tinkling chimes grew to a crescendo.

The combined effect stunned him, and he squeezed his eyes shut in reflex. Pressing on his eyelids with thumb and forefinger, he then shook his head to clear the daze. When a moment later he was able again to open his eyes, he looked down at the shimmering feather in his hand and recalled the strange wingéd creature.

Gasping, he glanced up at the now-empty spot where the creature had floated, and, whirling about, found himself alone in the clearing. From the path behind him, he heard the concerned calls of his friends. Mūk-Mudón slid the feather down inside his boot, not yet certain what to make of it, and equally unsure if he should share details of the encounter. He jumped up, renewed, and turned to race down the path, his voice receding into the night as he answered his companions' calls.

The following morning found them breaking camp with the dawn, the clear light drifting between the surrounding trees to illuminate their efforts. They moved with military precision, packing gear and provisions into tightened bedrolls, leaving nothing astray to hinder movement or sound warning to potential prey.

While the others refreshed themselves at a nearby stream, Mūk-Mudón alone remained behind at camp, following the early progress of the sun absent-mindedly as he pondered the events of the night before. Reaching into his boot to retrieve the feather, he stroked it, pulling the feather through a thumb and forefinger in meditation. As he did, a whisper of the creature's song sounded in his mind as if to stroke the feather was to strum a mystical instrument whose song only he could hear.

After a few moments harking to the music, on a whim he pulled an arrow from his quiver, fletching it with a thin cord and the strange feather, which, clumsy and nonsensical, dangled from the shaft.

He chuckled to himself, perplexed at what he had done, *By no means should this arrow fly straight.*

With care, he loaded the arrow back into his quiver, nock and feather end down, nestling it among the other arrows to prevent him from carelessly grasping the arrowhead. When the others returned, he stood, prepared for the hunt, and in good cheer they set out on the quest for their quarry.

For the first few hours of the morning, they moved together as a group, seeking sign of prey. As the morning lengthened, however, they grew frustrated at the lack of apparent game in the woods, and decided to split up, spreading themselves out in a line several hundred yards across as they moved forward through the woods in search of prey.

Since the first to claim a kill, of course, earned bragging rights for the day, all were eager and focused on the hunt. Mūk-Mudón, spread well to the right end of the line, and meandered down the shallow, ferny slope of a canyon, having located a stream running down the canyon's center. He stooped, filling his skin from the stream with one hand while he cupped his other and drank, looking up the canyon toward the source of the stream.

It was perhaps the clearest, crispest draught he'd ever drank, and it refreshed him immensely. He focused, catching a flash of movement at the end of the visible canyon. He reached for his bow, and following again inexplicable intuition, took the upside-down arrow from his quiver, to hold in hand alongside his bow.

He trod alongside the stream, following alongside it up the canyon. Mūk-Mudón glanced about, seeking sign of quarry, and was not disappointed. In the soft, wet earth of the stream-bank, a trail of clear hoof prints led away along the stream's edge, and over the rise at the head of the canyon. The stream babbled over the clean, grey stones of the gentle falls that spilled over the rise as Mūk-Mudón stealthily scaled it, ever focused forward for sign of his prey.

Surmounting the rise, Mūk-Mudón paused to survey the area. Before a mossy tree, the stream lay wide and shallow, a silver sheet spread beneath its roots. Mūk-Mudón had located his quarry, a fallow deer buck straddling the roots at the head of the stream, his graceful head bowed and adorned with a crown of sweeping, flat antlers.

Mūk-Mudón fitted his unwieldy arrow to string, where, drawn to his ear, the feather sang its quiet song again. Mūk-Mudón, hesitated, admiring the buck, its dappled flank glowing a faint golden green. He took stock of the beast, which appeared to be in his third year, a sorrel.

At the thought of taking aim with his weapon, Mūk-Mudón sensed a sudden warning in his heart, *Stop! Go back!*

He balked, lowering his bow. The drift of the feather attached to the arrow brushed across his hand, prompting him to look down at it. Abruptly, the music grew louder, and without words urged him to take aim, to fire. The buck's ears twitched nervously, as if detecting the murderous melody urging his death.

Mūk-Mudón raised his weapon, smoothly drawing back the arrow as he sighted down the arrow at his target. At that moment, the buck raised his thorny head aloft, and met Mūk-Mudón with his deep and liquid brown eyes. Mūk-Mudón heard again the warning cry, yet ignored it, electing instead to drown it out in the dissonant twang! of the bowstring as he let his arrow fly.

Surprise was in the buck's eyes as too late he recognized the danger. The arrow flew true, seeking the beast's heart, the trailing feather spinning in ever increasing rapidity to speed the projectile along with supernatural force. The feather pressed the dart along its way and guided the missile with deadly power to pierce the fallow buck's heart through.

Hanging from the arrow as a tail, the feather drifted across the bloody hole behind the creature's foreleg that the projectile left in its passage. The buck knelt slowly, crouching as if to rest, then, failing at the last, he sprawled stiffly on his side where he expired.

Until the creature's final breath, his eyes remained locked on Mūk-Mudón, who approached warily, as a creeping regret stole over him. The feather hummed a cheerful, greedy tune as it lay against the still-warm pelt of the dead sorrel. Mūk-Mudón reached down to detach it from the arrow and found the quill red with deer heart's blood.

A certain and decisive derangement took hold of him as he gripped the bloodied tip, and, unable to control himself, he began to etch his madness on his skin. Strange and arcane symbols, words from shadows deep, poured from his cursed pen as time and time again he made ink of the creature's life-blood. Their bloods mingled as he scrawled upon his flesh, the feather now alive with deeper purpose.

It's true that Mūk-Mudón knew not what he wrought, though it's not certain he'd have cared, with knowledge too of what he'd gain. For he was in truth reborn, a profane vessel for near-immortal strength and cunning covered in the blood of a pure and vital creature watered at a remnant of the shattered streams of Gan. The feather gave the final stroke, a fragment of fallen Malakím's glory to imbue and seal in mystery the transaction that was made. And when all was finished, the beast's life spilt upon the forest floor, Mūk-Mudón took, also, his crown as trophy, a helm for his own head. For when affixed as battle dress upon his gilded helm, the flattened antlers swept back as wings, with spurs framing his face in danger.

The wounds etched upon him had closed, his skin thirstily drinking the blood thereupon, and healing without a scar. The feather had likewise swallowed the blood that covered it from quill to vane in gory use. It had taken on a talismanic quality to Mūk-Mudón, and he had wrapped the quill from tip to downy barb in a length of cord, tying it off tightly. He'd secured the cord around his neck as a crude necklace, then slipped the arrangement under his tunic to conceal the feather. Mūk-Mudón understood now why the wingéd creature had offered him the feather, for through it, he was guided and empowered to do extraordinary things.

As Mūk-Mudón approached, carrying his kill, to his friends it seemed that he had grown, not in stature, but in presence–a charged presence that now eclipsed and gripped them. As was tradition, they celebrated the hero of the hunt, though Belláphorus, Imafel, and Cloust did so with somber reservation.

Conversely, Mūk-Mudón brimmed with positive energy and good humor as he recounted his tale of the hunt. Well, all but the final chapter. As he spoke, the others sensed some omission, some absent and important element, and so probed him for greater detail, interested to know more.

Mūk-Mudón, unwilling to reveal anything regarding his frenzied, dark ritual, instead peered intently into the eyes of each friend in turn as he spoke his fiction. As he did so, a peculiar force extended from his being to press on the minds of his friends, overriding their curiosity by the force of his will. Soon enough, the three nodded acceptance of his deception, each now assured that what he spoke was all they ever need know of his hunt.

Mūk-Mudón was ever their leader at war-camp, but on the hunt, he had been a peer. Now his looming, unnatural presence provoked increasing deference in his friends, which he grew to recognize as the evening wore on. The others seemed resigned to his clear superiority, and accepted it as the natural order, their spirits dominated by the strange force within him.

While in the past, the yawning expanse between him and his peers would have alarmed him, this new Mūk-Mudón regarded it as further proof of his ascendancy beyond the mortal constraints that yet bound his friends. With cool and calculating lucidity, he likewise realized his prime concern was no longer for the trivialities of comradery and friendship, though their loyalty remained useful to him. He was certain he would master the art of leadership, and as he would any other endeavor to which he bent his sublime genius. The evening wound down more quickly than most, and the subdued Belláphorus, Imafel, and Cloust drifted early to their bedrolls, leaving Mūk-Mudón to gaze out distantly over the campfire's dying embers.

Not long thereafter, as his fame grew, Mūk-Mudón gained, too, a moniker, The Western Sorrel. For it was in his third year as Warlord that he slew the sorrel buck and returned in changes sudden and peculiar to behold. Belláphorus, Imafel, and Cloust would agree that Mūk-Mudón left them on the hunt and returned a different man, picking his way easily through the brush with the fallow buck across his shoulders, eyes curiously bright and with over-broad smile on his face.

Chapter Eight

The Bunker

YEAR 26 OF THE IMPERIAL AGE

For the most part, Nat's first day at school was thrilling, and full of new, interesting experiences. Swept along with the rest of the Etom children entering the Bunker, Nat passed through the shadowy arch of the old shell and discovered it warmly-lit inside. Peculiar, skeletal ribbing ran athwart the interior of the shell that provided the ceiling of the entryway. Beyond the shell's edge, rafters diverted oaken roots that attempted to intrude upon the school, their tendrils poking through the packed earthen ceiling. Six shallow, round depressions ran along either long side of the Bunker, three on each side, leaving a flat, open space through their midst down the center of the school. Somewhere beyond the bobbling heads of the taller students in front of him, Nat heard a clarion voice call the students to gather in the center of the great hall.

He followed the shuffle to the center of the hall, the larger Etom jostling about at the front of the crowd still screening the speaker from view. Moments later, a gangly lot of the eldest students broke away from the group, moving carefully to avoid stepping on the smaller Etom. They gathered at the foremost cavity on Nat's right, and spread out to seat themselves along its edge, engaged in excited conversation. Not accustomed to seeing so many other children together, Nat stared after them until someone brushed past, stirring him from his reverie.

Another group of Etom, a bit younger than the first, passed as they worked their way to the closest hollow on Nat's left. Now the crowd had cleared in front, Nat caught a glimpse of the mysterious speaker at the front of the room, a bright yellow etma holding a long, narrow sprig, a wand, with which she conducted the students about the Bunker.

To Nat, his Mama was beautiful, and formed the basis for his standard of beauty, but this . . .this was different. Nat's golden eyes grew so wide his eyelids seemed to slip down behind the dewy orbs, his scalp pulled back, and his mouth stood open, chin drooping comically.

Stunned by the beauty before him, Nat watched, uncomprehending, as she waded into the crowd, and with a sweep of her wand sent the older children off to their designated places.

Satisfied she'd sufficiently winnowed the students, she turned to face the remaining group, which consisted of the youngest students. Somehow, Nat had ended up at the forefront of the group and stood stock-still as she approached.

Looking down at him kindly, she inquired, "Why, hello there! And what might your name be?"

Nat's eyes shifted from side to side as, yet frozen, he attempted to recall his name, whatever it might be, from his sudden and inexplicably blank mind. An awkward and silent moment passed.

"Are you a bit shy, then?" she asked with a lilt, as she leaned down, extending a hand in greeting. "My name is Kehren. I'm the Headmistress here. Now what is *your* name?"

Another moment passed, yet more awkward, and silent but for the ringing in Nat's ears. Still, he couldn't muster a response, and his tongue seemed stuck to the bottom of his mouth. All the moisture in it seemed to have vaporized, perhaps streaming from his ears like steam from a kettle.

A wild though occurred to him: That *explained the ringing!*

From off to his left, Nat heard a loud and obnoxious voice chime in, "I think he's a bit daffy. Don't you?"

The grating voice pricked him into action, and Nat wheeled about to locate its owner, as his grimace deepened, aghast as he was at further embarrassment.

"Oh! Well, it seems he's not *entirely* dense. That got 'im moving!" a large-mouthed, pale-pink young etma exclaimed in the same irritating tone.

"Rae!" Kehren spoke in warning, calling Nat's attention back to her. A look of ire darkened her gracious features, a single brow arched over a menacing, steely glare, "You are at *school.*" Certain he desired never to

Nat's Pink Nightmare

have Kehren level such a glare at him, he turned to note Rae very reasonably withering beneath the Headmistress' gaze.

"Now apologize. *Now,*" Kehren forcefully directed.

Rae, head hung low, glanced up at Nat, eyes wet with unborn tears. "I'm sorry," she said with sincerity.

Nat, his paralysis now broken, offered a bright smile. He knew what to do. Mama had taught him always to forgive, and she always forgave *him* and said so.

"I forgive you," he said. "My name's Nat! Sorry for not saying so sooner."

Rae likewise brightened, and said, "Hello, Nat. Nice to meet you! Do you think you might want to be my friend?"

Though Nat intended to respond in the affirmative, Headmistress Kehren interrupted the conversation "Well now. That wasn't so hard, was it, Nat? It's very nice of you to join us this year. We're pleased to have you."

She then straightened and turned to the group, introducing herself once more, "Hello, children! I am Headmistress Kehren, and I will be teaching your class this morning. Your usual instructor is delayed on a journey. We hope he will join us tomorrow, so you can meet him, too. He is very wise and will try to make learning fun for you this year!"

The Headmistress then took a moment with each new student to learn his or her name, and welcome returning students back. She politely shook each small and tender hand, letting each one know how glad she and all the teachers were to have him or her at school. Nat thought it was a fine welcome, and his smile remained as Headmistress Kehren led them over to their "pod," as he learned the ring-shaped depressions were called, which was the farthest back on the left of the hall.

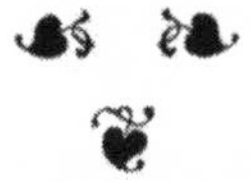

Whilst on their way back to the pod, Rae sidled up alongside Nat, and whispered to him, "Don't worry. I'll help keep you from making a fool of yourself again." Nat slowed some, shaking his head at her gall. He was just been flabbergasted when the Headmistress greeted him, but Rae had made it worse!

She looked back at him inquisitively, noting his shocked expression, "What did I say?!?" Before Nat could respond, a brawny, hulking shape shoved between them, knocking Nat to the ground, and spinning Rae aside.

"Move it!" a hoarse voice demanded, the speaker not bothering to face them as he plowed onward to catch up with the rest of the class.

Nat winced, but didn't cry. He'd fallen much harder before, so he didn't much mind the fall. Being pushed down, however, was new to him, and he didn't know what quite to make of it, other than that he didn't like it.

Rae, however, was indignant, her pale pink cheeks glowing magenta as she shouted after the bully, "Rosco! You! You . . . !"

She pursed her mouth shut, the curse falling silent on her lips as she remembered the Headmistress' earlier admonishment.

"That's Rosco," she told Nat. "He can be *really* mean. You'll want to stay away from him."

Nat nodded in slow agreement, eyes still fixed on Rosco's misshapen, moss-green bulk as he shambled to the pod and lurched down to his seat.

The two made their way over to the pod, Rae chattering the whole time (well, except for breathing; she *had* to breathe) as Nat quietly absorbed the information she shared, enjoying the company. He had grown used to it always being just him and Mama, and he savored the change.

Before today, whenever Nat had encountered other children in the village, mothers pulled their children aside, warning them not to talk or play with him. When Nat had first noticed the rejection, he was hurt, and cried a little before deciding it wasn't worth getting upset over. He still had Mama, even if he didn't have friends, and that was enough.

Also, some of the customers at Mama's booth were very nice to him and commended him on his cheery helpfulness and general good manners. Their acknowledgement helped to soften his loneliness, and

Nat had taken a particular liking to one customer, an elderly genletém named Shoym.

Shoym always had a smile and friendly word for Nat, and sometimes sweets. Nat had come to think of him as a kind, old uncle, and knew Mama liked Shoym as well. In any case, as pleasant as these kinds of connections were for Nat, he had lacked the carefree companionship and friendly fellowship of Etom his own age, and thus now found himself in unfamiliar territory.

His present circumstance aside, Nat couldn't recall a single exchange with another child that had lasted more than a few seconds. He smiled, grateful for Elyon's blessing. Mama had taught him since he was a hatchling to thank their Creator for every good gift. Nat followed her instruction, and joy always followed, just as it did now in the stream of Rae's of breathless babble, which flowed soothingly by as Nat meandered alongside to find a seat around the lip of their pod, far away from Rosco.

Once more, the Headmistress' attention fell on the pair, late as they were (tardy, really; tardy is what you call it in school).

"Decided to join us, did you?" she noted with disapproval as she glanced over top of a sheaf of papers.

Aware Rosco watched them through narrowed, spiteful eyes, Rae quickly recounted that Nat had taken a spill, omitting Rosco from the telling, and that she had helped him get up and over to the pod as quick as they were able. Kehren considered further chastening them, then relented. It had only been a few moments after all. Besides, the first day of school required some flexibility.

The Headmistress looked at Nat and Rae again, and gave a stern warning, "Let's see that it does not happen again, yes?"

Eyes bulging, Nat and Rae nodded with enthusiasm, both feeling very fortunate to have avoided further censure, "Yes, ma'am!"

Kehren suppressed a smile, always amused how seriously young students took school.

Regaining composure, the Headmistress looked out at the beaming faces, and addressed them, "Well, class, shall we begin?"

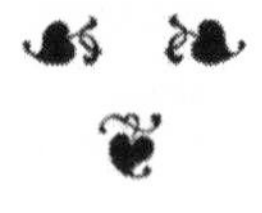

A few hours later, it dawned on Nat: he'd not expected school to be so exciting. It wasn't quite lunchtime yet, and he'd had his first crush, made a new friend, discovered a new enemy, and learned alaafeh, the first symbol in the albijaat, the Etom set of written letters.

They were finishing up with their lesson, in which they first learned how to recognize, then reproduce the symbol. After lunch, Headmistress Kehren promised they would explore the multiple pronunciations of alaafeh.

The promise of a tasty morsel and the playtime that followed it on the horizon, Nat knuckled down to the work of writing the symbol, a considerable feat that he tackled with unblinking focus, while a quirky sneer lifted the corner of his mouth. Though most students in the class easily managed the sweeping strokes of the character, for Nat, it proved difficult due to his meticulous nature. Any variance from the beautiful calligraphy that served as the example was a failure in his mind, and he, with painstaking deliberation, attempted to copy every nuance.

The Headmistress had tasked each student with writing the letter 10 times, a task most completed within a few minutes. Nat, however, found himself engaged in a fierce struggle with his own hand, which would not cooperate with his mind.

After several minutes waiting for Nat, who was the lone student still working on the assignment, Headmistress Kehren told him she would let him complete one more before they broke for lunch. Desperate to perfect the symbol, Nat bent low over his desk, bamboo pen gripped so tightly in his fist that his hand began to cramp and ache throbbingly. Nat relaxed his grip, took a deep breath, then drew a slow, deliberate mark across the page.

Looking down at his work, his seventh attempt, and a near-perfect reproduction of the example calligraphy, Nat grinned broadly as a shadow loomed over his desk.

Presuming it to be Headmistress Kehren, Nat, without looking up, exclaimed, "Look! I think I got it!"

A coarse whisper greeted him, "Now that's just great, inchworm. Maybe we can get some lunch now?"

Nat whipped around to face the speaker, none other than Rosco, who smirked unkindly as he narrowed his eyes to appraise Nat's work.

Rosco continued, "But, you know what? I don't think it's quite right yet. Let me help."

Dipping his pen into Nat's nearby well, Rosco flicked great spreading droplets onto Nat's page, and stalked away. Now Nat knew it wasn't nice hit people, but, in his anger, he considered it before deciding against it. His hand hurt already from writing, and he recalled Mama's instruction to forgive, even when others didn't deserve it.

Instead, he smiled, pleased at his accomplishment, which was something Rosco couldn't ruin, and so he stood up and presented his work, including the final copy, explaining that an accident had marred his final page.

Even though the ink blotches obscured Nat's last copy, Headmistress Kehren was taken aback by his talent. Slow as he was in producing the work, Nat had nevertheless managed to create a stunningly similar copy of the calligraphy she had provided the class.

"Well done!" she congratulated him, and dismissed the class, Nat beaming as he left the pod with Rae for lunch in the common area.

Contented after their meal and a spirited frolic, the pair returned to class on time. The Headmistress was preparing for the next phase of their lesson on alaafeh, which covered the multiple pronunciations contained within its haamjal.

After a few moments settling the class, Headmistress Kehren began, "The name of each character in the albijaat is called its haamjal, and each haamjal provides a pronunciation guide for the character it represents. The first haamjal of the albijaat, 'alaafeh,' contains all three of its pronunciations."

Nat focused intently. Desperate to understand, he scrunched his face in concentration as he listened, hanging on her every word. She had written each character of the albijaat on the blackboard at the front of class, and as she pointed to each one, moving from right to left, she recited its haamjal: "Alaafeh, bid, jaam, talt, eepe, waaw . . ."

Nat's concentration fell into consternation as he struggled to keep up with the rest of the students. For many of his classmates this was their second or third year of instruction. Even Rae, though at times stumbling, continued in the recitation, her familiarity with the albijaat apparent.

His considerable optimism having already been tested today, Nat was almost at the point of tears, his light blue skin tinged with ashy grey, when he heard again a whisper of melody, and the shimmer of a familiar light overhead caught his eye before it disappeared into the shadowy spaces in the ribbed ceiling.

Though he didn't understand just how, Nat found hope in the moment. A smile returned to his face with his color, and encouragement slipped neatly into his mind. He might not be able to keep up, but he could follow the class as close as he was able. He began anew, repeating each haamjal in sequence just behind the rest of the class. A few of the nearby students heard him echoing the class, and snickered, though not cruelly. It was fine. Really. He would figure this thing out alright. Just give him a minute, and he would have it.

Their school day ended with repeated recitations of the albijaat, the Headmistress increasing the speed of the recitation with each pass. Though Nat didn't have it memorized yet, he continued to follow as closely as he was able, his confidence growing each time.

Rae noticed how hard Nat was trying and thought to herself how brave he was to speak up. Nat might not have noticed, as Rae had, but all the other first-year students had remained silent. Rae, as a second-year student, looked back on her first day of class the year before, and remembered how terrified and embarrassed she had been. She hadn't spoken a single word during recitation, simply out of fright, though she had begun to remember parts of it by the end of the lesson. Rae admired Nat's sunny courage, a shy smile stealing over her face as she watched him fight through the albijaat, her pale pink cheeks glowing a burnished rose as she turned away abruptly, afraid someone might catch her watching him.

Nat's first day at school ended in a chaotic rush for the Bunker's exit, where he stopped a second to say goodbye to Rae. After, Nat broke away to stand alone under the brilliant, yellow dandelion his Mama had pointed out to him before she sent him into the Bunker, excited to tell her about his day, but enjoying the earthy smell of the flower, the buzz of bees overhead, and the last of the season's sunny warmth. A few moments later, he saw Mama rush into the clearing before the Bunker, cheeks flushed from exertion.

Nida spotted him under the dandelion where she had told him to wait and smiled in appreciation as she waved him over. *What a great kid!*

He ran to her with abandon, still young enough to not care who knew how much he still loved his Mama. His stubby legs carried him into her open arms, where she lifted him in a warm embrace, turning about as she did. They held one another tight, each unacquainted with the other's absence, so constant was their companionship, and found that to miss each other had been a good thing. Nida couldn't resist kissing Nat's tender cheeks, which bubbled around his sappy grin, and he giggled as she tickled him.

Nida set him down and took his hand to walk home as she asked about his day. He told her about his new friend, Rae, and about how hard he'd work to write an excellent alaafeh, making certain to mention how Headmistress Kehren had praised his work. He told her how hard it was to remember all the haamjal of the albijaat, and that he hadn't let it stop him, but did his best to recite the albijaat with the rest of the class.

"I'm very proud of you, Nat," Nida said. Nat beamed pleasurably in response as joy carried them onward to partake together in the comfort of hearth and home.

Chapter Nine

Battle at Za'aq Ha Dam

ADVENT OF THE IMPERIAL AGE

Now in his thirtieth year, facing Parác, the great Warlord of the East, Mūk-Mudón with a chuckle offered more levity than his friends had seen in him since their hunt in the wooded west. Oh, there had been other hunts, but they never knew him again as before, and never had the four alone set out to hunt again.

The three had remained with Mūk-Mudón, loyal to him now more than ever. His magnitude expanded like a star in the heavens, and they were as satellites, their orbits ever broadening to escape collision with his immensity. His legendary status now prevented the kind of intimate friendship they had all enjoyed in the past, and assuredly precluded any affectionate calls of "Baby Mooks!" as much from reverence as a vague fear of his response should they take such liberty, even in private. Each harbored anxious thoughts that something dangerous now inhabited their friend, though they dared never express them to one another.

Mūk-Mudón had drawn them all together, and in his detachment, the trio had drifted apart as well, each preoccupied with his distinctive command: Belláphorus over Heavy Infantry, Imafel over the Scout Regiment, and Cloust over the Artillery Barrage. Each had aged, weathered by a life of war, while Mūk-Mudón retained a youthful vigor that belied his years, with the singular loss of his baby-fat cheeks accounting for time's passage.

The trio also bore the weight of war in another regard, for though with honor they spilt blood in battle, their murderous deeds had left them Marked. Belláphorus, renowned for his strength and skill in battering foes with a great war-hammer, had proven no less capable of doing so with whatever stood at hand, and was known to appropriate man or beast as a flail should need serve. A great fiery beard covered his scarred face, terminating in numerous leather-bound braids from his jaw and chin. It was his strength that served him best in bloody work, and it was his great bare arms that bore Marks of his deeds, as writhing black brands stood in deep, twining bands twisting over shoulder, arm, and hand.

Imafel remained a vain creature consumed with the shape and enormity of his moustache, a magnificent and ridiculous handlebar affair, and with his sparse beard, bestowing excessive attention upon them both. Despite his self-absorption, none among Mūk-Mudón's forces doubted that Imafel was the most capable and cunning scout their army possessed. The Western forces depended heavily on the intelligence the stealthy Scout Regiment collected.

Indeed, it was Imafel and his group who had surveilled Parác's camp and had quietly concealed the mire. Due to his natural affinity with clever and quick creatures, it was also he who had trained the lemurs in their mission escorting the Elephants across the mire.

In any case, some conjectured that it was Imafel's constant posturing with jaw and chin cupped in the crook between his thumb and forefinger that had eventually Marked his cheeks in the arching black stains that terminated just beneath his eyes.

Imafel had first discovered small black diamonds on his cheeks in the reflection of the wash basin as he stooped to wash his face early one morning. No one in camp had dared mention the blemishes, aware how much he valued his appearance. He had stalked about, glaring every which way until encountering Cloust.

His tall, powdery friend had stared with concern as Imafel's blood rose to meet expected scorn.

Rather, Cloust had smiled and complimented him, "No matter. I think they make you look rather dashing!"

Imafel's anger deflated, turning to amusement as he smiled back in exasperation at his old friend. Cloust's small affirmation instantly transformed Imafel's concern over his marred countenance into curiosity, and he strode to a well-polished bronze shield to take a second glance in its reflection. After a few moments, he chuckled to himself. He pursed his lips, narrowed his eyes, arched a brow, and assumed again his most dashing pose. With face cupped once more in hand, he found he was rather pleased with his new ornamentation.

Cloust possessed extraordinary awareness and visual acuity that defied explanation. His Marks had shown up quite suddenly the morning after he single-handedly dispatched over 100 enemies in the rocky hills of some horrid, nameless wasteland. He alone had remained in the scout's perch on the ridge overlooking the battlefield to cover the retreat of his unit. As his unit had departed, they planted what unspent arrows remained to them in a ring around Cloust.

At the outset of his defense, he had removed his turban and upper garments for freedom of movement, prepared to sacrifice himself to stop the enemy's advance. His bald, albino head, arms and trunk shone in the moonlight, as his articulate, yet deadly skill with the bow transformed him into a translucent, waxen figure flowing from one kill to the next with graceful, murderous efficacy.

With the advantage of higher ground, Cloust had mowed down the advancing foes as they clambered up the rocky hillside over stone, brush, and fallen comrades. Having spent his final arrow, Cloust met in close combat a group of three foes–a she-leopard, a man, and a bear–each somewhat winded from the climb as they mounted the ridge.

The first to recover from the climb, the leopard prowled, slinking about in attempt to blindside Cloust. The man, swarthy and in dark armor, clutched a double-bladed battle-ax in his right hand as he stalked toward Cloust, still chuffing from the climb. Behind them both, a great Grizzly, the left side of his maw crusted in Blight, shambled on all fours as he huffed and snorted from exertion.

Aware of the spotted cat's quick, powerful leap, Cloust identified her as his most immediate threat, and baited the creature to pounce, dropping his bow and feigning a step back as if to flee. She took the bait, coiling and bounding in one fluid movement. From sheaths slung across his lower back, Cloust drew two identical, wide, blades, each about 2 feet in length. Rolling forward into the beast's leap, Cloust positioned himself beneath the startled leopard, who now overshot her target. He thrust the blades up into her exposed ribcage, leaving them in her chest as she passed, the force of her leap driving the blades deeper as she limply struck the ground.

While the cat still fell, Cloust pivoted on his right knee, right hand sweeping over the ground to pick up his bow from where he had dropped it, and continued to turn in a circle, his flowing robes fluttering open as he stood to meet the hacking downward stroke of the man's battle-ax. Gripping the bow at both ends with either hand, Cloust held the bow upright, using the force of his rotation to parry the battle-ax aside and downward with the center of the bow. He snapped both wrists in the direction of the parry, carrying his enemy's blade aside, and leaving his foe off-balance and with back exposed. Stepping behind his opponent, Cloust flipped the bow so the string faced outward, and threw it over the man's head, catching it under his bristled chin. He placed his knee in the small of his enemy's back, leaning back heavily to wrench the bow and garrote the man with the bowstring. All the while, he kept his eyes trained on the Grizzly, who had recovered from the climb, and even now lumbered ever nearer.

Cloust was well aware he stood no chance against the Grizzly should it charge, and instead wrested his felled foe's battle-ax from where its blade lay buried in the earth to rush the surprised beast. The great bear blanched as Cloust dashed toward him, turning the unblemished side of his face warily toward the threat even as he reared back, intending to snap his great jaws around Cloust as he approached. While still at a full run, Cloust raised the battle-ax, and hurled it, aiming for the Grizzly's exposed eye. Without waiting to see if the ax reached its target, Cloust juked aside to sprint for his blades, still buried in the downed she-leopard.

Meanwhile, the bear's reflexes had saved his eye at the last moment. As he fell back down to all fours, the ax's blade glanced instead off his thick, furry brow, and opened a nasty gash over his eye. Warm, stinging blood poured into the eye, temporarily impairing the bear's vision.

Cloust, with some effort pried his blades from deep in the leopard's chest and turned to face the hairy behemoth that now raged at the pain of his wound and frustration of his hindered sight.

Cloust watched the Grizzly for signs of an impending charge and observed that for which he had hoped–the bear's other eye was likewise almost useless, the crust of Blight on its maw had covered all but the barest slit around it. Quietly, Cloust approached the bear, stopping several feet away, blades held in either hand at his sides. After a few moments moaning and pawing at his bloody eye, the bear, also stilled, turning only his head to sniff the air.

For a moment, Cloust forgot that the beast could snap him up for a meal and watched the Grizzly with wonderment as he attempted to locate the oddly quiet yet oh so fragrantly present Cloust. At last, the moment arrived for which Cloust awaited.

The bear stood on his hind legs, hoping to better detect his opponent. In a flash, Cloust lunged, stabbing the bear in the heart with both blades. Leaving the blades imbedded in the beast, he rolled clear, landing in a low and ready crouch. The bear staggered in silence, stunned at the unexpected assault, then fell straight back, tumbling down the scrabble of slope he had worked so diligently to surmount.

Cloust left his blades in the fallen Grizzly, bundled himself up against a night grown cold, and picked his way back to camp, entering the tented pavilion unnoticed and unannounced to fall asleep on his cot. He awoke late the following morning to the surprised exclamations of his unit, who had presumed him dead when he failed to inform the sentries of his return the night before. Those who discovered him roused the camp, who cheered the return of their commander.

Cloust blandly accepted their praise. He wasn't one to seek attention but noticed the triumphant expressions of his soldiers turn to shock as, slack-jawed, they stared at him. One of the braver souls pointed cautiously at Cloust's forehead, and Cloust turned to seek his reflection in a still bucket of water.

On his forehead, just over his eyes, stood two perfectly round, black spots about the size of a coin. Reaching up with his left hand to touch the spots, he noticed the palm and inside of his hand with which he gripped the handle of his bow had also turned black. Looking also at his right hand, he found patches on his fingers and thumb where he gripped arrows in preparation to shoot. Throwing his head back, he laughed boisterously, those gathered around him staring in wariness.

What a wild night! he thought, still laughing.

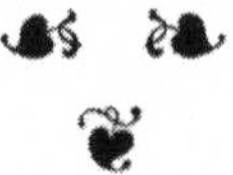

Even as growing Stains Marked the bodies of Belláphorus, Imafel, and Cloust, Mūk-Mudón yet remained unmarred although he had undoubtedly spilled the most blood of them all. By now, he should have been a patchwork of Marks, with maybe even a touch of The Blight.

Adding to his mystique was how he'd developed at a frightful pace after their hunt in the Western wilds. While he had yet remembered his friends' loyalty and abilities, it was not simple friendship that motivated him to elevate each of them to the pinnacle of command. Mūk-Mudón had also learned how to inspire excellence in those around him, bringing out their greatest potential, and imbuing them each with enhanced ability to lead and to use best their natural talents in battle.

Thus, was the army of the Western Sorrel strangely energized, as though lightning had struck Mūk-Mudón, chaining each to him through the furcated electricity of his will, prowess, and charisma, as it passed from commander to subordinate, and so on and so forth down to the lowliest foot soldier, each one now seething with terrible energy on the battlefield.

It was this deadly, charged fervor that Mūk-Mudón leveled now at his enemy, Parác, hefting it by force of resolve and focus of perception as any other might heft a spear in hand in preparation for the lethal cast. With interest Mūk-Mudón watched the progress of his Elephants, as the first in the column broke over the edge of the mire onto solid earth, and the Mahout that straddled the Elephant in front of the turret pressed behind the mighty beast's ears to signal the charge.

Each Elephant wore a helmet of sorts, designed to protect their foreheads, used as battering rams, with plates of armor, while a barbed mail ran down their trunks. Their trunks were deadly whips scourging those who might avoid the trampling of the Elephant's mighty armored feet and shins, and the spearing thrusts of their iron-tipped tusks. Beyond that, the Elephants lacked any defenses beyond what Nature afforded, any added weight potentially slowing the already-burdened animals beyond effectiveness. As the first Elephant began his ponderous, yet nigh unstoppable acceleration, the drummers, too, quickened their pace to mask the ruckus.

The army of the Western Sorrel matched the drummers' tempo with chants, stomps, and pounding of shield. Nevertheless, as more Elephants left the mire to begin their charge, the assembly fell into a quaking cacophony, a steady rumbling that shook the field.

Mūk-Mudón looked leftward for any reaction from the right wing of Parác's forces, the armored Elephants yet bearing down on them unnoticed. The first Elephant was a mere fifty yards or so from their position when the soldiers of Parác's right wing noticeably stirred, their commander whirling a scimitar overhead as their standard-bearer waved the pennant wildly from side to side to signal a sudden change in formation.

Ah! They've finally noticed the trap! thought Mūk-Mudón.

With very little opportunity to shift defenses and confront the armored, grey juggernauts, Parác's right-most regiment wheeled clumsily within the confines of their ranks, flailing in attempt to form a shield wall before the oncoming assault. The first of many Elephants struck Parác's forces, the mighty beast pitching enemy soldiers high in the air while pressing several into the ground underfoot. The first was the tip of the spear, and the Mahouts drove the charge as a chevron pointed at the heart of Parác's army. Mūk-Mudón straddled a magnificent dappled white charger with reins and bridle plated in golden laurels and stood now in his saddle to raise a hand beside his helm, thrusting it forward to signal the next phase of his plan.

Parác studied his enemy, his tawny brow furrowed in a mixture of consternation and concentration. The rumbling of fifty charging War-

Elephants overpowered the coordinated commotion of the drums in the Western Sorrel's camp to reach him from the right. Disquieted, Parác turned to face the disturbance and signaled the straggling front line to his right to turn about and close around Mūk-Mudón's Elephants as they drove into his flank, bowling over his unprepared forces with scarcely any resistance.

Thankfully for Parác, Haspades, the commander over the Artillery maintained a level head, and in an instant surmised their sole chance of stopping the battle-frenzied pachyderms was to engage them at range. The bulk of his ranged forces Parác held in reserve behind the main force, intending to shower the Western forces after they had broken formation in the melee.

Haspades, recognizing their great need to deter the Elephants' further foray into the Eastern army's flank, ordered a full barrage from bow, and ballista, firing into their own lines to meet the charging force. Though callous, his strategy was the correct one, for they could not be concerned with striking their own men, whose lives were regardless forfeit should Artillery fail to stop the Elephants.

The effort was effective, for, though the Elephants' heads and forelegs were armored, the remainder of their great, grey bodies were not. Similarly, the Mahouts driving the Elephants, and the spearmen in their turrets were not thickly armored, and so depended on speed and the higher ground afforded them by their steeds for protection. Arrow, spear, and javelin poured into the riven battle line, piercing friend and foe alike. Many an Elephant and rider fell in that first barrage, and the remaining Mahouts struggled with wounded and panicked steeds. In retreat, the Elephants veered eastward, far behind enemy lines, and ran parallel to the mire's edge to maintain their distance from Parác's rear echelon. Parác's right wing front was recovering, and Haspades' Artillery deterred any forays into their supply complement.

Though he no longer held much affection for any Man or Beast, Mūk-Mudón hated to waste such noble creatures and their trainers, both of whom lived in a respectful harmony that he admired, even as he admired the might and dignity their combined disciplined produced.

No matter he thought. *Better they are spent here in my service than in nameless, purposeless dissipation. Besides, their sacrifice proved a worthy diversion, and cost the enemy dearly.*

Chapter Ten

Dust

Throughout Parác's entire army, attention had turned to the ailing right flank the moment the Elephants had struck. The disciplined troops of Mūk-Mudón had fallen silent at his signal with each man and beast tapping the shoulder or flank before them in rehearsed signal to still themselves. When the Elephants' attack had garnered sufficient attention among Parác's troops, Mūk-Mudón signaled again for his army to inch forward as quietly as they were able, closing the distance between the armies with their approach yet unnoticed.

Across the battlefield from the elephantine chaos, the sounds of battle dwindled, time seemed to stand still, and a comforting loneliness settled over Mūk-Mudón. In this moment, he exerted prodigious mental force, and all grew still to him, a euphoric sense of invincibility filling his being. While in this state, he was able to influence the will of his troops, who he now commanded wordlessly to maintain focus forward on the enemy. In similar manner, he planted a suggestion of fear among the Eastern forces to magnify the threat of his Elephants. Thusly dominated and distracted, none on the battlefield observed him grasp the golden links about his neck and draw out the feather given him that moonless night so many years ago. Upon his other palm, he laid open a weighty, leather bag filled with a peculiar, powdered mixture of burgundy and yellow ochre.

The powder represented years of painstaking perfection. Mūk-Mudón, having learned the secret of the migas' venom in his contest against Imafel, had subjected himself to plentiful and agonizing experiments to extract, synthesize, and amplify the quickening effects of the venom, while removing the painful, dulling effects thereof. He dipped the plume into the bag, coating it heavily, then held the quill between his palms, the feather standing upright between his hands as he began to rub his palms together, spinning the feather to shake the powder from its barbs.

While he did so, began to blow, the powder now forming a cloud, which gathered before him, hemmed in by his mystical prowess. Three times in all he coated the feather, and three times he blew, an ever-denser cloud billowing in deepening saffron and vermilion yet remaining in place between him and his troops.

Mūk-Mudón closed the pouch and put it away, then spread the fingers of his right hand as a fan, the feather fixed beneath his thumb and jutting between his two center fingers. Holding his hand high, Mūk-Mudón closed his eyes and lowered his head in concentration. With a sudden slash of the air before him, he drove the gathered cloud to spread among his troops in winding wisps and tendrils. The soldiers of the Western Sorrel inhaled deeply, and the enchantment was complete.

From afar, it might seem strange how great a distance the Western forces covered in such a short span of time, the great mass gliding silently over the rock-strewn plain. Strange, too, was the lack of attention the Eastern army gave the foe before them, their focus affixed to the charge against their right wing. Mūk-Mudón's spell yet compelled his troops, who moved under his control at supreme speed to close on the Eastern forces. His commands positioned the Western army directly before Parác's front line at the left edge of their formation.

It wasn't until the tips of Western spears lay in the sides of the Eastern vanguard that their army stirred. Awoken as if from sleep by the death-cries of their comrades, they turned to meet their enemies, who now stood inscrutably before them. Stricken with alarm, Parác's troops made a valiant, yet bungling stand, which Mūk-Mudón and his army broke without much resistance. Parác, stunned at the speed with which his opponent dismantled his front line, hesitated, then roared the command to encircle the enemy from the right.

Meanwhile, a gap opened in the right side of Mūk-Mudón's formation, and a column of great, armored she-bears, Grizzlies all, poured forth from the gap at a full run. Looping around the left end of the Eastern formation, they punched a hole in the exposed flank, causing the left end of the line to sag back as the Western shield wall yet pressed forward.

To Mūk-Mudón's left, Belláphorus' Heavy Infantry deployed in a broad, immovable cluster, forcing Parác's advancing right wing to wheel around them to reach the rest of Mūk-Mudón's army. Meanwhile, the armored Cavalry of rhinos, boars, buffalo, and other fearsome charging beasts, most with lancers astride them, streamed from Mūk-Mudón's main formation, picking off the soldiers of Parác's straggling right wing as they attempted to form up. Imafel commanded the swift beasts and the birds of prey to harass the right wing, creating an environment of devolving chaos as Parác's troops swirled in confused eddies, unable to defend themselves from Mūk-Mudón's nimble assault.

Parác, muttering to himself in disbelief, watched as the left flank folded. The bears responsible for the failure still raged among his troops though they formed a ring of spears about them to encapsulate the ursine threat. Parác observed now Mūk-Mudón's main force pressing in on his collapsing left wing. If left unchecked the enemy in short order would reach the center of the formation, from which Parác directed a substantial, if not confused force.

Parác called all his forces to gather against the Western shield wall that yet pressed ahead on his left and withdrew support from the troops still attempting to envelop the enemy on the right.

They will need to fend for themselves, he thought with resignation.

Now that their forces had met in melee, Parác intended to smash in from the right, a blunt-force tactic that relied on superior numbers in immense concentration at the point of contact with the enemy. Slowly, the Eastern line shifted, each man at the front turning to his left. The maneuver necessitated every soldier hold shield and spear in off-hands to present the shield to the right where the enemy still threatened.

Focused on bringing the force of his right line forward into the Western formation, Parác didn't anticipate the inherent weakness in forcing his troops to fight and defend with their off-hands, an awkward feat that bucked against the conditioning that training wrought. In addition, while their shields were between them and the enemy, they now marched sidelong to the enemy, unable to withstand a direct onslaught. Nonetheless, the Eastern forces drove on from the right, congregating in greater numbers to amass at the center of the formation.

Mūk-Mudón smiled slyly as he saw Parác's right line shift, expecting this opportunity. As the center of the opposing army became a swirling cluster, and the Eastern troops all jockeyed for position in drive at the solid Western line, Mūk-Mudón by will alone signaled Belláphorus to advance with Heavy Infantry.

In an instant, Belláphorus' solid knot of soldiers became a dagger driving deep into the enemy formation. At the tip of the dagger, Belláphorus bellowed the Heavy Infantry's charge, all the while swinging with tremendous might and deadly precision his war hammer as his unit plowed through Parác's weakened right wing. The Heavy Infantry was well-suited to the task, each man a mighty tree armored from head to toe, a stout buckler in one hand, weapon of choice, be it mace, flail, axe, or polearm, in the other. Their unit was not swift, but instead pressed forward, their enemies unable to halt the intensity of the assault.

Mūk-Mudón turned aside and signaled Cloust at his right, and the Artillery unit sprang out from behind the main force, taking aim at the milling scrum that had formed beyond the enemy's front line. They let loose a barrage, arrow, bolt, and javelin arcing over the enemy's front line to find their targets in the jumble pressed between the main force and the sweeping Heavy Infantry. The result was devastating. A fortunate few of Parác's infantry managed to pull up their shields in time, but most fell, skewered by the piercing missiles.

The precision of Cloust's Artillery was such that many of those who surrounded the Grizzlies in the midst of Parác's camp fell, though none of the bears were harmed. In the fray, the bears struck out at nearby enemies, clouting them with massive paws and bellowing fiercely. Following the sound of Grizzly roars, the Heavy Infantry changed direction, intent on rescuing their allies.

In the meantime, Cloust had shifted the Artillery's focus to harass their enemy counterpart. Haspades commanded his Artillery to a defensive position, and took meager losses, launching a volley in response. Their work done for the time being, Cloust's forces folded back in behind the main body, avoiding serious losses as the enemies' arrows glanced harmlessly off the interlocked shields of the phalanx.

Though Belláphorus and Cloust had blunted the power of Parác's drive at Mūk-Mudón's main force, the substantial numbers of the Eastern army won them through to press the left side of Mūk-Mudón's phalanx. Mūk-Mudón obliged their forcefulness, and signaled the formation to wheel counter-clockwise, swinging the front of edge of their formation through Parác's weakened left wing, to present the right side of their formation to the enemy.

Normally, such a maneuver would spell certain defeat for any shield wall, for soldiers in such a formation held a shield in the left hand to protect themselves and their neighbor's right side. Thus, equipped with shields in the left hand, the wall was vulnerable to attacks on the exposed right side.

Mūk-Mudón, however, accounted for this weakness, recruiting an elite group of left-handed warriors and designing them special shields to curve overhead and meet the upraised shields of their right-handed comrades. These left-handed warriors, the Solaxay, comprised the right side of Mūk-Mudón's formation, and carried no spear, but used both hands to support the weight of their heavier shields, which bore jagged teethed along the bottom edge to facilitate planting them in the ground in a holding action. Sarissón, the right-handed allies just left of the Solaxay, carried special spears called sarissa, which were longer than ordinary. A round opening at shoulder-height in the Solaxays' shields allowed the passage of the sarissa, and thus enabled the Sarissón to thrust past the Solaxay and attack the enemy line.

Mūk-Mudón's method worked well in mitigating the common weakness of the phalanx's right side and presented quite a surprise to Parác's troops when the Western Sorrel's formation held along the right, leveling the opposition.

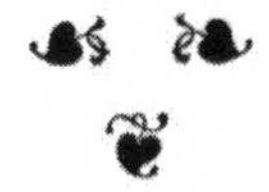

Mūk-Mudón Surveys the Battlefield

Turning his steed to face the central formation of the Eastern armies, Mūk-Mudón searched the horde for the enemy's command complement. There, enthroned over his armies on a litter carried by eight, sat Parác, who leaned forward from the edge of his throne, brow visibly furrowed in consternation as he watched the battle turn against him. Perhaps Mūk-Mudón beckoned him with uncanny force, perhaps it was simple chance, but the two Warlords' gazes met across the field, their wills locked in struggle for mastery as neither dared flinch.

Though not endowed with the fantastic abilities of Mūk-Mudón, the Eastern Warlord was no trifle; many a trial had tempered his will and ferocity, and neither did he offer any quarter here. The momentary contest passed, and without concern Mūk-Mudón broke gaze to direct his army. Aiming straight for the opposing Warlord, he clicked his tongue and sauntered forth, his dappled stallion whickering eagerly for battle.

Alas, Mūk-Mudón's steed faced disappointment, for the enemy line was in such disarray at their approach that the shield wall trod over enfeebled opposition to reach the core of Parác's forces, who now huddled protectively about their ruler. A hush fell over the assembly as Mūk-Mudón's phalanx opened, the ranks spreading like wings to either side of him as he ambled forward coolly to address Parác from atop his charger. Chin grasped between crooked forefinger and thumb, Mūk-Mudón took stock of Parác across the war-torn field, now strewn with the shattered armaments and chilling flesh of the fallen.

Removing hand from chin, he proffered it, half-open, to Parác, "I've come to request your surrender, and offer quarter to any Man or Beast in your army for refreshment and recovery if only he swears fealty to me. You have seen for yourself what my army and I are capable of, and I have a place in my ranks for anyone who wishes to join me, yourself included, Honorable Parác."

Though Mūk-Mudón spoke without raising his voice in the slightest, each Man and Beast on the field heard him clearly, no doubt due to his inexplicable abilities. Murmuring arose in Parác's camp as the enemy warriors debated the offer. Many were terrified at the display of the Western Sorrel's obvious strategic mastery and his unearthly facility in dismantling Parác's formation. Whether they were willing to voice their misgivings, many in the Eastern camp believed their defeat imminent, if not certain, and Mūk-Mudón's words yet wheedled their way into the cracks that doubt lay in the wall of their combative will, ever widening the gaps until the determination of many crumbled, collapsing within them as their belief in defeat became reality.

Parác observed the effect Mūk-Mudón's offer had on his army as the faces of Men grew ashen and the tails of beasts drooped limply. Parác's blood rose in fury, and the veins of his neck bulged in rage, then grew black as the Stain crept up from beneath the collar of his lordly tunic. Parác's temper had won many a contest for him, for as most lost control of their faculties when enraged, Parác grew ever more keenly focused. In this state, he showed no hesitancy in brutality, nor fear in charging into danger. Nothing would distract him from the target of his fury until he had gained satisfaction or perished in the attempt.

Now, his acrimony fell upon Mūk-Mudón, and seizing his spear from its stand upon the dais, he stood, eyes ablaze as he descended a stair of bare human backs, his slaves diving into place beneath each footfall. Never once did he take his eyes off Mūk-Mudón as he stalked forward, unslinging the single-edged battle axe into his left hand whilst preparing the spear in his right. The armies made way for the Warlords, as Mūk-Mudón likewise alit from his stamping steed, striding forward as he drew his leaf-shaped blade from its scabbard.

Approaching Mūk-Mudón, Parác held the shaft of his spear high, the tip pointed downward at an angle, the center of the shaft balanced on the handle of his axe. Without delay, Parác attacked, thrusting downward at first, and lunging forward as he raised and pulled back on the axe in his left. The result was a thrust that scooped upward at the end to almost piercing Mūk-Mudón in the throat. And it would certainly have done so, if the Western Warlord hadn't leaned back at the last moment, batting the spear away with a sweep of his blade, the Eastern forces' cheers falling as the Western army's excited shouts arose.

Grinning mischievously, Mūk-Mudón eyed Parác, who retracted his thrust, then swept the weighted bludgeon at the end of his spear across his body, crooking the shaft in his left elbow in an unsuccessful swipe at Mūk-Mudón's helmed head. The golden-haired Warlord circled back and to his left, out of harm's way, twirling his sword jauntily and winking at his red-faced opponent.

Growing ever more incensed with the impudent Mūk-Mudón, Parác pivoted to his right, aiming a horizontal slash with the spear's broad tip at his enemy, catching the cocky fellow by surprise and on his heels with the sweeping stroke. Mūk-Mudón managed inelegantly to put his blade between his torso and the spearhead, preventing a wound, but pinning his sword a moment between spear and armored plate.

Parác took advantage of his opponent's momentary delay in extricating his blade and released the shaft of the spear from the crook of his left arm to swing his left arm in a tight arc. Snapping his wrist smartly, he buried his ax in Mūk-Mudón's helmet at the base of the left antler, severing it and wounding Mūk-Mudón, whose startled blue eyes appeared for the first time to understand the seriousness of this deadly game. Parác breathed shakily, sweat dripping from his brow, red from heat and exertion, as he stood over the mighty Western Sorrel, who listed heavily to his left, then fell to his knee, the entire time bright blue eyes staring past him in shock.

In the stunned silence, no blood yet poured from the wound, yet so grievous it seemed that none anticipated Mūk-Mudón's survival. He slumped over his left knee, head down, still kneeling as if in defiance of final defeat, even in death. Parác considered his felled foe, engrossed in internal debate over the fate of this upstart from the West who had proven such a thorn in his side.

While a magnanimous victor might consider turning his opponent's body back over to his troops as a sign of respect to honor the fallen leader, Parác was of another mind. He would decapitate this fool that had dared oppose him and then parade his head around the kingdom as an example to those who might harbor treachery in their hearts.

Without turning from Mūk-Mudón, Parác gestured for his armor bearer to come forward, calling for the saf'kafir, a gleaming, golden scimitar sufficiently long and broad that it required both hands to wield it. His armor bearer hurried forward with the requested implement, wrapped in ceremonious, scarlet silk, and bowed out of the way as Parác grasped the blade. Slowly and deliberately he positioned himself to Mūk-Mudón's left, looking out in pointed derision at the Western forces as he readied himself.

Planting his feet wide, Parác raised the saf'kafir high over his head in both hands, and the world seemed to stop altogether. In the stillness, Mūk-Mudón gasped, stirring, then rising as he staggered backward. A wide-eyed Parác uttered a strangled cry, terror clear on his face, for from behind Mūk-Mudón's clear, blue eyes welled a black, oily pitch, which rolled down the fair-haired warrior's cheeks in dirty streaks, and ran down the collar of his armor, no doubt to stain the feather hanging over his heart. The wound in his head too gushed black, and his eyes continued to pour forth the foul Stain, as the whites and then colorful irises turned glistening obsidian.

Mid-stagger, Mūk-Mudón's body seized, pitching his head backward at a shocking and unnatural angle, as a deathly croak rattled its way up his throat. In the wide-eyed silence, the croak first resonated an earthy, low note, building in pitch into a throaty battle-roar. An invisible force buoyed the brightly armored figure, bent impossibly backward with head and arms thrown back, perched daintily on the tips of his toes. On every exposed inch of Mūk-Mudón's skin, the cursed glyphs etched long ago now stood out, black as Stain, and crawled about his body as if they held a life of their own. Mūk-Mudón's roar ended, and he pitched forward with a sudden, lunging step that cracked the hard-packed earth, his left gauntlet and right sabaton sinking inches into the ground.

Mūk-Mudón's head hung low over his extended right knee, and none could see his face. Back heaved from seething breath, and hand shook in iron grip around the hilt of his leaf-bladed sword, which had yet to fall from his hand. Rising with face downcast, Mūk-Mudón straightened and lifted up his countenance, now covered in running, black gore, to confront Parác.

Jet-black eyes twinkled, bright with a sinister light under Mūk-Mudón's golden brows, and a predatory grin, bright as polished bone against the dark stigma that marred his face, spread wolfishly across his face as he turned to his enemy. The air around Mūk-Mudón shimmered as waves of heat over scorching sand while Parác exhaled tremulously, his trepidation and uncertainty clear.

Mūk-Mudón stepped back and raised his sword hilt high as if drawing a bow, the tip of the blade angled across his chest. He extended his left arm in line with the blade, and his hand open with palm facing Parác, who readied himself shakily, his distress evident in every motion.

Mūk-Mudón breathed in slowly, nostrils flaring as his chest rose and he filled his body with air. Briefly, he closed his eyes, now near to invisible against the black field of his Stained face. Parác noticed, and, mistakenly thinking it an opening in his opponent's defenses, started forward.

Mūk-Mudón's eyes flicked open with ferocity, locking onto Parác as he advanced. The surface of his glassy gaze reflected every armored glint and every sun-borne ray to mesmerize Parác, who faltered with an empty grin upon his face, suddenly seeking his own reflection in the depths of silvered gleam. An expression of yawning horror soon replaced Parác's grin as he was drawn in, finding instead unfathomable, cheerless light as from the far side of the most distant star, streaming away into oblivion. To Parác, the passing moment seemed an eternity. His soul, grown ancient and weary, dwindled within him, and he knew no more.

Belláphorus, Imafel, and Cloust had picked their way through the throng to watch the duel unfold. From their vantage nearby, it appeared only a moment's hesitance passed over Parác, whose expression in the space of a heartbeat shifted manically from daft to aghast. The trio imagined the slow horror that he experienced in that moment, each man familiar with Mūk-Mudón's strange abilities.

An almost imperceptible flicker of Mūk-Mudón's leaf blade, a silver flutter a hundredfold faster than they'd ever seen from him, and Parác's limbs and entrails exploded over his attendants in a gory shower to leave Mūk-Mudón standing alone. Calmly he wiped his blade across his cloak to remove the blood before smoothly sheathing it. He extended a casual hand to catch Parác's decapitated head, blown sky-high in the flitting furor, as it fell.

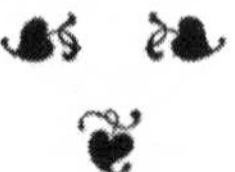

Standing triumphant before the amassed forces of the known world with his wound yet darkly seeping, Mūk-Mudón once again called on those gathered to pledge their fealty to him and to his dynasty. Man and Beast trembled before his terrible strangeness, and fear lent his bountiful charisma overwhelming power. None gathered could resist his offer, nor did they desire to do so.

Mūk-Mudón's feats had dispelled all disloyal ambition and lingering defiance, and the weight of his will yet dominated their minds, bending their thoughts even as each bent low in subjugation. Mūk-Mudón peered over the assemblage, haughty and certain of his superiority, his right to rule these warriors, and through them, the world.

A hot and dusty haze blew in from the West, carrying a low whistle, and something else–a shadow that closed over all to darken the glittering sheen of Mūk-Mudón's triumph. An impetuous Mūk-Mudón squinted into the haze, perturbed at the disturbance, and curious to discover what arrived on the fell wind. He perceived familiarity in the haunting melody whistling on the wind, and gasping, dropped Parác's severed head in the dust.

Perhaps it was their close acquaintance with Mūk-Mudón and familiarity with his powers that allowed the trio to see what now approached him in the dusty cloud. Whatever the reason, time ground to a halt for the rest, but Belláphorus, Imafel, and Cloust joined Mūk-Mudón to observe a silvery figure, wreathed in obscure, grey mist as it floated toward the Warlord, breaking through the dusty cloud and shedding ashen streamers upon its approach.

Though Mūk-Mudón knew well already what approached, his friends could only glimpse alabaster limb and great silver wing as they cut through the diminishing gossamer strands of mist until before them floated the incredible creature from that fateful moonless night during their hunt in the Western Wild so many years ago. Mūk-Mudón's friends drew close, as did their world, sounds growing muffled, and the throng gathered about them becoming indistinct shades, then disappearing altogether within the deepening haze. The strange wingéd beast paid them no mind and focused on Mūk-Mudón instead.

"It would seem you have achieved your goal," he spoke, his voice a sweet chime. Mūk-Mudón gawked in silence, for once uncertain how to respond.

"You're welcome," the creature intoned.

Over the years, Mūk-Mudón had traced his immense success back to his meeting with this . . . thing . . . and the power granted him through the talisman, the feather, that yet dangled wet beneath his armor. Oh, he may well have become an effective Warlord without the queer giftings of this beast, but since that day, he had become untouchable, always a league ahead of any situation, any opponent. No doubt he owed innumerable victories to the beast, and for that he was grateful.

However, he was curious what, on the day of his great triumph, the creature wanted, and, his curiosity getting the best of him, he blurted out, "Who are you? What do you want with me now? After all this time?"

Chuckling slyly and circling Mūk-Mudón, an indolent eye ever fixed on the grimy warrior, he answered.

"The name . . ." he spoke, trailing off dramatically before a sudden pivot to face Mūk-Mudón ". . . is Helél. I've simply come to reclaim what is mine."

"I believe you've got it right *there*," he said, pointing at the exact spot beneath Mūk-Mudón's armor, "and I would very much like to have it back. Now, please."

The word "now" hung on the densely charged air around the pair, resounding with more force every few moments as though an echo inverted. Meanwhile, Helél's lips remained sealed in a prim, smug smile.

The moment Helél had first sounded the word, the feather leapt inside the armor, scratching a tinny screed along the inside of Mūk-Mudón's breastplate as it tugged against the chain around his neck, seeking to restore itself to Helél's plumage.

"Now!" Piercingly, the word cracked the air about them. The feather broke from its chain and dragged Mūk-Mudón forward a stumbling step while he reeled to keep himself from careening into the dust.

"NOW!!!" The word boomed as thunder. Mūk-Mudón, prepared this time, lowered his stance and braced himself as the feather lurched violently beneath his breastplate, dragging him forward in shallow ruts left by his sabaton as Helél's strange power drew him forward.

The point of its quill facing outward within the armor, the feather spun ever more quickly, a dark and silvery radiance emanating from beneath Mūk-Mudón's collar. A glowing spot appeared on the outside of his breastplate, and he felt heat building within his armor as the spot glowed red, then brightened to a brilliant yellow until the feather burst forth from the armor, splashing molten metal as it flew to the very place from whence Mūk-Mudón had plucked it and rejoined its fellows upon silvery wing.

Enraged and wide-eyed, Mūk-Mudón, intending to stride forward and take back the feather by force if needed, instead shivered deeply, so deeply in fact that his armor rattled, and his face grew ashen as if he were on the point of death. All thought of taking the feather back fled his mind, as did any consideration of advancing in his armor, which had grown to such exceeding heaviness that it was all Mūk-Mudón could do to prevent himself from falling under its weight.

Seeking relief from the burdensome armor, Mūk-Mudón removed his helmet, and his friends, having drawn their weapons to flank their leader, caught his attention with their gasps. Mūk-Mudón turned to Belláphorus, who stepped back, horror in his eyes. Shaking his head gently from side to side, in sadness Belláphorus spoke two words, "Oh, Mūk-Mudón . . ."

Mūk-Mudón loosened the straps of his ruined breastplate, which dropped to the sand with a dull thud. For a moment, he felt some relief from the crushing weight that had afflicted him. Looking down, he saw now his body, withered to accompany the gaunt and hollow visage that moments earlier had taken his friends aback. Mūk-Mudón stared, shocked at his sunken chest, protruding ribs, and stick-like limbs, the skin covering them now paper-thin with powder-white, dusty channels crisscrossing where black etching once lay. The crushing weight returned to pulverize his earlier relief at removing his breastplate, falling now instead upon his heart as full of sorrow he looked up at Helél.

Helél, smiling gleefully, explained "You've no idea how you've sold yourself for ambition. From that moment in the forest when you took my feather, you've given yourself over piece by piece, as have all who've pledged themselves to your service. Until now, I've been content to leave what you owe with you and yours, but time has come for me to collect."

Mūk-Mudón groaned and hung his head, a deep weariness overwhelming his soul.

"Oh no!" Helél exclaimed. "Don't you worry! You won't remain thus. You will yet prove to be very useful."

Mūk-Mudón raised his head, glancing up at Helél in hopeful misery.

"That's more like it," Helél chimed with cheer, "Now let me show you!"

As he spoke, Helél raised a taloned hand before him, pausing for dramatic effect as he looked Mūk-Mudón in the eyes, and snapped his fingers.

As Helél snapped, Mūk-Mudón burst into a cloud of grainy, black dust, which settled into a mound among his armor. Floating eerily, Helél approached his remains while Belláphorus, Imafel, and Cloust stared on in stunned paralysis.

Helél chuckled darkly, beautifully, as he approached "What an admirable pile of dust you've become."

Helél hovered low over the black mound and gathered the sooty substance in both hands. With dust-filled hands cupped together he closed his eyes, smiled in triumph, and turned his face up to the sky. The haze around the three friends cleared, and they could hear again the din of the crowd around them.

Helél flung the dust into the air and flapped his wings in fury, blowing the dust over the gathered army. As those standing closest to him, the dust fell upon Belláphorus, Imafel, and Cloust first. Like Mūk-Mudón, the three burst instantly into the same black dust, and what remained of them joined the noxious maelstrom already spreading over the troops. The same fate awaited all, Man or Beast, as the swirling cloud grew in ever-widening range with Helél laughing at the center.

Those at the outer edge recognized the danger and attempted to flee. The dust, however, sought them out, and pulverized them all. The last succumbed, and the dust fell to the earth, leaving the fated plain of Za'aq Ha Dam a funereal black.

Helél called out to the dust, "Mūk-Mudón!" and the shadowy form of the once great Warlord rose to stand before him, a gritty and dark figure cast in the pure black smut that now covered the plain.

Helél eyed the figure and spoke "You shall yet lead these fallen here to establish an Empire at my command. Now! Go forth and conquer!"

Without a word, the coal-black golem turned to extend its arms over the battlefield. As it did so, the figures of all Helél reduced to dust now rose up from the plain. Uttering an unearthly and inhuman shriek, Mūk-Mudón commanded the army forward, its advance speeding upon a fell wind, guiding devastation across the land.

Gazing with hatred into the heavens from under glowering brows, Helél muttered, "There. Maybe *that* will get His attention," then vanished from the plain, leaving the wind to howl a lonesome dirge over the corpse-strewn battlefield.

The days that followed were dark indeed for all creatures, great and small. The army of dusk apparitions spread across the known world, ransacking those who opposed them, and subjugating everyone who surrendered, which all eventually did.

Walls and gates did nothing to deter the dark army. Many a fortress fell to the strange creatures, the Nihúkolem, as they became known, who floated over walls, blew in through cracks between wooden slats or walked through steel bars to materialize in deadly form behind enemy lines.

None could stand against a foe through whom weapons passed as if through a puff of smoke while they slipped very real blades between the ribs of their enemies. They were dust, yet with souls distinct, enslaved to Helél's service, leashed to Mūk-Mudón's will, and imbued with power to retain solid form when it suited the Empire's purpose. Immortal, yet accursed, they blanketed the world in shadow, and Helél ruled all from the shadows, Mūk-Mudón ever his shaded figurehead, a puppet emperor over an empire of dust and shadow, the Empire of Chōl.

The Empire dominated every aspect of life, exacting deep tributes and taxes, much of which was set aside to reward those who proved loyal to the Empire through the betrayal of friends and family. Even under severe taxation, reporting an acquaintance for complaints against the Empire, a friend for insulting the Emperor, or a brother for considering revolt made wealthy the cruelest of souls.

Helél enlisted his shadow army as secret police, their service no longer needed in battle once the world surrendered. Subjects of the Empire whispered reports of their strange abilities and seeming invincibility, adding to their fearsomeness. Though capable of speech, the Nihúkolem only spoke at need, and then only to those they oppressed. Between the shadowy Nihúkolem, verbal communication was unnecessary, cumbersome even, as information passed between all in an instant, unbound by the limits of distance. Frightening too was their ability for swift travel across great distances as specks coursing along the world's great winds to appear without sound warning, shadowy spectres further darkening an already desperate and darkened world.

Decades passed, and the world languished under the Empire of Chōl until, one day, a message passed in secret among the abject citizenry. The whispers spread far and wide for the wild hope, the absurd joy in even its consideration. In this age, a pauper born to the lowest of the lowly in a cruel and joyless world would herald the world's deliverance.

Chapter Eleven

Asara Ascendant

YEAR 29 OF THE IMPERIAL AGE

It was the first day of the month, Asara, so named for the star that climbed across Endego's sky each year in the tenth month of the Etom calendar. Near the end of the month, the star would reach its apex, shining its brightest with ruby light before a sudden decline in the sky as it dimmed, its prominence diminished until the following year.

Hurrying in the crisp, cool autumn air of Endego, Nida arrived at her marketplace stall after sending Nat off to school. Nat, now a couple months into his third year at the Bunker, had found fast friendship with a young etma, Rae, and was excelling at school. Ruminating on their many blessings, a smile rested on Nida's face, care-worn as the purse slung about her neck. Her smile was proof not of some fleeting joy, but one forged in the frenzied heat of almost endless exertion and tempered in the frigid cold of lonely despair.

"Lovely." The word hung ripe in the spice-laden, fragrant air of the bazaar, though she had not spoken it.

She looked around her booth to identify the speaker, alarmed and curious, before heading for the exit to see if she might encounter someone outside. As she was leaving her tent, a scrap of rolled parchment tied to a small leather bag on the ground caught her attention, giving her pause as she stooped to pick it up, presuming it to be another order for a tapestry.

She continued outside, looking about the market, which was close to deserted this time of day, and, failing to encounter anyone in the vicinity, she turned with perplexity to the parchment in hand. Lovely, the note began in flawless script, drawing a gasp from Nida before she continued with bated breath to read, her hands trembling:

Lovely Nida,

We would be most pleased if you might accept our invitation to a gathering in honor of your work. We heartily encourage you and your son to join us in celebration of your accomplished artistry at our hall beneath the olive tree the evening of the final Friday of Asara. With eagerness, we await your response in the affirmative, which we hope you will send by post with our compliments at your nearest convenience.

Your Friend,
Master Shoym

P.S. There may be dancing . . .

A small leather bag containing a few grains for payment of post on her response hung from the cord that was once wrapped around the parchment.

However peculiar he might otherwise be, Shoym is very thoughtful, Nida considered with appreciation before the import of the invitation struck her.

The olive tree! Nida's mind reeled, flattered by the invitation.

The olive was the lone tree of its kind in the grove, just as their rubber tree, and carried with it an air of mystery. The Etom inhabiting the homes around the tree were not all wealthy, though a fair number of them were, and yet they were somehow inexpressibly *different*.

The hall beneath the olive tree held even more intrigue for Nida, who recalled the muted music passing through its walls as she happened by on occasion. Not somber music, but not bawdy or jaunty either. The music was . . . it was . . . *lovely*.

There it was again! Planted in her thoughts as a hand might press a seed into warm and yielding earth. If ever she had been curious to discover what was behind those walls before, her curiosity now doubled. No! Tripled!!!

For all Shoym's oddity, he and his acquaintances had demonstrated unfailing friendship and kindness. And . . . something else. Something familiar. Excited and nervous, Nida made up her mind. She and Nat would go and see what these mysterious Etom were up to under the olive tree.

Looking about for a scrap of parchment, plume, and ink, she scrawled her response with shaking hand, tied the rolled note closed with the same leather cord from her invitation, then at once headed out to pick up Nat from school, determined to carry the invitation to their postmaster this very afternoon, and grateful to pay with the grains Shoym had provided. Nat and Nida were headed to a party!

Over the past few years, Nat had come to enjoy school very much. Though he had other friends, his friendship with Rae had grown paramount, and the pair spent a great deal of their time at school together. Because of his constant rejection before starting school, it had taken Nat until his second year at the Bunker to ask Rae if she might want to play with him after school. She, of course, said "YAAAAS!!!" and it was during their first play-date she'd revealed to him her greatest secret, something reserved for only the most trusted to know: Her mother was Headmistress Kehren!

She had told no one else at school for fear the other Etom children might treat her differently. It was, in fact, this fear that had drawn her to Nat, in whom she recognized the same, and in sharing her secret, the pair became the closest of friends, sealed in fervent trust. He promised to never mention it, though now he knew, the clues had been there to see in the dynamic between Rae and the Headmistress.

Regardless, their friendship kept them out of trouble for the most part, making class a joyous endeavor, and one at which they excelled. Barring excessive whispers and giggles, that is. It was on one such recent occasion, hunger weighing on their minds, that they broke from their studies for lunch, Nat and his classmates scrambled to the center of the Bunker.

Older students rolled out round, wooden tables and set them up, spacing them evenly throughout the clearing in the center of the Bunker for all to eat around. Meanwhile, the younger students gathered seats from either side of the testudinal entryway to place around the tables. The oldest students clustered around the tables in the center, leaving those around the edges for the younger folk, where Nat and Rae found themselves in the company of their classmates.

The Etom often wrapped meals in large leaves for storage, or for portability, a practice known among Etom as "green-kitting," as in "Whatcha got for lunch there? Green-kitting it today, I see." Only the wealthiest might carry their lunch in rot-resistant, carved wooden boxes of cedar or teak, so most of the children in Nat's class, including Nat, broke out leafy packets, unwrapping them with abandon to fall to the tasty morsels within more quickly. For her part, Rae produced a beautiful, golden teak box, placing it primly before her and draping a square, woven napkin over her lap before opening the lid, where lay utensils atop a tasty-looking delicacy.

The smell of Rae's savory dish wafted across the table, giving pause to the other younglings, many of whom stopped eating mid-bite to stare as many a crumb fell from open mouth to table. Even Nat stopped a moment to glance at Rae, who seemed unfazed by their gawking as she chewed contentedly on her meal.

Pausing after she finished her first few bites, Rae sighed, and pushed away from the table, calling out to the others, "Well, then! Who would like to try some?"

The table erupted in cheers as the teeming young Etom moved to sample Rae's delicacy.

From over Rae's shoulder, a brawny paw swept in, capturing her box, lunch and all as Rosco, in mock politeness, drawled, "Don't mind if I do."

Nat, upset at the offense, hopped up, "Hey! That's Rae's!!!"

Rosco, easily a head taller than Nat, cocked one brow and furrowed the other, unintimidated, yet amused that this ridiculous whelp would challenge him.

Nat, about as near to rage as he was capable, locked eyes with Rosco, gold eyes gleaming, and pointing at the lunch-box in Rosco's hand, "That's not yours, Rosco! Give it back!!!"

Hungry, and losing patience with the situation, Rosco reached for Nat with a free hand to topple him, stopping mid-motion as Headmistress Kehren's voice rang out from across the Bunker, "What seems to be the problem here?"

Disappointed and grumbling, Rosco gently set the lunch-box back on the table next to Rae, and snapped the lid shut with a sweep of his hand.

Leaning in close to Nat, he whispered with menace, "This isn't over yet, blue-bug. Not by a stretch."

Rosco turned to face the approaching Headmistress, feigning a smile that appeared more a pained grimace as he explained nothing was the matter, just a simple misunderstanding over Rae's offer to share her lunch. Headmistress Kehren asked Rae if she had offered to share her meal, glancing at her for confirmation. Rae nodded, unsure if she should tell the whole story before she heard Nat pipe up.

"But that's not what happened! Rae offered everyone a bite, and *he* tried to take it all!" he spoke, pointing up at Rosco, who now seethed behind a less and less convincing smile.

The Headmistress took a deep breath, shoulders heaving over her crossed arms, then asked Rae, "Is that what happened, Rae?"

Rae once more nodded, regretting it even as she did. Rosco was equally nasty to everyone unless they got on his bad side, which she had no doubt just decided to do. She was loath to consider how cruel he might be now he was angry with her, but also knew that Rosco was already mad at Nat and hoped to divert some of his ire. Rae appreciated that Nat had stood up for her and wanted to return the favor.

Rosco blubbered, "I don't know what they're talking about, Headmistress! They're fibbi—"

The Headmistress cut him off, "Rosco, I don't want any more trouble from you today. Normally, I might send you to detention, as you already know. You don't need another detention, so I'd like to give you the opportunity to apologize and skip the detention. Now don't you think that's gracious of me?"

Rosco's face contorted with anger for a moment before he gave a sullen response, "Yes, Headmistress. Very kind. Thank you, ma'am."

Rosco muttered an insincere apology to Rae and Nat and stalked away darkly. Though he didn't so much as glance in Nat and Rae's direction, they felt hot wrath radiating from him as he left. The two glanced at one another, uneasy as they considered how Rosco might retaliate.

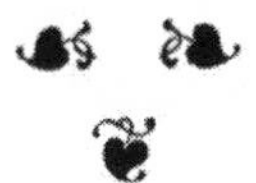

In the carefree fashion of young children, Nat and Rae soon forgot the dark cloud of Rosco's rage threatening overhead. Rather, the sunshine of playful friendship broke through, lining storm clouds with the silver of their mirth. Back in class, Rae's appreciation for Nat grew as she reflected on his courage in confronting Rosco. As was her custom, she gazed over at her friend, careful not to alert him to her surveillance, a smile betraying her affections.

Rosco marked the intensity with which Rae attended Nat, and an unkindly smirk wrinkled his lips as he considered his options in getting back at the two. It would be outside the Bunker, and he would encounter them unaccompanied to exact his retribution. He couldn't wait to lay hands on Nat. The meddling little blue bug thought he could stand up to Rosco, who held his own with the third-pod students in the schoolyard simply due to his size, cruelty, and willingness to act on it.

Granted, Rosco wasn't the brightest student, and had been due to rotate up to the third pod this year if not for failing his promotion exam the year prior, but he was a clever enough actor to manipulate the instructors. In fact, most teachers underestimated him due to his academic failings, in error thinking him a bit slow, and incapable of performing many of the offenses he perpetrated. If not for the presumption of the staff, coupled with Rosco's uncanny ability to avoid being caught in the act, he would have long ago been ejected altogether from the Bunker for his misdeeds. He was beneath scrutiny and enjoyed the low profile that resulted.

Today, he would watch for an opportunity to deal with Nat after he left the Bunker and would save Rae for another day. He already knew the exact tree under which she lived and would find it easy enough to intercept her the following morning on her way to the Bunker.

Class let out with the Headmistress' reminder to complete the evening's assignment droning through the periphery of Rosco's awareness while he observed Nat's departure inconspicuously as he could. Rosco waited a few short moments after Nat left, then got up to follow, able to easily track Nat's singular pale blue head bobbing along in the crowd toward the exit.

At first, it seemed Rosco would find opportunity for revenge this afternoon, when Nat left his classmates to stand alone in the clearing in front of the Bunker. Rosco hung back under the arch of the Bunker's entryway, ready to move again as soon as Nat did.

Without warning, Nat hurried across the clearing, and Rosco started, concerned that he might lose his trail. Rosco pulled up as he spied Nat hailing his mother, their greeting audible though unclear to Rosco across the still-crowded expanse. A passing and frustrated disappointment crossed Rosco's face, then transformed into a scowl of bitter determination. He might have to wait for another day, but he *would* find Nat alone, and when he did, he would make him pay.

As they left the clearing, Nida asked Nat about his day. At first, he brightened to tell her before his face grew a frown.

He spoke with care to avoid mentioning Rosco's name, "Well, there was a bigger etém who tried to take Rae's lunch. She'd already offered to let everyone at the table try it, but he took it anyway. I stood up to him, and the Headmistress came over to stop him, but I think he might be mad at me now." He finished, sadly looking down at his hands.

"Well," Nida comforted him, "I think it very brave of you to stand up for your friend, and *most* people will get upset if you stop them getting what they want. I bet you and this bigger etém make friends before long. Just be yourself."

"After all," she said, ruffling his zalzal, "you are *very* likable."

Nat returned a faint smile. His Mom was often right about things, but while he'd avoided getting on Rosco's bad side for the last few years, something told him that Rosco might *stay* upset with him for a while, and he didn't think they'd ever end up friends. He hoped his Mom was right and didn't want to let Rosco ruin the rest of their day. His smile perked, reassuring Nida that all was well.

"Are you quite finished now?" she said, teasing him. "It might be time for someone else to share now, don't you think?" Nat smiled up at her, nodding vigorously.

"Now it might surprise you, my darling son, but your mother has become something of a local celebrity. Why, just today I received an invitation from our good friend Shoym to a showing of *my* work. Can you believe it?" Nat stared in mute uncertainty. What was she talking about?

Nida shook him in mock frustration, "It's a party, Nat! In *my* honor, no less, and we've both been invited!!!"

Though he'd never been invited to one, Nat knew what a party was.

A toothy smile broke across his face as he bounced up and down, shouting, "A PARTY!!! I *LOVE* PARTIES!!!"

"Then it's decided," Nida continued, "We shall go to the party, which is not until the last Friday of this month." Nat was crestfallen to wait so long, but Nida countered, prepared for his disappointment, "I know it's a long wait, but now we have time to get *ready* for the party."

"Get ready?" he responded, bewildered.

"Of course, Nat. We *must* wear special clothes for such a special occasion, mustn't we? I have some wonderful ideas for yours, but first I need you to pick what color you'd like them to be. See? We've arrived!"

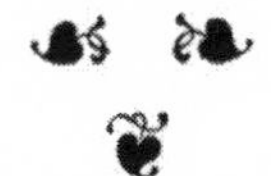

Their conversation had carried them to market, and more specifically to the stall whence Nida purchased many of the yarns and threads for her work. It was a spacious booth, with brilliant skeins of yarn and radiant bolts of cloth arrayed across broad tables slanted to angle the wares toward the shopper for easier viewing. Of course, texture was an important factor in selecting a suitable material, and the tables were low enough that it was simple enough to pass a hand over the various available fabrics and weaves.

"Nida! And Nat, too!" a cheery voice greeted them from across the shop, as an elderly she-shrew shambled toward them. A dark scarf was wrapped about her head, and matronly robes skirted her cinnamon-brown fur.

"Granna!" Nida replied, "It's good to see you!"

"Likewise, dear," Granna croaked. "And to what do I owe this pleasure?"

"Why, we've been invited to a *party,*" Nida confided, leaning down to put an arm around Nat. "And we're here to make sure Nat here looks a proper genletém for his first social engagement."

"Well then! You'll be wanting to browse some of our finer wares, no doubt? Come with me," Granna spoke over her shoulder as she waved for them to follow.

Nat and Nida accompanied her to the rear of the booth where laid across the table were some of the finest fabrics either had laid eyes on: purple linen, white silk, blue velvet, not to mention numerous richly-patterned fabrics and varieties of delicate trim.

Nida, gripping Nat from behind by both shoulders, bowed to whisper into his ear, "Go on, son. Pick one."

Nat stepped forward, peering about the table, until a scrap of blue cloth, both deep and brilliant, caught his eye as it peeked between crimson damask and sultry pinstripe. He reached for it, brushing his fingers across its velvety crush, then tugging to see if there was more.

Granna clicked her tongue, "Ah, that's a fine cloth. Let me see about it."

She removed the surrounding bolts of cloth, setting them aside, and revealing an entire bolt of the blue velvet, of the color called cobalt.

"That one," Nat stated with absolute certainty.

They left Granna's shop, Nida carrying a healthy swathe of the cobalt blue velvet and some white linen tucked neatly under her arm in a packet of brown paper, a roll of golden zig-zag ribbon secreted away in her purse.

"But what will *you* wear, Mom?" Nat had asked before they left the shop, his eyes blinking forlornly. He really was a good kid and believed that his mother needed to have clothes at least as special as his own for the upcoming festivities. He even felt a tad guilty she had purchased the cloth for his finery at the neglect of her own.

"Awww," she answered, favoring him. "Don't you worry, son. I've got something at home that should just about do the trick. It just needs a touch or two . . ." She trailed off, absent-minded and apparently lost in thought as she considered the alterations she might make to her garments.

They walked together, enjoying one another's company in silence until they had almost reached their home under the rubber tree, Nida breaking from her reverie to ask what might be good for supper. The two chattered back and forth, discussing the evening's plans as they entered their home, a wordplay both intimate and commonplace in loving homes. The evening wore on in cozy comfort, a fire lit within against the failing light and falling night. The two gathered to dine at the simple and smoothly-worn table in the kitchen, exuding a warmth no fire could match.

Nat's pure, shining enthusiasm at the prospect of the party perked a similar, yet mellowed excitement in Nida, who smiled peaceably as she considered the upcoming revelry. They washed up after the meal, Nida in playful manner prodding Nat to dress for bed, a doleful adoration in her eyes for his fleeting child-likeness as she watched him scurry away, squealing with happiness as he went.

As she swept again beneath the table, following up on Nat's work to ensure no crumbs, chunks, fillets, cutlery, or stoneware remained, she chuckled to herself, *Details are lost on my young one.*

He's getting better, though, she thought, relocating a spoon to the sink, and a small crust of bread to the wastebin.

It wasn't long ago he would have simply dragged the broom around the room, a track of miserable filth trailing behind. The table cleared and ready for work, Nida spread the velvet upon it, tracing with her finger a dozen different patterns before heading for her shears.

Nat busted into the room, clad in a fleece singlet (complete with backside dropchute), and circled the table in apparent attempt to lose either or both his eyes on Nida's shears.

"Ooooohhh! You're getting started, huh? What are you going to make me? A jacket? Some pants? A *kilt?*" he inquired with manic energy while darting to and fro beneath Nida's arms as she prepared to cut the cloth. Usually such a tolerable, sensible child in many ways, Nat nonetheless was, on rare occasions, hyper-active to an obnoxious extreme. This was one such occasion.

Frazzled, Nida poked her head out the front door for a moment for some fresh air, and to check for a full moon, recalling after a breath or two that it *had* been a very big day for them both. They both needed to calm down, and Nat was a confounded emotional snarl of excitement and exhaustion.

Okay, she decided. *Time to put him to bed.*

The clothes could wait until after. Nida came back in just the nick of time to intercept Nat leering over the fabric, shears in hand. Having narrowly prevented unknown travesties against the materials purchased for the festivities, Nida bustled Nat up to his bed in the loft overhead. A lengthy prayer of gratitude to Elyon preceded kind and loving goodnights, and they exchanged embraces before Nida nestled Nat deep under mounded covers. A sweet lullaby sounded from her lips while she caressed Nat's head, the youngster sighing contentedly in response as his eyelids drooped over weary, golden eyes. Her chorus, oft-repeated, she resounded yet again, softening to a whisper until Nat's eyes closed with finality.

Creeping quietly down the spiraled case, she stopped in the kitchen, turning about as she paced, then halted in internal debate with herself.

No! I mustn't stop. It's now or it's never!

Striding with determination, Nida went to her modest chamber, once shared with her lost love, and opened with temerity the closet at the back of the room. She reached hesitantly for a bundle on the overhead shelf, shrinking back briefly before gathering the bulk, spitting against the dusty cascade she brought down with it, a reminder it had remained untouched close to six years.

Anticipation paired with anxiety as Nida took a shuddering breath and carried the bundle out to the table. She dusted off its exterior, then stood back to examine the wax-covered cube.

Going to have to crack it open, she surmised. Nida rummaged through the bottom of her pantry shelf before locating a stout wooden mallet usually reserved for tenderization.

The fertile hesitancy remained, provoking uncertainty. Nida plowed onward in welcome distraction yoked to pinking expectation. Unsure what force might be necessary to penetrate the waxy shell, she timidly rapped the object. The mallet produced a minute crack in the shell, and a surprised gasp from Nida. She struck again, more confidently, and opened a wider gap. Tears fell unnoticed from her eyes. Nida swung full force at a section unmarred, the shell breaking apart and falling to the floor, where it shattered, a hundred thousand scales skittering drily across the room.

Beneath the shell lay several rubber tree leaves folded protectively over the contents. The leaves still supple, Nida nonetheless opened them gingerly for the delicacy of memories contained within. Her breathing ceased to shake, catching altogether at her first glimpse of the shimmering, white silk beneath. She scarcely dared caress the wedding garments, her gown and her beloved's vestments, protected from the elements all this time. She wept, overcome with emotion as these concrete reminders of their wedding day produced within her both memories shockingly vivid and bereavement stingingly poignant. There she remained, unaware of time's passage. Her hands sank into the tender crush, and she sobbed, gasping until her soul had emptied itself of tears.

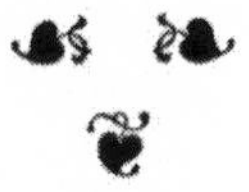

Late in the night, Nida had awoken, still bent over the table, and shivering in the cold autumn air, her breath puffing visibly in the lunar glow. She had swept away the detritus of the waxy packing and had stuffed the leaves into the wastebin before reclaiming the wedding garb to hang alongside her drab, everyday affairs in the closet. In the end, she had folded away the velvet for Nat's clothing, then retired to her rough, yet familiar pallet where rest had come swiftly, soundly.

Well before the sun's rise, Nida was up, kindling the stove to prepare breakfast, and, more importantly, tea. To savor the rich, dark nectar was to sample a portion of Elyon's own life-giving essence, as if fallen from the heavens for the benefit of all. The first sip in the darkened day was spirit-lifting ambrosia and had helped keep Nat alive on rare mornings when both awoke grouchy.

Thankfully, this was no such morning, and in good cheer Nat bounded down the spiral staircase from his loft, whistling a lilting rendition of the prior night's lullaby.

Still stirring the pot of porridge before her, Nida turned her head to smile at him, "Good morning, son! How did you sleep?"

Seating himself at their table, Nat propped an elbow on its surface to rest his face on the palm of his hand as he answered distantly, "Good. Good. Except I dreamt you were crying over a wilted flower. I was worried at first, because you seemed so sad. But your tears must've watered that flower, because then it bloomed again. A big, white one. A lily, I think? You were so happy. How about you, Mom? How did you sleep?"

A few words into Nat's response to her simple question, Nida had stopped stirring the porridge in dumbstruck awe until Nat had asked her how her rest had been. A hot bubble of the swelling porridge popped, spattering on the back of her hand.

"Aaaaahh!!!" Nida exclaimed, spurred into sudden action by the pain as she dipped her injured hand in the cool water of the washbasin and turned around to stir the pot of porridge with the other.

Nat jumped up, concern etching his features, "Are you alright, Mom? Is it bad?"

"No, no," Nida winced, "it's not too bad. Here, get me some bowls so I can get this off the stove."

Nat scrambled for the bowls, as Nida pulled her hand from the water to examine the burn, now a sizable red spot on the back of her fuchsia hand where the steaming dollop of porridge had landed. It would be fine, she saw. It would just be tender for a day or two but didn't seem it would blister.

Nat returned promptly with the bowls, "Here you are, Mom!"

"Set them here on the counter, dear," Nida directed, "I'll spoon this up right away, and we'll eat together while I finish my tea."

Nida scooped the porridge into their bowls, finishing each with a generous helping of honey over top before they settled in at the table. As they ate, she showed Nat her hand, which he gently stroked while Nida reassured him it wasn't serious. After, he asked about his new clothes for the party. With skill Nida deflected his questions regarding the particulars of the outfit and winked at him playfully.

"It's a secret, dear. A *surprise,*" she added with a mischievous smile.

Cocking a pointed finger back and forth in the air, Nat nodded with hooded eyes, "Oooooh, so it's a secret, is it? I gotcha, Mom."

Nida chuckled at his precocity, unsure from what strange fount this peculiarity of personality sprang, but appreciative nonetheless. They finished their breakfast quickly, each looking forward to a full day, and gathered their things before they departed, leaving their home dark and cool in their absence.

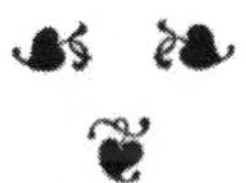

The next few weeks, Nida and Nat said their farewells outside the Bunker, the excitement of the upcoming event growing within them. For her part, Nida focused on her work, while Nat played with friends, studied hard, and avoided Rosco as much as he could. Every day they found one another under the dandelion outside the Bunker, a sweet reunion each time, followed by a hearty feast at home, then bedtime for Nat, and loving labor for Nida, who worked tirelessly on their ensembles for the party.

Thursday morning, the day before the party, Nida bid goodbye to Nat outside the Bunker, letting him know he would need to walk home by himself because she needed to deliver an order that afternoon.

"Maybe I can ask a friend to walk with me?" he inquired with hopeful expectation.

Nida smiled agreeably, "Sure. Maybe your friend Rae?"

Nat blushed.

"Sounds like a great idea," she said, and pat him on the back to usher him off to class. Rosco watched the exchange, unknown to Nida and Nat, then fell in far behind Nat, trailing him to their pod, where Rae rushed over to embrace Nat in greeting, his eyes bulging noticeably as he struggled to breath under Rae's affectionate constriction. Rosco chuckled unkindly at Nat's discomfort, and slipped around to the back of the pod to await the start of class.

The day passed without much event for Nat, and before the lunch period was over, Nat told Rae that he'd be walking home by himself that afternoon, shyly adding that he would very much like her company. Rae, already well-accustomed to walking herself home, thought it a marvellous idea, and responded with enthusiasm (meaning loudly) in the affirmative. Ever lurking about, Rosco overheard their plans, and sneered grimly, pleased at the opportunity.

After class ended, Nat and Rae gathered outdoors to situate their packs, Rosco watching at a distance from beneath the Bunker's shadowed entryway. The two struck out, and Rosco waited until they were almost out of sight to pursue them, unwilling to risk being found out so close to school.

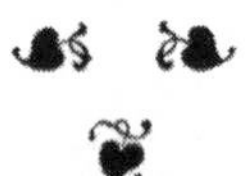

One could sense the autumn chill on the air, and a noticeable frenzy of activity among living things also signaled the first frost as the creatures rushed to prepare.

In her excitement, Rae tugged at Nat as she urged him aside from their route homeward, "Come this way a bit. I want to show you something."

Curious to see what she wanted to show him, Nat willingly complied, Rae's fervor energizing him. They passed under the shaded fronds of many a willow before traversing Potter's Arch, a rustic, wooden bridge over the Üntfither, one of several streams passing around and through the wispy village grove of Endego.

Past the bridge, a clearing opened around a gnarled and silvered tree with dusky green, oblong leaves. Homes great and small spread beneath its branches, though one peculiar structure among them, a rectangular building of cut stone that stood at least twice the height of the nearby homes, held Nat's attention.

Rae, for once quelled, hushedly approached the edifice, guiding Nat by the hand until they stood a short distance away, peering from the cover of a great stone, where they set down their packs. From inside the structure a haunting, beautiful melody drifted to them, music unlike any Nat had ever heard. In the clearing, it seemed all else grew still to give heed to the tune, and in the sacred silence, the drifting symphony swelled, unique voices of wind, brass, and stringed instruments growing distinct, the crack and blast of percussion and tympani interspersed rhythmically among their dulcet tones.

"Come on!" Rae urged, "Let's get closer."

At first Nat hesitated, but Rae would be neither dissuaded nor delayed, for indeed she had already trotted up to the side of the building and was following the wall toward the back of the structure, searching for an entrance.

He rushed to catch up with her, and together they discovered a black iron gate standing open at the rear of an enclosed courtyard that opened off the rear of the building. A covered walkway ran the larger part of the courtyard's length, beginning a few steps inside the stony walls. A door into the building stood open at the end of the walkway, the glow of candlelight and sound of music beckoning within.

"Wait! We're not going in there, are we?" Nat asked his friend, hopefully.

Rae took Nat's question as a challenge, a dare, and a devilish glint lit her eyes as she asked, "Why? You're not afraid, are you?"

Nat stammered his denial even as Rae gripped his hand to bolt forward, dragging him toward the glowing entrance while his incompliant feet stuttered over the walk.

Once inside, the pair spotted several doors leading off what appeared to be a foyer lit with oil lamps along the walls. Right before them stood a set of closed and forbidding double doors, and from a door to their immediate left, they heard sounds of hard work, perhaps hammering or digging.

Next to this one, another was cracked open, the melody growing louder as they approached it, and dim lamplight flickered within. Rae pressed gently on the open door, and the two peered around its edge, their eyes reflecting the dancing flame that lit the room.

They ducked inside and closed the door behind them, their eyes adjusting to the meager light shining from a lamp mounted on a nearby stand. Finding the stand light and portable, Nat carried it along. The room, though somewhat narrow, in its length seemed to run the width of the building, the lamp's scant illumination dwindling in distant shadow. From behind a closed door and several steps away along the right, music resonated, surging to shake the room at times. Against the wall opposite this door lay what appeared to be large, half-assembled, wooden frames.

Taking an interest in the frames' construction, Nat walked deeper into the room, Rae huddling near him to remain in the lamplight. Nat was mildly disappointed to find nothing but frames in various stages of manufacture along the left-hand wall. However, as they passed the door on their right, he swept the lamp that way, then stood, frozen in contemplation, as the light revealed what hung upon the wall.

Rae came alongside him, and transfixed the two remained, examining the image before them. Upon further inspection, Nat with certainty identified the image as one of his mother's tapestries, now framed with care and hung as if a masterpiece, a work of art, and not a mere decoration. It was one of her earlier works, Nat now recalling with clarity the many hours he'd spent on it as a grublet when it lay spread across the floor, the wondrous shapes and colors spilling forth from Nida's lap as she worked from her rocking chair at home.

He remembered now the primal delight of tracing the soft, inky darkness and of touching the stars blossoming within the celestial cloud that swirled across the weave. The symphony grew indistinct to Nat and Rae as they walked along the wall to the next tapestry, an expansive continuum of blues, azure above and aqua below meeting in unbroken, silvered horizon. Clouds streaked across the shifting sky as whitecaps crested atop the churning sea, and a sense of awe began to surge within Nat.

His mother had, of course, told him the tales of King Elyon, often while crafting the tapestries now before them, yet the care and reverence with which they were handled here stirred something new within him. The unspoken tale entrancing him, Nat imagined he felt a breeze within the storeroom walls, then heard a tinkling chorus arise among the nearby score, its melody slowly softening until it stopped.

A bright and tiny light, a star in smallest form, descended through the ceiling high overhead. The sudden brilliance drawing his attention, Nat followed its course, his golden eyes shining in unbroken focus. The light struck forth with sudden speed, and piercing Nat above the eyes, transported him mind and soul. In the darkened storeroom, he slumped down to the floor, Rae gasping in surprise as she crouched over him attentively, while unbeknownst to the children, a mysterious figure observed their drama with interest from the shadows.

Chapter Twelve

Speaking Life into the Land

That star that had transported him from the confines of the now-forgotten storeroom glowed and hummed merrily, resting at Nat's side. Within the spark's melodic polyphony, Nat detected meaning, a hidden speech that warmed and guided him as understanding sprouted within.

Nat found himself a guest among the earliest memories of the fabled land of Gan. And where else could he be? For the sky and earth were full of Elyon's speech and song, a soaring symphony to imbue everything that has breath with His life-giving nature. Before him, a palace stood forth from the land, an alabaster pinnacle of stone that shone there in the daylight, the abode, no doubt, of the great King. The star had set Nat before the courtyard gates that stood outside the palace walls where Nat remained, awestruck in the still and unadorned expanse.

The palace gates boomed open, and Nat gasped as Lord Elyon strode forth, majestic and inscrutable. The young etém was as nothing, just a speck before the King's frightening goodness, an unrelenting and foreign virtue that made Nat tremble. Though well beneath His lordly notice, Nat felt compelled to bow, and found it nigh impossible to view the King directly for fear. In his distress, Nat noticed an approaching assemblage of fauna: An Elk, a bear, and quite a few he couldn't put a name to. Where they gathered round their holy King, each bowed its head in homage, not in servility, but in recognition of their Lord's primacy. Finding himself not alone in obeisance, Nat took heart, and a burgeoning peace calmed him.

In reverent silence the King stood within the palace gates to whisper some deep and wonderful thing to the earth, through which a glowing white sprout broke without a sound, crumbling the rich, reddish soil as its trunk rose and expanded. The shoot grew up beyond His waist, and slow beams of silver and gold light laced the air all about the trunk, budding branches following shortly thereafter to trace the neon paths.

The King spoke, His words echoing now far and wide though without effort He spoke, "Behold! The Tree Ha Kayim!"

Leaves, shimmering as rainbow scales of a fish, unfurled upon the branches, and spread the light of the Tree Ha Kayim in wondrous patterns that shone upon the King, the land, and the creatures, all of whom crept closer in awe.

From beneath the tree's spreading roots, a spring burst forth. The King sighed, as did the land, and leading due South a trench opened, through which the spring's waters ran sloshing from one side to the other as they raced to their end in a shallow pool miles away. Nat glided with the river South, the star obliging him to go.

Wheresoever the waters overflowed the banks, tall grasses, flowers, and every kind of growing plant at once took root, spreading where they found place. The stream of water that issued from beneath the roots of the Tree Ha Kayim, shining as crystal and pure as light, cascaded over a narrow precipice not far from the royal gates, casting prismatic flashes in pristine sunlight.

A passenger to its will, the star elevated Nat to observe the land from above. From overhead, Nat watched the waters flow from the palace in the North to the center of the land, where they diverted also due East and West, with the Southward stream yet unbound along its course. The springwaters split into ever smaller streams and rivulets as they spread life throughout the land in a network pattern of veins and capillaries resembling those within a leaf.

All creatures of the land ran thereafter to drink at the stream, and every green and growing thing stretched forth leaf, branch, and root, seeking its tributaries and growing fruitful in its nourishment. As all gathered at the stream, so now did the Nat and his astral companion, who dipped them over the Southerly flow to speed them to its end.

At the southernmost end of the trench, they found the pooling waters whirling, then rising over the banks to splash the rich, red earth. Here, too, green life arose, ringing the pool. Most notably, on the pool's far side and opposite the Tree Ha Kayim, another Tree sprouted, this one a rich, nutty brown, and glowing with faint green light, as it rose through the now sodden earth.

As the trunk of the tree thickened grew tall, its bark became gnarled, and its branches stretched forth, toward the great sheets of thick grey stone that now arose from the ground to ring Gan with a formidable wall. In the wall's only gap grew the second Tree, its uppermost branches grasping the top edges of the wall on either side. Wherever wall and tree touched, slender branch reached deep into stony crevice until they stood as one, the Tree an arboreal sentry over the southern reaches of the land.

From where He still stood before the palace gates, the King spoke yet again, the words resounding in Nat's ears even at great distance, "Behold! The Tree Ha Datovara!"

Along its tawny limbs, a million multicolor blossoms bloomed, each bud a vessel of fragrance releasing its refreshment into the air as it opened. As soon as they bloomed, the blossoms stirred in wafting wind, and in each nexus of perfumed petals, a budding drupelet surged.

Each drupe grew to size, the Tree fruiting fully in an upward gust that stiffened to detach and carry off the petals, the Tree discarding them in disuse. The remnant of that primal morn, the flowered breeze lingered over the land, each petal a prism casting light in kaleidoscopic shower to the blessing of those below before dispersing hither and yon, even outside the wall.

Nat marveled at the sight, recalling tales told of the world's morning, in which all trees sprang from far-flung fronds strewn about on a mysterious wind. Among the Etom, every grove, even Endego's, owed its origins to these, the first and only flowers of the Tree Ha Datovara, which, pressing into the virgin soil of the world, sprouted trunk and limb and leaf, a forest grown from every petal.

Nat stood in isolation at the beginning of the world with none to tell, save the light at his side. It appeared the star sensed his loneliness, for its shine shifted to an amber glow, and its song grew sweet as it drew close to his chest. Warmth blossomed against Nat's skin, and his host carried him over the pool before the Tree Ha Datovara. Nat appreciated the creature's attempt to comfort him, and found he rather liked the strange spark.

Appreciation ended abruptly, however, as the star whirled Nat about to face him skyward over the pool, eliciting a strangled cry from him, "Urk!"

His guide whistled an apology as it turned a shade of orange.

Suspecting what came next, Nat managed to shout "Wait!" before the star dropped him. Flailing as he fell, Nat plunged into the water, ever reaching for the orange flame that yet hovered over the surface. Kicking and struggling toward the light, he broke through the waters to find in its stead the warm flame of a lamp upon its stand, and Rae jostling him vigorously in attempt to awaken him.

Chapter Thirteen

Asara Paramount

Sitting up from where he lay upon the cold and stony floor, Nat blinked hard at his friend Rae in the dwindling light, unsure just how much time had passed. For her, it had been mere moments, though panic had prolonged her suffering.

"Nat! What happened? Are you alright?" she asked, throwing her arms around him in relief.

She released him and stood, prepared to depart the strange place.

From his place sitting on the floor, he stared at her in wide-eyed wonder. "Rae! Rae, you'll never believe what I saw. *Who* I saw. It was Lord Elyon! I could hardly look at Him. He's so good and . . . scary."

Rae's looked at her friend, frowning doubtfully.

"Did you hit your head when you fell?" she asked with skepticism.

She hadn't found anything wrong with him when she'd checked him over, but she was no doctor.

"No! No, Rae. This was real. I was *there,*" he answered, pointing at the nearby tapestry of the Tree Ha Kayim standing before a palace.

Rae imagined she heard the creaking of a door hinge and chose to humor him in hopes they might leave, "Ok. Ok. Let's talk about this later. Right now, we need to get out of here."

They both stood to leave, suddenly aware that the music had stopped.

Nat swept the lamp before them as they advanced with caution, calling quietly ahead, "Is anyone there?"

No response forthcoming, the pair hurried along, Nat setting the lamp aside carefully before they exited into the foyer. Finding the area still deserted, they sprinted out the back door, traversing the courtyard in seconds, and fleeing through the iron gate, unaware that eyes still followed them.

Making their way back to the stone they'd hidden behind earlier, they stopped to catch their breath in the dwindling light. It was getting late, and after resting, they arose urgently to gather their packs and leave for home. Suddenly, a hand fell on Rae's shoulder and slammed her back into the rock.

"Oooww!" Rae exclaimed, as Rosco leaned in, leering inches from her face, his breath hot on her skin and smelling curiously of peppermint as he pinned her against the rock.

"Feel like sharing now, princess?" he mocked. "Maybe you'll think twi—agh!" he exclaimed, recoiling from the switch Nat whipped across his left cheek.

Nat stood stock-still, switch clutched in white-knuckled fist, poised to strike again.

His golden eyes gleamed, and a grimace replaced his usual sunny smile, "Leave her alone, Rosco!"

Wincing, yet undeterred by the stinging welt across his face, Rosco turned on the smaller etém, advancing too quickly for Nat to effectively swing again. Rosco caught the switch and wrenched it from Nat's hand mid-arc, then planted a hand in the middle of his chest, and shoved him, hard.

Nat tumbled backwards in reverse somersault, sprawling on his belly, where he spat dust from his mouth, furious tears running muddy tracks down his face. Rosco was just so, so . . . *cruel*! Being such a good-natured youngster, Nat didn't quite understand it. Rosco, meanwhile, had returned his attention to Rae, who hadn't been idle while he was distracted with Nat.

From the moment Rosco had turned on Nat, Rae searched frenetically for some form of defense. In short order, she spotted a round stone sunken part-way in the ground nearby. It was smooth and looked substantial enough to threaten Rosco. She scurried to it, sliding the last few inches on her knees, and tearing her skirt (Oh! Mother would never let her hear the end of it!) while she used her fingers to dig tracks around the edges of the stone to loosen it.

Out of the corner of her eye, she saw Nat fly backwards, propelled by Rosco's push, and tugged on the stone as hard as she could with both hands pushing down into the earth with her feet in hopes she might free the stone. To her surprise, it came quite easily. So easily, in fact, that Rae swung it overhead, and she almost toppled over backwards with the unexpected force of it. She recovered her balance with Rosco now striding toward her and held the rock overhead in both hands before stepping forward to hurl it at the bully.

Rosco stepped aside as Rae clumsily loosed the stone, chuckling as it arced ponderously past him. At first dismayed at missing Rosco, Rae uttered a disappointed groan. Her disappointment became a frightened warning cry and time seemed to slow, the stone flying on a collision course with Nat, who still laid in the dirt.

Nat, unable to avoid the hurtling projectile in time, cried out as well, and hid his head under trembling hands in dread anticipation of the impact. Watching through spread fingers as she covered her face, Rae looked on, horrified, as the rock continued on its course, certain to strike her friend. Rosco also stopped, turning to watch, a satisfied sneer on his face.

At the last moment, a stranger stepped in, inserting a hard, black case between Nat and the stone, which bounced off the case with a loud "CRACK!!!"

The three children froze in shocked silence, and the stranger spoke, patting the case, "Well, I certainly hope the old gal is alright in there. No doubt broke a string at the very least. Now then, what's going on here?"

Focused as they had been on the melee, none of the three young Etom noticed the newcomer's approach. Now each one stared at the handsome, young genletém who stood before them, an inquisitive look on his face. His skin was a muted, buttery yellow, and he wore a black hat, a bowler, which he sported jauntily tipped back on his head. He wore a white linen shirt, the sleeves of which were rolled up to the elbows, and a black vest, colorfully embroidered with two large brass buttons down the front. Between his vest pocket and upper button of the vest hung a gold watch chain. His plain, black pants had a neat crease, and his low, black leather boots were well worn, though they had a proper shine above a dusty scrim around the soles.

Dumbstruck as the trio was, the stranger offered again, "Maybe one of you will share with me what's happened here?"

Pulling a clean white kerchief from the breast pocket of his vest, he reached down to his case to dust off the rough, circular scuff left by the hurtled stone, "By the looks of it, things were about to get right nasty. You, there. What were you doing with these two?"

He fixed a stern gaze on Rosco, who blanched at the air of authority this intruder carried. Looking at Nat and Rae, Rosco shook his head, muttered something about their luck, and fled the scene, the newcomer taking a few quick steps after him before skidding to a stop in a dusty swirl.

Instead of pursuing Rosco, he turned to help pick Nat off the ground by the elbow, offering a hand in introduction as he did, "Hello there. My name's Dempsey. Are you well enough to stand? Looks like you took quite a fall."

Nat took a few shaky steps, still trembling from the confrontation before he nodded furtively, grateful for Dempsey's intervention.

Dempsey called Rae over with a quick wave, "And you? Did that other etém hurt you?"

Rae shook her head, hesitant tell the strange genletém too much. Their parents hadn't approved this diversion to the olive tree, and their delay in heading home was proving much longer than she had anticipated. Now it was getting late, and their parents could well be concerned at their absence. She just wanted to be on their way, so they might have time to get cleaned up before their parents got home, too.

Oh, well. Her parents had taught her that honesty was best, so she mustered her courage and spoke, "I brought him to hear the music from the strange building under the olive tree there, and we lost track of time. The other etém was mad at us because of something that happened at school."

"He caught us here, and was going to hurt us, so we're very glad you came along, but we don't want to get in trouble with our parents, so will you please, please, please just let us go now?!?" Rae ended plaintively, pleading Dempsey for release with hands clasped together before her.

Dempsey contemplated his response for a moment, before he answered, "Listen here, I play at the temple over there," he gestured over his shoulder with a cocked thumb, "almost every afternoon. I'll let you go on two conditions: first, I need both your names, and second, I need to know that, should this bully ever trouble you again, you'll let an adult know, even if it's just me. You know where you can find me now, and when, so I expect you will."

"You should both know what happened today was dangerous, and you," he locked eyes with Nat, "nearly had your skull bashed in. I need some peace of mind that I haven't turned you out to be brained later by that misfit. Now, will you two agree to my terms?"

Nat and Rae looked at each other, then back at Dempsey, and nodded their agreement.

Nat went first, extending his hand to Dempsey, who shook it warmly, "I'm Nat, Master Dempsey. Thank you very much for helping us."

Rae curtseyed self-consciously, well-aware of the tears in her skirt and her general dishevelment, "My name is Rae. We appreciate your help, but we really must be going. We'll both probably be in trouble as it is for just coming out this way without permission, never mind the scuffle. If it's all the same to you, we should be on our way."

Dempsey sighed, rubbing his hand across his face, "All right. You've met my terms, young Master Nat and Mistress Rae."

"So, I'll let you go n— Hey!" Dempsey exclaimed as the two rushed to collect their things.

Rae called over her shoulder, "Thanks again, Master Dempsey! Your music is delightful! Maybe we'll come listen again and see you then?"

Dempsey shook his head, turning his bowler in his hands as he muttered, "Geez. At least let a guy finish, will ya'?"

He chuckled, wishing them farewell and good evening as they disappeared into the dusky shadows beneath the willow, then turned to retrieve his case and saunter back to his home beyond the olive tree.

Nat deferred to Rae, who was in a panic at the prospect of her parents beating her home and escorted her there before turning homeward himself. They arrived at their destination on Cliphook Lane, a stately home with a spreading, well-trimmed lawn through which ran another of Endego's tributaries, the Altfither. Two small bridges crossed the stream where it met the circular drive, which forked in either direction just inside the palatial gates. Rae peered through the brass bars of the gates, then breathed a sigh of relief. Neither of her parents' coaches were parked in the drive. She had made it in time.

"Please, Nat. Not a word of this to anyone if you can help it. You're a mess. Your mother will wonder what happened to you. I'll forgive you if you tell her but hope you don't."

Nat had never lied to his Mom, and didn't plan to start now, but maybe she wouldn't ask him what happened. "I-I'll try, Rae. I don't like lying, especially not to my Mom. I should probably get going now. Hope you have a good night."

He went to leave, but not before Rae embraced him fiercely. "Nat, you're my very best friend."

She released him, and he took a bewildered step back while she slipped through the gates then dashed for the large double doors of her home. Watching to make certain she'd gotten inside safely before he left, Nat raced for home, weary, yet exhilarated from the day's adventure.

Nat was not quite so fortunate as Rae.

His mother had beat him home by a narrow margin, and was searching through the house frantically, calling his name, a note of desperation in her voice, "Nat! NAT! NAAAT!!!"

From outside their home, her heard her and burst through the door. "Here I am, Mom! I'm right here!"

Nida rushed to him, and clutched him close in embrace before she noticed the state he was in. Looking him over, she saw he was covered in dust from head to toe, and had scrapes on his hands, forearms, and head. "What in the Elyon's holy name have you been up to, Nat?!?"

Nat spluttered, unsure where to begin, before making a full confession, the words pouring out of him in a jumble as he told her Rosco had caught them after school, and he'd done his best to protect his friend, just like his mother had taught him. Nat ended his tale in tears, his face downcast, sure that his mother was disappointed, but desiring to be honest with her.

There he stayed, seated at their kitchen table, staring down despondently at his hands, before he felt Nida grip his shoulder to reassure him, "Nat, dear, thank you for telling me what happened. I'm proud of you for defending Rae. It sounds like this bully needs to be taught a good lesson, though I'm not sure who should be the one to do it. I need to think about it. I don't want to rush it. In the meanwhile, just do your best to stay away from him, and let a grown-up know right away if he tries to hurt you or Rae again. Will you do that for me, Nat?"

Nat looked up, his face a muddy mess from the mingled dust and tears there, but happy that his mother understood his heart, and nodded, smiling through his tears. In the rush to tell his tale, he had left out some of the details, such as their trespass of the temple, and, more importantly, his strange vision therein.

Since it had not been Nat's intention to deceive Nida, perhaps he might be forgiven the omissions. For now, however, he was home, and Nida took care to draw him a warm bath and cook him a fine supper before putting him to bed with a tale of Gan and prayers, a lullaby on her lips once more as he drifted into slumber.

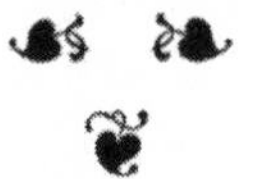

The day had finally arrived! Nida and Nat were a blur of activity on this, the final Friday morning of the month. There would be neither late deliveries nor unauthorized excursions today. Nida and Nat would both race home to prepare for the celebration as soon as they were able. Their excitement over the upcoming event was apparent as each went about their usual, mundane morning tasks with unnatural fervor.

They bustled happily out the door and to the Bunker, Nida reminding Nat to stay away from Rosco and come right home after school. Nat was happy to oblige his concerned mother, and offered the ironclad promise of youth, complete with pinky extended to shake in solemn affirmation. A pinky promise among Etom was as good as gold, and Nat put his reputation on the line with his promise, not that Nida was concerned about him doing otherwise.

Yesterday's events were an anomaly, and she needed to let him explore a bit more now he was getting older. Today, though, she needed him home right away, and didn't want him crossing paths with Rosco after class besides. Nat was a wonderful child, and she trusted him. She smiled at him affectionately as she released him from her embrace and sent him on his way into the Bunker, watching until he disappeared from her view, as was her custom.

Nat was bursting with excitement as he hopped down into the pod next to Rae, who looked much better than she had the night before when they'd parted ways.

"Did you get into trouble, then?" he asked.

Smiling conspiratorially, she answered, "Not a bit!"

"Have you seen Rosco about?" he inquired nervously, sweeping his golden gaze around the pod and beyond into the Bunker, intending to keep his promise, and, thus, his distance from the brutish bully.

Rae noticed him looking around, and ribbed him playfully, "You're not scared, now are you?"

Truth was that she'd never expected Rosco to come after them like that, and yesterday's assault had frightened her. That Nat, small though he was, had stood up to Rosco so bravely impressed her, and had inspired her defense of him in kind, even if she had come close to braining him in the process.

Nat, looking sad for a moment, answered, "A little, but only because I don't like seeing *anyone* get hurt. I know he's mad at us, but I hope he'll stop now."

Rae was amazed that Nat was concerned for Rosco but didn't believe Rosco would stop until he'd gotten his revenge, whenever and however he might.

Catching their eye as he entered across the pod, Rosco slinked down into his seat, a sullen expression on his face, and a glaring red welt across his mossy green cheek where Nat had struck him with the switch the day before. Rae stifled a laugh as Nat shushed her and swatted at her absentmindedly, concern on his face as he looked across the pod at

Rosco, who glared straight ahead, determined to ignore his classmates' curious glances and speculative whispers.

Nat and Rae passed their day with peripheral, passing concern for Rosco, losing themselves in the study and play of the day until they found themselves once again outside the Bunker, parting ways at the end of the week.

Nat left Rae to join his mother as she waited for him across the clearing.

Nida greeted him, "Hey there, Nat! How was your day?"

"It was great, Mom!" he exclaimed.

Nida gestured toward Rae as she left the clearing. "You *must* invite your little friend over for supper one of these days."

"Uuuh, eeerm . . . alright. Maybe next week?" Nat responded shyly.

"Why, Nat! You're not embarrassed of your mother, are you?"

Nat blushed a glowing violet, and answered, "No. That's not it. I don'—"

"Nat," she interrupted, "I'm just teasing. I know you'll ask her over soon. I'm just excited to get to know your friend is all. Now let's get moving for home, and after, the party!"

She pumped her fist in the air as she said "party," and Nat followed suit, one hand in hers and the other extended in a fist as he jumped in the air, "Hurray! A party!"

The two continued in the same exuberant spirit, laughing at times, skipping at others, as they made their way home, the joy of the forthcoming celebration on their minds and in their hearts.

Somehow, Nida had managed to evade Nat's inquisitive forays into her chamber and keep the design of his clothes secret by hanging his newly crafted outfit on a nail in the wall behind her clothes. Now was the time to reveal to him the garment she had tailored with love for the occasion.

Nida made him wait outside her room in the common area, closing the door behind her as she went to the closet for his attire. Outside her room, Nat stood listening with head cocked attentively to one side as she rustled about. Moving so quickly she startled him, Nida swung the door wide open and pulled him into her chamber to view his garment, which she had draped over the edge of her bed for presentation.

Accustomed to the rough weave and drab palette of coarse, inexpensive fabrics, Nat timidly reached out to caress the fabric, the trim, the cuffs of his clothes, unable to believe how his mother had transformed the raw materials into this, this finery the like of which he'd never worn.

Tears in his eyes, he turned to his mother, "Is it really mine, Mom? It's *lovely*. I can't believe it could be mine."

Nida, choking back tears of her own, spoke haltingly, "Why, of course it's yours, Nat. Don't be silly. Let's go try it on!"

She shooed him out the door and up to his room to change, then swept her own door closed as she sashayed merrily to the closet. Pulling aside her everyday garb, Nida found her own garment, a wedding gown now made fit for a ball, and pulled it out to begin changing, humming happily as she did.

Nida had found modifying her wedding gown an emotional challenge, suffused as it was with bittersweet memories of Jaarl, now lost to them, and of the sun-kissed life that had died along with him. Once she had made the decision to press on, the challenge diminished with each snip and stitch, as if crafting in homage to her widowed life. When she had lost Jaarl, she had discovered the lifestyle they had knit together no longer fitting to the occasion, and out of necessity trimmed the domestic frivolities that comprised what she had once considered happiness.

In a vacancy of heart as empty as Jaarl's deserted place setting, a mysterious, abiding security began to grow. Nida's confidence in surmounting the challenge of raising her son and fending for the two of them alone likewise grew. Time passed, and Nat occupied Jaarl's once-empty place, and happy he was to fill the place before him, and Nida's as well, with spatters of mash as he flung his arms about and spluttered obliviously in his high chair.

In short, Nida's new lifestyle had proven a work in progress, and she had been unsure at times how to proceed in even the most trivial of matters. Memories of her husband's faith and her own burgeoning confidence in Elyon, uninformed though it was, buoyed her. In the same way, transforming her flowing white satin wedding gown into a dance-appropriate and much less involved dress for the ball had been an act of faith.

She'd reduced the amount of fabric in the main body of the dress, also shortening the skirt to a few inches below her knee, whereas before it had drifted so heavily as to sweep the floor. She'd removed the blooming sleeves at the shoulder, leaving finger-width straps to support the bodice, and from the sleeves had crafted delicate white gloves that rose just past the elbow.

She simplified the bust to a few folded layers across the front, with the waist cinched just below it for an uncomplicated and comfortable form that swished pleasantly around her knees as she pirouetted about the room. Using Nat's leftovers, she'd fashioned a gold-fringed, cobalt blue hooded cloak with white satin lining, which proved a both comfortable and warm enough covering to traverse the village on their way to the olive tree. As she finished dressing, Nida enjoyed the fruits of her labor over the prior weeks, especially pleased given the limited time she'd had to complete the garments. She again swung her door open energetically, excited to see how Nat liked his new clothes.

Nida entered the dining area of their home just as Nat came down the spiral staircase from his loft, one hand gliding over the rail as he slowly, reverently smoothed over the crush of velvet and folds of linen, delicately fingering the stiff, zig-zagging gold trim.

Lost in thought, he didn't notice his mother poised in expectation at the bottom of the stairs, though he began to call out to her, a dopey smile on his face, "Mom, I still can't belie—"

The words died on his lips as he raised his eyes and saw her, "Mom!"

He hurried down the final steps to her to catch up her white gloved hand in both of his, "You are *BEE-YOOTIFUL*!!!"

Nida blushed and thanked him, then told him to turn around so she could view him in his ensemble. He wore velvet breeches terminating below the knee, and a short velvet jacket hemmed at his midriff over a formal shirt of fine, white linen. As he turned, Nida straightened and tucked, ordering him to lift an arm or look up at the ceiling as she adjusted the fit.

He'd had no idea what to do with the linen cravat, which she now tied loosely around his neck, draping the folds over his chest. His jacket had a short collar that stood straight up, and its front had neither lapels nor buttons. Its close-fitting sleeves allowed for remarkable freedom of movement, and its short bottom hem ended over the trimmed and tasseled linen sash Nida tied around his waist.

Last, Nida pulled up his linen stockings, securing them under the gold-trimmed cuff of the breeches with a smart little brass button. Beside scuffed and weary brown leather shoes for daily wear, Nat owned one other pair of shoes–shiny, black formal shoes that fastened with a leather strap through a square, brass buckle over the instep. These Nat had worn only once before, and thus he and Nida engaged in an epic struggle to shoehorn his feet into the unbroken leather, succeeding after some time, prolonged strain, and repeated pounding on the heels to finagle feet into inflexible footwear.

To be certain, Nida's son looked very dapper, and he preened somewhat, sauntering about the dining area, and obviously very pleased with his attire. Almost every night over the past weeks, Nida had instructed Nat in some common Etom dances in preparation for the party tonight, rehearsing with him the steps and movements until he began to gain some familiarity with them.

Though time was limited before their departure, she took Nat through the choreography once more, pleasantly surprised as they traversed their rugged kitchen floor by how much he'd retained in the short time they'd had. Nida made certain to praise him for his dancing, hoping to inspire enough confidence that he'd participate tonight.

The sun winking beneath the horizon, Nida fastened the cloak about her shoulders, and called her son to depart. Nat sprang to respond, bounding across the room while Nida stepped aside to hold the door open. Nat sped past with Nida on his heels, and she spun to close and lock the door. Once outside, she cocked an elbow aloft and cleared her throat to catch her son's attention. After several such signals, Nat took eventual notice, and ceased his absentminded dawdling, removing hands from pockets to stand at attention beside the walk, his own crooked arm held aloft as he sheepishly looked back at his mother. Nida chuckled, stepping forward to slip her arm into his, and they at last were on their way to the party.

Night drifted down, a dusky grey gossamer screen falling over Endego, the flutter of fireflies as golden beacons heralding the advent of starlit sky. Passing beneath the drape of willow fronds, and over the chuckle of fervent stream, Nat and Nida hurried on their way. They rounded the trunk of a shaggy willow and spied from afar the temple where only yesterday Nat and Rae had met Dempsey. The temple lay radiant under the olive tree, for the well-lit rectangular building shone as if made of gold.

The two gasped in concert in the spectacle of it, and turned to one another before Nida patted Nat's arm, "Come on, then. Let's go have a closer look."

Nat nodded, and they set out for the brilliant structure, approaching timidly as they encroached upon its light.

A friendly greeting floated across the expanse, and Shoym stepped forth from the brilliance, his shadow cast long over them, cavorting playfully with his approach, "Nida, dear! So very glad you've come! And Nat! Am I to understand that you've visited us before?"

Nat at the Ready

Nida interjected in the awkward silence as a flustered Nat struggled for words, "Let's just say this is his first *official* visit, and leave it at that, shall we?"

Nat smiled at his mother with appreciation for the rescue, and produced his heartiest greeting for Shoym, extending a rigid hand as he barked, "Very nice to see you again, Master Shoym!"

Shoym, chuckling, cocked his head and cupped an ear toward Nat, "Eeeeh? What was that again, Sir Nat!?!"

Nat almost repeated his greeting but stopped himself short as he caught the mischievous smile on Shoym's lips. Nat giggled, and Shoym ruffled the his zalzal affectionately before offering a hand to Nida to guide her up the burnished steps into the shining temple, Nat following close behind. As they passed through the courtly gates, tall enough to reach the top of the temple, Shoym told them of the temple's significance.

Nat gaped at the gates, covered with ornate carvings of Nature, Men, and wingéd Beasts, and plated with what must be gold, before Shoym's words caught his attention "... which is why you see the Malakím included in the carvings. The entire structure is a monument to Elyon, and we've included as much of His story and that of Gan within its walls as we were able to collect."

They passed through the large, open entrance hall, the floor of which was composed of highly-polished stone, Nat noting the impressive columns supporting the ceiling, stamped at their capitols and bases with a strange fruit that he didn't recognize.

Here and there a friendly greeting sounded from the Etom they encountered before they passed into a long hall lined on each side with columns, and with rows of long benches (Shoym called them 'pews', but Nat thought they smelled fine) across the floor, a single aisle running down the center of the room to the front of the hall to terminate at a broad, low stage.

"... and this, is our sanctuary hall," Shoym finished.

A podium stood centered on the stage, a large, dark curtain draped across the back wall, covering it side to side and top to bottom. At the front of the hall, past the benches and before the stage, a considerable group of Etom stood milling in the orchestral pit, the din of their various conversations growing as the trio approached.

Spotting a young etém breaking away from the gathered crowd, Nat recognized Dempsey's familiar face and voice as he hurried up the aisle to greet them. His appearance much improved since their grimy encounter the day before, he wore a smart black jacket with long tails, short black breeches, white stockings to the knee, and the same weathered black shoes, though now polished to a reflective shine free of dirt and dust. Nat also noticed a small swath of Stain behind each of Dempsey's ears, now visible in the absence of his bowler.

He hailed Shoym heartily, "Dear Master Shoym! So very nice to see you've arrived this evening. Is this the guest of honor, then?" he inquired, turning to Nida to offer his hand in greeting.

"Why, among all her fine qualities, did you fail to mention her beauty? She is *lovely*!" Dempsey exclaimed as he kissed her hand.

Nida, silent in surprise at Dempsey's overtures, blushed, then turned to Shoym, and enquired in a steady, still voice, "And who, Master Shoym, may I ask is this charming genletém?"

Shoym gestured toward Dempsey with an open hand, "This, dear Mistress Nida, is young Master Dempsey, a respected member of our community, and quite an accomplished cellist in our orchestra. I hope you will forgive his excitement. I've merely shared with him, and many present tonight, your exceptional character and ability."

Recognizing Nida's discomfort at his words, Shoym added, holding his hands up before him in a posture of defense, "Without embellishment, I swear before Elyon!"

Resilient though Nida had grown, her trials had not prepared her for the challenge of receiving such complimentary praise, and she found herself scarcely able to incline her head and thank Shoym.

Following Nat's birth, and the subsequent alienation Pikrïa had devised, affirmation became a distant and remote memory ever dwindling in slow retreat from ready recollection. Head still down, she blinked back tears now surging up from the abandoned well of her honor, regaining composure as she forcefully exhaled, and looked up to find the smiling face of Dempsey awaiting her.

The moment lingered pleasantly until a subtle lowering of the lights in the hall caused them to stir, the first strain of viola now resounding as the artist ran her bow across the strings. The sound of the orchestra tuning their instruments in the shroud of deepening shadow at the front of the great room lent a pensive warmth to the dimming hall.

Nat intently watched the various musicians tending their instruments while Dempsey excused himself to rush and join the orchestra. Shoym ushered Nat and Nida to their seats at the front of the room, just left of the orchestra. After Nida cajoled her son into his seat, she settled in herself before turning to thank Shoym, but he had unexpectedly left their company.

From his seat, Nat observed that all the musicians were dressed in the same black attire as Dempsey, rendering them almost invisible now the lights were down. He sat stock-still in the spectacle of it all, and the orchestra quieted while a solitary figure crossed between the audience and the orchestra pit, visible when he passed the low lamps illuminating the lip of the stage.

A gleam broke across the conductor's weathered profile when he opened a shuttered lamp before turning his back to the audience and ascending the rostrum. The conductor placed the lamp before him on the podium, from which he produced a slender white wand, his baton. He flourished both hands as he raised them, baton in the right, in preparation for the performance, and Nat heard a whispered shuffle of movement in the pit as the orchestra shifted in readiness. He imagined Dempsey perched at the edge of his seat, embracing his cello in left arm, fingers poised on the strings, and bow hovering over them in anticipation of the first stroke.

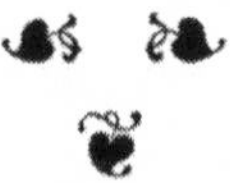

A resonant, low hum started from the bass strings, enveloping the audience. Nat sat mesmerized in the crescendo as first cello, then viola, then violin added their voices to the strain, the vibrations now palpable in the hall. At the back of the stage, the black curtain rose along with the music, attendants on either side of the stage directing their lamps at the back wall, across which hung a peculiar contrivance. Two sets of rails ran parallel from left to right across the breadth of the stage's back wall, and a pair of stagehands, also in black attire, wheeled a tall and vaguely cubical apparatus draped in black from a well-concealed door at the far left of the wall behind the stage.

Nat watched the two stage hands with curiosity as they wheeled the apparatus to the where the rails began on the left side and flipped up the back edge of its drape. The top of the contrivance reaching well overhead, one of the hands climbed a stepladder, then appeared to attach the device by some means to the rail. The top of the device met the upper rail precisely, and Nat assumed its bottom met the lower rail in similar fashion when the other hand stooped to repeat the procedure his partner had completed up top. Both stagehands scurried away to secrete themselves behind the hidden door again as the music faded to the forlorn piping of a lone flute.

From the far right of the stage a masculine figure dressed in scarlet top hat, jacket, pants and black boots strode boldly across to where the apparatus waited. A bit of theatrical magic, a spotlight, illumined him as he went by. His right hand resting on the upper edge of the device, he turned to face the audience, a golden vest peeking out from beneath the lapels of his jacket as he removed his stovepipe in the left hand with a sweeping flourish and bowed low over his extended left leg, the heel of which he cocked. The figure rose grandly from his bow, peering out from under his brow as he straightened, and Nat caught his breath.

Gripping his mother's arm and shaking it with excitement, he exclaimed in whisper, "Mother! It's Master Shoym!"

And indeed, it was Master Shoym, who stood solemnly, now gripping the drape over the apparatus in his right hand and cradling his scarlet top hat against his left hip as even the piping flautist fell silent.

In the silence, Master Shoym's voice boomed forth, "In the beginning!!!"

The stringed instruments quivered excitedly from the orchestral pit as he whisked the drape away, then flung it aside, revealing what appeared to be a tall wooden box. In the next moment, he tossed his hat with a twitch of the wrist to send it spinning off in the opposite direction. Nat followed the hat as it skated to a rest at the lip of the stage before returning his attention to Shoym, who it seemed had removed a narrow, lengthwise sliver of the box. Shoym stepped to follow the spotlight as it glided to the right, leaving the strange device and the section he had removed veiled in shadow.

In the susurrating hum of stringed instruments, Shoym spoke with clear and solemn intonation, "In the beginning, The Lord Elyon spoke the universe into being, His first words—"

The music died away again, and Shoym turned to face the apparatus as he spoke quietly in the stillness, Nat and the audience straining to hear, "Let there be light."

The orchestra sounded with horns stabbing, kettledrums pounding in steady crescendo, and strings quivering anew as the spotlight shifted to display the stunning image of a swirling, nebulous coruscation against the wall to Shoym's right. Even in the commotion of the hall, Nat heard his mother inhale sharply, the flutter of her hand as it flew to her mouth catching the corner of his eye in the mellow shade. Nat tugged at her arm with concern, noticing the emotive gleam of tears cascading down her cheek.

"What is it, Mom?" he asked.

"Why, dear Nat," she responded tremulously, "I do believe it's mine."

Nat took another look at the wall, Shoym having affixed the image, held within a large frame, to the rails along the wall. Shoym walked several feet to the audience's right, shifting along the rails the portrayal of starry, brilliant cloud on field of midnight black.

Upon further inspection, Nat identified the image with certainty as one of the tapestries that he and Rae had discovered behind this very stage the day before and wondered what might come next.

The answer came in form of light, a familiar, brilliant form arising from amidst the galaxies to linger high within the hall, casting rays into high ceiling, corner, and wall. Nat recognized the twinkling shape from his earlier encounter, a preamble to recollection, an expectation come to mind.

The answer came in form of light, a familiar, brilliant form arising from amidst the galaxies to linger high within the hall, casting rays against high ceiling, corner, and wall. Nat recognized the twinkling shape from his earlier encounter, and in preamble to recollection, an expectation filled him, though he struggled to recall why. Suddenly Nat remembered, and with the memory stiffened, drawing in a heavy breath, his heart catching in his throat as the star sped toward him. Once more, it flashed before Nat's eyes as light caught his mind away, his head lolling to the side in gentle surrender as he beheld again a vision.

Chapter Fourteen

The Sunder

Once again, Nat found himself in the land of Gan, though things had matured, since his prior journey, the land grown lush and showing signs of cultivation. At his side floated once more his companion spark, chirping chipperly in salient song.

Nat stood in a clearing beneath the prismatic falls just south of Elyon's palace, its spire silhouetted over top the nearby rise in the light of dawn's first blush. Unlike Nat's first vision, several moments passed without event, and he peered about expectantly in the absence of some dramatic happenstance. Discovering none, he turned instead to his shining guide, with whom he'd yet to become acquainted.

"Hello, there. Can you understand me?" Nat asked the brilliant orb, which bobbed gently in place before his face.

The star revolved, ejecting colorful plumes of light as the rhythm and melody of its song changed. For a moment, an answer tugged at the edges of Nat's perception. Desperate to discern the star's response, Nat's mind leapt to grasp the meaning, which seemed instead to send comprehension skittering away.

"You just tried to answer me, didn't you? I'm sorry. I'm having some trouble understanding you. Would you mind please trying again?" Nat pleaded.

Shifting again and rolling ever so slightly, the sparking orb sung out once more, and this time, Nat imagined he heard a voice fading in and out of his awareness, *I . . . you are . . . one . . . trouble . . . me. You . . . too hard.*

Nat gawked, amazed to understand the creature's distinct words, albeit incompletely.

It hummed again, *You . . . trying . . . hard.*

Nat cocked his head, brow furrowed in perplexity.

Again, it whistled, *You . . . trying too hard.*

"I'm trying too hard?" Nat responded. "Give me a second, okay?"

He took a deep breath and prayed Lord Elyon help him understand, his face growing serene as he relaxed, trusting Elyon would help him, then returned his attention to the task at hand.

"I'm ready now. Please try again!"

The star sang out once more, and now in Nat's mind, he clearly heard, *I said you are the one having trouble understanding me. I can hear you perfectly, Nat. Been listening for a while now, actually.*

Nat gawped, "That's amazing! How do you know my name?"

I was present at your birth. Just ask your mother, if she's not already told you the tale, and I've visited you since. King Elyon assigned me to guide and protect you, Nat.

Curious, Nat ventured, "Do you have a name?"

The spark spun, and brightened, throwing off a prismatic shower as it danced around Nat's head, singing merrily, *Why, yes! Yes, I do! It's been quite a long while since anyone has asked it. My name is Astéri Ha'vimminkhulud, of the Malakím, a messenger of the Lord King Elyon, and quite at your service.*

"Asteriskaboom?" Nat asked, perplexed.

The sparkling star dimmed, drooping low over the ground, its color now a gloomy lavender and its song pitching low and dissonant before it repeated drily, *Astéri Ha'vimminkhulud.*

"That's long," Nat responded. "Can I just call you Astéri? I can remember that."

The compromise seemed to cheer the star, and it brightened once more, though not quite to its former brilliance, *That will suit me just fine, Nat. Please call me Astéri.*

"Then may I ask you another question, Astéri?" Nat began, "Why haven't you spoken to me before?"

Though possible, it is much more difficult for me to speak to you in your, your . . . temporal manifestation, which is why I've brought here.

Nat asked, "Temper-what-now?" a puzzled expression on his face.

Yes. Well, maybe I can explain it better to you. Astéri floated over the nearby stream where it exited the pool beneath the waterfall, *Think of your 'temporal manifestation' like this stream. In it, time flows in one direction, and . . .*

Onto the water Astéri flung a bright spark, which did not fade, but floated on, carried atop the stream before Astéri continued, *Like this spark, anyone who lives within your 'temporal manifestation' is powerless to change his or her direction within the current. This is the lot of all creatures since the Sunder, that time flows ever onward until Elyon declares an end to the ages. Though we may observe what has occurred, we cannot change it.*

"But if we're not in my 'flow' now, then where are we?" Nat asked.

Flow! Astéri chimed. *I like it! Well, let's say we're no longer in the natural flow, but observing it as spectators. As Malakím, we are not subject to the Sunder like the rest of Nature or even our accursed brethren, the Shedím. We may yet sit upon the banks as it were of your flow and choose where we wish to enter it.*

"What's happening with my body right now? Last time, you scared Rae pretty bad," Nat spoke miserably. "I'd hate to think how frightened Mom might be right now."

Ah, yes. Astéri answered, dulling some, *Regrettably, I was unable to introduce your being back into your flow at the exact moment I had retrieved you. It's not a precise art, though I promise I will do my best to return you before the flow has carried everyone else along too far.*

"I guess there's not much to be done at this point, right?" Nat asked. "After all, I'm already here."

He looked around with curiosity. "Why *am* I here, by the way? I mean, I like getting to know you and all, but not much else is happening."

Astéri glowed, flitting left to right, and resonating meditatively, *I'm glad you asked, and your timing is wonderful, Nat. If you'll just be patient and watch, I'm sure you won't be disappointed, though I warn you what you see here today may disturb you.*

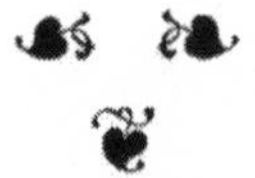

A nearby path opened into the clearing about the falls from the embrace of trees that overshadowed its level course. Nat peered into the shadows for long moments until almost giving up the watch. At that instant, the bare forms of a Man and a Woman stepped from the dense shade into the morning's early light.

"Is that Kessel and Pethiy?" Nat asked.

Indeed, Astéri responded. *Now watch. I'm sure you'll find this instructive.*

With some dismay, the Etom remembered the race of Man, long feared among the diminutive race for their destructive and exploitative nature. Often enough, Etom villages had fallen victim to the heavy footfalls of Man as they crushed homes and fields, determined to carry off the wee creatures as slaves, for they were quite handy in producing fine goods requiring the nicety of detail that miniature scale afforded. Some Etom were used for entertainment, least cruelly as actors in plays opposite puppetry, and most as gladiators pitted against various pint-sized predators.

The Etom learned early on to remain hidden, settling far away from the civilization of Man, and thus avoid contact with the larger bipeds. Etom fathers and mothers all told their children to stay away from Men, warning them with tales of their cruelty toward the Etom for fear a curious young one might wander close and be captured.

Kessel, the first Man, and Pethiy, the first Woman, were first in notoriety among all members of Mankind, and the first of their kind that Nat had seen with his own eyes. Yet, when Nat observed them among the abundance of that verdant garden, he felt pity. Pity because, stately beneficiaries of Elyon's wondrous gifts though they were, Nat knew them to have thrown away the company of their King, forsaking the plentiful bounty of Gan to toil in the wilderness, and exiling the great remainder of Creation along with them. For a moment, it tore at him, the painful fruit of their folly. He wondered dismally for what purpose Astéri had brought him here, and to what woeful event he might bear witness.

Astéri and Nat glided along, following the fated pair, who wandered without aim, yet southward, ever southward. From his prior visit, Nat knew what lay to the south, the Tree Ha Datovara.

Though this day had been long in coming, neither Kessel nor Pethiy spoke of it, both unconsciously recognizing that their curiosity about the Tree's fruit had now captivated their imaginations. Not willing to admit their deep fascination with the Tree and its polychromatic fruit, both made sure their conversation along the way was light and did not hint at their ultimate destination, though both with certainty knew it.

The forest opened into a lane several yards wide on either side of the stream flowing from the Tree Ha Kayim. Low, lush grass covered the ground alongside the waters that ran straight to the Tree Ha Datovara, the branches of which high overhead spread a leafy canopy over the forest below. A green and golden glow surrounded the Tree, illuminating the wide-eyed faces of the Man and Woman.

Astéri, its usual, twinkling light grown subdued, and cheery song fallen mute, carried Nat to a high branch not far from the Tree Ha Datovara to watch events unfold. His guide now silent, Nat recognized an altogether different tune floating on the breeze.

Upon entering the clearing, the Man and Woman, too, noticed the song—deep, dark music from beyond the Tree. They both realized it had been playing for some time but couldn't place exactly when it had begun. In any case, the song served to draw them nearer the Tree at a quickened pace once they were aware of it.

Their desire now exposed, they cared not that the other knew, and both savored the breathless, heart-pounding sensation of approaching the forbidden. It was altogether new to them, and the novelty grew more intense with each step closer to the Tree. In a moment of clarity, both recognized their folly, and stopped while still a good distance from it. Realizing that they could not return from this decision, they looked at one another in hesitation. In prolonged agony, they fought temptation, wrestling against curious desire, and ultimately deciding they enjoyed intimacy with Lord Elyon too much to ever jeopardize it. Their minds made up, they together turned from the Tree and the allure of its fruit. Then the music stopped.

While they had yet neared the Tree, the music had grown louder. The silence was deafening in its place. Both froze in place, unsure what to do. A musical voice called down from the branches overhead.

"Why, hello," the voice spoke its melody.

Curiosity seized them in its grip, irresistibly wrenching them around to peer up into the branches of the Tree for the owner of the voice. Ten or fifteen feet up, a dazzling creature lay along a branch, dangling a lazy arm and leg, his head propped up on a fist. His tail swished hypnotically, swinging beneath him in slow, lackadaisical arcs.

Dazzling was the only appropriate word for his appearance, for he shimmered and danced in their vision like an emerald mirage. It took the Man and Woman a moment to ascertain why he glimmered so. He was covered in shining, sparkling green scales, his blood-red eyes gazing down on them bemusedly through slitted lids.

From his perch alongside Astéri, Nat shouted, "No! Don't listen to him! Just go!!!"

Alas, we can do nothing to alter the past. The flow is set, forever unchangeable. Astéri informed him with dejection.

Helplessly, Nat watched on, already certain of the outcome.

The creature spoke again, "Leaving so soon?"

His voice buzzed and echoed pleasantly in their minds, and along his body, scaly gills fluted musically in beautiful, seductive counterpoint to his words. Without sharing a word, they decided to stay a moment, intrigued by this new and interesting thing.

"What brings you two way out here, then?" the creature asked.

Kessel and Pethiy stayed fixed in place, staring dumbfounded at this odd being.

At last, Pethiy couldn't bear it anymore, and took a step forward to speak, "What do you know of this Tree and its fruit?"

The creature reached out with a long finger to caress a nearby piece, which shimmered and flitted kaleidoscopically as it swung and twisted this way and that on a sturdy stem.

"Oh, *this* fruit?" he asked. "It's simply the best fruit to be found in all of Gan. Perhaps best even among the fruit *outside*, too."

Both turned and looked at one another, expressions equal parts alarm and excitement on their faces.

Outside? They both thought. *How did this creature know about the outside? Was he from there? How had he gotten Inside, then?*

None in Gan desired to leave the safety and bounty of their land, and the two marveled that this strange creature had so casually admitted his knowledge of the lands outside their walls.

Almost as if reading their thoughts, he spoke once more, "You could know more, too, if you'd like. You needn't leave this place, either."

The pair seized fiercely on his statement, interest apparent on their faces.

"How?" Pethiy asked.

"Why, you need only taste *this,*" he spoke as his finger again prodded the nearby fruit, which shimmered again, casting its dancing, hypnotic light on their upturned faces.

Fighting her own desire, she protested, "But the King told us never to eat of this fruit, or we would die!"

The creature with a sly smile answered, "Now did he *really* say that?"

He produced a piece of the fruit, and tore it open with marvelously white, pointed teeth to reveal glistening, delicious flesh and colorful, fragrant juice, which ran down his glittering hand.

"See," he said silkily, leveling his gaze at them, "I've tasted it, and do *I* appear dead to you? The Tree's fruit will make you as wise as the King. I dare say that's why He wishes to keep it for Himself!"

The lie had a powerful effect on their naïve and innocent minds. Any defense of the King's goodness withered within them as the two believed the worst of it, and in that moment, they saw the King as a cruel deceiver intent on keeping them from greatness. Any remaining restraint they had disappeared, and both started for the Tree again, determined now to taste its fruit.

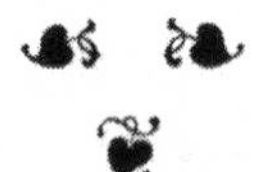

Unlike all other fruiting plants in Gan, the Tree Ha Datovara, itself subject to the King's edict, did not offer up its fruit at their command. Instead, the scaly beast flicked a sharp talon through the stem of the dangling fruit in a flash, and it tumbled toward the ground.

Gasping in concern, Pethiy stepped forward quick and light, and extended her hand to catch the fruit. Now that she held it, her hunger was uncontrollable, for the cool texture and weight of the fruit lent themselves to the obvious appeal of the fruit's aroma and appearance. And the creature's words yet buzzed and clicked, pacing her mind restlessly.

As wise as the King!

She couldn't resist any longer. She bit through the thin, bitter rind into the sweet, juicy flesh beneath, staining her mouth, her lips, her hands. It was unlike anything she had tasted before. Her eyes shone unnaturally as her mind raced and her thoughts soared loftily. Possibilities never before considered streaked through her mind, casually smearing her ordered paradigm in passing to produce a mild and intoxicating confusion within her. She found it pleasant to dwell in the chaotic skepticism that developed to smash through the upright naïvety of her drastically changing mind.

She recognized the particular and exceptional position that she and the Man held in Gan, their deep import in its affairs. She turned around, and the Man cowered beneath her sharp and demanding gaze. The fruit had already replaced the gentle tenderness heretofore ever-present on her face. In truth, he seemed less to her than he had moments before, for she now considered herself something greater in having tasted the forbidden fruit. She strode toward him, the fruit outstretched in offering, disgusted at his fear, but desiring still to share with him the blossoming, sensual transformation already begun in her.

He must *understand!*

She compelled him eagerly, "Take, eat!" and to his shame, he all too willingly complied.

Together they devoured every bit of the fruit, licking fingers and lips for every last drop of its versicolor juice. Kessel's eyes, now hard, and bright, caught the glittering beast, a nasty grin on his face, leering at them as he hung from the tree by an arm, his foot planted against its trunk, and tail twitching cattily. Kessel looked down at himself, and at his mate, both naked and covered with the stains of the juice.

He felt bare, exposed unlike ever before, and recognized their nakedness as though formerly clothed, their garments now torn from them. Glancing back up at the beast in the tree, Kessel saw the triumph in his face, and at last understood, as his heart plummeted, how the beast had tricked them. Their choice to eat the fruit had been a decision to believe this, this *stranger* over King Elyon, who had only ever cared and provided for them!

Feverish desire and a single lie from the beast had shattered their enfeebled trust in Him who had ever proven trustworthy. Shame and rage both lit Kessel's face, his blood rising hot. His foolishness now produced within him a deep self-loathing, and a curious and furious desire to lash out in violence against the queer creature. However, even as he stood to do so, the two heard in the distance the voice of King Elyon calling for them.

Kessel and Pethiy stood still as statues, dismay painting their features as the juice painted their skin. A fierce desire to hide themselves and their act took hold of them, and they both raced to edge of the pool, plunging into the water to remove their stain. While the pure, crystalline, waters indeed served to remove the stain from their skin, the rainbow shimmer did not dissipate in the waters. Horrified, they watched as the swirling colors blended in the glassy waters, turning a dirty black that crept through the pool toward the mouth of the stream descending from the Tree Ha Kayim.

What the stain touched, it changed. All living creatures that met it grew somehow darker, too, and, for the first time in all remembrance, Nature began to turn on itself. A glossy-eyed bullfrog lashed out with its long tongue to snatch a dragonfly out the air and consume it, loudly gulping down its victim. The cattails along the edges of the pool darkened to a sickly greenish-black and wilted until their heads dipped into the pool.

From above, Nat watched, horrified, as all the while, the inky, murky stain spread through the water, its effect lurching over the edges of the now swampy pool as the darkness inched through the grass.

Kessel and Pethiy leapt from the water to flee the corruption but had nowhere to run. Where could they go? Recognizing their hand in the spreading calamity, terror bloomed within the two humans. All their safety, all they had, was tied to the King they now feared to face.

Their fear redoubled as King Elyon strode through the trees at the end of the clearing. He laid eyes on the duo, who stood shaking at the epicenter of the sickness that troubled His land. Aware the King could reduce them to dust at a word, they trembled, and fell to their knees.

King Elyon knew what Kessel and Pethiy had wrought, yet instead of wrath, a deep sadness etched His features while the guilty pair argued their justification across the expanse. He spotted, too, the wretched, gleeful face of the scaly, green beast still watching the destructive scene unfold. The instant the King's searing gaze fell on it, the glistening beast's eyes went wide, and he turned to flee up into the branches.

Without hesitation, the King spoke, "Forevermore crawl, Serpent!" The beast's arms and legs vanished in chaff of shiny green scales, the creature growing stiff as a nearby branch while falling to the ground to land with an 'oof!' and a 'thud!' Recovering, the cowardly Serpent hissed, and slithered away in swift retreat through the roots of the Tree Ha Datovara to disappear beyond the wall.

King Elyon turned his attention to the Man and Woman, and spoke, "You two have no understanding of the suffering you have brought upon yourselves and upon this world. Woman, you will now know pain in bringing forth life, and your desires will ever set you and the Man at odds."

"You, oh Man, will no longer rest in my provision, but must now toil to survive. Both of you will live under the weight of what you have wrought upon this land, as will your children, and your children's children. For truth, you will surely die as I told you when I forbade you to eat the fruit, yet not for a time."

"You both, in your foolish wickedness, have likewise corrupted my holy Speech, and have distorted the harmony between yourselves and between all creatures. This very moment, they turn on one another as the filth of your stain reaches them. Look! It poisons even the *land* I created for you to enjoy"

"But . . ." He paused, weeping into His hand, "but most grievously, you have sundered the connection between you and me. No longer may we walk together in friendship as we have in the past. You are my own, my children, and precious to me, but the price demanded to restore our friendship pains me bitterly. As My Word stands eternal, One will come, a Kinsman, to pay the price for the evil you have loosed this day. Justice demands payment for this travesty even as My love for you compels Me to ensure it is paid."

The Man and Woman hung their heads in shame, making feeble attempts to cover their nakedness, their exposed flesh. The King looked aside with resignation at two large beasts circling one another in preparation to attack, and spoke once more, destroying the beasts within their skins, which, empty, fluttered to blood-stained ground. Inclining His stately head toward the vacant skins that lay spread upon corrupted earth, He commanded, "Cover yourselves. Quickly! I must depart."

Two fierce Malakím swept down from the sky to flank King Elyon on either side as He strode away into the forest. The stain yet crept across the land and drew upstream ever nearer to the Tree Ha Kayim. Leaving Kessel and Pethiy for now, Astéri and Nat followed the trio as they marched northward and saw that the King had managed to arrive at the palace before the poisonous corruption reached the Tree Ha Kayim.

Outside the arch of the palace gates, King Elyon turned, standing before the Tree Ha Kayim, and straddling its stream. He drew his blade, which shone with a blinding white light, and held it before him in both hands with blade pointed down at the stream. With a roar that shook the land, he raised the blade overhead and drove it down into the stream, sundering the Tree Ha Kayim's connection to the land.

While King Elyon's mighty roar grew quiet, the shaking continued. The palace rose as if a crown upon an earthy disc. The stream of the Tree Ha Kayim spilling forth still from its broken bed, the King stood before the palace gates as He ascended into the heavens, looking grimly down upon the land.

Down below, the situation could hardly seem more disastrous. As Astéri transported them back to the Tree Ha Datovara, Nat observed the effects of the infectious stain, which continued to produce dire results in everything it touched as it saturated the whole of Gan.

At first, the Tree Ha Datovara, having drunk of the water of Tree Ha Kayim for so long, seemed impervious to the horrible effects of the accursed stain. Kessel and Pethiy remained near the Tree, watching helplessly as the hours passed. They wished that the Tree Ha Datovara might yet stand, for who knew what greater catastrophe might befall Gan if it, too, were corrupted?

While the pair considered their fate in the darkening world, they glanced from time to time at the massive Tree, searching for any sign of its defilement. For long hours, it stood as ever, its vital presence unshaken until Pethiy noticed a single shadowy vein snaking up its gnarled root, tainting and discoloring the bark a dark and deathly grey. The vein continued up the trunk, and was soon joined by others, which streaked up the trunk and into the snarl of branches to split the bark as wounds ripped open to expose the tender flesh beneath.

Eventually, the entire trunk, branches, and leaves turned the same sickly, gray. The Tree shuddered and shook, before its trunk twisted with a short, sharp snap. Thousands of leaves, mottled black, fell shaken from the tree. The two beneath it staggered back in silence as darkness fluttered down over them.

The stain also affected the wall, and the Tree's shaking now opened cracks in the stone on either side. The branches, intertwined in stone, now strained against the wall as the Tree appeared to sag backwards at the middle, while its uppermost half hunched forward heavily. The effect of the spreading corruption on the wall was devastating, rendering brittle the once strong stone.

With the Tree's movement, great stone slabs on either side toppled forward dangerously, breaking away from the wall to crash down and shatter against the earth. Branches that still gripped the stone twisted and squeezed, exploding it and sending great, cracking fault lines racing through the great, crumbling wall. In jagged ruin, the wall fell all around Gan to let whipping sand pour in from outside. If the Man and Woman had not already retreated from the Tree to escape the foul crush of falling leaves, the collapsing wall may well have killed them.

Even as shards of the exploded wall sprayed forth, passing through their airy forms, Astéri moved them to a better vantage to view the aftermath. Several chaotic minutes passed as Kessel and Pethiy sought cover from the stinging sand, carried on a bitter wind that raced in from outside their once-prosperous land. After a time, the wind died down, and the two chanced a hopeless glance as they lifted their faces from within the crooks of their arms.

The wind had stripped all remaining leaves from the Tree Ha Datovara, as well as from its neighbors. The Tree stood crooked and bent against the alien expanse of bleak blue sky and orange dunes framing it behind. Small, sandy drifts spotted the land, and the wall was utterly devastated, standing now as sparse, craggy teeth encircling what remained of Gan.

Though the Tree Ha Datovara's branches held no more leaves, its fruit still dangled from crisp and twisted black stems, each piece a gray, sagging reminder of its former glory. Kessel spat grimly, attempting to remove its taste from his mouth. A more hateful flavor he had never known, yet its sickly-sweet savor persisted in his mouth, and its fragrance lingered in his nostrils. It was perhaps best the taste prevailed, for it would serve as an enduring reminder of their folly.

The Man and Woman turned wearily to one another, each grasping the other's hand, and into the wilderness they ventured. Their forms grew dim to Nat, and their world receded into darkness, as he awoke in the sanctuary hall to an elbow in the side and the concerned face of his mother.

Chapter Fifteen

Asara in Decline

In the darkened hall, only the rhythmic tinkle of chimes remained as Shoym recounted how Lord Elyon had separated open sky from endless waters, revealing yet another of Nida's tapestries. True to his word, Astéri had returned Nat to almost the exact moment he'd left on his historic jaunt, and none was the wiser for his absence, save Nida, who'd supposed Nat had dozed a moment, hence her prodding.

The reedy chuff of woodwinds and intermittent clash of cymbals accompanied the expansive continuum of blues, azure above and aqua below meeting in an unbroken, silvered horizon about a third of the way up the tapestry. Clouds streaked across the shifting sky as whitecaps broke atop the churning sea, and a sense of awe began to surge within Nat while he watched and listened, enraptured. His mother had, of course, told him the tales of King Elyon, often while crafting the tapestries now displayed before them, yet never had he experienced such worshipful reverence in the telling.

Creation flowed across the stage along with the growing number of tapestries that now lined the back wall as Master Shoym regaled the audience. His imagination alight with impressions from his visions, Nat watched the ground swell beneath the waters, the sun, moon, and stars materialize in the sky, the seas and skies come to teem with life, the soil bulge and break as every kind of creature bound to its rugged surface, the Etom among them, arose to embrace the wondrous new creation. In his mind's eye, he saw from the fledgling earth the Tree Ha Kayim spring forth, with flowers, trees, and every good thing to eat following.

Last came the creation of Man, whom Nida had depicted among the abundance of the verdant garden of Gan, a Man and Woman bathed in light symbolic of the gracious and unique communion they and they alone had shared with the Lord Elyon.

"Kessel and Pethiy!" Nat exclaimed under his breath. With eerie accuracy, Nida had recreated their likenesses, the resemblance close enough that Nat's recognition of them was instantaneous. His recent vision set concrete within his mind, Nat felt again heart-dropping disappointment at first sight of them, and as a cloud of bats screeching forth from dank cavern, a hundred accusations flew in flurry at their figures from dark corners of his mind.

No, he thought as he spotted the shimmering Serpent draped among the Tree's branches, *that's not the whole story.* Though the error of Man was inexcusable, the nefarious beast shared the responsibility.

Nat, immersed once more in the spectacle of the narrative and its orchestral accompaniment, observed again the catastrophe of the Sunder, then the emergence of the horrific Blight, and the violence of war-torn ages pass by until the back wall was strewn with the images of their shared history. Shoym's stack of tapestries growing thin, they arrived at the Battle of Za'aq Ha Dam.

Once again, the fate of their world had rested in the hands of Men, and once again Helél had deceived them, first enslaving the triumphant forces under Mūk-Mudón, then subjecting the world to the Empire of Chōl through the Nihúkolem chained to the will of Helél's puppet king. It was on the horrific image of the world's inhabitants, cowering in fear of the Nihúkolem that Shoym ended, a final melancholy note trailing off into the dark and absent reaches of the hall. Nat shook his head, wincing as the lights came back up, and Shoym approached the audience, stopping at the front lip of the stage.

"I'd first like to thank all of you for joining us this evening," Shoym began, "and we are grateful for the efforts of all of our musicians, stagehands, and countless others who helped make this night a success."

"Most importantly, we would like to thank the etma who provided an invaluable contribution, enriching not only tonight's presentation, but our very lives. Miss Nida, would you and your son mind very much standing please, so our congregation may see you?"

Nida turned to Nat, and asked, "Will you be alright? It's a bit strange with so many looking at us."

Nat responded, smiling bright, "I'll be fine, Mom. I already know how great you are. Why don't we let all these people see, too?" Whether to offer her support to Nat, or vice versa, Nida grasped his small hand in hers and stood slowly, a shaky breath leaving her frame as she arose.

All across the great room, eyes met them, some familiar, some not, but all friendly.

"Here she is!" Shoym exclaimed. "Thank you, Nida! Your masterful work has made our remembrance of Lord Elyon more vivid and has allowed our community to realize plans long in the making. Would you all stand with me and honor her with a round of applause?"

The audience sprung to its feet, clapping with enthusiasm, a hundred beaming faces surrounding Nida and her son, the warmth of their adulation overwhelming Nida as she looked around. Alerted by the splash of her joyful tears on his hand, Nat too, smiled up at her with pride.

After several long moments of steady applause, the audience quieted somewhat, and Shoym called from the stage, "Thank you for your help in honoring dear Miss Nida. Alone, I could never convey just how thankful we are for her work. Now, let us remember the One for whom we have gathered, and thank Him for guiding us to Miss Nida, for inspiring us to our creative efforts in sharing His story, and for giving us another day of life to share our joy in Him with others. To our Lord and King Elyon!!!"

The applause began anew, yet more thunderous than before, this time accompanied by shouts of joy, praise, and celebration. Nat, unsure how to respond, felt his mother squeeze his hand gently, and looked up to where she smiled down at him through her tears. While Nida did not applaud or shout, she closed her eyes, raised her face to the sky and in silence thanked the Creator, the Lord Elyon for directing their path to Shoym and this community. Watching his mother reassured young Nat, who likewise closed his eyes, and put his head down, smiling as he too thanked Elyon for blessing his Mom, whom he knew had worked so hard for their survival as long as he could remember.

Time passed in the glorious tumult following Master Shoym's invitation to worship, yet neither Nat nor Nida could say just how much. In the aftermath, Shoym encouraged all present to gather outside the hall for refreshments and conversation. Nida guided her son out a door left of their seats, where they found themselves in a wide, open corridor, a galleria, whither a many of the audience had already flocked, clustered in groups and engaged in lively discussion.

Throughout the galleria stood numerous tall tables with tops round and small, and atop low, long tables placed along the walls spread a sizable buffet. Having worked up a considerable appetite over the course of the performance, Nat's eyes bulged with appreciation upon spotting the buffet, and he salivated in hopeful anticipation of a bountiful meal. Noticing her son's attentive perusal of the buffet tables, Nida chuckled and gestured toward the food, patting his shoulder as she took him to collect a well-deserved supper.

While Nida had been preoccupied with the spectacular showcase of her handiwork and feeling a bit self-conscious that her designs were on such noticeable display, it had not escaped her just how mesmerized Nat had been with the production. Other than a short nap at the beginning, Nat had been very well-behaved, and had earned the reward of a good meal. After supper, she had plans to locate a dessert or two for him as well.

Collecting a meal from the buffet turned out to be more challenging than anticipated, however. Well-wishers and congratulators complicated the task, interrupting their foray to the buffet, and intercepting them at every step with, "Hello!" or "So nice to see you here!" and "We really enjoyed your work!"

Nida would normally be quite interested to greet them all, especially given their gushing praise, and she was already acquainted with many from the market. Right now, however, she was overwhelmed with all the attention, and felt hungry, weak, and irritable, though nonetheless grateful.

As a small crowd began to press around them, a confident, clear voice rang out from the periphery, "Hi there! Do you think you might give the dear etma and her son a moment, please?"

Through the press of crooked elbows and swinging legs, Nat spied Dempsey, who continued, "I'm certain they are both very pleased to speak with you, but it seems they could use some refreshment. What do you say we give them some space, so they can eat, and then return in a while? Maybe only a few at a time?"

Most of the group broke away happily with apologies and promises that they'd speak later, but a few obtuse individuals hung about until Dempsey offered the pointed and perfunctory "Thank you!" as he shooed them away.

One or two scoffed as they moved off, Dempsey following them a step as he bid them farewell with some sarcasm evident, "No! Truly! Thank you ever so much!"

Wheeling about, Dempsey leaned in to speak to Nida, "I must apologize for their rudeness. I trust you and your son will find the way to your meal now unobstructed, though I won't make any promises. Our lot is a sociable bunch. It's agonizing for introverts, hermits, and those who generally like to keep to themselves. One can't sneeze without someone showing up on the doorstep with a casserole, but they mean well."

"Not that I'm complaining," he contended, registering the inquisitive look on the pair's faces before the color rose in his own to turn his cheeks a bright orange.

"Oh! But I *am* rambling. So sorry! Perhaps we might continue this conversation later?" he finished abruptly.

Before Nida could reply, he'd hurried away down the galleria, furtively greeting those he passed with a hurried word and fleeting handshake as quick and light as a hummingbird.

Bemused, Nida turned to Nat, and asked, "Did it seem to you Master Dempsey was behaving oddly, Nat?"

Nat, having met Dempsey now on a couple of occasions, stared after Dempsey with mouth agape before responding, "Yes, I do, Mom. Do you think he has a fever?"

A snort of laughter escaped her as she answered, "No, dear Nat, I believe him to be in perfect physical health."

"It's his mind I'm concerned about," she muttered not unkindly, a minute grin on her lips.

"Did you say something, Mom?" Nat enquired.

"No, no dear. Let's go get ourselves some supper now!"

With that, mother and son proceeded to the buffet without further incident or interruption, enjoying splendid repast seated together on a bench in a warmly-lit corner of the galleria.

Feeling rejuvenated after their meal, Nat and Nida welcomed the renewed attention of those milling about the galleria and introduced themselves to groups clustered about tables and benches as they worked their way down the galleria. Everyone was interested in Nida's work, and complimented her thoroughly, much to her embarrassment, evident in the ever-present blush on her face.

Nat, on the other hand, glowed with pride for his mother, very pleased at the recognition she received. Several commended the behavior of the wee gentletém, lauding at times the finery of his attire. This, of course, served to heap more honor on his mother when he informed them that she had also made their clothes, adding to her chagrin and to Nat's mischievous delight.

Approaching the end of the galleria, where double doors opened into the temple's grand entrance hall, the pair noticed the growing and melodic swell of music. Both doors were propped open, admitting a bright, yellow glow and the sound of a celebratory psalm into the galleria.

As they stepped into the hall, Nida and Nat spotted dancers in its center, arms interlocked to form a ring as they revolved and chanted heartily before the assorted instrumentalists, who provided energetic accompaniment. Drawing closer, they saw two rings of dancers, the outer ring composed of all etém stepping in one direction, the inner composed of etma stepping in the opposite direction.

The etém faced in toward the etma, who were turned out to face them, as they chanted in call and response, punctuating their words with a leap, stomp, or clap of the hands, all in time with the music.

After a few lines, the dancers paused, each etma laid back in her partner's arms as the music came to full stop.

After a brief pause, certain of the instrumentalists clapped their hands in time: one, two, three, four times, the dancers springing up on the next beat to begin a vigorous and quick-stepping dance, each couple turning and pivoting about in revolution about the dancefloor. Nat, awestruck by the choreography of the dance, stood on the periphery enjoying the spectacle.

Nida, however, wistfully recalled dancing with Nat's father, and, as the song came to an end, moved away from the dance floor to stand along the wall opposite the musicians where she could still see Nat. The dance drew many difficult memories up from the forsaken well of romance within her soul, a hollow bucket hoisted on a cumbersome chain and carrying the empty hopes of long-dead dreams of intimacy.

The dance floor began to clear, and though she was not tearful, her face conveyed the forlorn sadness of one beyond tears. It was in this moment that her eyes met Dempsey's across the now-empty floor. He'd been busying himself with some cumbersome instrumental maintenance common to cellists when he'd glanced up.

Noting the distress on her face, he cocked his head, brow furrowed in concern. Nida, embarrassed that he had caught her thus in melancholy reflection, was pleased the dance floor began to fill again in preparation for the quadrille, pairs of couples squaring off about the floor and obstructing their view of one another.

Dempsey, undeterred nonetheless, lay his cello against his stand and hung his bow, and with an apology, parted company with the other musicians. In haste, he skirted the crowded dance floor to where Nida stood against the wall. She'd seen him coming as he'd rounded the crowd, and for a moment was compelled to dash away, considering it the easier option when confronted with answering his concerns.

Instead, she'd stayed, attempting to regain composure behind a frozen mask of cordiality when he flew to her side, softly gripping her elbow for attention, a world of care abundant in his eyes. A wordless and emotional exchange bridged the speechless pause. Their hearts seemed petrified, afraid to beat and break the private silence.

"Are you quite alright, Miss Nida?" he began, at last. "I saw you from across the hall, and, I don't know. I thought . . . I thought you might need some assistance. Would you mind telling me what is the matter?"

Dempsey, in clear discomfort at addressing Nida's dejection, had still come to offer aid, however unsure he might be. While just a little, his thoughtfulness thawed Nida's frozen mask and the heart that hid behind it, eliciting a shrouded smile at the corners of her mouth.

Dempsey's eyes brightened, and his anxious expression turned to one of cheery confidence, "Well, I'm happy to see that the matter is not a lost cause, whatever it may be, and that I was able to help somehow."

Rather smug now, Nida noted to herself with some humor.

Dempsey continued, "Actually, I had intended to ask you this earlier, but the time didn't seem quite right . . ." He trailed off in distraction as he looked up and about, tugging at the cuffs peeking from under his jacket sleeves.

He's anxious, she thought.

Dempsey, struggling for words or to still some inner tumult, halted in his speech, "Well, erm, I was quite hoping you might, well, consider giving me the pleasure—"

A tug on Dempsey's sleeve intruded, and he turned to identify the source of the interruption. Nida flushed, unbeknownst to Dempsey as she realized he'd been attempting to court her. She then noticed that Nat stood at Dempsey's elbow.

"I don't feel so well. It's my stomach," he complained feebly.

Nida clucked her tongue in exasperation. Perhaps that second dessert had been one too many. No matter now, they would have to depart so she could care for the ailing youngster at home.

Sensing her need to leave, Dempsey offered, "I do hope we'll see you again. If you couldn't tell, our community is quite taken with you. As for myself, well . . . I'd like to get to know you better."

Nida, unaccustomed as she was to chivalrous attentions yet recognized his overtures, which she welcomed with reservation by extending a polite invitation, "Feel free to visit me some time at my booth in the market. Do you know where it is?"

Though Nida couldn't recall ever seeing him in her shop, he replied, "Little spot tucked away in the corner, isn't it?" Realizing he may have volunteered the information too readily, a flush crept up from his collar, turning his yellow cheeks a burnt orange as he sputtered.

With an unguarded smile at his agitation, Nida assured him, "Yes, that's the one. I'm sure we'll see one another there. Now, however, we must bid you farewell."

Nat, now a sickly, washed-out turquoise, offered a weak goodbye, and they began their trek home, stopping at times to let the sick child rest. For all his digestive difficulties, Nat was in high spirits, as was Nida, and they nonetheless enjoyed their fitful journey home, Nida recounting the highlights of the evening, and Nat interjecting with his favorite moments as he was able.

Upon their arrival home, Nida herded her son off to bed where she sat with him, offering him sips of soothing herbal tea and replacing the cool, damp cloth on his forehead while he rested.

"Mom?" Nat inquired, his young voice soft. "Did you ever, I don't know, see anything strange?"

Not sure where her son was headed, Nida answered with a perplexed question of her own, "Strange how, son?"

"Well, almost like the stories we heard tonight, when Lord Elyon showed His servants visions or dreams. Like that."

"Why, son?" Nida returned with a flippant chuckle. "Has Elyon been showing you things?"

Nat grew very still and fixed her with a somber gaze to nod in affirmation.

"I think He has..." Nat whispered.

Nida grew serious at her son's assertion and, her words cautious, asked, "What kind of things, Nat?"

With brow furrowed in atypical angst, Nat looked up and away for a moment, then locked eyes with her again to reply, "You know the Tree Ha Kayim?"

Nida nodded, urging him to continue.

"I've seen it," Nat breathed. "And the Tree Ha Datovara, and tonight I saw...I saw..."

He blinked at the mournful tears that started in his eyes as he recalled the horror of the Sunder, that separation from Elyon and the life He intended for Creation.

Regaining himself, he resumed his tale, "I saw the Sunder and the birth of the Stain tonight – the very moment that Kessel and Pethiy fell.

Nida chuckled, though this time with nervousness, and tried to reassure her son, "Of course you did, Nat. We all did. Just as we all saw the Tree Ha Kayim and dozens of other eventful moments from history. My own hands wove the images while most times you watched. There's nothing strange about that."

"No," Nat dissented, shaking his head. "Not like that. I was there, mom. My friend, Astéri, took me."

Nida's alarm grew at the mention of the strange name, and she asked, a sharpness in her voice she didn't intend, "Astéri!?! Who is this Astéri? How do you know him?"

Eyes wet with threatening tears and mouth drawn down in a dismayed frown, Nat ventured the admission, "Astéri is...well, he is...Malakím."

Nida sat back in wondering shock, then inquired, "Astéri is Malakím? And how did he come to you, son?"

"He told me he'd been with me since my birth, hidden from sight until recently."

Nida considered the strange circumstances of Nat's birth – the melodic and brilliant, sweet-smelling manifestation that had touched Nida when Nat had hatched. She had long stored up the memory in her heart, pondering the significance of what had seemed such a blessing at Nat's birth.

Nat, she reasoned, was honest to a fault and, with his golden eyes, saw with a clarity that sometimes stunned her for the depth of his insight. All at once, she believed what he had told her and asked for him to tell her more. To tell her all.

The hours passed as Nat related all he'd seen, his confidence growing while he told the tale, and Nida questioned him on the plentiful, fascinating details of all he'd witnessed. At the close of his recollection, Nida cautioned him not to share what he had seen with anyone else.

"I won't, mama," he yawned. "I promise."

"And you'll tell me if you see Astéri again, or if he takes you anywhere else?"

"I will, mama. I won't. I promise..."

Nat's pledge drifted on the late night air as, at last, he fell into a slumber still and serene.

Chapter Sixteen

Portents

The Saturday of the following week dawned upon a chill and frosted morn, Nida and Nat awaking somewhat later than what was their usual Saturday custom due to the late hour of their arrival home the night before. Just as they had sat down for a late breakfast when they heard a sharp rapping at their door. Nida was hesitant to answer the door, odd as it was to have visitors this time of day on a Saturday yet pulled on her housecoat and went to the door, which she opened warily. Their threshold stood vacant but for a familiar-looking scrap of rolled parchment. Written thereupon in a familiar scrawl were these words:

Dearest Nida,

I despise leaving a message for you thus, but we have need of some secrecy. We believe we are being watched, and that treachery may have brought us to the attention to the agents of Chōl. Great changes stir the world abroad, giving cause for vigilance and hope. We have received news that may affect us all, you and your son included. If you wish to learn more, come after nightfall tonight, and find the lantern hanging near Potter's Arch over the Üntfither. Swing the lantern three times toward the stream, and three times away. Someone will come to escort you. Your discretion is appreciated, for your safety and ours.

Your Friend,
Master Shoym

Closing and locking the door behind her, Nida with shaking hands placed the note in the pocket of her robe, Nat eyeing her with interest.

"What is it Mom?" he asked. She had begun trembling upon reading the name of the accursed empire, Chōl, cruel fear gripping her soul. For all the terror that Man had brought upon the Etom, the Nihúkolem cast an ever-darker shadow over all. Even in Endego, some yet sought to ingratiate themselves with the dark powers.

Pikrïa, she thought, then shook her head to banish the painful memories that followed, snapping at the heels of the name like a ravening pack of wild dogs on the hunt, Nida's very soul the prey. Nida had long suspected Pikrïa's association with Chōl, and not many in Endego would cross the old etma, whose Blight had already begun to turn her face into a crusted, inscrutable mask when last Nida had seen her years ago. Though Nida had yet to receive word of her death, last she knew, Pikrïa was in poor health. She returned to her senses, aware that Nat was now tugging at her robe, worry for her on his young face.

She apologized, "I'm sorry, Nat. No one was at the door, just a messenger leaving a note. I'll tell you more about it later. Can we eat breakfast now?"

Nida did not want to risk Nat accidentally sharing the details of their secret meeting with the wrong Etom, but she would tell him more as they prepared to leave at nightfall. He was very good at following instructions, and Nida thought she could trust him to remain quiet while on their journey.

After breakfast, Nida read the note again before throwing it into the stove, watching closely to ensure it had been altogether consumed before closing the door, confident that the message was destroyed. The two passed their day in the familiar and beloved recreational activities of a typical Saturday: a trip to market for provisions (Nida rewarded Nat with a sweet for his exceptional behavior, as usual), a quick meal of kabobs at one of the stalls for lunch, followed by a stroll along the Altfither in the crisp, fall air, Nat swinging a long twig as he raced along the bank, swashbuckling nefarious villains found only in his imagination.

Nida took joy in these mundane, comfortable pleasures, unaware of the upheaval their lives were to undergo. The sun shone with the curious cool cast of autumnal afternoons, signaling the impending arrival of the dusk, which came earlier each passing day. Nida called Nat to follow her and turned homeward to prepare for their nighttime journey.

They arrived home with enough time for Nida to prepare supper before they set out. She was eager to depart under cover of night as soon as they were able, curiosity and caution compelling her. During supper, Nida shared the contents of the note with Nat, taking care to stress the importance of remaining quiet during their journey to meet with Master Shoym.

Nat, excited though he was at the prospect of a secret nighttime meeting, pledge with solemn promise he'd do his best. The pair bundled themselves up against the chill and breezy air outside, Nida pleased that the weather provided a pretense to cover themselves with stocking caps and scarves, and thus protect their identities to some extent. She didn't expect to encounter anyone on such a cold, blustery night, but one never knew, and Shoym had urged care. Nida left the lamps lit in the kitchen, and pulled the drapes, hoping the effect would make a casual observer believe they were still home.

Nida led Nat off the darkened back stoop of their home, the two skirting the rubber tree until they found a path on the side opposite their home, which took them most of the way to the Üntfither, though considerably downstream from Potter's Arch.

The path terminated, however at Galfgallan Road, one of the main thoroughfares through Endego. It was a well-lit and well-traveled lane of packed earth spanning a considerable gap between the diminished undergrowth of two matronly weeping willows. Given their desire to pass undetected, and the warning in Shoym's message, the usually warm and homey lamplight escaping the windows of homes on either side of Galfgallan Road seemed to her the eyes of predators lying in wait.

The path to the Üntfither that she sought was not straight across the road, but further up, requiring they travel, exposed, alongside Galfgallan Road either before or after crossing, further adding to her worries. Nida huffed with anxiety and looked down at her son. For his part, Nat was his usual chipper self, and was doing a wonderful job of keeping quiet. Sensing his mother's disquiet, he squeezed her hand and smiled reassuringly. Nida, encouraged by his fearlessness, and emboldened by her concern for his safety, uttered a silent prayer to

Elyon, and soon found peace of mind sufficient she might weigh their options.

Traveling along the road on the near side would have them pass a number of homes before crossing while there were almost no homes opposite their current position. Nida knew the trailhead on the opposite side ran dangerously close to a large home, but that was unavoidable. At least if they crossed now, they would pass in front of the homes on this side at a distance, shrouded in the shadows of the dry underbrush growing along the road. They had yet to leave the trail to begin their crossing, and tall, flaxen grass, sparse as it was, surrounded them on either side. Nida whispered the plan to Nat, and they prepared to step out of hiding.

A few steps from where they hid, they heard someone clear their throat. At once, Nida clapped a hand over Nat's mouth to prevent a surprised outcry and dragged him down with her into a crouch. She instructed him to lay on his side, flat against the screen of grass, and did likewise herself as she considered what they might do if confronted. She supposed that they could just pretend they were out for a walk, however unlikely it might be in this weather, in the dark, with a child.

No! Even as Nida considered it, it seemed impossible to believe. Regardless, she didn't have much time to worry about their predicament, for even as she did, a foot stepped out across the path, followed by the darkly-clad form of a constable, the silver crest of his bobby helmet gleaming under the streetlamp. Nida stifled a gasp, sure he would hear her as he meandered across the trailhead, twirling his club by its strap.

The constable stopped halfway across, his back to them as he lingered, looking this way and that way–every way, in fact, except in their direction. After several long minutes, he continued down Galfgallan Road, whistling a jaunty tune, which receded into the distance as Nida let out her breath in relief. She rose, signaling Nat with an open hand to stay put while she went ahead to peer around the corner in the direction the constable had taken. He was out of sight, and perhaps had taken a turn off Galfgallan on a designated patrol route. Nida turned toward Nat, beckoning him to come.

Nat lay still, instilling cold panic in her as she wondered, *Is he alright?*

She approached him with caution, looking about to ensure they wouldn't be spotted. As she neared him, lying quiescent on his side, Nida heard a softly purring snore. Here they were, hiding from detection by an evil empire on their way to a secret meeting with possible dissidents, and the child had fallen asleep! Nida stifled a laugh with a mittened hand, then covered his mouth while she shook him to wake him. Nat's eyes flew open, golden orbs flashing in the lamplight, before he arose to join his mother at the edge of the pathway, where she scanned the area before grabbing his hand to hurry across.

Once on the other side of Galfgallan Road, they hugged the edge of the underbrush that yet remained, taking advantage of the intermittent shadows to cover them as they sought the trailhead, which lay just before reaching the first home under the willow this side of Galfgallan.

The three-storey home's sinister windows leered as they crept toward it. They were near the pathway when a well-dressed etém exited the large home's front door and proceeded briskly down the walk to the street. Nida just about froze, but forced herself to keep moving, tugging at Nat's hand to speed up. The gentletém stopped at the road's edge, producing his pocket watch to check the time and glance the other direction up the street as Nida and Nat reached their path. Nida glimpsed the chap turning his head in their direction, and ducked into the path, yanking Nat out of the stranger's line of sight as she did.

The pair raced down the path to the Üntfither as quickly as they dared while maintaining their silence, only stopping once they had reached its banks, well out of view of Galfgallan Road. They sat down hard, both breathing heavily from the exertion and the mental strain of avoiding apprehension. After a few moments, Nida decided they had recovered enough to continue, both finding the way forward much less difficult now they followed the deserted path that ran along the Üntfither.

No less vigilant than before, Nida continued to exercise her senses, common and otherwise, as they grew close to their destination. She expected their final meeting place wouldn't be far from where Shoym had instructed her to signal her arrival. Even now, she spotted the lantern past Potter's Arch as they rounded a bend in the stream, and she hurried Nat along, whispering encouragement for him to keep moving though she knew he was tiring.

Stopping out of sight several yards from the lantern, Nida surveyed the area thoroughly for anything amiss. Having satisfied her cautious sensibilities, she and Nat stepped out from cover, heading straight for the lantern, which hung by a hook from a low post beyond the bridge. Without hesitation, she grasped the lantern's ringed handle, removed the lantern from its hook, and swing it as instructed: three times toward the Üntfither, and three times away. She set it back in the hook, and turned to await their escort, and recoiled, almost yelping. Their escort stood a mere few steps away, clothed in all black and with face covered besides. The stealthy figure, perceiving her surprise, reached up, to pull down the mask and reveal a familiar, yellow face.

"Dempsey!" she rasped.

Nat shushed her and squeezed her hand to remind her not to be quite so noisy.

Dempsey also motioned for quiet, then gestured for them to follow, guiding them between two thick stands of brambles nearby. Once they were hidden betwixt the brambles, Dempsey opened a camouflaged hatch, exposing a gaping black maw in the earth, a stairway down into darkness. He motioned for the two to enter, which Nida did with some misgiving, now keeping Nat at her side as they descended the stairs, disappearing underground as Dempsey closed the trapdoor behind them.

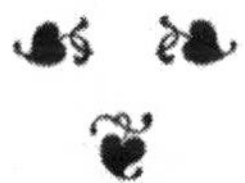

With an apology, Dempsey pressed past them in what seemed a narrow corridor through the stifling gloom.

"Bear with me a moment while I light a torch," Dempsey requested breathily a few steps ahead of them.

Nida and Nat heard the scrape of a match as Dempsey attempted to strike one, feeble sparks bursting before eyes made sensitive in the dark. Scrape . . . scrape . . . *phoom*! The match flared, noisy in their speechless confinement, and Dempsey touched it to the torch that rested in an adjacent sconce before replacing the matchbox in a small recess next to the sconce.

They were in a level tunnel with wooden beams supporting a rough ceiling and walls of red earth. The heat of the torch soon filled the space, and Dempsey seized it from the sconce then called them to follow. Slowly, the trio advanced, Nat and Nida crowding Dempsey to remain in the torch's warm glow out of unconscious aversion of the looming shadows that threatened to engulf them from behind.

In her constant disquiet, it was all Nida could do not to peer over her shoulder into the incomprehensible, trailing obscurity. After several dozen steps, she imagined that the air had freshened since they'd entered the tunnel, and a few steps later discerned a slight breeze. The guttering flame of Dempsey's torch confirmed her observation, the consequent duskiness revealing a faint light farther down the shaft.

The increased flow of air invigorated them all, while their heavy clothing, intended to protect them from the cold weather outside, now proved burdensome in the warmth of the underground channel. Nida removed her mittens and stocking cap, stuffing them into the large front pockets of her parka, and told Nat to do so as well, providing them a modicum of relief from the sultry heat. Voices drifted to them down the corridor, close enough to be heard, yet too distant to be distinct. As they approached the now-apparent aperture through the right-hand wall of the tunnel, Nida recognized Shoym's robust, clipped inflections among many voices issuing forth.

The trio stepped from the tunnel into an open, circular chamber constructed of rough-hewn stone. In its midst, a convocation of perhaps a dozen elderly Etom sat, forming a ring around a shallow, round recess where an animated Master Shoym stood, manifestly engaged in debate with other members of the council.

They entered as Shoym, his usual ashen complexion brightened to a flinty grey, finished an impassioned argument "... and I still say that the time for action is now. It is better to risk detection in pursuing the truth than to fail to act and remain ignorant! This matter is too important to us all. We must know!"

A matronly Etom the color of eggplant, and a small, circular Stain standing out on her forehead, offered dispassionately from the periphery, "What do you propose we do, then? If the Empire discovers us, the Nihúkolem will obliterate us, and our families along with us. I agree that some action is appropriate, but reckless abandon in the pursuit of more information is not the wisest course. How do you intend to minimize the risk to our community?"

Dempsey whispered into Nida's ear, "That's Chief Counciletma, Agatous. She is fair and circumspect, but wary.

Noting the arrival of Dempsey, Nida, and Nat, she directed a sidelong glance at Nida, and, nodding in her direction, continued, "We all know how our last scouting mission fared. We learned next to nothing and suffered loss besides. What reassurance do we have that we won't fail again?"

Shoym, now aware that Nida and Nat had arrived, glanced over, a pained wince appearing on his face, before returning his attention to the assembly, where he scanned each face before imploring with finality, "Please. We must do something. No matter the cost. Send more. Send a hundred. Take the time to train every last one but send them."

He returned to his seat around the forum with nary an acknowledgement of the visitors, and slumped with resignation, hand on his forehead in troubled meditation. The council members murmured, each to his or her neighbor, before an aged etém, chalky white but for the beard of Stain along his jaws, called from Agatous' side for a vote on the matter.

"That's Talcalum," Dempsey advised again.

Nodding her head in acknowledgement, Nida wondered, *What is it they seek?*

While her curiosity was piqued, she felt they were interlopers in this business. Nida counted the assembly, arriving at a total of eleven council members seated around the forum besides the Chief Counciletma, who made an even dozen.

Talcalum spoke again, "So. What say you? Aye or nay? I for one say 'Aye!'"

A bilious and severe avocado-toned gentletém called from his seat next to Talcalum, "Nay!"

His neighbor followed suit, then hers, for a total of three against the proposal, and one, Talcalum, for it. The vote traveled clockwise around the room, some for, some against, with Shoym electing to send them.

The vote circumnavigated the assembly, at last arriving, tied, at Agatous, who considered her words soberly before she directed her gaze at Shoym, "Master Shoym, I believe I speak for us all when I say we appreciate your passionate dedication to this initiative. We understand what great personal price you have paid in its pursuit. It is for that reason that I trust you will guarantee the utmost discretion in selecting candidates capable of secrecy in their mission, and that you will strive for excellence in their training to give them the greatest chance of their safe return?"

Shoym, anticipating Agatous' vote in the affirmative, was beside himself as he responded, eyes blazing with resolve, "Chief Counciletma Agatous, fellow council members, I will dedicate my very being to the success of this mission, and to the safe return of our brothers and sisters from the wild."

Agatous closed her eyes in thought before opening them, her clear gaze falling again on Shoym, "Then, dear Master Shoym, I entrust this effort to your capable hands. I vote 'Aye!'" Heated discussion among the council members broke out to interrupt her until Talcalum quieted them.

Not in the least discomfited, she continued, "I also propose the formation of a commission to aid Master Shoym in his efforts. Master Talcalum, will you call the vote, please?" Though there remained some bickering in the council, Agatous' proposal passed without resistance now the first vote had passed, most council members seeing the good sense in supporting Shoym's success.

As the meeting broke up, Dempsey led Nida and Nat over to Shoym, who was gathering his things distractedly.

"Master Shoym?" Dempsey asked. Shoym, looking up, brightened as he saw his visitors.

"Why, Mistress Nida! Young Master Nat!" he exclaimed, "So glad you came! I'm sorry you got caught up in this official gobbledygook. It's not interesting, but quite important, mind you!"

Shoym beckoned them to join him in a nearby antechamber, a parlor of sorts designed for conversation where a number of sofas and lounge seats surrounded low tables.

"Sit, please. Sit," he directed as Nida and Nat found comfortable seats. Shoym relaxed into a deep easy chair, his weariness apparent to Nida while Dempsey remained standing in alert readiness at the entryway nearby.

"Well, you received my note, of course, and made the effort to join us this evening. Now, I'm certain that you're wondering why I contacted you?" he asked, directing a piercing look at Nida.

Nida was indeed curious, and unbidden her first question flew from her mouth, "Why did the Chief Counciletma look our way when she spoke about past losses?"

Shoym looked away, a grimace on his face, "I suppose I should have shared this with you earlier. I am sorry I didn't. It's about your husband, Jaarl."

Time for Nida slowed, moving forward with every ponderous beat of an aching heart, her vision a darkening tunnel with Shoym's piteous face standing at the end.

A long moment passed before she could muster the strength to ask, "What? What about Jaarl?"

Shaking his head sadly as he stared at the floor, Shoym began, "As you may have realized, we've sent out scouts before, several years ago. We weren't nearly careful enough, nor were they well-prepared for the dangers of the mission."

"I met Jaarl through my son, Killam, years before, and saw the influence they had on one another. They were good for one another. Killam shared our knowledge of Elyon with Jaarl, who grew to revere and trust Elyon, and Jaarl shared his passion for life with Killam."

Wet with grief, Shoym's eyes shone as he spoke. "Jaarl put his whole heart into everything, a trait that inspired Killam. Killam was always so reserved until he met Jaarl."

Recalling their friendship, Nida nodded her head as tears slid down her cheeks, Nat snoozing comfortably on the sofa next to her, exhausted from the journey.

Shoym continued his tale, "It wasn't long after you were married that we received important news requiring some investigation abroad. Killam was set to go alone until Jaarl found out."

Shoym began to weep, "No one thought they would be gone long, but nobody has seen them since they left, and that's been—"

"Over eight years," Nida finished grimly. "Why didn't he tell me?" she whispered, mostly to herself.

She was grateful Nat was sleeping. She didn't want him to hear this. "What could have been so important as to abandon his wife and unborn child?"

"And now you're thinking about sending more out there to . . . to . . . disappear?" she asked him in disbelief.

For all his grief over his own son's vanishing, Shoym looked up at her, sobering in an instant to answer, steady and collected, "It will be worth it, considering what we seek. At times, even I lose sight of this fact, but Nida, I hope you appreciate that our council, which represents over a hundred families in Endego, has authorized us to do just that."

Nida's distress visible in her countenance, Shoym appealed to her, "I can tell that you're upset, and rightfully so. Please give me a moment to explain."

"Our people have been watching for a long time, which I'm sure you recognized during your visit to the temple last night. Your work is important in preserving for us not only the history of our world, but in teaching our kind the nature and the ways of Lord Elyon. Decades ago, upon first sighting of the Nihúkolem, we received a prophecy, one that spells salvation for all people, great and small."

"In it, the King sends an emissary, a Kinsman of the first of Men, come to cleanse all of the Stain, and deliver us from the Empire of Chōl, from the oppression of the shadow army and the detestable Shedím!"

Shoym spat with disgust, and returned to his tale, "When we sent out Killam and Jaarl, we had received word through our network that such a One had appeared in the land. Our scouts were to seek out and confirm the fulfillment of the prophecy."

"Since we lost touch with Killam and Jaarl, we have indeed received reports that seem to indicate the Kinsman has arrived, though we've been unable to contact Him. However, our most recent report declared the unthinkable, that the Empire of Chōl may have captured Him. Furthermore, it would appear that our Enemy is at high alert, and many of our informants throughout the Empire have fallen silent."

"That is why it is so important that we seek Him, that we find Him, wherever He may be! I know it must seem quite mad, but do you understand now, Nida? The very fate of our world rests on finding the Kinsman!" Shoym implored, peering into Nida's eyes as she leaned back against the sofa, exhaling sharply.

Nida considered what Shoym said, as well as the sincerity with which her own husband had believed. Weighing the truth of it in her mind, she found herself compelled to believe for the wild hope of it but remained skeptical.

A dull ache at the back of each hand reminded her of her own Stain, appearing there as tiny, twin spots in recent years, its murky presence destined to spread until the day she died.

Someone to deliver us all from the Stain and *the Empire?* she pondered. *It doesn't seem possible.*

The wraithlike Nihúkolem were invincible, and the rumored Shedím wielded unknown powers that had subdued even the mightiest of Men. All creatures feared their deathly empire, for word had carried that since the Battle of Za'aq Ha Dam, the enslaved souls of many thousands of soldiers inhabited the dark and ethereal creatures to enforce the will of the Shedím.

Nida shuddered involuntarily, the skin tightening across her body. *Creepy!*

Nida looked long and hard into Shoym's eyes, still moist from his tears, then asked, "So what is it you need from me? Other than Jaarl, my son and I have almost no connection to your group. Surely you can't imagine that I would volunteer to wander out into the world with my son in tow on your fanciful crusade?"

Shoym steeled himself once more, and Nida assumed the worst before with caution he spoke, "Before Jaarl embarked on his excursion, he told me something. Something about your son."

Nida's misgivings surged, and she blanched, leaning away to stare at Shoym in oblique confusion.

Shoym recommenced in a whisper, "Nida, but for the fact that Jaarl, his father, told me this in expectation that I might convey it to you, I would never dream of bringing something like this to you. About your son— Jaarl believed that he would be instrumental in our search. He couldn't tell me how, exactly, but he believed that Elyon had spoken to him about your son. It may be the only gift that he was able to leave Nat."

Nida sat, stunned and shaking her head in short, dizzied arcs, unable to respond except to ask with a sob, "How? How do you expect my son to help? He just a child, and he's supposed to help find this . . . this savior of the world!?!"

Without her realizing it, her voice had risen to a shrill echo throughout the empty council chamber.

His head down in abashment, Dempsey glanced over at Nida from his post at the entryway, feeling sorry for the young widow and her son. *Why shouldn't she be upset? First her husband disappears on a secret mission she knew nothing about, and now this?*

Shoym likewise understood her distress, but took her hand instead, "Nida we ask simply that you join us. See who we are, what we are about. We want you to learn what Jaarl believed in, and why he was willing to risk himself for it. Will you at least consider doing that? Please?"

Nida swallowed hard, and nodded weakly, "I will consider it, Master Shoym. I will."

"Thank you," he responded, "Now maybe you would like to accompany us for a tour? There is much more to this place than you know."

"Master Shoym," Dempsey interjected, nodding toward the slumbering Nat, "Perhaps some refreshment is in order first? They've had quite a journey tonight already . . ."

Aghast, Shoym replied, "Why, yes. Yes. Of course. Please forgive my lack of consideration. What would you and your son like?"

Nida countered, "Do you have any tea? I would very much like a strong tea right now. Nat might enjoy a bit of fruit or some juice, please."

She went to her son, and woke him with the promise of a snack, which roused her growing etém without delay.

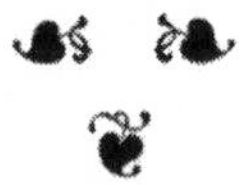

On a silver tray, a young etém brought in four delicate teacups on saucers, a bowl of sugar with teaspoons, and a small silver samovar of rich black tea, then returned with the tray half-full of tea biscuits. The other half of the tray contained raspberry drupelets for Nat, who, with his mother's assent, fell to them greedily, his lips soon becoming stained with the vivid, red juice.

Observing the child's voracity, the attendant hurried away, to return promptly with several linen napkins. Nida thanked him with a smile, happy to see her son regaining his strength, while she enjoyed the aroma and flavor of the hot, bracing tea. She even took a biscuit or two, and within minutes her sense of calm returned.

She recalled all that Shoym and his community had already done to support her small family, the sense of welcoming friendship they had shared with her, and their connection with Jaarl. She remembered, too, how Jaarl and Killam had been more brothers than friends. The relationship had run deeper than she had realized, and this presented an opportunity for them to learn more about her long-absent husband: What he believed and what he valued. As much for her as for Nat, they needed to explore this unknown aspect of Jaarl's life.

Having provided the tea at Nida's request, neither Shoym nor Dempsey had taken any out of courtesy to her. Her ruminations over, Nida turned to Shoym as she began pouring him a cup of tea, "Master Shoym, I have decided to join you provisionally. I want to learn more."

"Do you take sugar?" she asked, tongs and sugar bowl in hand.

"Two. Thank you," he answered, encouraged.

Placing two granules of sugar into the teacup beforehand, she passed it to him on a saucer with a teaspoon, "Given the potential dangers to us, I hope you understand that I reserve the right to sever ties with your company any time I see fit?"

She finished, filling the other cup, "Master Dempsey? Sugar?"

"No sugar for me, please, though I do appreciate the tea," he reached forward, offering a work-worn, calloused hand for Nida to rest the saucer in.

"Thank you," he said, taking a sip, his eyes lingering a moment on hers as he did. Clearing his throat, he returned to his duties as sentry, intermittently sipping his tea.

Undaunted, Shoym rejoined, "Mistress Nida, I assure you that you need not fear us in any matter. We desire peace and freedom for all, and that includes you and Nat. If you elect to part ways with us for the safety of your family, we won't protest."

Pushing off the arms of his chair, Shoym sprung up, beckoning them to accompany him, "Now, are you quite ready to see what it is we're up to? I think you will find it quite interesting."

With quick, practiced strokes, Nida wiped the stains off her son's purpling face as well as she was able, then grabbed his hand and stood up to follow, "Lead away, Master Shoym!"

Chapter Seventeen

The Eben'kayah

Opposite the now-sealed doorway through which they had entered the large council chamber, they saw another, to which Dempsey led the quartet. He inserted an odd-looking key in the handle and turned it. Nida imagined she heard a distant bell ring through the wall before a narrow slit at eye level in the thick door opened.

A set of dark eyes appeared in the slit, and Dempsey leaned close to mutter something to the Etom on the other side, evidently a password. She heard a key run into the lock from the other side, and a clear chime sounded in the chamber before the heavy, cumbersome door slid open, leaving them face to face with a surly-looking, stout and tawny Etom. He waved them through brusquely, slamming the door shut behind them as they hurried down another earthy tunnel, this one much better lit than the one they'd come through earlier.

While Dempsey led the party forward, Shoym provided necessary commentary to satisfy Nida's curiosity, "See here the support beams, which are of some of the most durable wood you can find around Endego. Of course, we smuggled them in through various routes."

"We've recently bolstered our security, and have several ways of entering our complex, though only a few of us know them all. We must always be careful to leave ourselves a means of escape in case we are ever discovered."

They rounded a corner and encountered another door. Through the door's slit, Dempsey hailed the sentry, this one a friendlier lot, who repeated the earlier process: the chime ringing inside, a password whispered, then the bell tolling without before the great thing glided open.

The four of them stepped through the door onto a gangway overlooking a cavernous, open area several storeys deep, the walls and floors constructed of grey stone.

"These are our training grounds and armory, Mistress Nida," Shoym said. "Let's have a closer look, shall we?"

He directed them across the gangway to a staircase on the left that led them down to the main floor of the grounds, where nearby a group of sooty Etom in thick aprons, blacksmiths, worked bellows and pounded glowing steel.

The smiths worked behind a brick partition that enclosed them on two sides, shielding the rest of the chamber somewhat from the heat from their work. The smithing area was open toward the wall behind the gangway, and, jutting from the chamber's left side took up about half its width. The smithy was about as deep as it was wide and standing likewise enclosed as its mirror opposite on the right was the armory. Within the armory stood rows of spears in stands, blades hung on hooks, and various helms and breastplates, formed of leather, carapace, and other durable miscellany, sat in bins staged about it.

Set between the forge and the armory was a broad corridor, through which they passed, Shoym and Nida side by side in front, Dempsey and Nat behind. Once past the forge and armory, they found the space open, with designated zones for swordplay, obstacle training, and instruction in foraging outside the village.

In each area, Nida observed Etom of all sorts engaged in active training. Here a young etma not quite an adult attempted the obstacle course, excelling as she crossed a narrow plank and high-stepped through raised hoops, yet finding difficulty with the climbing frame as her grip broke and she fell into the muddy pit below.

As the etma slogged her way out of the mire, Nida's attention turned to where an aging etém swung a wooden training blade, testing its balance as his junior approached to spar. The older etém took his stance in graceful readiness, poised as the younger rushed in, swinging recklessly. With a blinding, quick parry, the elder deflected his attacker's blade, and responded with a smooth riposte to his opponent's mid-section, knocking the younger Etom down. The youngster clutched his chest where the blade had struck as he struggled to get up while the elder etém, his sword put away, approached, offering to help him up with one hand while shaking the finger of the other in admonition.

Voices nearby drew Nida's focus to the survival training, where a group of Etom gathered around a stately etma, who produced assorted herbs, nuts and berries from a basket before her on a small table. Nida overhead her speaking as she raised a small, leafy sprig before her, "... so, you see here how the veins and stem of the leaf are purple? This is one to avoid. One nibble of this, and you will spend the day squatting behind a tree, if you take my meaning."

The nervous chuckles of the students faded, the quartet moving onward through the training hall, for that is what it was. Nida catalogued the various faces present and the disciplines practiced, intrigued by the level of apparent sophistication employed.

Despite the general appearance of unswerving focus upon their arts, instructors and students alike marked the passage of the strangers through the hall, which Nida observed in momentary, yet steady glances affixed them as they slid by. A measured clarity in their gazes caught Nida's attention, somehow reminding her of her first encounter with Jaarl. With greedy teeth, aching memory gnawed at the moment, and Nida flew from it, retreating hastily to present awareness.

They reached the far end of the hall, and out of courtesy Dempsey prompted her and Nat to proceed ahead of him through a narrow defile. She fell in behind Shoym, who guided them through a short passage and up a lengthy flight of stairs.

"These are our stores, in case we need to a remain in hiding or give provisions to our scouts when they set out," Shoym explained as they traversed a long, low room with numerous rough and sturdy wooden shelves stacked with crates of foodstuffs and bags of grain.

Past the shelves, large wooden barrels lined the walls and a modest mill stood in the center of the room. Four beams jutted regularly about its circumference to enable a quartet of Etom to rotate the wheel that powered the mill. The turning of the mill lifted a large stone on a pulley inside the closed chamber at the center of the mill, and a ratchet within then dropped the stone on the whole grain in the chamber, pounding and crushing it until useful. Once the grain was ground, the resulting flour was removed through a hatch in the chamber's exterior. The mill assembly stood in the way of a narrow staircase at the far end of the storeroom, requiring the group circumnavigate it to depart through a hatch in the ceiling above the stairs.

Shoym turned to face Nida and Nat, placing his index finger before his lips to signal for silence before he ascended. He paused in the gloom beneath the hatch, the faint clatter of keys tinkling together in the enclosed space as he fumbled to unlock it. A sliver of silver light fell across their upturned faces at Shoym's eventual success, a freshet of crisp air stirring them as they arose into a room of grey stone with lofty ceilings as evinced by the high window through which argent moonlight poured.

In near silence, Dempsey and Shoym gingerly lay the door back into the floor, the faint 'click' of a latch sliding into place scarcely audible from beneath the heavy flagstone that camouflaged the entrance. A faint golden light peeked from beneath a nearby door, which Dempsey approached, hearkening in the dark before gently pushing the door open to peer out.

Confident all was clear, he waved them forward, Shoym again leading as they advanced together into a warmly-lit lobby already familiar to Nat, and off which several doors opened. Shoym led them through a set of double doors to their left to enter the long, broad galleria off the sanctuary hall of the temple, now made eerie in the dismal stillness of the late hour.

Shoym took a quick jog to the left, opening one of the doors through which the Nat and Nida had exited just the Friday before, and ducked in, beckoning the others to follow. Though the sanctuary hall was unlit but for the dim stage, from the invisible, warm, and breathy press, Nida perceived the seats were quite full.

Through the crowding murk Nida pursued Shoym's inky form with Nat trailing close behind until Shoym stopped at a row near the front, whispering directions for them to take their seats, "They knew we'd be along presently, and saved us all a spot. You and your son are quite dear to us, Mistress Nida."

She tucked into the row, finding four seats remained at the end of the row when she bumped blindly into the occupant of the fifth, encountering the stately elder, Talcalum, recognizable by his firm, yet kind voice, "Steady there, miss."

From the next seat over, a voice hissed "Quiet!" in the familiar, acrid tones of the Counciletém Nida knew only as Master Sour Avocado. Nida politely apologized, excusing herself before she sat down, happy that at least her immediate company was pleasant.

What is going on here? she thought, her paradigm in flux as she attempted to integrate the events of the past few days.

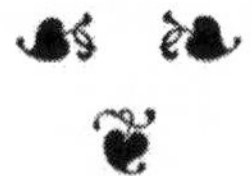

Almost as if in response, the lights of the stage rose, and through the door behind the stage exited Chief Counciletma Agatous, who spoke with power even as she approached the lectern, addressing those congregated, "I have word that most of us have arrived. If you know of kin or friend that could not join us tonight, please make them aware of the plans we discuss tonight in light of current events. You are all well aware we only call a full covert assembly in case of an emergency. We believe this to be just such a case."

A swell of speculative murmurs and mutterings arose within the sanctuary hall until Agatous, projecting forcefully from the stage, called the meeting back to order, "Please! Please quiet down, and I will explain everything!"

The roar diminished to a hush, and she continued, "We have received reports through our network that the prophesied Kinsman has been found."

Anticipating the din that erupted, Agatous made no immediate attempt to press on through the animated and excited chatter of the crowd.

Having granted a few moments for gesticulation amongst the congregation, Agatous quelled them once more, and continued, "Our reports tell us that the Kinsman has been found. However, we have also received the disturbing news that He may be in the Empire's custody."

She paused, the dismay clear in her countenance, "We're not certain what this means for the prophesy, but we have determined that inaction is not an option."

Grave silence greeted her in response to her announcement as the gathered Etom sat, stunned.

"A large number of messages have poured in, warning that the Empire is agitated, and that the Nihúkolem are on the move in a way we haven't seen since their appearance many years ago. Additionally, a great many of our contacts have gone silent, whether from fear of detection or because the Empire has captured them, we don't know. Earlier tonight, our Council convened to discuss a course of action, and we have determined that it is paramount we ascertain the veracity of these reports, no matter the cost."

"We have commissioned Master Shoym to prepare fresh scouts for a foray to discover where the Kinsman is and what his fate may be. We call on you for support as we initiate a new reconnaissance program. It will not be easy, but we ask that each of you consider how best to serve our community. If you are so led, please consider joining our scouts. While we hope and pray that each one will return to us, such a likelihood is slim at best, and the greater number we send out, the more probable our success will be. For decades, we have awaited liberation from the Empire, and for ages, we have waited to be cleansed from the Stain. The Kinsman presents us our best chance at freedom from both. Do not hesitate in the face of fear!"

"Along with our training needs, the likelihood of an increased Imperial presence in our village necessitates we accelerate all current efforts with the utmost discretion. The manufacture of weapons and procurement of provisions must at a minimum double, meaning each household should institute immediate and strict rationing so the surplus may go into storage. Foraging for smithing materials must also take precedence over individual needs."

"Beware any new faces you encounter in and around Endego. Anyone you do not know is a potential spy. We never know who the Enemy might send to infiltrate us, so look out for friends or family members that take sudden and renewed interest in your affairs. For all intents and purposes, we are in a state of emergency."

"Talk to Master Shoym if you would like to volunteer as a scout. Pritch or Hardy will help with weapons, and Alcarid will give direction on rationing and food storage. Now more than ever, you should use the secret paths to get home. Be safe and hold onto your hope. We are the Eben'kayah, and we still believe! May the blessings of Elyon go with you!"

With that, Agatous departed, and the assembly broke, the lights in the hall coming up to allow Etom to depart in safety.

Shoym reached across Nat to lay a hand on Nida's wrist, "Please be patient and wait a moment for the crowd to clear. Unlike those that live nearby, you two have a long way home. We'd like to help make the journey a bit more manageable, if you'll allow us."

Nida nodded her assent, awareness dawning that their life had just undergone drastic change, and that she would need all the support she available to weather the upheaval. Given what she'd learned, she might have some closure regarding Jaarl's disappearance, though only time would tell. Nida also foresaw the turn of events as a potential answer to unspoken prayers for the sense of community that she and Nat craved.

No! That we need! she resolved with fervor.

Her thoughts returned to something Agatous had said in closing the assembly that had piqued her interest.

While they waited to depart, she wondered if Shoym might satisfy her curiosity, and ventured, "Master Shoym, who are the Eben'kayah?'"

"Why, Mistress Nida, that is what we call ourselves," he responded somberly. "We are the Eben'kayah, the Living Stones, and so was Jaarl, you should know. We believe the whole truth of our history, a history you helped us tell last night."

Nida sat in silence, looking down as she pondered Shoym's words.

Much of the throng had dispersed, and Shoym beckoned to the same door by which they had entered the hall, taking up the rear behind Nida and Nat while Dempsey led them back through the double doors into the lobby. Straight ahead was heavy door, a thick bar across it, which Dempsey removed deftly and set aside, propping it in the nearby corner. Holding up a hand for them to wait, Dempsey swung the door open, its well-oiled hinges turning quietly before he disappeared into the darkness.

Shoym spoke to Nida, "I'm afraid that this is where we must part ways for now. I bid you farewell. We will contact you soon, so be on the lookout for our message. Dempsey will see you safely home. Here he is now! Hurry!"

He ushered them out the door, where they found themselves under a short, covered walkway, the moonlight cascading about them through the thick, stone pillars. Dempsey walked them to the end of the walkway, signaling them to hold once more as he peered about. Nida, a firm grip on Nat's hand, took stock of their surroundings, identifying the walls of a courtyard adjacent to the rear of the temple, a black iron gate before them.

Dempsey led them out of the courtyard, pushing the gate open without a sound. With appreciation, Nida realized he had unlatched it on his short excursion moments ago to ensure a stealthy departure. Nearby, she heard the running waters of the Üntfither, steadfast in its flow, and growing louder as Dempsey conducted them along a narrow path hidden amongst the withering grasses and reeds.

They arrived at the shore of the stream, Dempsey turning aside to tug at something beneath the scraggly mass of thin, leafless branches overhanging the bank, and drawing out a canoe. Placing the bow in the water, he gestured for Nida to step into the boat, Nat close behind her. Once they were aboard, Dempsey pushed off from the shore, leaping into the stern as the current pulled the canoe downstream. From within the boat he produced a paddle, with which he directed the course of the boat as the Üntfither propelled them along. While the stream wouldn't carry them all the way home, they could disembark somewhat close by, and traveling along the water varied their route in case anyone had noticed them on the outward journey.

Despite the secrecy of their expedition, Nida enjoyed the tranquil babble of the stream, and the moon overhead shimmered hypnotically on its rolling surface. She turned to find Nat also mesmerized, a dreamy grin on his face making plain his content. Glancing back at Dempsey, she encountered intent focus as with vigilance he scanned the way ahead.

Admiration for him stole over her, edging its way into her heart. There was more to him than met the eye, that much was certain. He caught her gaze, and smiled as he turned the boat to shore, their aquatic adventure coming to a close as they cut lazily across the current, the mirrored moon-sheen breaking in their wake. They slid across the shoreside shingle, stopping with a low, wet crunch before alighting.

Once ashore, Nida and Dempsey took momentary stock of their surroundings while Nat leaned on Nida, exhausted. After some whispered discussion, Nida was clear on their location, and determined the safest route home. They tarried a moment while Dempsey found a spot nearby to hide the small boat in the underbrush. He would retrieve it at a more appropriate time.

Before they parted ways, Dempsey whispered to Nida with concern, "Please let us know if you need anything. Anything at all. Things may get difficult, but we're here for you, and for Nat."

He spoke this last with a smile as he laid his hand on the etém's head with affection.

"Good-bye," he said, then replaced his mask and turned into the night, disappearing in the shadows a few steps away.

With that, Nida tugged at Nat to rouse him for the journey, and they set out for home. The village was very quiet at this hour, and even the breeze they felt earlier had fallen still. The journey from the Üntfither to Sylvanfare, the lane leading past their rubber tree, was uneventful, and they slipped stealthily from shadow to shade through the slumbering neighborhood.

They arrived at the Sylvanfare's shadowy edge, Nida looking about before they stepped from cover. All was clear as they scurried across, until from high over the lane's distant end, they heard a jagged shriek descending, growing closer by the second. Nida nearly froze, which would have spelled their doom, but she instead yanked a petrified Nat the rest of the way across the lane. She shoved Nat into cover a short way down the path to their home and crouched near the path's edge to see what had made the horrifying noise.

Down the moonlit lane, an ebon missile struck the ground, a ring of soot billowing from the impact. The terrifying shriek had stopped at the moment of collision, yet in its stead Nida heard an angry, static buzz over the sound of Etom up and down the Sylvanfare coming to investigate, loudly inquiring of neighbors about the commotion. Nat gingerly crept up to his mother from behind.

"What is it Mom?" he whispered.

A dark and flowing figure arose within the settling dust, coalescing as the particles flocked to its form, and the droning intensified.

The Nihúkolem! They're here! Nida realized with sudden, shocked fright, her skin tightening in uncomfortable reaction.

"Nihúkolem! It's the Nihúkolem!!!" a frightened male voice echoed down the lane.

The rest of those roused by the tumult took up his cry, proclaiming the news with loud shouts, followed by the sound of several doors slamming shut up and down the lane.

Nida didn't hesitate to see what came next. She hoisted Nat in a piggy-back carry and bolted down the path, dashing pell-mell for their front door.

Down the Sylvanfare, a shrill female scream pierced the distant cacophony, "Cairn! It's taken my Cairn!"

Nida shook her head as she ran, her face contorted in empathy, distressed at her own impotence, her inability to assist her weeping neighbor or captured husband. Nida reached their door, sliding Nat off her back with her one hand and clutching for the key with the other. She quickly unlocked the door, Nat diving inside before her. Nida turned and bolted the lock, trembling as she turned and slid down the door, her back against it as she sat down heavily, exhausted.

Nat crawled over to her lap, where he curled up, and asked "What was that thing, Mom?"

"I'll tell you about it tomorrow, dear," she answered, "Let's get you into bed now. Quiet, please, and no lamps."

Nida helped Nat out of his heavy coat and shoes, then walked him up to his loft, where he fell asleep in an instant, drained from their adventure.

Though she and Nat hadn't known them well, Nida wept for Cairn and Wenga, an elderly couple that had often greeted Nat and Nida with kindness from the garden in front of their home when they passed by.

What will become of them? Nida wondered as her head met the pillow.

She resolved to check on Wenga, determined to help however she might as merciful sleep overtook her.

Chapter Eighteen

Community

A palpable gloom settled over Endego with the arrival of the Nihúkolem. Though not a constant presence in the village, the Etom could never be certain when one might come drifting into the grove, perhaps to carry away another for interrogation, perhaps to watch with pitted, empty eyes that shifted unpredictably about their churning forms. More often than not, the Nihúkolem came alone, though occasionally they arrived in pairs. Forms of Man and Beast patrolled the village, gliding eerily through the wooded byways.

Those few who returned from questioning were often catatonic for a day or two after. It had taken poor Cairn a solid week to recover himself, and even after, he would often retreat to his room for hours, shaking his head as he wept in bed, inconsolable. Nat and Nida visited the couple when they could, but nothing they or Wenga did could draw Cairn out when he regressed.

Nida educated Nat on the Nihúkolem, recounting what she knew about the Battle of Za'aq Ha Dam and the subsequent enslavement of Mūk-Mudón's army. Not surprisingly, Shoym, Dempsey, and the Eben'kayah were quite knowledgeable of the Nihúkolem, their tradition of history supplying a number of answers to Nat and Nida's questions.

More often, however, their focus when they met with the Eben'kayah was training and preparation. Though she was quite willing to contribute, Nida would never volunteer as a scout and potentially leave Nat an orphan entire. Instead, she and Nat gathered what surplus they were able from their own garden to give to the community.

Besides the training, storage, and council areas, the Eben'kayah had a substantial canning facility in the temple, though it was not hidden. It was, in fact, the room concealing the hidden passage in its floor, which in the darkness Nat and Nida had been unable to see clearly. Jars of preserves, pickles, and other provisions sat on shelves lining the canning room's walls, except for that under the window.

Centered beneath the window sat a wood stove, the stovepipe feeding up and out the window. On one side of the stove sat a short counter with a cupboard beneath it, and a nearby rack held jars, lids, pots, and miscellaneous canning supplies. The pantry was always kept well-stocked, though fresher items were rotated down into the hidden storeroom and the older brought up for immediate use. Anything approaching its shelf life they donated to needy Etom in the village, so nothing went to waste, and Nida was proud to participate in blessing others, an aspect of her life denied her until now.

Nat and Nida began to feel more comfortable within their new community, and each struck up friendships among the Eben'kayah. Trips to and from the temple were frequent, and more than once, Nida considered how convenient it might be to move closer, though she was loath to leave their home under the rubber tree.

Soon enough, however, it became apparent that it better served the Eben'kayah that they continue to live near the rubber tree. On a crisp, spring Saturday evening, Nat and Nida took a stroll to the temple for the customary gathering. Etom trickled in as the evening wore on. No assembly was scheduled for the evening. It was a time to converse and organize their efforts. Nat played with a few of the Etom children running up and down the galleria, bringing a smile to Nida's face. It still blessed her to see him play with other children. They had found a sense of belonging here that nurtured both their souls. Before many had arrived, Pritch and Hardy, Etom uncommonly seen outside the forge below, together approached Nida in the galleria with a request.

Covered in grit, Pritch spoke up first, "Excuse me, Miss Nida? Might we have a word, please?"

"Of course!" a surprised Nida answered.

Neither one of the smithies had spoken a word to her before, and for the most part kept to themselves. In general, Pritch's expression was neutral at best, while Hardy wore a perpetual frown.

Pritch spoke under his breath in covert tones, "Miss Nida, am I to understand you have access to Endego's sole rubber tree?"

A likewise grimy Hardy cocked a brow and stared at her in inquisitive silence.

"Why, yes. That's right. What's this about?" she asked, a tad curious. It was no secret where she lived.

Pritch looked down the galleria while Hardy surveilled the opposite end.

Pritch whispered hoarsely, "Might you see clear to provide us with a bit of latex? Raw, mind you! This is all very top secret. Hush-hush and all, understand?"

Hardy's frown deepened, and his lowering brow pressed his eyes down to slits as he nodded in stolid agreement with Pritch.

Bemused with the pair's seriousness, a smile tugged the edge of Nida's mouth as she consented, "I will absolutely share my latex with you. How much do you need?"

Pritch glowed with appreciation, his excitement clear, and he took her hand in his calloused paw, "As much as you can spare, Miss Nida, and thank you!"

Beside him, Hardy's frown had improved to an impassive, blank expression, and he lifted a single thumb, an enthusiastic twinkle in his eye. The stout pair toddled away back to their cavernous forge, their thick leather aprons scuffling along the ground.

After her conversation with Pritch and Hardy, Nida wandered back to the canning area to deliver a few jars of preserved tomatoes she had lying around from the prior harvest. One of the jars she had marked with an emblem of flame to forewarn of the contents' spiciness. She had infused these tomatoes with chili for a fiery treat.

She returned to find the long table for supper set in the galleria, where the Eben'kayah enjoyed a regular meal together on Saturday evenings. Nida called after Nat, who streaked by at the head of a game of tag with the other Etom children, their squeals of delight a joyous cacophony echoing through the confines of the hall. Nat skid to a halt and turned in response, which resulted in a pile-up as the wave of those behind broke over him to knock him down.

Nida approached the giggling gaggle of children that lay atop her son as she called, "Nat, dear! Are you alright?"

A blue arm shot out of the mound, the hand waving as Nat's muffled voice arose from the heap, "Yeah, Mom! I'm fine!!!"

The other children extricated themselves, dispersing to join their own families at table until Nat alone remained, flat on his back and limbs sprawled. He lifted his head to prop himself on his arms, violet blooms on his cheeks from exertion, and tongue sticking out one side of his mouth as he gave his head a kooky waggle. Nida smiled, a happiness welling within for her son, who she knew had long yearned for this kind of play, this kind of interaction with other youngsters that she had been unable to provide.

"Come along, dear," she said, "Let's go get something to eat."

Nat galloped up to a couple of empty seats at the table, and Nida joined him while an elder beseeched of Elyon the customary blessing on their meal, their fellowship, and their very lives, giving thanks for all as he ended the prayer. At first, Nida had found this practice peculiar, yet now looked forward to the regular acknowledgement of Elyon as provider and appreciated the opportunity to thank Him for his many blessings. Just another of the many things among the Eben'kayah to which she had grown pleasantly accustomed.

How did I manage so long without these other Etom? she mused. *Just. Only just.*

They set to their meal of roast qábēs, a sheep-like creature about the size of a mouse whose wool was useful. Nida knew the creature had been broken down for its pelt, hide, sinew, bones, and meat, all of which were processed or preserved beneath the temple. From a single such beast would come fleece, leather, armor, tools, weapons, and food. Nothing would be wasted.

Down table someone cracked open a jar of Nida's spicy tomatoes, eliciting loud compliments and exclamations of delight, which drifted her way to bring a smile to her face. Shortly thereafter, handkerchiefs fluttered out to stanch the tears and mucus flowing down the faces of those Etom who were unaccustomed to spicy food. She looked over at Nat, who stuffed a roll in his greedy mouth while a morsel of tender qábēs yet poked from between his lips. She smiled but asked him to slow down and remember his manners.

There would be no worship gathering in the sanctuary this evening, yet Nida's heart swelled with thanksgiving to the One who made it all, the glow of contentment carrying her through the meal, dessert, and conversation afterward. The kinship she felt with these Eben'kayah was amazing, and she drew closer to them in mutual reverence for Elyon and shared mission. Even the scarcity and toil they suffered as they poured their resources into training the scouts and prepared for potential calamity made every meal a celebration, a feast such as this in particular.

Though extravagant, the Saturday evening meals brought together all Eben'kayah, from poorest to richest, on a foundation of common belief in the promises of Elyon. Each Etom contributed as he or she was able, the Eben'kayah giving honor and offering friendship in equal measure to the lofty as to the lowly. There were conflicts among them, of course, but it seemed none threatened the bond of peace they shared. Thus, Nat and Nida enjoyed the rest that the fellowship of the Eben'kayah afforded and departed in the afterglow of communal warmth.

Weeks passed, and of the first harvest of latex, Nida gathered a cask's worth for Pritch and Hardy. Before the Saturday evening meal, the grim and grimy pair received the tribute heartily, excited to experiment with it, and pleased with Nida's promise of more.

She made certain to share what she knew of preparing the latex for use, mentioning the effects of heating the latex, and of adding morning glory juice. They pondered the information in stony thought, then each offered a thumbs-up as they nodded their expressionless approval.

Before returning to his work in the forge, Pritch spoke up, "By the way, Miss Nida, Master Shoym asked to see you below if you have the time."

She and Nat had not returned to the secret grounds beneath the temple since their mid-night journey months ago, so at first, she was taken aback at the request.

Nida preferred Nat not accompany her but knew she could entrust him to one of the other mothers in the galleria, so nodded, "Yes, I will join him. Where will he be?"

"If it's all the same to you, we wouldn't mind taking you right to him. Seems the least we could do in exchange for this," Pritch said, patting the cask of latex as Hardy nodded in sober agreement.

"Yes, please," Nida responded, "I would appreciate that."

She didn't particularly care for the dank underground and would enjoy the company. She excused herself a moment to ask another mother to watch Nat and told him to be good while she was away, then returned to Pritch and Hardy, following them as they descended into the dark. Though she was initially uncomfortable below ground as before, Nida soon acclimated, her growing familiarity with the surrounding passages and chambers lending her confidence.

It wasn't far to reach Shoym, who presided over the bustling training hall, both hands braced against the rail of the gangway high atop the far end of the hall. As they approached their forge, Pritch and Hardy pointed him out to Nida, then hurried off with the cask of latex, impatient to begin their research.

Nida waved up at Shoym, catching his eye. He offered a smile, warm and quick, then beckoned her to join him up on the gangway before returning his attention to the ordered commotion of the training hall. Nida ascended the nearby stair to the walkway, growing a bit winded in her haste before she reached Shoym.

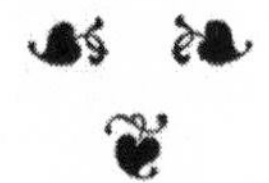

"Master Shoym!" she exclaimed in salutation over the din of the crowded hall below. "You asked for me?"

Shoym's face was set in determined concentration as he surveyed the hall, and for a moment he did not respond. Nida, uncertain if he'd heard her greeting, was about to speak again when he straightened suddenly, striking the rail with his hand as he did.

"By the Great Trees of Gan, they're coming along wonderfully!" he shouted, the look of tense focus on his face breaking to make way for a brilliant smile. "Nida, dear! So glad you're here."

He turned to put an arm around her shoulder companionably, "I have a favor to ask of you, if you're willing."

"Sure. What might you need?" she inquired.

"Do you see the climbing walls along the left of the hall there? Toward the front where you came in."

She nodded affirmatively, though unsure where the conversation was going. "I see them. How can I help?"

She'd taken interest in the climbing area during their first time through the training hall, noting the various surfaces built into the wall: one of ivy, another of wood planks, and a third of craggy stone.

Looking at Nida, he spoke, "I understand you're quite a climber. Maybe all your time spent scaling that rubber tree of yours?"

He stared vacantly out over hall before he continued, "I would like to put your expertise to use as a trainer if you're agreeable. Our volunteers could benefit from your experience. Etom are good climbers, but we need excellence from our scouts. Their lives may depend on it."

Nida considered Shoym's words with care before responding, "You know I will never volunteer as a scout myself. I couldn't bear to leave Nat or put him in harm's way on such a journey."

Shoym stirred, disappointment branching across his features before Nida continued, "Still, I wish to help, and am more than happy to help train our scouts."

Shoym went from crestfallen to elated in a heartbeat, and exclaimed, "Thank you! Thank you, Miss Nida!"

Smiling, Nida interjected, "Master Shoym! I have some conditions, if you'll hear me out."

"Of course. Of course. What is it, dear?"

"I will need to bring Nat with me to the training hall. I won't neglect him, and he won't be in the way. Also, I may need some help with tending my garden and my shop. I can't afford to neglect them, either. Can you find me some bright and trustworthy Etom to help?"

"I'm sure we can find a few assistants for you, Miss Nida. A couple come to mind now, and I'll introduce you later. Right now, might we discuss some details on your way back upstairs? A schedule perhaps?"

The two of them made their way down the stairs and through the training hall, conversing conspiratorially, heads together as they walked. Nida stopped at the climbing wall to take a closer look, eager to inspect the surfaces.

"We'll need some special equipment, too," she said.

"Anything you need. Just put together a list. Sooner is better than later in case we need to make it ourselves," Shoym responded.

Nida lay her hand against the rough, rocky surface, and looked up the wall, assuring herself, *I can do this, Lord Elyon help me.*

Feeling heartened, she turned to Shoym, who stood several steps off, and followed him out of the hall, and back upstairs.

"Mom!" Nat cried, spotting Nida upon her return to the galleria.

He ran to her, and she caught him up with much effort to embrace him.

How big he's gotten! she thought. *I won't be able to pick him up much longer.* The thought elicited a ferocious affection, Nida's embrace intensifying until Nat could endure it no longer.

"Mom . . ." he gasped. "Mom, you're squishing me. I can't breathe."

She chuckled as she released him to the ground. "I'm sorry, Nat. Are you alright?"

"'Course! See?" He breathed with a loud huff, then said, "I *am* hungry though. Can we eat?"

Finding the table set, and food served, Nida and Nat took their seats among the gathered Etom, happy to join their fold.

Chapter Nineteen

A Mile in Her Shoes

At home the following evening, Nida jotted down a list of climbing equipment for Shoym, which was as follows:

Large coil of rope
Climbing hooks
Powdered chalk
Roll of canvas
Several fleece blankets
Sturdy belts
Spool of strong cord
Leather gloves
Durable shoes
Weighted packs

We'll need one climbing hook, belt, pair of shoes, pair of gloves and pack per trainee, and one each for myself. Please size the shoes to each Etom. We'll be putting them to hard use.

She made sure that Shoym received the list early the following week along with an old pair of her own shoes for sizing and checked with Pritch and Hardy a few days later in the forge to answer any questions.

The smithy was abuzz with activity as Pritch and Hardy directed their crew around the hot and hazardous forge under the red glow of the furnace. She'd forewarned Nat about the potential dangers of the forge, so he stayed at her side, obedient, but with eyes wide in interest. Nida approached the pair to ascertain if they needed help.

"Well ma'am, we're just not sure what you mean by climbing hooks on your list here," Pritch said quizzically as he pored over the stained parchment.

Nida enlightened them, "The hooks should have a loop in the end to attach a rope, and bend in three or four different directions at the top. We'll be throwing the hook with a rope attached, so it needs to be strong, but light. The idea is to catch the hook on something above, usually a tree limb, and anchor it to climb the rope, you see?"

The stoic Hardy cupped his chin in hand and offered a solitary and next to imperceptible nod as Pritch agreed, "I think we see what you're after, Miss Nida. You'll be using it to, er, grapple the terrain as it were."

"Yes! That's precisely it. Any other questions?" she asked.

"Now that you mention it, we were wondering how much weight you'll be wanting in these?" Pritch asked, pointing at a pile of leather packs on the table.

"Ah, yes! They need to train under realistic conditions, so do your best to match the weight and balance of a full pack" she answered. "I'll take the roll of canvas and fleece blankets if you have them, and any shoes you've fit to our trainees. I need them for a project."

They led her over to the armory, where she spotted the roll of canvas wrapped around a long dowel and leaning against a shelf. A half-dozen folded fleece blankets sat on the shelf, and four pair of stout, leather shoes sat lining the wall nearby.

Pointing at the farthest pair, Pritch informed her, "Those are yours. Hope the fit is right."

She grabbed her shoes first, lifting her left foot while bracing against the wall so she could match the new shoes to the ones she wore. They appeared to match quite well, though she would need to try them on to be sure. Nida nodded approvingly. She tied each pair of shoes together by their laces and tossed them over the end of the canvas roll, which she then slung over her shoulder, the shoes dangling against her back as she headed back over to the forge.

"Nat, love, could you get the blankets there for me, please?" she called over her shoulder.

Nat snapped to attention with a mock salute, "Ma'am! Yes, ma'am!"

He pulled the blankets off the shelf and followed at a short distance, intent to stay out of his mother's way, yet remaining close enough to satisfy his curiosity.

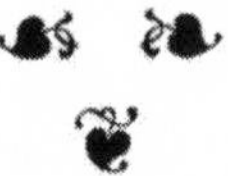

Nida had come prepared today with a fresh cask of latex, and a bottle of morning glory extract, which she brought over to a workbench in the forge, setting down the canvas and shoes atop it. Nat arrived a moment later to set the blankets beside the other materials. Nida put the latex aside for a moment and took a coarse file to one of her new shoes, roughing the smooth leather of the sole and the sides of the shoe just above it. She was careful not to tear the stitching of the shoe and did the same with its mate before noticing Pritch and Hardy, who stood nearby with mouths agape.

"What have you done to your new, beautiful shoes?" Pritch asked, incredulous.

It was clear that he and Hardy were appalled at her seeming mistreatment of their handiwork.

"Sorry, gentletém. I know rubber won't stick to a smooth surface. I'm roughening the leather to give it something to adhere to. I honestly don't know if even this will be enough to keep them from falling apart."

Hardy held up a finger to ask she wait as he dashed to a corner of the shop, and returned, awl in one hand and mallet in the other. Using the awl and mallet, Hardy pierced the edge of one of the soles as he worked his way around the shoe, knocking holes between the stitches holding sole to shoe.

Observing the technique, Nida understood, and was delighted, "Well done, Master Hardy!"

Hardy nodded smugly, eyes closed, as the shadow of a smile passed fleetingly over his lips. The holes would allow the rubber to seep into edges of the sole, forming rubber "fingers" to help grip the shoe as they hardened. Along with the coarsened leather, these "fingers" would help provide a more secure attachment of rubber to shoe.

Reaching for the awl and mallet, Nida asked Hardy, "May I?"

He handed the tools to her and pointed at the table with both hands open in a "go-ahead" gesture. Nida took the second of her shoes and tested the awl on it, finding the leather resilient, yet ultimately pliant when she applied force. She did as Hardy had, knocking holes through the sole until she'd finished perforating its edge. Eager to complete the project, Nida enlisted Pritch and Hardy in filing the remaining three pair of shoes while she used the awl and mallet.

After, Nida turned her attention to the roll of canvas and stack of blankets. Laying a blanket atop a stretch of canvas she'd unrolled on the table to ensure their approximate uniformity, she cut out several rectangular strips of each material with a pair of shears. She repeated the procedure with a second blanket, cutting four rough circles from both cloths. Bringing the ends of one of the rectangular canvas strips together, she formed a cylinder, one end of which she sized to a circular piece on the table. She sewed the ends of the cylinder together, flipping the seam inside, then attached one of the circles to its end to form a small bag, perhaps two handbreadths tall. Using the matching pieces of fleece, she made a liner near-identical for the canvas bag. Within minutes, Nida's needlecraft produced three more rough canvas bags, complete with liners.

"Did you by chance have the spool of cord I requested?" she asked Pritch, who produced it readily from a dim shelf beneath the worktable.

Using the cord, Nida measured around each bag, tying off a loop before cutting it. In this manner, she made two such loops for each bag, then stood back a moment to appraise her work, and consider her next move.

Spotting a rough pot near the furnace, Nida raced over to retrieve it as Pritch, Hardy, and their assistants watched her closely. They'd worked with the latex a fair amount by now but were interested to see her technique. Nida emptied her latex into the pot, filling it almost to the top. Afterward, she took the bottle of morning glory juice, and poured several drops into the latex, stirring it with a long iron spoon until she'd mixed in the juice altogether, repeating the process until she'd emptied the flask altogether.

Finding the heat of the furnace too intense to work with the latex, Pritch and Hardy had set up a small, rudimentary brick oven stove with an iron flat top along the cavern wall. Nida snatched up the pot, stirring it as she went, and placed it on the stove, which she found warm, but not hot enough for her needs.

She opened the oven door, and found the embers smoldering within. Using tongs in one hand, she tossed in a few large chunks of coal from the nearby coalbin and stoked the fire until it became too hot for her to bear, the whole time stirring the latex in the pot. She slammed the oven door shut and flipped the latch before inspecting the latex, which had begun to thicken as it heated.

Never before had she added so much morning glory juice, though she'd observed its ability to strengthen the resulting rubber a number of times. She wanted this batch to be tougher than any other she'd produced and was not disappointed. The latex grew ever thicker and darkened until black as it continued to heat. Unwilling to wait any longer, Nida removed the pot from the stove and took it to the workbench where the shoes, canvas bags, and loops of cord waited.

She set the pot on the table and looked inquiringly at Pritch.

"Tongs?" she asked.

From the murk beneath the table, he produced a set of tongs, again without delay. For the second time, Nat wondered how he found anything down there. Nida threw a matching pair of looped cords into the pot, stirring them in with the tongs, then lifting them out one by one to slip them over top their corresponding bag, which she had stood on the edge of the table. She rolled the rubberized loops down the side of the bag until they rested against the surface of the workbench, then did the same with the other sets. She returned to the first pair of loops and discovered they had stuck together as they had cooled. She gently loosened them from one another, then slid them back off the bag.

The rubber around the cord had firmed up, turning the loops into hoops, albeit somewhat fragile ones. One at a time, Nida dipped the hoops into the rubber for another coat, removing them at once so the heat could not soften the layer beneath and deform them. She spaced them out on a clear corner of the table to cool and proceeded to the next phase of her project.

Before moving on, Nida took a moment to tuck all of the shoelaces inside the shoes, then gripped one of the shoes by its collar before lowering it into the pot. She dipped the sole in the dark rubber up to the point they'd coarsened it, leaving the shoe a moment to allow the rubber to stick. She took the shoe out and cautiously set it upside-down on the table, then did the same with the other shoes. Starting in order with the first shoe she'd dipped, she repeated the procedure twice to form a substantial layer of rubber on the soles and lower edges of the shoes.

She stirred the rubber again to prevent a "skin" forming over top it as it cooled, then inspected the rubberized hoops of cord she'd made earlier. Matching them up with one another first, then with the specific bags she'd measured them to, Nida inserted them one at a time into their respective bags. One of the hoops she pushed down to the bottom of the bag to stabilize the circular base, then suspended the other near the mouth of the bag, tension holding it in place.

Taking the one of the bags, now a free-standing, stable cylinder, Nida placed a fisted hand inside it, and slowly pressed it down into the rubber, base first. The bag was just a tad taller than the level of rubber in the pot, and she pressed the bag down to the bottom before removing it with the tongs. She delicately set the bag upside-down on the bench and proceeded to rubberize the remainder in similar fashion. After each had cooled long enough they had stiffened, she used the tongs to dip just their bases in the rubber, remembering to dip them in the same order each time.

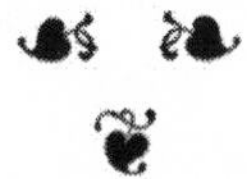

Nida set the last of the bags on the table, again upside-down, and returned to check the first and see if it had cooled sufficiently to handle. Finding its surface still supple, yet no longer tacky, she took the shears to the outside of the bag, cutting two vertical slits into it a short space apart, perhaps a third of the way down the bag. With her stir-spoon, she smeared the cuts with rubber inside and out, then held them open to keep the edges from sticking to one another as she blew on them to speed the rubber's cooling.

This she did twice, explaining that the rubber would keep the slits from tearing open further. While she was at it, she heavily slathered the rubberized ring of cord in the base of the bag to secure it in the bottom. To give the rubber time to cool before moving to the next phase, Nida repeated the same with the other bags, then cut eight equal lengths of cord, which she dipped once in the rubber and placed them on the table to cool.

Nida gathered the fleece liners together to pair it with its matching bag, then trimmed two finger widths off the top edge of the liner. Inserting the liner into each bag, Nida folded the top edge of each rubberized bag inward, over the liner and the upper rubberized ring of cord, then sewed the liner into the bag, securing it in a wide seam.

Finding the slits she'd made in the side of the bag, she rotated the bag a quarter turn clockwise, took up the shears again, and made two new vertical slits through the seamed top, spacing them a few finger widths apart. As she had done with the slits she'd made before, she double-rubberized their edges inside and out, then waited for the rubber to cool around the slits.

Nida took the spool of cord and measured around the outside of the bag, cutting segments perhaps a hand breadth longer than the circumference of each bag. This she threaded through a slit in the side of the bag, the cord between the liner and the bag's interior, and, with hand inside the liner, inched the cord around the inside of the bag until she could pull it out the other slit. Pulling on the ends of the cord, she drew the liner closed within the bag. She tied bulky knots in the ends of the slack to prevent them falling into the bag through the slits, then made loops of the rubberized cord through the slits in the seam for a belt to pass through. Having equipped each bag with drawstring and belt loops, Nida stepped back, satisfied with the fruits of her labors.

In contemplation, Nida probed the rubberized sole of one of her shoes with a finger, finding the rubber now cool and resilient. She waved the intrigued Pritch and Hardy over to demonstrate.

"See here? This rubber is much more durable than anything I've made before. And its natural elasticity will provide traction while climbing."

"We're excited to see how these hold up," Pritch said with Hardy at his side, their stoic expressions seeming to indicate the opposite.

"You get me my hooks, packs, and chalk, and you won't have to wait long, gentletém," Nida said winningly.

"We've got your chalk right, here, ma'am," Pritch said, reaching once more into the shadows beneath the worktable, and drawing out a dusty canvas bag. "It's in the raw, so I hope it meets your needs," he said, holding the bag out to her and shaking it.

With a pleasant clink, the bag produced a puff of fine white powder from between its rough weave. Nat, who stood at eye level with the bag, sneezed as the chalk dust met his nostrils.

"Bless you, son!" Pritch exclaimed before turning back to Nida. "You'll have the rest of your supplies by the end of the week. "I presume the bags you've made are for the chalk?"

"Correct, sir!" Nida confirmed.

"Now that we've seen what to do with them, we can finish the bags and shoes. You should be able to test them after dinner on Saturday," Pritch said with pride.

"Stupendous!" Nida cheered. "Thank you both very much. I'll see you Saturday evening, then." And with that, she and Nat departed the forge and the training hall to locate Shoym aboveground.

Chapter Twenty

Leaders Among Etom

They encountered their dear friend just inside the main doors of the temple, where he was bidding farewell to a large and noisy family who were very active among the Eben'kayah.

"Good night, Master Haarfanell! And a fine evening to you as well, Madame Grüntha!" Shoym shouted after them into the descending gloom.

Shoym rubbed his brow and chuffed as he pulled the doors to. He appreciated their contribution, but by the flowing waters of the Tree Ha Kayim, they were a boisterous and exhausting bunch!

Realizing Nat and Nida stood quietly a short distance off, Shoym came to and greeted them, "Mistress Nida! And young Master Nat! It's very nice to see you here this evening. To what do I owe this pleasure?"

"Well, Master Shoym, we came to see how preparations for the training were coming, and, of course, to speak to you," Nida responded cordially.

"And did you find everything in order? Pritch and Hardy treating you right?" Shoym inquired.

Nida answered, "Absolutely! They have been nothing but helpful, and their work is top notch. We should be ready to start first thing next week, which is why I wanted to speak to you."

Shoym stood at the ready, "Yes, dear? What might you need?"

"I hadn't really thought of it before, but how many will I be training?" she asked.

"Of course! Let me just see here," he said as he dipped a hand inside his jacket to produce a folded parchment about the length of an envelope, but a little wider.

He pored over it a moment, counting under his breath as he skipped the side of his finger down the margin of the page, then smiled and looked at Nida, "Why, you've had quite the turnout, Mistress Nida! Thirty-one will be joining you for training. Very impressive!"

Nida's breath locked in her chest, and she uttered a wheezing cough before she rasped incredulously, "Thirty—?" She cleared her throat, "Thirty-one?"

She'd expected perhaps a dozen at most and had been comfortable considering that number of students. But... so many? She shook her head uncertainly until Shoym reassured her, bracing her with a hand on each shoulder.

"Mistress Nida, I know it's quite a lot, but there's no one else in whom I have such confidence. You have proven time and again you are up to this. Now if you will just believe it," he pleaded. Shoym's voice grew resolute, "'Anything is possible to him who believes.'"

Nida looked up at once, meeting Shoym's blazing eyes, a hundred memories of Jaarl speaking the same soared up from the depths of her recollection, a shining eagle cresting the edge of a pained chasm, its rays striking her tender heart.

"Where—?" Sudden tears sprung from her eyes, and she turned her head, embarrassed because she wept. "Where did you hear that?"

"A thousand times from your husband's lips, though he did not author this truth. It is found in the chronicles of Gan, among the very words of King Elyon. Jaarl was especially fond of the phrase, as you well know."

Nat drew close in consolation to grip her arm, and Nida dried her tears, "Thank you, dear Shoym. I will be ready. No! I am ready and willing to train as many as needed. Count on it."

Eyes dewy with emotion, Shoym responded, "I do, dear Nida. I do."

Observing Nat's prolonged and gaping yawn, Shoym shook the sentiment of the moment, and ushered them to the doors. "I'm certain your son could do with some rest, yes?"

He bid them a very fond farewell, and the pair departed, Nat looking back over his shoulder as the great and beautiful gates slipped closed behind them.

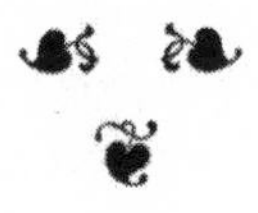

Saturday evening came with Nida in throes of anticipation both thrilling and distressing. She and Nat arrived early at the temple, well before the meal, such was her eagerness to ensure the equipment was meet to the rigors of training.

They hurried below to the forge, and from there Pritch and Hardy directed them over to the armory, where they found all as Nida might have imagined it. The hooks were placed in a row on one of the long shelves across the wall, the chalk-bags sat on the shelf beneath the hooks with leather gloves peeking from each one, and the large canvas bag of raw chalk rested on the floor at the end of the shelf. The packs were grouped in a corner, the coil of rope suspended by a hook in the wall above them. Belts hung by their buckles from a long rod protruding from the wall next to the rope, and the shoes sat in tidy formation on the ground next to the packs.

She ran a hand over one of the multi-pronged hooks, and hefted a pack to test its weight, finding it more than adequate, then gathered one of each to assemble a kit. She'd worn her climbing shoes to the temple, hoping to break them in some before testing them in earnest, and had found their level of traction far superior to her usual smooth leather-soled shoes. She cut a substantial segment of rope, estimating the full height of the climbing wall and then some. It was a simple matter now to attach rope to climbing hook through the loop at the end of the hook's shaft, then threaded the strap of a belt through the loops of a chalk-bag before cinching it around her waist.

Nat tapped her on her arm, "Mom, do you think it might be alright for me to try, too, please? I don't have the special shoes . . ."

Nida indulged the child, and he followed suit in preparing himself in the same fashion as she, finishing up by throwing the chunk of raw chalk she offered him into his chalk-bag with a toothy grin. They looped their ropes over their shoulders, and headed for the climbing area, Nat's rope draggling on the ground, a coarse tail etching a trail behind him in the dust.

They reached the wall, catching a few sidelong glances from others training in the hall as they made their way over to it. Nida dropped her coil of rope to the ground, tucked the gloves into her belt and dipped a hand into her chalk-bag, bringing out the rough block within to "paint" her hands with the powdery substance. She replaced the chalk in its bag, then dropped into a crouch, snatching the coil of rope up in her left hand and the hook in her right before she arose.

Hook in hand, she warned Nat away, "I need you several steps back, dear."

Nat gave her a wide berth and plopped his own rope down where he stood to watch. Nida approached the climb, looking up the sheer wall, and glancing to either side before she began twirling the menacing hook slowly on the end of the rope as she returned her attention to the wall.

Using the momentum of the whirling hook, Nida slung it up the wall forcefully, aiming for a sturdy loop of a branch about halfway up the vegetative surface. The hook flew true, two of its flukes catching over the branch, as the rope trailed behind with a shallow wave running down its length. Nida tugged on the rope a few times to secure the hook's bite, then, gripping the rope, leaned back to entrust her weight to it, and began to stride up the wall with unhurried, fluid grace.

She found the shoes' additional traction helped immensely in scaling the wall, and the chalk kept her hands dry and her grip on the rope sure. It was a matter of moments before she reached the hook. She wedged herself amongst the ivy to pull up the rope and then bind it to the branch from which the hook still depended.

Standing out on the branch, Nida clung with one hand to the ivy while again twirling the hook for a throw, this time aiming for the top of the course. She found it awkward to throw from her perch on the wall and learned from several failed attempts that the steep angle of the throw required precise and subtle control before finally succeeding.

Nida's hands and shoulders ached from steadying herself in the unnatural position, so she took a moment to rest and assess the situation. Unable to see what she'd latched onto with the hook from her narrow vantage on the wall, Nida decided to tug and yank on the rope from various directions before trusting her weight to it. Nat cheered her on from below, and she noticed a small group gathering behind him to watch her ascent.

They've come to see what the new trainer is made of, eh?

Nida stepped out, rope in both hands, to continue up the wall, and looked straight down, evoking a mild, queasy dizziness and instant regret.

It must be the nerves, she thought. *I've completed more difficult climbs than this.*

She looked again at the growing crowd.

Never had an audience before, though. If I'm not careful, they'll find out what I'm made of, inside and out, she thought with wry, dark humor.

Nida recovered her composure and again strode up the wall, confidence growing with each step. Before long, she summited the top of the wall, and discovered her hook hung upon a wooden rail surrounding the narrow platform atop the course. The rail seemed sturdy enough, but would need reinforcement, as would the platform, given the number of climbers slated to train.

She removed the hook from the rail and unfastened the rope from the its end before securing it to the rail over top the rocky portion of the climbing wall. The combined weight of multiple climbers and continued duress would soon weaken the current rail, though she found it suited her current need.

Pulling on her gloves and gripping the rope in one hand, Nida dropped a leg over the rail, winding the rope around the other, then over and behind the opposite shoulder in preparation to rappel. She stood a moment with both feet against the wall to take stock, venturing another peek over her shoulder down at the ground where her welcoming committee, headed by Nat, waved up at her, shouting and whistling. Having conquered the course, her earlier apprehension melted away.

She spoke aloud to herself, a mischievous smile on her face, "Well, I might as well give them something worth cheering, huh?"

Instead of walking her way down the wall, Nida took a couple quick steps down, one hand on the rope above, the other holding the rope beneath her backside as a brake. She hopped out from the wall, releasing the brake a bit for a short swing down, her shoes scuffing audibly as she struck the wall. Without delay, she jumped out a bit further for a longer, deeper swing as she dropped much farther.

In the relative silence of her swing, Nida perceived the din of voices below had grown quiet. Her feet, positioned close together, slammed loudly into the wall, breaking the silence as she bent her knees, crouching into the impact, and absorbing it. From her coiled position, she sprung out as powerfully as she was able without hesitation, swinging wide of the wall, and dropping rapidly.

Pritch and Hardy's gloves held up well, and it was only during this final phase of her rapid descent that Nida detected the scorching friction of the rope's swift passage through her gloved hands. In some part of her mind, Nida detected the stillness that had stolen over the hall, and envisioned all eyes focused on her antics. She banished the distraction, the wall now looming before her as she swung toward it, bracing for impact while clamping down on the rope to brake her descent. She spread her feet wide this time, bending her knees deeply as she violently met the wall, her feet throwing dust and grit into the air upon impact. The collision forced the air from Nida's lungs, causing her to grunt, and she squatted so deeply in reducing the brunt that her backside struck the wall, though without much force.

Nida cautiously peeked down around her arm to see how far she'd come and discovered that she was mere steps from the bottom. Her last bound down the wall had been just shy of half its height, and indeed she felt the repercussions of the impressive drop.

Nat rushed up to her with concern, "Mom, are you OK? You hit the wall *hard*."

She had impressed him, and Nat thought he'd never seen his mother, flushed from excitement and exertion, look so lovely.

Nida stepped down from the wall and released the vise-grip she'd had on the rope, her fingers momentarily cramped and frozen.

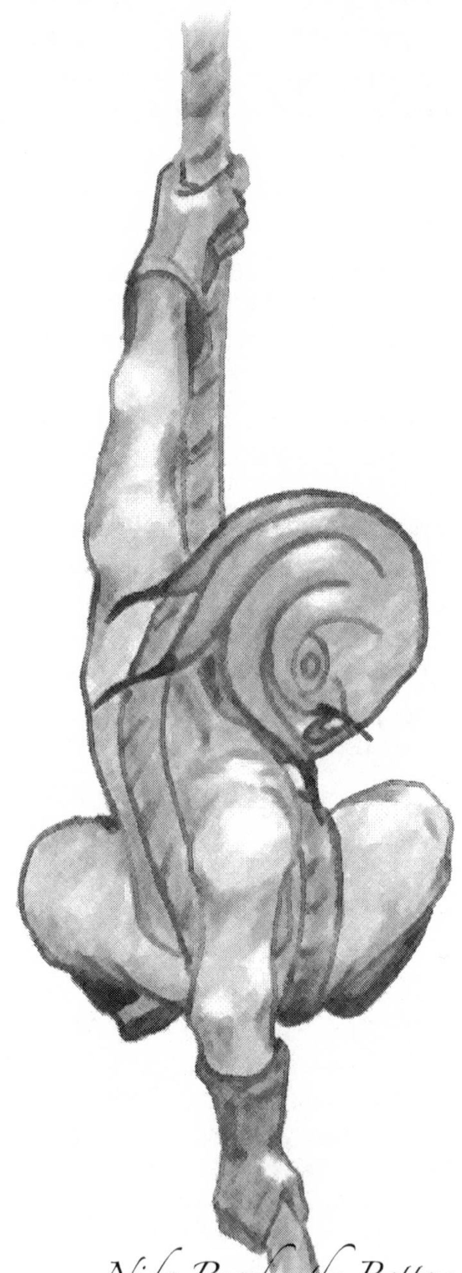

Nida Reaches the Bottom

"Yes, I'm fine, dear," She responded, then stood up straight, stretching tall as she flexed her hands, a dull ringing in her ears as she swung stiffly about on stilted legs to meet the crowd that had followed her progress down. A number of her audience cheered and whistled as they grouped around her.

"I've never seen anything like it!"

"Are you OK?!? That last bit looked painful . . ."

"When do you start training? I think I want to join."

Nida offered perfunctory replies through a heartfelt, yet wincing smile as she gingerly walked off the pain. The huddle followed her about, their interest in her well-being and in learning to climb from her apparent.

If Nida's plan in pulling a stunt coming down the wall was to reduce enrollments in her classes, it had backfired stupendously. Not only had she shown the supreme utility of her climbing skills, she'd made it look fun to boot! She sent no fewer than a dozen of her flocking fans to Shoym for registration and expected from the buzz following her feat that she would see at least a dozen more on her rolls before too long.

Oh well, she thought, *I still did what I came to do.*

And indeed, she had. She'd successfully tested the new gear, and herself, which was more important. Having proven herself against the climbing wall, Nida gained confidence in her abilities to lead, and the excitement she'd inspired among the scouts also bolstered her morale.

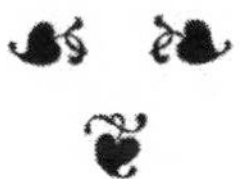

When all was said and done, Nida ended up with over fifty students, the majority of the scouting program participating. At the start of the program, Pritch and Hardy had difficulty in keeping up with demand for the gear but caught up within a couple of weeks. The delay in production helped Nida acclimate to the growing demands on her time and energy since not all registered for the training were able to start at the same time.

In addition, Nida found limiting the size of her classes necessary since it was too difficult to communicate the niceties of technique and prepping the equipment to any more than a dozen or so at a time. It took her the better part of a month to ramp up the training program to include all fifty-plus enrollees, resulting in a total of five weekly sessions.

By the time she began instructing her newest students, Nida had identified and recruited a few of the more talented climbers under her tutelage to begin teaching the new trainees. Nida foresaw a number of them becoming skilled instructors and planned to turn a session or two completely over to them as they matured. In this manner, her training program provided accelerated instruction and additional support for those who might be struggling.

In the time it took her to get the climbing program up and running, Nida coordinated with Shoym to staff her stall in the market, finding the three trainees he provided more than adequate to the task. All three were honest, bright, and hard-working, which allowed Nida to delegate and release responsibility for her shop to them. If she'd found any of them otherwise incapable, it would have distracted her from properly training the scouts. When she asked Shoym about compensation for the help, he insisted the Eben'kayah had gotten the better end of the bargain and would accept nothing from her. Nevertheless, Nida made certain to leave a few grains here and there for her young helpers, who were always appreciative of the unexpected reward.

Though much younger than the trainees, Nat developed quite a knack for climbing, and Nida grew both proud of him for his abilities, and afraid for him because of his daredevil tendencies. Perhaps it was his upbringing dangling from her back and swinging from a rope high on the rubber tree, but Nat was fearless and calm among the heights of the climbing arena. It was his element, and he soon adopted the fluid, easy grace that his mother demonstrated clambering over stone, brick, and branch.

If it made Nida uneasy to watch her son scamper and leap around the climbing surfaces, it outright unsettled several of the scout trainees, especially the less experienced, who could only watch him with wary, flinching eyes and halted warnings caught behind half-gnawed lips.

His antics aside, Nat inspired others in the training program, and was always ready with a smile and a word of encouragement. All elements of the training program strained the mind and body, as Shoym had intended, and many times Nat was there to cheer on a trainee struggling through a challenging task. His good humor was infectious, and uplifting to such an extent that instructors and trainees alike made him the unofficial mascot of the training program, well-respected and well-loved among them all.

Also, he wasn't long in making yet another important contribution, an epiphany of phraseology that took place during a cross-discipline meeting of all trainers. Shoym led the meeting, checking in with everyone and soliciting feedback. A guest at the meeting, Nat was present with his mother, and, as usual, remained politely quiet. This day however, the cumbersome terms "training hall" and "storeroom" received heavy usage throughout.

Suddenly, Nat interjected, eyes bright and smiling "I've got it! Forge and Forage! You see? Forge and Forage!"

In confused silence, the group looked at Nat, then Nida, for some explanation. They clearly did *not* see what he was talking about.

Just as perplexed as the others, Nida, too looked down at Nat, and asked, "Why, Nat. Whatever do you mean?"

Still beaming with excitement, Nat explained, "Well, we don't just forge weapons and armor in the 'training hall.'" He threw up air quotes with his hands for emphasis. "We forge skills, minds, bodies, too. The Forge! You know? And what do you do in 'the storeroom?' You *forage*. Soooo . . ." He looked around at everyone with expectation. "The Forage! Forge and Forage!!! Yeah?!?"

Laughter started slowly among the trainers, one or two snorting, then giggling.

Chuckling gave way to great guffaws, Shoym the loudest as he agreed, wiping a tear from his eye, "Young Master Nat, that *is* quite catchy." Turning to the others as the laughter quieted, he asked, "Don't you agree?"

Around the room, heads bobbed in agreement, and Shoym declared, "Well then! Henceforth, the 'training hall' and 'storeroom,'" Shoym imitated Nat's air quotes satirically before continuing, "shall be known as The Forge and Forage! Now, unless anyone," he looked back at Nat with a smirk, "has else something to contribute, I say we should adjourn."

Still smiling, the trainers all shook their heads, and the meeting ended on a positive note. Nida looked down at her son, and chuckled.

"What?" Nat asked. "What's so funny, Mom?"

Rolling her eyes in bemused exasperation, Nida walked away to prepare for her next class, leaving Nat still shrugging in self-satisfied bewilderment.

Truth be told, Nat's new-found climbing abilities augmented a healthy confidence in himself as his academic knowledge likewise grew. A year passed, and then another, his continued friendship with Rae meanwhile flourishing. Though he didn't have another friend quite so close, he had found many at the Bunker and among the Eben'kayah.

The name of the Etom school, the Bunker, took on new meaning under the sinister watch of the Nihúkolem, for the shelter the weathered shell provided away from unwelcome surveillance. Inside the Bunker, Nat forgot the looming threat of imperial Chōl, and he enjoyed a certain peace, his conflict with Rosco notwithstanding. In fact, Nat had on occasion found opportunity to demonstrate kindness to the bully, assisting the bigger etém with his work when no one watched.

At first, Rosco had refused in angry. Nat, however, had persisted, and Rosco after some time received the much-needed help, albeit grudgingly. For all intents and purposes, Nat remained Rosco's secret tutor. Secret, that is, but for the exception of Rae, who discovered the deed and marveled that Nat would choose to aid their antagonist. It was from the Eben'kayah that Nat took the lesson of mercy, even in the face of hostility and hatred, and the lesson served him well. Rosco would be loath to admit it, but by the end of their fourth year together, he would count Nat among his friends, so great was the help Nat supplied.

Besides Nat's clandestine friendship with Rosco, Rae began to notice other changes in her friend, and might have chalked them up to the changes that accompanied him growing up, but for one element: Nat was keeping something from her. Something big.

Sure, they still spent time together in and out of school, learning and playing together, but though Nat hadn't spoken a word of it, word got out that she was the Headmistress' daughter. That fact, coupled with her family's substantial wealth, had left Rae with two demerits against her popularity among the "normal" children of Endego, and she was insecure her friendship with Nat would be affected.

So, it was with some reservation that Rae invited Nat out to her palatial home for her tenth birthday, and she was hesitant that he might treat her differently afterward. At first, Rae had been dismayed at Nat's expression, eyes saucer-wide and mouth agape, upon receiving him at the door the night of the party. He had simply never experienced a birthday celebration on that scale.

Rae needn't have worried, however. Despite her misgivings, Nat remained a constant friend and her closest confidante, for what it's worth among children. Still, Rae sensed Nat shouldered a substantial secret, perceived in his evasiveness and his regular, unexplained absence from her company.

On a whim, Rae once stopped by his house to say "hello," and found the home dark and windows shuttered. Being an assertive young lass, she'd knocked several times at the empty and quiet residence to no avail. She didn't mention it to Nat at school the following day, but tried again a few nights later, discovering his house was once again vacant.

Unable to contain her curiosity any longer, Rae confronted her friend at school, blurting out, "So where have you been at night, huh?

I've come by twice now, and *you. don't. answer!"* She punctuated the last three words with sharp jabs to Nat's shoulder. "Where were you?"

At first, Nat balked, shifting his gaze side to side before answering, "My mom has me helping out with the shop, and sometimes we're out late. That's all."

"You've been *helping out* as long as I've known you. You've never been out so late before," she'd said.

Nat took a deep breath, "Look, it's actually super boring. If you must know, the shop hasn't been doing so great, so mom's been working extra, and dragging me along."

He finished, looking embarrassed, whether because he lied or because he told a shameful truth, Rae couldn't tell.

Withholding judgement for the moment, she let him off the hook, "OK. OK. You don't need to say more. Geez. Just thought it was weird, you know?"

Nat was relieved, and offered, "Maybe we can do something Thursday? I'll talk with mom today. See if I can get out of helping her for the night."

"Sure. Sure," Rae had responded distractedly. She didn't fully accept his explanation and had a sense he'd not given her the whole story.

Oh well. When he's ready, I'm sure he'll tell me, she thought. Except he didn't, or at least not yet, and it had been months since their conversation. She gave up prying, intending to wait her friend out, but Rae had never been the most patient etma, and sooner or later would force the issue.

It ended up being sooner, rather than later, the occasion arising during lunch period at school when Nat declined the invitation to her upcoming eleventh birthday celebration at the end of Asara, just over a week away.

"Rae, I'm sorry. I want to come, but I just can't. Mom says we have to do something else that day," he offered plaintively.

At first disappointed, Rae grew angry, her pale pink cheeks flaring apple red, "But you're my best friend, Nat! My *best* friend! Can't you just do it another time?"

"I already asked, and Mom said 'no.' Maybe we could have you over to our place another time? I bet I could get Mom to bake you a cake? You love Mom's cooking."

"Nat!" Rae scolded, "You need to tell me what's going on right now!"

"Huh?" Nat said, shaking his head, bewildered, "What are you talking about?"

"You know what I'm talking about!" she said, her voice rising to a screech. "You're never home! You're spending time with Rosco, but don't have any for me! What is going on with you?"

Nat's eyes bulged as he attempted to hush Rae, "Quiet! Quiet. OK? Give me a second."

Though they were a distance from any others, Rae outburst had drawn unwanted attention.

Nat thought hard for a moment, chin in hand, then spoke again, "Can you wait 'til tomorrow? Please? I just want to talk to mom first, yeah?"

Though not entirely satisfied, Rae agreed to wait, and they finished their lunch in silence before returning to class, a palpable chasm between them. Nat lamented the growing distance and promised himself he'd talk it over with his mother that very night. In his mind, he formulated a plan, and hoped his mother would agree to it.

Chapter Twenty-One

Full Measures

Just under two years had passed since Nida and Nat had joined the Eben'kayah, and the years had been good to them. At home from after a day at the market Nida prepared herself for an evening of training and mused over the circumstances Elyon had orchestrated to bring them into the fold. A contented smile on her face, she considered the goodness of their lives and of their Lord while stirring a pot on the stove. Nat burst into the house, cheeks flushed violet from apparent exertion, and words flying from his mouth as he entered.

Nida shook her head in confusion, brow furrowed and hands up as she asked her son to start over, "Whoa! Whoa. What's all this again?"

Nat took a deep breath and began again, "Mom, Rae knows something's up. I don't know how. I haven't said a word. I swear!"

Nida went to the door then the window to ensure no one was nearby to overhear their conversation, then whispered, "Nat, what did she say? Tell me."

"She knows I've got a secret, but not what it is," he explained, "and she's upset I can't go to her party at the end of the month. That's what set her off! We were just sitting there. Just sitting at lunch! And out of nowhere, she asked me —"

"What did you tell her, Nat?" Nida interrupted.

"Nothing, except that I would tell her everything tomorrow. I can, can't I, Mom?" Nat pleaded, "She's the only one I trust around here, and doesn't she deserve to know, too?"

Nida had already thought this scenario over, realizing that eventually Rae might discover their secret–the secret of the Eben'kayah.

Nida spoke, "Nat, I need you to make a deal with Rae. If she's willing to wait until the night of the party to learn more, I'll let you go to her party."

"Really, Mom? I can go?" Nat asked with hope.

"Yes, dear, as long as Rae agrees to wait. I know that you were supposed to help make preparations for the evening's festivities, but I'll make sure to cover it with Shoym." Nida softened, and looked a moment at her son, caressing his cheek tenderly. "I know how important Rae is to you, Nat, and I want her to join us among the Eben'kayah, too. I'm inclined to believe this may be Elyon's way of doing just that."

Nat's lips quivered, and his eyes shone, "I hope so, Mom."

"The second thing is that I want you to do is invite her to the temple the night after her party, but—and this is important—don't tell her where you're taking her. It'll be a surprise. Can you do that, son?"

Nat nodded with enthusiasm, "Yes, Ma'am!"

He was excited to go to the party and of course had wanted to tell his closest friend about the Eben'kayah for years now.

Nida continued, "Her party's in the afternoon right after school, yes? If you two can leave her party early in the evening, you'll arrive before we get started. Do you think she'll go for it?"

"She'd do anything to have me at her party! Thank you, Mom!"

As expected, Rae jumped at the opportunity to make sure her best friend was at her party and saw no reason they couldn't leave on their mysterious journey before dark. After a couple hours at Rae's party, most of her guests were ready to leave anyhow, so it wasn't difficult to steer everyone out the door before Nat and Rae headed out, the sun already well below the horizon.

Rae was curious as to their destination, which Nat's use of various, discreet shortcuts only heightened. The final leg of their journey took them to the large stone where Rosco had ambushed them while they listened to the music pouring from the temple, a fact that did not escape Rae's notice. She mentioned as much to Nat as they once again crouched in cover at the stone's edge, Nat shushing her as he examined the area to ensure they could cross unobserved.

The temple sat in shadowed silence, and appeared vacant to any prying eyes, especially those of the Nihúkolem or their informers. A flitting shadow overhead caught the corner Nat's eye, betraying the passage of a hawk, and Nat decided the front entrance was too dangerous to chance. He rounded the other side of the stone with Rae on his heels to plunge into the underbrush after locating one of many hidden paths to the temple. They pushed on in relative silence, Rae suppressing the myriad questions that arose in her mind in favor of the stealth she knew Nat preferred. It was all very exciting and mysterious, and Rae trusted she would soon discover the secret Nat had withheld from her so long.

Soon, they arrived at the rear of the temple, an iron gate before them a few paces from their cover in the brush. It was the very gate through which they had entered the temple together what seemed a great while ago. Cupping his hands around his mouth, Nat chirped in imitation of a cricket once, twice, thrice.

Though Rae detected no sentry on the other side of the gate, moments later it quietly swung open, inviting them into a courtyard at the rear of the large stone structure. Nat grabbed Rae's hand, prompting her to move, and they passed through the gate, a flicker of movement catching Rae's eye, and startling a gasp from her. She fought down the urge to scream as a figure, hardly distinguishable from the surrounding darkness, swung the gate shut behind them.

They passed into the shadows of a covered walkway, Nat moving with confidence in the darkness. Another shadowed sentry opened the dark port before them, a gleam of light escaping from beneath a wide and nearby door right before them when at last they had entered the building.

The door behind closed with a muted 'click,' and Nat spoke again, "We should be alright now we've made it inside."

He tugged her toward the door across the dim foyer, "Come with me. There are some people that I want you to meet. That I *have wanted* you to meet." Bracing herself as Nat opened the door onto a warm and glowing light, Rae followed her friend into the unknown.

The sight that greeted Rae as they stepped into the temple galleria was several small clusters of Etom conversing in subdued and pleasant tones. The faint, muffled clamor of many voices spilled from a doorway propped open at their left, the dim light of the sanctuary hall silhouetting the movement of several figures within.

Near the open door, Rae recognized Nat's mother chatting with a vaguely familiar, pale-yellow etém whose back was to them. As the pair approached Nida and her companion, Rae noticed Nida touch a flushed cheek with her hand in a gesture she'd seen from her mother when her father said something charming.

Oooo! Rae thought. *She* likes *him!*

"Mom!" Nat hailed. "We made it!"

Nida looked over her suitor's shoulder, waving them over, as the stranger turned, a friendly smile on his face.

"Dempsey!" Rae exclaimed, identifying the figure.

"Why, I know this young lass! Pummeled any bullies lately? Or just innocent instruments?" Dempsey offered with a mischievous grin.

Rae shook her head, speechless at the encounter.

"You've grown a bit since I last saw you. You here with this rascal?" he asked, slapping a hearty hand on Nat's shoulder.

"Yes. Yes, sir," Rae stammered uncharacteristically at Dempsey's familiarity.

"Dempsey, please," Nida intruded, "Can't you see it's a bit much for her?"

Dempsey looked inquisitively at Rae for a moment, then apologized, "I'm sorry, Rae." He shook her hand, "It's good to see you again. I'm glad that you came." He looked up at Nida, "What do you say we head in now? They'll be starting soon, and I am needed up front."

Nida agreed, "Yes, let's." Addressing the children, she swept them inside the hall with an open arm, "We'll find our seats together." Taking the lead, Nida headed to three open seats she'd spotted near the front.

Dempsey followed them to their row, then passed down the aisle to the front as the trio shuffled politely past the attendees, doing their best to avoid trampling toes. Nida, Nat, and Rae settled in to their seats, Rae sweeping her gaze around the hall in wonder. It was to her advantage that Nat was at hand, for he explained some of what to expect, and answered any questions she had.

From the tuning of the orchestral instruments to the turning of the final tapestry, the Eben'kayah reproduced the performance given Nat and Nida's first night in the temple exactly two years before. The end of

Asara marked the annual celebration of Gan's history, and a comprehensive review of all the Eben'kayah believed. Rae sat in awe, much as Nat and Nida had, absorbing the beauty of the spectacle until its very end. Nat and Nida arose as the lights came up to proceed to the galleria for refreshment, Rae following in a thoughtful daze.

They reached the galleria, and Nat asked, "Rae, are you alright? You haven't said anything for a while."

"I'm not sure yet," she responded, shaking her head, "What was that in there? I've heard bits from my parents and teachers, but not all of it."

"Rae, dear," Nida began, "That is our history. Much of what we know since the beginning, but not all by any means."

"What do you mean?" Rae asked. "And who was the King with the huge sword at the beginning?"

"That's King Elyon, Rae!" Nat exclaimed, excited. "The Creator. The One who made it all. Made us, too."

"But they told me no one really knows where we came from! How do you know it's true?" Rae asked.

By now Dempsey had joined their conversation from his place in the orchestra, and jumped in, "My young friend, our people and others like us have recorded history since its dawning. What you saw this evening is the culminated effort of generations of dedicated members of our tribe since we first sprang forth from the earth of Gan and learned to speak from Man."

Nida spoke just above a whisper, "Rae, we understand this is a lot to take in. If you look around at our community, we hope you will see the benefit of our beliefs. Come on, let's get you something to eat, OK? Nat, would you take her with you to the buffet?"

"Sure!" Nat blurted, grinning from ear to ear at his mother's proposed combination of two of his favorite things: food and spending time with Rae. Nat grabbed Rae's pale pink hand in his sky blue one, and for a change dragged her to the tables, her feet skipping irregularly beneath her while she caught up to her friend.

Nida and Dempsey watched Rae and Nat from a distance, enjoying the muted giggles and prattling conversation not quite audible from their vantage. Tinged by concern, Nida's happiness at their youthful cheer was incomplete, and Dempsey caught her dimming disposition.

"It's a risk, I know," he said in response to Nida's mood.

Nida laughed, startled that Dempsey had read her with such faculty, "I'm believing for the best. Only Elyon knows the outcome. I hope that neither one is hurt."

"There's no guarantee of that, as you well know, but I hope the same. Think we can help them somehow?" Dempsey wondered aloud.

Nida frowned in concerned thought before she answered, "Pray. We can pray. And be available for them. Anything more may drive Rae away."

Dempsey nodded with appreciation, "Right. She needs to make her own decision." He straightened, blinking brightly, and attempted to lighten the mood, "Well, they shouldn't be the only ones to enjoy themselves. Join me for a bite?"

Dempsey gestured to the tables and looked to Nida expectantly.

Nida cheered, favoring Dempsey with a smile as she assented, "Of course, my good sir." In mock formality, she continued, "And whither shalt thou conduct me?"

Dempsey humored her wit, "My good etma, wouldst thou join me henceforth at yon table of buffet to purloin a leg of roasted beast from amongst the provender displayed therewith?"

"Oh wow!" Nida chuckled. "You've taken it to another level. Was that another language? Let's get something to eat."

It turned out that they needn't have been so concerned about Rae's reaction. An observant and precocious child, she'd already noticed the many changes in Nat, and knew him to be an even better friend for his involvement with the Eben'kayah. His credibility with Rae outweighed any doubts she might have had, and if he believed, then without long speculation, she did too.

Nat and Rae's friendship thus restored, they enjoyed a curious and unbroken season of respite from daily worry, though the specter of the

Nihúkolem yet loomed. In time, Nida, Nat, and Rae introduced first Rae's mother, Headmistress Kehren, and then her father, Tram, to the Eben'kayah. They, too, had noticed a favorable change in their darling child, who for all her wit and charm had often behaved in a stubborn, spoiled manner.

Tram and Kehren saw a different child emerging–one altogether kinder and more considerate than before. It was to their credit that Rae's parents received the promises of Elyon so readily, for it became apparent that not many among the Etom in Endego would. The need for secrecy was ever present, and it grieved the Eben'kayah when every so often a family from the community would disappear without a trace, the Nihúkolem snatching them out of beds in the night to dark destinations. Even so, their remnant remained faithful, and strength increased among them.

Nat and Rae continued their studies in the Bunker and went out of their way to involve Rosco as much as his pride would permit him to bear the disgrace of being seen in their company. Nevertheless, Rosco softened as he grew closer to them, and eschewed his former hoodlum companions. Recognizing the worth of what his new friends displayed in their ways, Rosco cast off his brute exterior to reveal a wise and gentle soul in the nurture of Nat and Rae's fellowship, and that of the Eben'kayah.

As is the nature of all seasons, even this one came to an end. The Eben'kayah of Endego continued to send out a steady stream of scouts in pairs, hoping to discover something new regarding the Kinsman. Mission protocol dictated each pair of scouts continue in the general direction assigned them until they succeeded in gathering critical intelligence, or three months had passed, whichever came first.

If Endego sat at the center of a clock's dial, Shoym directed most scout teams to move out along its hourly graduations, while others he sent to a specific location based on prior intelligence. It was in this manner that the Eben'kayah sought for some sign, some portent of their expected Deliverer. Limiting time on mission and pairing the scouts improved chances of success and scout survivability. Time and time again, the teams returned empty-handed, having gained only wounds and scars for their trouble, and many never returned. Their fates unknown, the Eben'kayah had naught else but to presume them dead or captured. It was in desperation, therefore, that the council convened to discuss what additional measures they might take to prosper their heretofore fruitless endeavor.

After the Saturday evening meal, Shoym invited Dempsey and Nida to attend council as observers, stating that he might need their expertise. After leaving Nat upstairs with several grandmotherly etma tending the children, the trio arrived at the meeting. Nida noted that almost all of the other scout program trainers were also in attendance and wondered what was at hand. Agatous stood in the center of the council-ring to call the meeting to order, the discordant clamor of debate around the ring falling to a hush as she began.

In measured tones, she spoke, "It's certain that you are all aware that our reconnaissance over the past two years has yielded us little new intelligence."

Taking her seat around the ring, she looked favorably at Shoym, who stared in defeat at the cold stone floor of the chamber, and prompted him with gentle words, "Master Shoym, I do hope you won't take this is as any indictment of your character, your determination, or your methods."

Shoym lifted his head at her address, his eyes shimmering with frustrated tears of disappointment.

Continuing, Agatous honored him, "Every one of us has witnessed how capably, how intensely, and how consistently you have striven for the success of our mission. However, the hour now grows late, and large segments of our network and our community around the world have fallen silent."

"Our numbers here in Endego dwindle, as presumably they do among the Eben'kayah in every land. The time for half measures is over, and we can no longer delay. After some discussion with Shoym,

Talcalum, and Alcarid, we propose to launch several larger, extended expeditions at the same time to find the One we seek."

From across the chamber, a concerned voice arose, "How long will they be gone?" It was Gimble, a squat and friendly mauve etma involved with supporting families among the Eben'kayah.

Agatous swept her gaze over the council gravely before answering, "It is our intent that none return until they achieve success."

A momentary silence that followed broke under the murmurs and protestations of the council until Shoym's voice rang out over the tumult, "Please! Please! Let Madame Agatous speak her piece."

Nodding appreciatively in his direction, Agatous continued, "Thank you, Master Shoym." She met the eyes of the council once more as she spoke, "Under Shoym's leadership, our training program has succeeded in training close to every Eben'kayah for survival in the wild. Even those who have yet to complete the training are more disciplined and better prepared than ever for the rigors waiting outside the grove. Adversity has made us stronger! More unified!"

"Which is why we further propose that every Eben'kayah in Endego depart on expedition. But for a small remnant, all others will be sent. Those who stay behind will relay communications between groups from hiding. Alcarid has assured us we've sufficient provisions to supply those that stay and give those headed into the wild enough until they acclimate to surviving on what they forage. It is with lengthy prayer and meditation that we propose this course of action."

Agitated furor erupted within the council chamber, and Agatous tried to regain control, undeterred, "Given the current state of affairs, we consider it a greater risk for the Eben'kayah to remain here!"

From her left came an ear-splitting roar, "Order! ORDER!!!"

The council grew still in surprise at the usually mild Talcalum, who stood trembling as he addressed them with passion, "How many more of us need disappear into the night!?! Better to hazard the journey in pursuit of hope than to remain here under *their* thumb!"

He cocked a blazing eye toward the surface as he finished. The council, comprehending his allusion to the oppressive Nihúkolem above, fell silent.

Agatous began again in the stillness, "As I was saying, to remain here bears its own risk, which we've seen, and our assessment is that it's a risk taken without benefit comparable to our proposed excursions. Our people have grown stronger under the current hardships, and we cannot shield them from this eventuality further. I believe we've all known in our hearts that it might come to this, ever since the Empire of Chōl spread its darkening cloud over all lands."

"And let us not forget: We may be small, but our King is great! We may be weak, yet He is mighty! He will not allow us to fail in our purpose!"

The council, no longer spurred by fear, but stirred by Agatous' exhortation, nodded in fervent agreement.

Gimble voiced her accord, "I second the Chief Counciletma's motion! All in favor?"

All around the ring, the council gave unanimous assent, before Agatous passed direction of the meeting to Alcarid, he whom Nida had once known only as Master Sour Avocado. Nida had at first found difficulty identifying any charity in the elderly etém yet had discovered his calculating and stern nature concealed a heart invested in the well-being of the Eben'kayah. He was a blessing to their community, and his ability to analyze the scenario with objectivity and logic was a great asset, especially when Nida's own concerns for those she'd come to care for had just about paralyzed her in consideration of their dispersion. Thank Elyon that He saw what His creation could not.

The council at once set to the task of organizing the Eben'kayah's departure from Endego, Gimble's extensive knowledge of their community's families proving particularly useful now. With her assistance, and that of the council, Alcarid loosely grouped the Eben'kayah's eighty-six families and the several "singles," forming a dozen teams of around twenty Etom each.

The scout training staff on hand at the meeting provided insight into the capabilities of the team members to ensure that each team contained Etom with complementary skills to round them out. Alcarid also assigned a scout trainer or assistant to each of the teams for additional support. Given their current leadership roles, the others would naturally look to the trainers for direction.

Team assignments now set, Alcarid brought Shoym into the conversation to set search parameters for the teams. Shoym called those involved in the discussion over to a table outside the council ring and laid out a map thereupon. It was the same map he had used to direct scouting parties since their mission began two years prior. Using a quill and straight edge, he had long ago drawn twelve rays intersecting at Endego, which he now labeled with the names of the different expeditionary groups.

Shoym had drawn on the name, "Eben'kayah," meaning "living stones," as inspiration, to decide on the code names for each group, which he referred to as "companies." At the one o'clock vector, he wrote the name of the first team, Company Ruby, then the second, Company Topaz, at the two o'clock, and so on until he finished at the twelve o'clock with the final team, Company Jasper.

They determined the general search protocol, which dictated that each team would travel half a day in the prescribed direction, set camp, then spread out in pairs from the camp for the remainder of the day. The larger group would allow for them to cover more ground and go farther than the pairs sent before. On-site leaders would have latitude to deviate from protocol at their discretion, which might occur if the group needed to circumvent an obstacle, or if they encountered new information and wanted to follow a lead. As a scout trainer, Nida received an assignment as well, leading Company Jasper to the 12 o'clock, due North.

Courses thus set, Shoym was preparing to rejoin the rest of council when Nida spoke up, "May I offer a suggestion?"

"Of course. What do you have in mind?" Shoym responded.

"Oughtn't we figure out exactly what each group should take on the journey now?" Nida inquired. "That way we can begin assembling our teams' packs from the Forage right away and identify any shortages we have on specialized supplies in advance. Imagine what kind of problems we will have if not everyone packs what they need, or if we found out right before we set out that we didn't have enough of certain essentials?"

"My goodness, Nida! Thank you for your foresight!" Shoym stated, horrified they'd narrowly avoided potential tragedy, but relieved that Nida had spoken out.

"What say you all?" Shoym asked, looking to the trainers for guidance. "What will our people need out there?"

After some debate among the trainers, they settled on a number of essentials each team would need for their excursion. Almost every Eben'kayah already possessed a pack, as they were used in training, which simplified the matter. Shoym created a list of the items to pass on to Alcarid to ensure the Eben'kayah would have everything on hand when packing for the journey.

With Shoym and his cadre thus occupied, the rest of the council and their aides worked to set a timeline for their departure in the interim. Talcalum suggested that groups leave one at a time over the span of several weeks, but after some deliberation, the council ruled out his scheme. It would cast too much suspicion on the Eben'kayah still in Endego if large numbers of their acquaintances departed without explanation. No, all but those chosen to stay behind in hiding would depart en masse under the cover of dark within a fortnight. Thankfully, the early spring showers were all but over, and the forthcoming mild summer weather would be optimal for adjusting to a lifestyle in the wild.

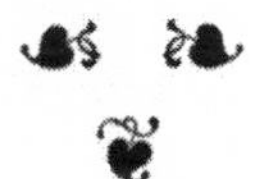

Shoym returned to the council ring with his crew in time to overhear his peers' determination, and jumped into the conversation to echo his assent, "As long as Master Alcarid confirms our stores sufficient to such a speedy exodus, I wholeheartedly concur."

Alcarid countered, "Master Shoym, I believe the council will find our preparations to be more than ample to the task. We might supply the expedition with what we have on-hand today if need be."

"Very well," Agatous rejoined. "Then we need only set a date for our escape. Would anyone object to the final day of Nisán? It's also the night of the new moon, which will provide us plenty darkness as cover for our departure."

Talcalum enthusiastically endorsed the idea, and prompted the others, "All in favor?"

As one, the council voiced their approval with a hearty, "AYE!!!" that shook the chamber.

"Before we adjourn," Agatous called out. "Mistress Gimble," she said, addressing the Counciletma, "Will you consider taking on the additional duty of answering any immediate concerns our people have with their group assignments? I'm certain they will come, and I know your specific expertise in serving our families will enable you to help them best."

Pleased at Madame Agatous' recognition of her role, Gimble replied, "Madame Agatous, it would be my honor."

Turning to Alcarid, she asked, "Master Alcarid, could you possibly provide me with a list of the assignments, so I can inform our people, please?"

"Of course," he responded, "but perhaps we ought to wait until Madame Agatous has announced our decision to the entire congregation?"

"Indeed," Agatous chimed in, "Gimble, your immediate task will be to assemble every last Eben'kayah you are able in the sanctuary hall tomorrow evening. Don't let slip a single word of our discussion here until after my announcement."

Impressed with the import of her role, Gimble nodded, "Yes, ma'am, Madame Chief Counciletma!"

"If I may, Madame Agatous?" Alcarid interjected.

"Yes, please, Master Alcarid," she said, opening the floor to him.

In gravity, Alcarid began, "I don't intend to throw cold water on the proceedings, but my mind inevitably turns to worst-case scenarios. While I am pleased we have a plan of action, I wish to know what consideration we might give to contingencies in the event we are found out and even raided before our set departure date?"

Around the chamber, heads nodded in accord with Alcarid's sobering wisdom.

After a contemplative pause, Shoym spoke, "I believe I can answer that, if I may?" He looked to Agatous for assent, which she gave with a quick nod of the head. "Our top priority must be to complete preparations for our departure. Now. Our people must make a coordinated effort to supply themselves for the journey within a week. Master Alcarid, I trust you will be responsive to any emergent shortage in provisions?"

"Without a doubt," Alcarid answered sagely.

Shoym continued, "Next, all Eben'kayah will need their group assignments as soon as possible. They must be prepared to rendezvous with their team members for departure at a moment's notice. If we are compromised, the plan should be to evacuate Endego at once."

Shoym's words hung glumly over a quiet council before Talcalum called a vote on Shoym's proposal. Though a difficult measure to swallow, the council passed the motion unanimously.

With that, Agatous adjourned their meeting, which left Nida's head spinning. *After all we've struggled to build in Endego, we're to leave it all behind on the basis of a few prophecies and some spotty intelligence?*

She shook her head and closed her eyes to utter a short prayer. She opened her eyes to find Dempsey once again smiling at her.

"You alright?" he enquired.

Nida took a deep breath and exhaled loudly before answering, "Yeah. Sure. Fine."

With a knowing and smarmy smile, he retorted, "Ok. Whatever you say. Keep it to yourself then. Shall we gather up Nat?"

She nodded shortly, joining him as he headed topside, and keeping the conversation along the way light and superficial, afraid to betray the disquiet she felt.

They collected Nat, and then bid one another a good night where Shirkrose Lane, which led past the olive tree, and Galfgallan Road intersected. Nida maintained her composure dutifully as she conducted Nat along the way home, not wanting to worry him prematurely. After following their usual nightly routine, she sent Nat up to bed where he fell asleep almost instantly.

On the lonely gusts whistling by outside, she heard the voice of despair calling her once more. It had been a while since she'd perceived its anthem, insulated as she had been amongst the Eben'kayah, but tonight it seemed she stood alone, a solitary tree outside the windbreak of their fellowship.

Praying tearfully as she went, Nida walked through every room, caressing each of the mundane treasures of hearth and home in farewell. In disruptive counterpoint to the wailing dirge without, a still and ironclad voice within spoke the truth of the blessedness she and Nat had enjoyed throughout their years here.

Finding herself upstairs at her son's bedside, Nida lay her hand gently on his head to caress the greatest of her treasures and comprehended the true wealth of memory that she would never leave behind. Blessedness would follow them wherever they might go. Through her drying tears, she saw her way downstairs to bed and, then, to peaceful rest. And shining with the sun tomorrow came to awaken a refreshed soul.

Chapter Twenty-Two

Readiness

A pleasant day preceded the evening meeting. When all called together like this, the Eben'kayah again impressed Nida with their unity. It had been one thing to sense their fellowship as an outsider, but how sweet it was to taste, to partake of the immensity of their conjoining in the love of the Lord Elyon. Minds and hearts, unified in sacred purpose, enveloped every individual in something larger on the inside than it appeared on the out.

The steady murmur of the gathering tapered off as Madame Agatous approached the lectern on the stage.

"Good evening, my friends," she began solemnly, "Thank you all for coming on short notice. I imagine that you all came prepared, recognizing the irregularity and urgency of our gathering signaled also its importance in these challenging times. It is with the council's unanimous support that I announce the following, and I ask that you remain seated and quiet until I've finished speaking."

Madame Agatous looked down gravely as she composed herself before resuming, "As of yet, our scouts have returned empty-handed from their journeys into the wild, if indeed they returned at all. We all agree that the importance of locating the Eben'kayah's Kinsman is paramount. It has also grown more dangerous for us under the watch of the Nihúkolem, who seem intent to cart off any Etom, Eben'kayah or no, whom they believe to be involved in our mission. We've lost several families already, and we daren't risk losing any more to them."

Agatous raised her voice in passion, "Our situation calls for our total commitment. Of time. Of resources. Of self! It is with this understanding that we call upon all the Eben'kayah of Endego to be sent in search of the Kinsman. We've all prepared for this. We've trained for this. We've lived for *THIS!!!*"

She paused, the hall utterly silent as she adopted a more moderate tone, "Now Master Alcarid has assured me we are well-stocked for our journey and has organized our departure in groups of twenty or so, each headed by one of our scout trainers. Families will travel together on the course Master Shoym has set, and group leaders will provide support. A very few of us will remain here in hiding to facilitate communication between groups in the event those sent out encounter any intelligence of substance."

"After we conclude here in the sanctuary, Mistress Gimble will await you all in the galleria with your group assignments. Take your family to her after we conclude here, and she will direct you to your group leader, who will help coordinate final preparations."

"Finally, we have set the date of our departure as the last day of Nisán. We do not have much time to get ready, but I know we are capable of completing this mission. Our Enemy would like nothing more than to prevent us from doing so. Please do your best to hold your peace. Not a word to outsiders!"

"After she has provided your group assignments, Mistress Gimble will be available to answer any questions your group leader cannot. Thank you and may our Lord and King Elyon speed us on His wings!"

With that, Agatous departed the stage, and though there was some uproar in the hall, understanding of the need for this action took root among the Eben'kayah. They were committed, to the last of them, and went to Gimble in as orderly a fashion as they were able. Nida found a spot at the far end of the galleria, and awaited the families assigned to Company Jasper. From what she recalled of the council meeting the day before, Master Haarfanell's family comprised a large part of the contingent on their own. Master Haarfanell and Madame Grüntha approached, their gaggle of six children, all elbows and accusations, followed. Grandma trailed behind the dust-up to make their party nine. Counting Nat and Nida, Company Jasper was already at eleven members, though Nida knew several more would join them.

From a nearby cluster of Etom standing in the galleria, Rae burst forth shouting as she ran full force to ensnare her friend in an embrace, "Nat! Nat! We're coming with *you*! We get to go together!"

Kehren and Tram followed right behind, walking at an accelerated clip to keep sight of their exuberant offspring.

Kehren caught sight of Nida and made a beeline for her, calling ahead, "When she found out we were in your group, she took off like a shot to find you!"

After catching up with their daughter, the couple greeted the rest of Company Jasper, and Tram encouraged Nida, "Honestly, we couldn't be more pleased to travel with you and Nat. Rae has her best friend, and we hardly know anyone else here, so it's good for us to have a friend in the group, too. Well, that, and you're one of the strongest trainers here. We haven't had much time to adjust to our new lifestyle, so we were a little worried until we found out you'd be leading us."

"I'm flattered, you two," Nida responded, blushing a vibrant red. "I know you've met Master Haarfanell and his family already. They're good, dependable Etom. All but the youngest children are already well-accomplished survivalists in one regard or another. I'm sure any one of them could help teach you any skills you need to brush up on."

She called over to Haarfanell, where Nat was acquainting Rae with the many children, "Isn't that right, Master Haarfanell? We're going to help each other out in the wild, yeah?"

With surprising coordination, the entire family responded, "YEAH!!!"

A few stragglers arrived shortly thereafter, and everyone greeted them to welcome them into the group. A tone of warm support now set amongst the members of Company Jasper, Nida gathered the adults and older children to discuss preparations. Nida was not one to procrastinate and wanted no delay in getting ready to leave.

After the council session the day before, Shoym had provided all the trainers with copies of the final list of necessities to pack for the long journey. She passed the copies around to the adults present, so they could familiarize themselves with it. Save any last-minute perishables, Company Jasper would have their packs loaded by the following evening. Given their plight, even the youngest would need to carry a pack, and stronger members would carry a bit more to compensate. They would meet the following night in the Forge for Nida to inspect the packs, and anything lacking they would gather from the storage beneath the temple.

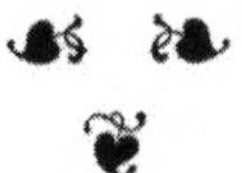

After Nida had given direction, she released Company Jasper to their respective homes to begin preparations. She and Nat did likewise and gathered what they were able from home upon arriving there. The following day was a blur, any time they might have had to themselves on a normal day was full of activity. Neither Nida nor Nat took any rest until they were ready to leave for the temple and sat down for a quick meal before they left. With no time to waste relaxing after supper, they collected their partially-filled packs and headed out to the temple.

Upon their arrival, the Forge and Forage was abuzz with Etom clamoring to sort out their packs. Shouts such as "pass me a flint, would you?" and "I need a bit more jerky over here" resounded throughout. After some maneuvering of their own in the Forage, Nat and Nita filled their packs from the list, leaving just a few items from the armory to collect. Down in the Forge, they spotted Master Haarfanell and his family lingering near the sparring ring to watch a group of young Etom practice their swordplay.

Nat and Nida were headed to meet the Haarfanells when from behind they heard Rae call in singsong tone, "Hey Naaaaat!!!"

She bounded toward them in typical style, the pack on her back jangling as it bounced up and down. To her credit, the weight of the pack didn't appear to slow her approach. Lord Elyon bless him, Nat flinched involuntarily, memories of numerous swooping, affectionate hugs surging up from his unconscious.

He relaxed just in time for Rae to wrap herself around him, pinning his arms to his sides. Nat's face betrayed no discomfort, just hopeful patience that his best friend would soon loosen her grip.

Huffing and puffing, Kehren and Tram trotted up to Nida and the entangled friends, each with pack in hand. Nida greeted them with warmth and together the five of them approached the Haarfanell family, their children quiet for once, so engrossed were they in the combat nearby.

Tram, anxious to bond with the only other adult etém on the team, called out, "Master Haarfanell!"

Master Haarfanell, who was pale grey and very tall for an etém, spotted them and smiled, lifting a great slab of an arm to wave them over. He extended a great paw to envelope Tram's chocolate brown hand in greeting, "Now, now then! None of that Master Haarfanell business! My *friends* call me Rippert, and my wife here is Grüntha." Grüntha was also tall for an etma and pear-shaped, her skin the color of sun-bleached brick.

With a nod and a quick shake of her hand, Tram acknowledged Grüntha, "Very nice to meet you, Grüntha."

Rippert beckoned toward an elderly etma, the same color grey as he and likewise tall, though somewhat hunched with age, standing with the Haarfanell children, "My mother over there we call Bōh'beh. With so many children underfoot, we're glad to have her help, as you'll be, no doubt. She's maybe one of the best foragers here and can whip up a tasty meal from whatever we find."

The rest of their company trickled in while Rippert continued.

All but one of their children were the same pale grey, and pointing to the tallest, he shared, "My eldest son there is Grippert, a strong climber. Next, we have Flippert, who's quite the acrobat. Then Trippert, who, wouldn't you know, is a fine wrestler?"

"He's followed by Slippert," here he added more quietly, as an aside, "He's a bit on the clumsy side, but don't mention it, 'cuz it hurts his feelings."

Tram gave a fatherly nod of agreement before Rippert continued, "Down on the end there you can see our youngest son, Mal. He's the baby, so the etma give him whatever he wants."

Finally, Rippert gestured to a young etma the same color as Grüntha, "In the middle there you see our only daughter, Suzaranakaltana, but you can call her Suzan or Su for short."

"We used to call her Lazy Su when she was younger on account of all her spinning about. Well, that, and her lazy eye. 'Bout the funniest thing I ever saw. When she was just a wee etma, she'd spin and spin and spin around, 'til she was about ready to fall over, so dizzy she was. So, I go to catch her, you know? To keep her from fallin'?"

"Well, I get 'hold of her and look her in face, and what do you know? Her lazy eye just kept spinnin' 'round and 'round in her head. I laughed so hard I almost dropped her anyways. The boys thought it was funny, too."

"Grüntha and Bōh'beh didn't think it was too funny, though. Still don't. And you better not let any of the etma catch you calling Su or her eye lazy anymore, or you'll never hear the end of it. I know I haven't."

Believing himself now thoroughly versed on Rippert's family, Tram thanked him and returned to where the Nida, Kehren and the others conversed just in time to determine the group was headed to the armory. Rippert and Grüntha gave the signal and rounded up their children to carry their packs down to the armory while the rest followed suit.

Once there, Nida coordinated with the adults to grab the remainder of the supplies on the list to distribute to the youngsters. All Eben'kayah were to be armed with a blade, even the children, besides a few machetes the group would need for clearing brush. A sword proving to unwieldy for the younger children, the Eben'kayah provided them instead long daggers, one of which Nat now unsheathed with sparkling eyes as Nida watched with chagrin. After he had thrust and swung the blade several times with what seemed to Nida altogether too little awareness of his surroundings, she made him sheathe it again, and gather with the rest of the team.

Along the far wall of the training hall beneath the catwalk, they placed their packs. Nida had every team member unpack and set the items neatly on the ground in front of their pack. Using her list, she checked that each pack contained the requisite items. After several times through the list, verifying the items became second nature, and her pace quickened.

When she had finished checking a pack, she would direct its owner to load everything back into it. Though some of the children and Rippert grumbled a tad, it was good practice for the daily realities they would soon face in the wastelands outside their grove. Nida was pleased to note that Nat did not complain, and though Rae began to do so, she soon fell silent when she saw Nat happily bustling to complete the task.

Once satisfied all was at the ready, Nida sent everyone home with their packs, convinced it would be best her team had the packs on hand in case of any sudden changes to plan. On her list, she had marked several items: flints, rope, and hardtack among them. These had all been running short when Company Jasper went to secure theirs, and Nida made certain to pass along the information to Alcarid, who was busy at the head of the Forage, on their way through to the temple.

The aging etém offered surprising gratitude when she presented the list of items running low to him, "Thank you, Mistress Nida! It's good to see *someone* is looking out for the common good here. I'll get my people on this right away!"

"You're welcome, Master Alcarid. Have a wonderful evening!" Nida responded in slight shock.

Indeed, as she and Nat departed, she thought, *I've never seen Alcarid look so alive. I guess you never know what might bring out the best in someone.*

She shook her head, smiling in mild amusement as she turned to usher Nat out, finding him stopped and staring at Alcarid, his bemused smile no doubt a reflection of her own.

"Mom, did I just see Master Alcarid *smiling*?" he asked in disbelief.

Giggling, she replied, "I believe you did, son. Will wonders never cease? How about we head home for some rest now?"

With a shrugging hop, Nat hitched up the straps on his pack, and chuckled, too, "Sure, Mom. That sounds . . ." He yawned, and blinked his weepy eyes, "That sounds nice. Let's go home."

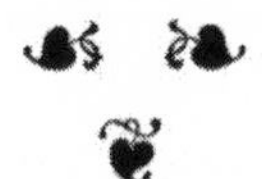

The rest of the week was uneventful, though the very air seemed now to hold a breathless, stifling tension as anticipation of their exodus loomed. Nida knew they were ready to go at a moment's notice should the need arise, and each morning she had Nat fill their waterskins afresh in case of sudden departure.

By the time Saturday evening arrived, Nida was relieved to head to the temple with Nat for the customary meal. Perhaps the company of her fellow Eben'kayah would give reprieve from the sense of constant, grinding vigilance under which they all now labored. Dempsey, Kehren, Tram, and Rae ate with Nat and Nida, who found their rest among the Eben'kayah, enjoying conversation and sustenance together as they forgot for a moment the inevitable separation from their loved ones and their homes.

After the meal, Nida reclined, satiated in body though her soul yet hungered. Their end of the table sat empty but for Dempsey and Nida as Nat went to play with Rae and the other children. She gazed after them with mournful happiness, envious of their innocent naïveté.

In her disquiet, Nida's apprehension grew. She believed the history of Gan and prophecies of King Elyon, but this was different. To leave with the Eben'kayah was to trust, to commit in a manner so ultimate she knew she could never return from it. Maybe the drastic transformation that might result was at the root of her fears. To change so much as to recognize herself no more was the source of her anxiety. Decided to bear not misgiving another moment, Nida gave it voice.

"Dempsey?" she ventured.

Caught in a moment of woolgathering, Dempsey faced her with a drowsy smile and eyebrows raised in response, "Yes, Nida?"

She glanced around before she began in a low voice, "Dempsey, do you ever wonder if what we plan to do, our leaving, I mean–do you ever wonder if it's the right thing to do? I'm afraid. Afraid to leave everything behind, especially since we don't have that much to go on, do we?"

Dempsey listened with thoughtful attention, nodding as he mulled over his response.

"Here," he said, offering a hand, "Come with me. I want to show you something."

"But Nat–" she replied.

"No worries. I think he needs to see this, too."

After collecting Nat, the three of them headed out in the direction of Dempsey's rather modest cottage, which sat just out of sight of the temple near the trunk of the olive tree. Nida and Nat had been there before, though only a few times for a supper here and there. It had turned out that Dempsey kept a tidy home and was a passable cook. But this was no social call, and Nida now approached the cottage, dim in the twilight, with mild apprehension.

With a quick turn of the key, Dempsey swung the cottage door open and asked them to wait a moment at the door while he lit a lamp. The amber glow of the lamp flared as Dempsey lit it, then washed over them as he swung it their way and beckoned them inside. It had been a while since Nat and Nida had visited, and it was obvious Dempsey had made some changes since. The walls, once adorned with paintings, were now bare, and a fine hutch that once stood in the corner was absent. Gone, too, were the dining table and chairs, leaving a solitary armchair against the wall near the kitchen stove as the lone seat left in the home.

"Come. Come," Dempsey beckoned, guiding them toward his room. "Take a look in here."

Nat and Nida looked into the room, finding it also empty. Neither bed, nor dresser, nor nightstand, nor shelf stood in the space, now vacant but for a simple bedroll on the floor. Leaving the room, Dempsey stood at the large picture window at the rear of his house, peering out into his moonlit garden.

Leaving Nat to gawp at the strangely empty home, Nida found Dempsey at the window and asked, "Why show us this?"

"Honestly, I know how distressed you are to leave everything behind," he replied, still looking out into the silvered nightscape. "I know I was when the Nihúkolem first arrived in Endego. From that moment, I believed we would have to leave at some point and began preparing for the eventuality."

He pointed out into the leafy rows, and continued, "It's difficult to think that these beds are the only ones left to me now, but I've learned to accept this is all I truly need."

Pulling his gaze away from the garden, he looked at Nida tenderly, "All I need, that is, except you, Nida."

Nida brought a hand to her face, uncertain how to respond. She had grown to care very much for Dempsey and admired him for all his work among the Eben'kayah, but this . . . this she wasn't sure about, especially right now.

In the sober, silent pause, she heard Nat jump about and shout from the other room, "We should bring Rae over here to plaaaaaay!"

The interruption resounded within, her maternal instincts clearly echoing her reply to Dempsey's advances, "Dempsey . . . dear Dempsey. I am sorry. As much as I might like to return your affections, now is not the time."

She looked apologetically into his eyes, and he nodded, took a deep breath, then exhaled in disappointment before he answered.

"I understand. You have . . ." he shifted his gaze toward his room, where Nat yet bounded off the walls, "responsibilities, and I accept that. I have always accepted that. You should know that I care for *both of you* very much. I can't think of a son I'd rather claim as my own. You've done a fantastic job raising him."

He paused and turned away to stare out the window again. "Your answer doesn't surprise me. As long as I've known you, you've been a mother first, as you ought to be. With everything that's happening right now, with all of us going our separate ways, and no assurance of what happens next, I guess I just wanted you to know how I feel."

Nida looked down at the floor meditatively, then spoke, "I appreciate you telling me, Dempsey. I hope you can believe that I'm disappointed, too. It's just . . . the timing."

Dempsey whirled around, a plaintive smile on his face, "Then can you promise me something, Nida? Can you promise me if we return, that you will give us a chance? Just the hope of it will sustain me."

With a mellow smile to herself, Nida recognized how pleasant a chord Dempsey's devotion struck among her heartstrings. Still looking down, she answered, "Yes, I will."

To speak the words revived a hope that long ago had died. Finding now her lover's eyes, she smiled brightly, and repeated from her heart, "Yes, I will."

Dempsey took her hand in his, and smiling gratefully, he said, "You've made our parting now more bitter, but for the sweetness of the hope at our reunion. Thank you, Nida. Thank you!"

At Potter's Arch, Nat and Nida took their leave of Dempsey, who insisted at the very least on seeing them to the Üntfither. Speaking now the night's goodbyes, Nida found that she might miss him. Just until the morrow, then. Just until the morrow.

Chapter Twenty-Three

What About Rosco?

A fine Sunday morning dawned over Endego, the signs of spring heard in the birds' song, and felt in the fresh air. Nat yawned and stretched as he sat up in bed, delighting in the cozy comfort of his warm blanket and soft pajamas before hopping down to slide into his slippers, which rested on the wooden planks of the loft floor, worn smooth by years of shuffling.

The scent of an especially tasty Sunday breakfast wafted up, eliciting thoughts of gratitude for such a great Mom. A tall stack of cinnamon-applesauce griddle cakes awaited him on the dining table, along with a deep jar of honey in the center of the table, and Nida's place setting opposite his. Bypassing the tasty meal, he ran up to Nida, who was still busy at the stove with the griddle, and hugged her around the waist, burying his face in the small of her back.

"Thanks for breakfast, Mom!"

Nida hadn't heard him come down and was at first surprised at Nat's unexpected show of affection.

He's been taking lessons from Rae, she thought, and smiled.

She patted Nat on the arm, and told him, "I don't think there's a better son in this whole world. Give me a sec, and I'll join you at the table, OK?"

He released her to sit patiently at the table, his feet lazily swishing back and forth beneath his seat. Nida brought the platter of cakes and a pitcher of juice to the table, and they took a moment to thank Lord Elyon for their many blessings, including the food, of course. Nat took a moment to drizzle honey on his cakes while Nida poured them juice, then fell to as if starving, demolishing the mountainous pile in short minutes. Nida had scarcely taken a few bites before he was reaching for more.

"Ah, ah, ah," she chided, "Just one more at a time, please. Let's give your body a minute to tell you if it's still hungry. Drink some juice, too, huh?"

Mouth already full of griddle cake, Nat nodded his head furtively and washed it down with a gulp of juice, which sloshed dangerously in his agitated cup. Nida suppressed a chuckle, and instead reminded him of his manners.

Stopping his fork mid-air as he reached for yet another cake, he asked, "May I? Please?"

Nida smiled, mystified at the amazing appetite of young etém, before giving assent.

Instead of skewering another cake, Nat hesitated, then recoiled, dropping his fork to the plate with a clatter as his contented smile disappeared, replaced with frownful care.

"What's wrong, Nat?" Nida asked in confusion.

Nat inclined his head, which moved back and forth in short, thoughtful arcs, his lips moving as if in some silent argument with himself.

He looked up at his mother with tears in his eyes, and broke his silence, "Mom? What about Rosco?"

As realization struck her, Nida came to share her son's concern. Rosco was one of the Eben'kayah, and was involved at the temple, though not as often nor as regularly as he might want to be. When Rae had first joined the Eben'kayah, but before her parents had, she'd not been able to meet with them very often, either.

Though Nat and Nida had attempted to reach them, Rosco's parents presented more of a challenge: With a high degree of confidence, the Eben'kayah had identified Rosco's father, Rufus, as an informant for the Nihúkolem. Nonetheless, Nida had witnessed the change in Rosco, his bully façade melting away in the warmth of Nat and Rae's friendship. Dempsey, too, could attest to how far the young etém had come, and it had been a memorable reunion between the two after their first encounter, when Dempsey had stepped in to stop Rosco's assault on Rae and Nat. Several seconds passed in silence as the mother and son contemplated a solution.

At last, Nida jumped up from her seat, and exclaimed, "I have it! We must bring him with us! As the leader of Company Jasper, I will take responsibility for him. Do you know where he lives, Nat? We will visit him *today*."

Nat, while taken aback at his mother's response, was regardless pleased, and answered back, "I do! And he should be home right now. Maybe we could see if Rae might like to come? Her house is on the way."

After a moment's consideration, Nida agreed. The more support they could bring, the more likely they would be to convince Rosco to join them. It was a great deal to ask him to leave behind his family so suddenly, but it might be worse for them all if the Nihúkolem got ahold of him. Swiftly, they completed their meal, and cleared the table before getting dressed. Within a quarter hour, they were out the door and on their way, walking briskly in the springtime sun.

Now Rae's father, Tram, was a merchant of no small repute in Endego, to which their palatial home attested. In recent days, however, Tram and Kehren had decided to remove the gates that once barred entry to their estate off Cliphook Lane. Out of kindness to their serving staff, they offered to build several cottages along the stream Altfither that ran through their grounds. They required no rent for the housing provided, and many had taken them up on the offer.

The result was a small, teeming community within the walls–a village within the village, replete with families outside their homes enjoying a beautiful Sunday morning in the warmth of the season. None of the families had yet to join the Eben'kayah, but Nida knew that Tram and Kehren were working toward that goal, and their astounding generosity was part of their plan.

Nat and Nida approached the great doors of the home, greeting the Etom outside in cheer. It was as if they could sense the blessing of Elyon on the home. In place of the sterile frigidity once present, light and life abounded. Excited to invite Rae on their adventure, Nat leapt up the stairs leading to the door a few at a time and banged the knocker into the door loudly and repeatedly.

Embarrassed at her son's lack of consideration, Nida felt compelled to chastise him. Before the words had left Nida's mouth, Rae was already on the doorstep hugging Nat, who jostled uncomfortably as Rae jumped up and down in excitement at the unexpected visit.

Rae spoke in rapid-fire succession, "Oh, my goodness! Nat! I'm so glad to see you! What are you doing here?"

Once he'd extricated himself from her, Nat gripped her shoulders and answered in wide-eyed seriousness, "Rae, we completely forgot about Rosco! What is he supposed to do when we . . . ?"

Remembering the secrecy of the matter, Nat looked around suspiciously before he whispered, "What's he supposed to do when we *leave*?"

Rae's mouth gaped, and her eyes waxed round as she, too, realized the gravity of Rosco's plight.

"Wow, Nat," she said, shaking her head, her spirits dampened for once. "I hadn't even thought about leaving him behind."

"Hold on, though, Rae," Nat said, not quite able to suppress his glee, "my mom said Rosco could *come with us*. How about that!?!"

Stunned by the announcement, Rae fell mute, though the twinkle in her eyes and smile on her face spoke volumes as she looked at Nida.

Retrieving her voice, Rae expressed her gratitude, "Thank you, Mistress Nida! Thank you so much! You're amazing! I'm going to tell Mom and Dad!"

Rae turned on her heel to race back into the house.

Before she had crossed the threshold, Nida raised an open hand, and exclaimed in a hoarse whisper, "Rae! Wait!"

Skidding to a halt, Rae paused just inside the doorway, and turned to face Nida.

"Why? What's wrong?" she asked.

Nida came close and whispered in Rae's ear, "Rae, the Eben'kayah know Rosco's father is an informant for Chōl. It's unlikely his parents will be coming, and we need your help to convince him *quietly* that he should come with us. That's where we're headed right now, and I don't want to involve your parents or anyone else unless we need to. Do you understand?"

Armed with new information, Rae recognized the need for secrecy, and nodded vigorously, "I understand, Mistress Nida. When do we leave?"

They walked a short distance farther down Cliphook Lane, where Nat pointed out Rosco's home. While Tram, Kehren, and Rae's home stood to the east of a willow's trunk, Rosco's was situated on its north, in perpetual shade. Tall and regal, its towers stood in gloom, as closed and still as the other was open and vibrant. Nida half expected a downpour and peals of lightning overhead as they stood down on the lane before the narrow walk up to the darkened door, stony ramparts high and razor-straight on either side.

Feeling diminished before the imposing structure, Nida asked Nat and Rae, "Have either of you ever been inside?"

A "Yeah," from Nat and "Sure we have," from Rae accompanied their placid nods, goading Nida from her nascent cowardice to lead the youngsters onward. The home's numerous windows seemed so many eyes looking down on them, their curtains veiling only malice.

Nida strode up the front stairs, Nat and Rae close behind, and gripped the knocker ring, enlaced in ghoulish fangs, hesitating a moment before assertively rapping the door. Long and thorny moments passed in waiting for the vaulting door to crack, and Nida had about given up when, creaking, the portal opened on a yawning, dusky rift. From the shadow of the empty void, Rosco's moony, green face peeked forth, his eyes brightly questing as they alit upon the trio. Though pleased to see them, Rosco face betrayed also his apprehension.

"Hey guys!" Rosco spoke in whispered shout, a smile tinging his lips. "Hang on a sec, OK?"

Like a turtle, he tucked his head back inside before silently he slipped outdoors, sweeping the door closed behind him.

Once on the stoop, he spoke again, his unease still apparent, yet abated, "What are you guys doing here? My parents don't like visitors, in particular those without an appointment."

Before either Nat or Rae could reveal too much, Nida jumped in, "How safe is it to talk out here? Might we be overheard?"

Rosco shrugged. "It's as safe a place as any around here. Why? What's up?"

This is not *optimal,* Nida thought, once more glancing furtively at all those baleful windows, *Oh, well. This may be the best chance we have.*

Fists balled, and lips pursed in vexation, she began speaking quietly and quickly, "Rosco, we've all come here because we care about you–as a friend and as a fellow Eben'kayah. Last week, the council reached a major decision that affects all of us. We must apologize for failing to realize that you were not told at the time of Madame Agatous' announcement last Sunday."

Rosco began to appear more concerned with what Nida was telling him than he was with his parents finding him out.

"What? What is it?" he asked, his brow seamed with care.

"Rosco, can you keep a secret?" Nida asked.

"Of course, I can. I've kept the Eben'kayah secret this long, haven't I?" he retorted.

Nida resumed, lowering her voice, "The Eben'kayah are leaving Endego. All of us. On the last night of the month."

The color drained from Rosco's face, turning him from mossy green to bland lime. Head in hands, he sat down hard on the top step of the stoop, looking back at each of them in turn. Nat and Rae looked at him with remorse, sorry now they'd brought Nida here on this awful mission.

"So where does that leave me, then?" he asked in accusation. "Alone again, that's what," he grumbled in misery and covered his head again.

Nida descended to a lower step and crouched down in front of the distressed etém to console him, "Rosco, please don't fret. We have a plan . . ."

At the mention of a plan, Rosco lifted his head, a glimmer of hope in his eye.

"A plan?" he inquired, desperation in his voice. "What is it? Tell me, please!"

"First, you should know it involves serious sacrifice on your part," Nida offered.

"Anything! I'll do anything!" Rosco spat.

Nida peered around to ensure that no one eavesdropped, lamenting once more how visible they were before the home's many shrouded windows, and said, "Rosco, we'd like for you to come with us. With Rae, Nat, and I. When we leave. Would you be willing to do that?"

Rosco stood up, smiling as he answered, "Absolutely! I'll need to bring my parents, too, of co–"

"No, Rosco. That will not do," Nida interrupted. "I hate to be the one to tell you this, but your father is working for the Empire. There's no telling how many of the abductions in Endego he's responsible for. You and you alone would leave with us."

The revelation about his father, and the terms of joining the others when they left threw cold water on the spark of Rosco's joy. He slumped down to the step again, dejected.

Nat and Rae sat down on either side of him and each put an arm around him comfortingly.

Nida continued, "I understand how difficult it will be to leave your parents behind, but it is the best thing for everyone. If you stay, and your father discovers your involvement with the Eben'kayah, he might feel obliged to turn you in. If he doesn't turn you in, and the Nihúkolem find out, then *your* family could disappear. At least if you come with us, you can protect your family and yourself. Your father will be able to honestly say he didn't know anything about your connection to the Eben'kayah, and you won't be here to answer any questions."

Her words hit home with Rosco, who looked up at her, tearful, yet determined, and answered, "You're right. I know it, but it's still hard. I'll come with you. Just tell me what to do."

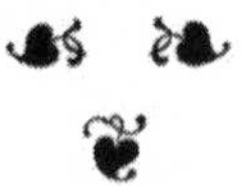

Nida told him they would assemble another pack for him and would be in touch to coordinate their departure. She laid a hand reassuringly on Rosco's shoulder before his young friends embraced him and they said goodbye. Striding out of the gloom to remember again the springtime sunshine, Nida, Nat, and Rae felt remarkably unburdened. Rosco waved after them, happy to have found such wonderful friends, before turning to enter the dark abode. And in the corner of a nearby window, the heavy curtain twitched.

The trio satisfied with the completion of their errand, they parted company after escorting Rae home, Nat and Rae exchanging promises to meet up after supper. In Nida's mind, she foresaw a pleasant and filling Sunday afternoon meal, followed hopefully by a nap. For his part, Nat likewise looked forward to the meal, and perhaps an adventure with his best friend after. The pair strolled home at a leisurely pace, satisfied to ruminate in the silence. The sense of freedom in the unscheduled day ahead permitted their souls to rest from the concerns and pressures of everyday life.

Potential, Nat thought to himself. *That's the word for it.*

He recently learned the word in physical sciences at the Bunker, the instructor describing the potential energy in an object, any object really, held aloft to fall.

Why, Nat mused, *There's potential in such common things. After all, anything can fall.*

High overhead, a cloud covered the sun in soft eclipse to cast a chilly shadow over them as they slipped inside their home.

Chapter Twenty-Four

Flight

Sated and happy after an early dinner, Nida went to lay down in her room, leaving Nat to occupy himself. He and Rae were planning to head off on some juvenile quest while she rested, so Nida expected he might be out when she awoke.

"Make sure you're home before dark, please!" she called drowsily.

"Definitely, Mom!" he shouted back, then bolted out the front door, slamming it closed behind him, and jarring Nida back awake again. She was briefly miffed, then smiled, chuckling at her son's exuberance.

May as well enjoy it while it lasts, she thought. *In a few years, he might be too worried what his friends think to get excited about anything.*

She lay back, sinking into the softness of pillow and quilt, and soon fell asleep.

Nat hurried back toward Cliphook Lane, excited to spend a few free hours with Rae doing whatever they liked. A sharp gleam off the waters of the Altfither nearly blinded him as he crossed over the bridge on the way to Rae's.

Strange, he thought, stopping to rub his eyes. *What was that?*

Nat leaned over the rail near where he'd seen the flash, peering with interest into the moving waters. A sudden spark shot straight up from the water to float so close to his face that he had to stare cross-eyed to get a good look.

Astéri! he concluded after a moment. *What are you–?*

No time for questions, Nat! Astéri blasted into his mind. *They're coming for you! All of you! Get out of Endego! NOW!!!*

With a pop, Astéri vanished, leaving Nat paralyzed on the bridge, his heart pounding frantically while he tried to figure out what to do next. Tram, Kehren, Rae, and Rosco were the only Eben'kayah he knew this far north in Endego. He would warn them first, then return to tell Mom they needed to leave. Realizing the fate of the Eben'kayah rested in his hands, Nat sprinted all-out for Rae's house, his feet clopping noisily on the wooden bridge as he set out.

Nat reached Cliphook Lane in short time, and veered left toward Rae's, flagging as he passed through the gates. Without time or breath to answer in kind the many "hellos" sent his way as he passed through the servants' village, Nat raised a few offended brows. He could only manage to wave a wordless apology while struggling on toward the manor door. Rae, expecting his arrival, reclined serenely on the porch swing, but leapt down as soon as she saw her friend lurching toward her in distress.

"What is it, Nat?" she asked, "What's wrong?"

Fighting to recover his breath, Nat managed a few words, "Must... go. Coming... for us all."

Confused fright on her face, Rae asked, "You don't mean...?"

Rae trailed off into dread silence as Nat nodded emphatically.

"Yes! Yes," he gasped. "Tell your parents to get ready to leave. Now. I'm going to get Rosco."

Nat pivoted to leave, but Rae, afraid for her friend's safety, grasped at him, stopping him in his tracks.

"Please," she said, realizing she couldn't ask him not to go, "Be careful. I have a bad feeling about this. Especially about that house."

Nat nodded earnestly, not willing to spend his breath on words. His walk became a trot, and then a sprint, and soon enough he was gone from her sight. Not willing to succumb to her distress, Rae shook her head, then vaulted up the stairs, and entered the house to seek out her parents.

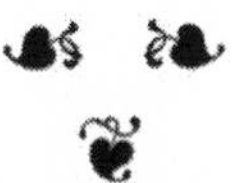

Back on Cliphook Lane, Nat continued left, to the north, as he hurried from Rae's house. Cliphook Lane, named such for its shape, hooked westward as it approached the north end of Endego. Thus, the lane crossed in front of Rosco's north-facing home as it straightened its westward course. Brush and high grass stood in the no-Etom's-land at the bend, screening Nat's view of Rosco's house. A sudden stitch in his side forced him to stop before he rounded the arc in the road. He stood there, wincing, as he attempted to gain control of his ragged, puffing breath. Nat's cramp subsided, and he began to shuffle forward again, only to be struck instead by a petrifying sense of foreboding.

Deep within him, a still, small voice spoke a single word, *Hide!*

His experience with Astéri had trained him to act, even when he didn't fully understand. Maybe this was just another message from his luminous friend? In either case, he didn't hesitate to slide into the tall grass along the lane, crouching low to make himself more difficult to see. Just as his cramp had, the sense of foreboding subsided, replaced by an alert watchfulness. Nat crept forward in the grass, seeking to gain a view of Rosco's home.

Discordant voices from down the lane caught Nat's attention, and he froze in his hiding place, desiring to locate their source before moving again. Shifting only his golden eyes, fixed open in unblinking resolve as he scanned the surroundings, he located the disturbance–Rosco and his father, Rufus, coming down the lane in his direction.

Nat gasped in concern for his friend. Nat had never met Rufus but knew the hunter green etém in a top hat worked with the Nihúkolem, which didn't improve Nat's opinion of him, and neither did what he observed now. For all appearances, the elder etém was shoving his son along the lane and prodding him with a cane while he berated him. Nat looked more closely and saw Rosco's hands were bound together with knots of coarse rope. They grew nearer to Nat's position as Rufus propelled Rosco down the lane and were soon close enough Nat could make out what he said.

"I already know where your stuck-up little girlfriend lives! Believe me, the Nihúkolem will be rid of her and her snooty family in no time. Now tell me where the little blue bug and that bright pink etma are! What is she? His mother? We're going to take care of the lot of them. And you!"

He thumped Rosco with his cane as he shouted, "You thought you were just going to up and leave, eh? After all your mother and I have done for you? You'll be lucky if all you get is a beating!"

Nat could no longer watch his friend suffer such abuse and intended to help Rosco escape. He was just going to confront Rufus when an icy breeze wafted over him from behind. Hunching his neck in surprise, Nat froze again in place, slowly turning his head. Before he could identify what had chilled the air so, a shadow fell over the patch of grass in which he hid, followed by the black paw of a Nihúkolem stepping over him into the lane, trailing dark, gritty wisps.

The dusky form of some wild cat, perhaps a lynx, passed overhead, slinking toward Rosco and his father. Rufus fell silent, and stood behind his son, whom he presented as a shield, or offering, or both. Crouching low over its front paws with tail twitching moodily, the beast mewled something unintelligible to Rosco's father. The contact was similar to Nat's experience with Astéri, though whereas the star's song was warmth and harmony, this was a deathly cold and dissonant unpleasantness.

A grating, static scramble of words invaded Nat's mind, *We will take the child. Where are the others?*

"Please, I can handle this one," Rufus began, "He's my son, after all."

If he believed appealing to some sense of consideration for his connection with Rosco would change the creature's mind, Rufus was sorely disappointed. The Nihúkolem growled in chittering cacophony and arose, inching forward menacingly. Rufus fell back as he thrust his son forward, his top hat tumbling from a bald and Blighted head. Rosco took a large, stumbling step forward, yet did not fall, though tears from his eyes betrayed the wound his father's lack of love inflicted.

From its roiling shroud of midnight black, the phantom cat repeated, *Where are the others?*

"You never said anything about taking my son. That should be worth at least double," Rufus bargained, "I won't say another word until you've agreed."

The Nihúkolem's growl rose to a caterwaul to express its displeasure.

My patience grows thin, insect. We will compensate you as we please. Now tell me where the others are before I decide to take you as well.

What wheedling courage had remained in his greedy soul now fled Rufus, who grudgingly surrendered, "At the other end of the grove. Under the olive tree. He told me there was some sort of stone temple. That's where they meet."

Stooping low and turning its head, the cat took Rosco sideways in its jaws, leaving his head and arms dangling from the corner of its mouth.

"Wait. Wait!" Rufus shouted. "What do I tell his mother? Will we ever see him again?"

The Nihúkolem ignored his questions, and without another sound departed. Rufus lingered in the road, watching as the creature left with his son, then retreated up Cliphook Lane in defeat.

Nat crept silently around his refuge in the grass to follow the beast's movement as it prowled by. Nat stopped at the edge of cover, watching helplessly from his vantage as Rosco strained to lift his head and look around. The desire to help his friend warred with the knowledge that he must still warn the rest of the Eben'kayah. The creature now past, Nat reasoned it might not spot him, and, though conflicted, he chanced spreading apart the stalks before him, revealing his face in hopes Rosco would see him.

Rosco, still sweeping his gaze about, caught sight of his friend in the grass, and locked eyes with him.

Rosco shook his head mournfully, his distress obvious, and even over the growing distance Nat clearly saw him mouth two silent words–*I'm sorry.*

Then the cat bounded up a tree, disappearing into its shadowy canopy, and, like that, Rosco was gone. Overcome with emotion, Nat stepped out from the stand of grass, reaching feebly after his friend, the pain of loss contorting his features as he wept.

Time was of the essence, and Nat knew it. After a few seconds mourning for Rosco, Nat wiped his tears on his forearm, grit his teeth, and sniffed to clear his nose. There was work to be done. Whereas a stitch had stopped him only moments before, Nat found now new strength in his limbs, which required no rest as long as he paced himself. He returned to Rae's house in time to catch them on their way out onto Cliphook Lane in their coach. A species of tiny hoofed creatures, chevrotains, pulled their coach down the drive as Nat arrived.

Nat waved at them to stop, and from the driver's box Tram called, "We were just on our way to your place. Jump in!"

Nat speedily complied and closed the door behind him with a click as he hopped into the cabin, finding himself face to face with Rae and Kehren inside.

"Rae," he started, stifling a sob that threatened to rip through him, "I was too late. Rosco's gone."

"Gone?" she said, horrified. "Gone where?"

"Rufus gave him up to the Nihúkolem!" Nat wept. "His own father! We have to warn the others. All of them! The temple isn't safe anymore."

Before Rae could respond, Kehren interjected, "You know this for a fact? The Nihúkolem know where we gather?"

Nodding exaggeratedly in his grief, Nat responded, "I overheard Rufus tell one of the Enemy all about the temple and watched as that *thing* carried Rosco off."

"We're never going to see him again!" he wailed.

"Oh my," Kehren breathed, grasping the urgency of the situation. Sticking her head out the side of the coach, she shouted up to Tram, "We need to hurry! It's an emergency!"

Tram nodded grimly and flicked the reins against the backs of the chevrotains as he shouted "Git!"

The animals increased their pace, and within a couple minutes, they were on Sylvanfare pulling up in front of Nat and Nida's home. Nat sprang from the coach and bolted down the path to his house. He burst loudly into the home, waking Nida with a start.

Sitting up in her bed at once, she called, "Nat!?!"

Nat was already at her door, panting as he explained again what happened. Before he had even finished, Nida was grabbing their packs, weapons, and waterskins, and urging her son back out the door.

As they clambered into the coach, Tram called out, "Where to? The temple?"

"Yes! And hurry!" Nida shouted back from inside the cabin, the coach lurching forward and tipping her back into the seat.

Kehren looked at Nida and asked, "What can we do? How do we alert everyone?"

"Many of the Eben'kayah live right near the olive tree. Including the council," Nida answered. "We'll warn them all first, and they can help spread the word. I hope there is enough time."

Nida put her arm around Nat in the seat next to her and soothed him, "I am so sorry, Nat. You did a great job today. By the end of the day, we may all owe our lives to you."

Though he appreciated his mother's words, they did little to console him. Nevertheless, he welcomed the comfort of her embrace, and nestling in her warmth, he dozed off.

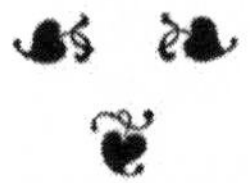

To Nat, it seemed an instant before his eyes snapped back open, Rae jostling him awake as the adults loaded the gear out of the coach and into the temple. They had pulled up near the rear gate, and Tram and Nida hurried inside to seek out anyone who might be in the temple above or the complex below.

Kehren herded the children inside to the foyer, where they waited for Tram and Nida to return. Apart from losing Rosco to the Nihúkolem, Nat and Rae found the waiting the most difficult part of their day. The chaos of the hours prior had kept them occupied, but the lull in activity left them to reflect on painful reality.

It was only a matter of minutes before Tram and Nida rejoined their party, several Etom in tow, including Pritch and Hardy. They had also activated the warning chimes that ran throughout the complex, which to an interloper might seem a pleasant, ambient melody. Nida hoped the chimes would be sufficient to warn away any unaware Eben'kayah who might arrive after they had left.

As the sole scout trainer on the premises, Nida took the lead, directing the others in pairs to the various Eben'kayah homes around the olive tree. She asked each pair to muster with their respective companies, and to instruct those they warned to do the same. Nida also directed everyone who had access to a pack and weapon for the excursion to strap it on before leaving the temple. They could leave nothing to chance. They might encounter the Nihúkolem at any turn.

Tram and Kehren asked if Rae could stay with Nida and Nat before they left on their assignment. Their fate uncertain, they each took a moment to embrace their daughter and kiss her goodbye before they left. If all went according to plan, they would meet outside the north end of the village. Near Rosco's house.

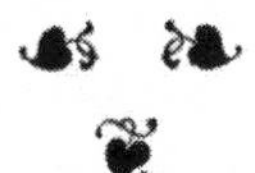

Within seconds, Nida, Rae, and Nat were the only ones left in the temple foyer. Nida helped the youngsters slip on their packs, which were heavy, yet not intolerably so. Once on their way, they stopped to bid a fond farewell to the temple gates, which perhaps they'd never see again, and then marched on toward Dempsey's house.

The last of the sun's light dwindled overhead, and the moon shed a sliver of light from its narrow crescent.

Well, it might not be a new moon, Nida thought, *but it's close.*

The darkness might help conceal them when they left tonight, though Nida was uncertain if the expedition was already lost. No matter. The things she couldn't control she left to Lord Elyon and focused on the task at hand. Tired and not accustomed to the weight of their packs, Nat and Rae lagged behind. As kindly as she was able, Nida cajoled and pressed them to hurry. Even so, it took them double the time to reach Dempsey's house that it ought to have, and Nida left them to catch up the last leg of journey while she steamed ahead to knock at the knotted wooden door.

Strange as it was for him to have visitors so late and unannounced, Dempsey opened his door cautiously, lantern in hand to identify his unexpected guests. As soon as he saw Nida had come to call, his suspicion turned to welcome, then to apprehension upon noticing the pack on her back and the weapon strapped to her waist.

Over Nida's shoulder, Dempsey detected the children trudging up behind her, and ushered his visitors into the house, "Get inside. Hurry!"

Once inside, Nida recounted the situation, Dempsey leaping into action to gather his own pack and exchange his house shoes for more appropriate footwear. While Nat and Rae could certainly have used a rest, necessity dictated they get on the move without delay. Dempsey's group was Company Beryl, heading out in a northwesterly direction along the ten o'clock. Given their groups' proximity to one another, Dempsey felt obliged to accompany the trio to rendezvous with their group before meeting up with his. Nida appreciated his offer and was glad to have him join them on what might prove an arduous journey with the children through the grove.

They set out immediately, the children struggling, yet not complaining. Nida had cautioned everyone to follow her lead as they stole through the shadows, and to remain as silent as they were able. Avoiding detection in transit across the village had been a necessity over the past months, and all of them had developed a certain skill for it. The packs, however, presented a challenge in this regard as well, their unwieldy mass and bulk hampering normal movement, let alone stealthy movement through brush and shadow.

At times, they saw across the way the fleeting frames of their shadow compatriots as they passed in secret through the shaded groves of Endego, some headed this way, some headed that. Only once did they meet any other Eben'kayah–at the Sylvanfare bridge over the Altfither, where earlier in the day Nat had encountered Astéri.

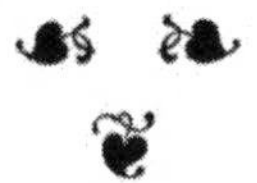

It was in the breathless quiet of the hunted that Nida, Nat, Rae, and Dempsey saw movement on the bridge, and fell still in the underbrush alongside the stream where they trekked. In muted moonlight, the imperfect silhouettes yet betrayed bulging packs like those they carried, and Dempsey with practiced woodcraft advanced to the bridge to intercept the group. Nida signaled Nat and Rae to follow her up to where Dempsey hailed their fellow travelers in the night.

Shocked to hear a voice from the darkness, the other Eben'kayah froze, and those who had yet to complete their crossing over the bridge fell prone along its rail. In the heart-pounding tranquility, word that they were well met passed back along their line, and slowly the prostrate figures stirred to join those who'd already scurried down the embankment to meet Dempsey and the others. Dempsey was already in discussion with the group leader, the swordplay trainer, Rroggold (spelled with two 'r's to indicate their trilling).

Rroggold and the rest of Company Amethyst had mustered nine of their number and were now headed to their point of departure due west of Endego to hopefully join the rest of their company there. Emergency protocol dictated that none of the teams were to wait more than two hours at the rendezvous before leaving. The risk of delay was too great, and the council had granted the scout leaders the authority to leave early if pressed.

Thus far, neither group had seen any sign of the Nihúkolem, though it was certain that at minimum they would be watching the temple now. The exchange of relevant information now complete, they brought their parley to an end, the need for urgency weighing on them. The companies shared embraces amongst its members, even between those not well acquainted, so vibrant the bond that connected them was. Likewise loomed the ever-present thought that their separation may be permanent or long-suffered, for who knew the will of Lord Elyon in this matter? As sober tears dried upon their eyes, they parted, some to the west, some to the north to slip gently into night.

Shortly thereafter on a trail along the eastern side of Cliphook Lane, Nat imagined he heard screams. Stopping, he gave tilt his head, and the others paused to watch him. Whether shifting winds or rising terror brought shrieking to their ears, there was no doubt among the team that the Enemy had found their friends. It mattered not to know the names of those accosted, for in the dark, the screams confirmed that they had lost them. Hurrying, they came to a clearing, and the company ground to a halt.

Whither to go? Soon the question struck them. To hazard crossing the clearing or the road to their left would leave them similarly exposed, the latter bringing them in dangerous proximity to Rufus' abode. Whether thus rebuffed he would continue to curry favor with the Nihúkolem was a risk they'd prefer not to take. No, better still to skirt the clearing on the right, which after some deliberation, they elected to do.

Within a few steps eastward, Nida at the rearguard heard a dread and scampering tread. Signaling a halt, she crouched low in the grass to peer astern, the others following suit. A pair of burdened Etom, indistinct in the shifting, moonlight-dappled murk, rushed down the trail toward the troublesome clearing.

At a couple dozen steps, Nida gasped in recognition, then arose to wave them over, calling as loudly as she dared, "Tram! Kehren!"

Identifying her in the tarnished silver of the paltry moonlight, Tram cried hoarsely as he spotted her, yet did not slow, "Nida!"

The others also stood at Nida's first call, and, as Tram perceived Rae among the group, his eyes grew wide with fright.

He altered course straight for his daughter, his pace yet unabated, and raised a shout that rang clear in the false tranquility, "Everyone! RUN!!!"

Without a pause, he snatched up Rae, and continued into the clearing, Kehren's feet beating a rapid rhythm in her passage. From the overgrown trail behind them burst an amorphous mass, pouring forth to unite in predatory form. Before the figure grew distinct, the band was on their feet, dashing all-out after Tram and Kehren. Nida and Dempsey took Nat's hand from either side to make sure he didn't fall behind. Ahead of them, Tram lowered Rae down along his side as he ran, her feet flailing until she touched down at a trot, keeping pace as best she could with the adults.

Behind them, they could faintly hear the gritty rasp of the Nihúkolem's footfalls, and compelled themselves to run faster, barking encouragement to one another through heavy breaths. Unrelenting, they crashed through the wispy grass that ringed the clearing's border, and Dempsey, praying safety, chanced a look over his shoulder.

Through frond and stem a curling black preceded the creature's pressing paw, which over grass and field carried it in speedy pursuit. The silence of the creature's passage belied the beast's proximity, and Dempsey called ahead to all to run faster. Kehren, Tram, and Rae passed into the trees, the shade offering some cover. A plan in mind, Dempsey broke away from Nida and Nat, slowing his pace as he headed straight for the trunk of a nearby tree. The beast, perceiving him as weary prey, took after Dempsey, who had been watching over his shoulder for such a moment.

Anticipating the Nihúkolem's pursuit, Dempsey ran full-tilt for the tree, glancing as he was able for the beast to approach him. In the creature's crouching pause, Dempsey foresaw its predatory lunge. He was nearly at the tree when he heard the characteristic rasp of the creature's movement and dove to the right. Unable to arrest itself midair, the beast burst headlong against the tree, splashing obsidian dust in every direction.

Unable to restrain himself, Dempsey uttered a celebratory "Woohoo!" as he reveled in the brief triumph. And brief it was, for the creature had already begun to reassemble itself, the slow drag of its elemental grit grinding together across the grass.

The group took advantage of the Nihúkolem's delay, however, to increase their lead, slowing again to a stealthy march when they had determined the distance sufficient. Dempsey once again took the lead in the tedious and nerve-wracking journey to the northern boundary of Endego, which was marked by a sudden absence of trees.

They were still some ways east of Company Jasper's rendezvous, near where Company Ruby was assigned to meet. Dempsey saw no sign of the other group, and hoped they were only delayed, not captured. Remaining among the trees of the grove for protection, they skirted the village westward where they were to meet Company Jasper. Growing close to the rendezvous, they rounded a large trunk, and spied several of the company gathered atop a broad and heavy stone, called the Anvil for its jutting shape. Even in the dim and argent light of the moon, five figures stood plainly limned, their movements shadow against starry canopy.

The fools! Dempsey thought, *They are completely exposed up there. They could bring the Nihúkolem down on top of us all!*

As if on cue, a large, dark figure swept in from the west, another, sleeker shadow breaking from the glade to their left, and passing close enough its murky cloud enveloped Dempsey at the front, whose head spun dizzily in the fog. Determined not to alert the Enemy to their presence, he gripped a blade of grass to keep himself from falling. The Nihúkolem struck their friends without warning, trapping those atop the Anvil, and rounding up with ease the few on the ground attempting to escape. Their cries echoed in the night, and Nat and Rae wept through shuttered eyes, hands clapped over their own mouths to stifle their own sobs.

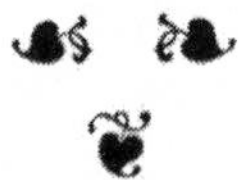

The Anvil stood stark against the night sky, its face so clear and empty, and in the stillness, it seemed yet echoed the shrieks of those abducted. Disheartened at the sudden loss, Nida had no strength to prod the others on.

They rested there in the underbrush without discussion until Nat spoke in the darkness, "Oughtn't we go see if we can find any others? Dempsey, we could check on your group."

Dempsey croaked, then cleared his throat, congested from disuse, "Nat, my good sir, I believe you may be right. It would be better than doing nothing."

Nida seized the opportunity to get what remained of Company Jasper on the move again, "Come on, then. Tram. Kehren. Rae. We've rested long enough. Any longer, and Dempsey may miss his rendezvous. Besides, it's better to occupy ourselves than just sit here. And think . . ."

Wearily they got underway, continuing around the village in cautious awareness of their surroundings. While the lack of enemy presence let them breathe more easily, the absence of Company Beryl upon arrival at the rendezvous only further discouraged them.

In the chaos of the night's events, they had forgotten protocol. Each company's runners were to use a predetermined hiding place, or "dead drop," to leave messages for the Eben'kayah who stayed behind in Endego. The method eliminated the risk of discovery a messenger might face in entering the village and allowed a single scout to collect messages from all teams by circumnavigating the village, thus reducing the likelihood of detection.

The dead drops came to Nida's mind a few moments into a search of the meeting site, and she reminded the others, "We've all but forgotten about the dead drops. We should look for a message from Company Beryl. Dempsey, you're part of their group. Do you remember where it is?"

"They didn't tell me anything except that it'd be under a rock," he replied.

They searched the meeting site several minutes for the drop, Kehren finally uncovering a tatter of parchment left tucked within a small wooden box buried in the earth beneath a stone. Kehren handed the note to Dempsey without a word, and in the seclusion of a nearby thicket, they chanced to light a match and read the scrap.

Company Beryl was gone. After waiting for Dempsey, the final member of their contingent, to arrive, all eleven of the remaining Eben'kayah had decided to leave rather than risk capture. Dempsey smiled at the message, happy not have held the rest of the company up. The remnants of Company Jasper were also pleased that Company Beryl had set out on their appointed mission. It gave them hope that others of the Eben'kayah had fared so well.

After some whispered discussion, they arrived at a plan. Without a doubt, they were glad to add Dempsey to their number, and Endego was no longer safe. They would return to the Anvil and set out northward according to their original assignment. Returning to where Company Beryl had hidden their message, they replaced it there for any other Eben'kayah seeking to know their fate before they set out for the Anvil.

Cued by the note Company Beryl had left, Nida located Jasper's drop, then scrawled a note of her own to leave near the sculpturesque stone, as follows:

All but we six are lost. We leave to find the Kinsman.

Company Jasper

Heartbroken though they all were, Nida urged her companions onward, sparking the flames of determination in her own soul as she did. Pressing on in the twilight, she looked back to see the same fire burned firm and resolute in their eyes. Questing northward, the valiant company disappeared into the tall grass, and overhead the dawning sun turned tops of bladed stalks to burning swords held aloft.

Chapter Twenty-Five
The Wilds

In the first several weeks following their exodus from Endego, the six travelers underwent a drastic transformation. Many things they had taken for granted at home they soon remembered with fond longing: a soft, warm bed, hot meals, honey, and so on. And on. And on. Likewise, the rigors of daily life in the wilds pressed in on them, and the nature of their new existence lay bare, delineating between the essential and the frivolous.

The Nihúkolem's raid on the Eben'kayah and the capture of over half their number critically diminished their capabilities. First, Haarfanell and Grüntha's older children were to have served as runners between Endego and their camp in the wilderness. Without additional personnel to serve in this capacity, Nida, Dempsey, Tram, and Kehren decided to disregard the agreed weekly messaging schedule, and to return with a message only if they discovered anything of import. Second, even if they had been able to send someone back, the company had doubts that anyone remained to monitor communications in Endego. Last, with a mere four adults and two children now available, their search capacity was severely curbed.

They altered their search pattern, spreading out along a line several hundred steps apart to sweep forward. As the stronger members of the team, Dempsey and Nida each took a solo position at either end of the line, while Tram and Kehren each paired up with a child. They remained in shouting distance of each other, prepared to signal if they encountered danger or spotted anything worth investigating.

The days wore on without any leads forthcoming, the lack of communication with Endego added to the sense of isolation Company Jasper experienced with the growing distance from home. But for their mission, and the bond they shared in Elyon, their band would have dissolved. However, as their leader on the trail, Nida reminded them of their purpose, and of their aim: locate the Kinsman and then call their people home.

The hope and vision of the Kinsman and the Eben'kayah's reunion buoyed the spirits of Company Jasper. Instead of aching for the comforts of home, the desire to complete their mission consumed them. Around the warming embers of the morning and evening fires, the adults discussed the honor of joining their fellow Eben'kayah on their sacred mission while the children soaked up their discourse, looking on with shining eyes. Slowly, subtly, over the months that followed, the thoughts of all turned ever toward the hope of the Kinsman, and the reward of pursuing Him with joy.

Their spirits revived, they grew more physically rugged, as the lonesome wilds molded their frames while leaving their souls untouched. Shoym had equipped each scout leader with a map showing the company's respective assignments and the boundaries of previous searches. He had also marked the map with points of contact and locations their prior intelligence indicated they should search. The map legend provided reference to a detailed manual in which Shoym had shared everything they'd learned thus far in their search. Now five months into their journey, Company Jasper found themselves far beyond the limit of the prior search, and any evidence pointing them to the Kinsman seemed distant.

Flying high on spiritual wings that had carried them so far, the company faltered as the belief that their mission was futile and endless began to take hold. In the cloying heat of scorching summer, they strode forth as on many days before. Toward the center of their line, Kehren and Rae marched together with Kehren asking her daughter to stand back at times to mow down vegetation with her machete.

It was a familiar process, and one often repeated, but for a tragic aberration on this blistering day. Kehren swung the blade to cut down a stand of grassy stalks to discover a boulder stood behind the masking screen. Accustomed to slicing through without meeting much resistance, Kehren struck without restraint while Rae stood back a couple steps, outside the cutting arc. Upon meeting the unexpected stone, the swift blade gave forth a spark, and shattered. Kehren cried out in surprise, then caution, but learned she was too late, for in the grass behind her lay her daughter, blood on her face.

The blade, breaking, had flown back with fearsome force, and struck Rae in the head. Kehren gave a shout to call the rest to her side. Perceiving the anguish in her cry, Tram was first to come, Nat treading on his heels. Through the brush on either side came Nida, and then Dempsey. Tram flew to Kehren's side, as she cradled her daughter's wounded crown, rocking back and forth over her senseless child, weeping.

"I've had enough," Kehren whimpered, "I can't go on."

Dempsey bent down over Rae, and asked tenderly, "May I see?"

Lips pursed in constrained grief, Kehren relaxed her arms and looked away, allowing Dempsey near. While Dempsey examined Rae's wound, Nida produced the map and rolled it out on the ground, seeking some form of nearby aid.

Trembling, Nat approached his mother, asking quietly, "Will Rae be alright? She looks like she's bleeding a lot."

Looking up from the map, Nida reassured her son, "We will do everything we can for her. We care just as much for her as you, Nat. I'm looking for a safe place in the area. Somewhere we can let her rest, and perhaps get medical attention."

Meanwhile, Dempsey had enlisted Tram to unpack the ointment and linen bandages. Pouring water over the wound to Rae's forehead, Dempsey rinsed away most of the blood. The gash was not very deep, and it appeared instead of the blade, the blunt backside of the machete had struck her, which was a blessing. What concerned Dempsey most was the force of the impact, which had knocked Rae unconscious. Minutes later, she still showed no sign of awakening as he wrapped her head in the bandage and applied ointment.

Completing what treatment he was able, Dempsey left her in the care of her now much calmer parents. In just removing the blood and dressing the wound, Dempsey had comforted the family, and he was happy to have helped as he stepped over to where Nida was still poring over the map, Nat crouched at her elbow.

"Have you found anything?" Dempsey asked.

"I think so," she replied, chewing her bottom lip. "Here," she said, pointing at a spot east of their position.

"Sakkan, eh?" Dempsey mused.

The map indicated an Etom village labeled with two question marks, which they knew to mean several things: The location of the Eben'kayah village was firm. However, the last report on Sakkan was at least two years old, and the Eben'kayah of Endego had received no response to more recent attempts to communicate with their brethren in the village.

Dempsey mulled it over, then asked, "Do you think it'll be safe? We might be walking into a trap."

Nida looked over her shoulder where Tram and Kehren hovered over Rae, and answered, "I don't think we really have any choice, do we? One of us ought to break off and scout it out when we get closer. See what we can see."

"OK," Dempsey deferred, not pleased with *any* of their options now, but unable to provide any better than what she proposed.

A harmonious sigh upon the breeze drew Nat's attention away from their conversation, and a patch of sunlight poking through the foliage overhead shifted irregularly to linger over the stone Kehren had struck with her machete. The wind blew again, stronger now, and with a decidedly western direction.

The gust rustled the overgrowth, Nat following its westward course with his eyes to discover another stone there, vines entwining its great, jagged surface where it arose from the earth as if a tooth in the maw of some great beast. The sun shone bright upon its pinnacle, and a mute whisper informed Nat of the setting's distinct familiarity. At the edge of recollection, a similarity pressed, and Nat concentrated, sensing the potential import of the memory. The discussion nearby intruded.

"Nat?" his mother called, approaching him where he crouched several steps away. "What is it? Did you see something?" she asked, the unspoken question apparent as she knelt beside him.

Did Astéri show *you something?*

His brow wrinkled in perplexity, Nat answered, "I don't think so. I just have a feeling. Does this place seem familiar to you?"

"I don't see how it could, for any of us. We've never been this far out before. And, Nat, I'm worried about Rae.

"Isn't her safety what's most important right now, especially if you're unsure?"

Nat nodded, conflicted and not entirely convinced, but certain Rae needed help.

Nida arose with a sigh, then walked over to Tram and Kehren, hoping she didn't have to work too hard at persuading them to take Rae to the village.

After hearing Nida out, Tram nodded in agreement, "I think it's our best chance for Rae. You said we'd scout the village first, right?"

"Absolutely," Nida replied, "If we think it's safe, we can see a doctor, rest, and resupply there. I think we could all use a break while we get our bearings again."

Their focus turned now from the mission, and they made haste for Sakkan after fashioning a travois for Rae to aid in transporting her. Though the map appeared to indicate a half-day's journey to the village, they encountered several obstacles that slowed their progress.

A few hours eastward, the dense foliage cleared, then the snarled turf underfoot gave way to a hard and stony scrabble the color of iron. After a short while, they arrived at a substantial precipice, stopping at its edge as they developed a plan. The view offered from the heights of the cliff was beneficial in scouting the surrounding area. Not far east from the cliff, they spotted the shimmering silver ribbon of a river snaking southward. Looking northward along the river's course, Nat spotted a large, wooden Man-made bridge, the spectre of which evoked apprehension in the Etom while holding the best promise of a speedy crossing.

Right now, they would doubtless need to rappel to the cliff's base, and Nida hoped their supply of rope was sufficient to the task.

Presenting another challenge would be getting Rae down, though Nida's mind was already whirring away to develop a solution.

Before long, they decided Tram would be first to descend, followed by Kehren, then Nat. Tram and Kehren would secure a perimeter, ensuring the area was safe before any children came down, and meanwhile those up top would send down the packs. Next, Nida would rappel, with Rae attached via makeshift harness. As the strongest climber, she would be most able to handle any unforeseen problems encountered on the descent. Dempsey would descend last as the rearguard.

Before Tram started down, they worked together hammering several ringed pitons into the rocky terrain atop the cliff, creating an anchor system to assist with the climb. Once Nida had secured the rope, she signaled Tram to start down. Both he and his wife had preliminary training in climbing before they left Endego, and with frequent use their skills had flourished in the wilderness.

Tram reached the bottom without event, as did Kehren and Nat, then it was Nida's turn. Taking the rope in a gloved hand, she approached the cliff's edge, stopping a few steps short to turn around. Dempsey had already tied Rae's hands together, and now positioned the child facing Nida to place her arms over Nida's head, her fastened hands ensuring her unconscious grip around Nida's neck wouldn't fail. Nida squatted, bending her legs deeply for Dempsey to throw each of Rae's leg over top Nida's thighs, then loop another rope over, under, around, and through their waists and legs.

Satisfied the etma were well-attached to one another, Dempsey nodded, "You're ready. The both of you. Please, be careful."

With a wry grin, Nida responded, "I couldn't imagine being otherwise," then stepped back over the edge of the cliff.

The first drop was the most difficult, the harsh yank of the rope as it stopped them giving Nida the opportunity to recalibrate for Rae's additional weight. The going was slow and difficult work, and Nida's hands were cramped around the rope by the time they reached bottom, but they did so safely. Dempsey, whom Nida now envied, swung as he rappelled, attesting to the relative ease of his descent.

They set up camp for the night some ways from the cliff, not willing to put their backs to the imposing wall if discovered. In the evening, Rae finally stirred, her eyes opening to a squint as she called for her mother, who rushed to her side, Tram right behind her. Nat, Nida, and Dempsey gathered nearby, but tried to stay out of the way.

"Hey there," Kehren said gently, "How are you feeling?"

Rae looked around, confused as she tried to lift herself on her elbows before slumping back down onto the travois where she lay, shaking her head back and forth gentle arcs.

"Rae, you mustn't try to get up," Tram warned, "You've been asleep for hours."

Kehren chided her lovingly, "You had us worried, dear."

"What?" Rae began weakly, "What happened?"

Kehren felt responsible for the accident, and looked down, ashamed, before answering, "It was my fault, Rae. I wasn't paying close enough attention and broke the machete against a stone. The blade flew back and hit you. I'm sorry, honey."

"Mom," Rae said, seeking her mother's eyes, "Don't. Please. I'm going to be fine. Right?"

She looked up at the worried faces of her friends and family for assurance.

"We are going to get you help, Rae," Tram answered.

Sensing an opportunity to jump in, Nat dashed to his friend, chattering excitedly, "We're taking you to a village over the river, Rae! And there's a bridge. A Man-made bridge!"

Rae smiled wanly, overwhelmed by Nat's energy, yet wanting to share in the excitement.

"Nat!" Nida called, "Give her some space! You'll have a chance to catch up later. OK?"

Chastened, Nat nodded, then smiled at Rae, "Later?"

Rae gave a mute nod, and Nat returned to stand with Nida and Dempsey.

Kehren returned to nursing Rae, asking once more, "How do you feel, dear?"

"Tired. Dizzy. Thirsty," her daughter replied. "My head *hurts*."

Dempsey was already prepared with a waterskin, and handed it to Kehren, instructing, "This is the only thing she should take for a while, and just a sip at a time."

Kehren nodded in acknowledge while with a supportive hand she helped Rae to lift her heavy, aching head and sip the water.

Through the night, they each took turns caring for her, though Kehren and Tram took the lion's share out of parental instinct. Still, the others were happy to help the worried parents rest, and Tram and Kehren appreciated their support.

The next morning, they set out early for Sakkan, determined to reach its outskirts by the end of the day. Now, as they headed east, the roaring rush of the river reached their ears, and Nida directed the company northward to seek the bridge, each one anxious for Rae's recovery.

They arrived at the imposing structure late in the morning, grateful for the relief the misting flow provided from the steaming heat of the noonday sun. The river here grew wider and shallower, making it an optimal place to span the watercourse. Though sturdy, the bridge appeared to have been recently built from rough-hewn split logs. The pungent scent of piney pitch that yet lingered upon the decking struck the Etom as they scampered up to it.

The little band crowded into the shadow of a post while Nida peered across the bridge and into the wooded glades surrounding the far side. A plethora of vegetation sprouted upon the road on either side, seeming to indicate it was seldom used, and Nida perceived neither movement nor threat in their surroundings. Nevertheless, she couldn't shake the waiting watchfulness she sensed from the environs.

Waving the others forward, she advanced, the group sticking as they were able to the meager shade of the bridge's railing to reduce their visibility. Nat followed behind his mother. After Nat came Dempsey and Tram carrying Rae in the travois as if it were a litter, its poles in their hands to reduce jostling the child and expedite their journey. Kehren followed as rearguard, her eyes questing to and fro for any sign of danger. The sense of exposure as they crossed the bridge was palpable and brought to their minds the chase across the clearing the night they had escaped Endego with the Nihúkolem lunging at their heels.

Though the river was not terribly wide, it seemed their trek in the open would never end. The blinding glare of the reflected sun on the golden-yellow slats increased the drudgery of their passage. The once-distant woods now arose before them as they approached the end of the bridge, and the road disappeared under the shadowy canopy as it arced away to their left.

Nida reached the final rail-post, and stood in its shadow, looking down the embankment to the right as she waved the others past. Nat struck out for the nearby underbrush, eager to get under cover, and the rest followed suit. Nida lingered at the rail-post, gazing down the shadowy lane that led away into dense and darkened forest, her skin tightening in chilly fear. Beyond the sun's piercing rays, some *thing* not visible along the way violently shook unseen boughs, the distant rustle of leaves surrendering to the shocking snap of twigs, and the striking crack of meaty branch.

Nida's eyes grew wide with alarm, and she tarried there no longer. Casting aside her caution, she dove down the embankment, directing her roll toward the underbrush as best she was able. Arriving at the foot of the slope in a dusty tumble, Nida was back on her feet again, scrambling to get out of view of the shadow she felt sure drew near. The others silently, yet furtively beckoned her onward from the concealment of the thicket, and she threw herself flat beneath the leaves, indifferent to the minor wounds she incurred.

The company watched from their refuge, the trees over the road twitching and twisting to mark the monster's passage. The creature remained just out of sight, the trees screening it from view, and a throaty grumble shook the earth. Through the leaves peeked ebon tendrils, wafting forth on languid breeze, the sure sign of Nihúkolem confirming the group's fears. In frustration, the creature yawped, a harsh, unnatural bark, then turning from the river's edge, returned to haunt the wood.

The Etom shared a weary sigh, exhausted from the ordeal. They lunched there in the underbrush, then arose refreshed to continue toward the village, Sakkan. They hiked along through oaky wood, and pleasantly green the sun shone through the lofty leaves above. It wasn't long before they came upon a fragrant meadow, which spanned the gap that yet remained between them and their destination. Across the expanse, they watched the bustle of the busy Etom village from the shadows of an oaken glade.

Nat observed Nida and Dempsey speaking in hushed tones, their heads together in conspiracy a short distance from the others. Nida spotted her son and smiled and waved before muttering some quick and final words to Dempsey.

The pair walked over to the others, Nida in front as she addressed them all, "Dempsey and I have been discussing our plan to get Rae some medical attention in Sakkan and have decided that he will be the one to enter the village. I will take the rest of you back into the forest to set up camp. I saw a spot not too far from here that should work nicely."

Tram and Kehren nodded grimly. Now that the company was here, danger spoke within their minds, alerting them of each potential threat. They offered Dempsey their gratitude as he prepared to enter Sakkan, and Nat, on behalf of Rae as well, hugged him in fierce farewell. Walking Dempsey to the edge of the meadow, Nida stopped and faced him, gripping his hands in hers as she gazed at him with affection.

"Be careful, Dempsey," she bade him farewell with tender care. "I expect you to return. Unharmed. And soon."

With a confidence not quite cocksure, Dempsey answered, "I will do my best, my lovely Nida," and embraced her with longing.

She stepped back from the meadow's edge, and Dempsey strolled out into the fullness of the summer light.

Chapter Twenty-Six

Sakkan

Dempsey crossed the meadow without event, and skirted the village of Sakkan, giving special attention to any sign of Nihúkolem activity in the village. To the best of his abilities, he determined the village superficially safe, then casually sauntered down one of the main thoroughfares in search of a market or bazaar–anywhere he might expect to encounter an Etom willing to direct him to a doctor.

Though no one stared openly, Dempsey perceived suspicious curiosity in sidelong glances and expressions of mild shock when villagers identified him as a stranger in Sakkan. He found it difficult to engage anyone in conversation, discovering that most kept their heads down to avoid eye contact as they passed, and several flat-out ignored his hails for their attention.

Dempsey arrived at the first major intersection of roads since he entered Sakkan and had his first real stroke of luck as he looked down the road to his left, spotting a swarm of Etom milling about stalls that stood in a wide clearing a short distance down the road.

A market! Dempsey thought.

Marching forth in determination, Dempsey reached the first of the stalls within minutes. The first several merchants he attempted to engage responded with a blank stare, obviously not excited to have dealings with an outlander. Not discouraged, but seeking an alternate approach, Dempsey stood back from the stalls to observe Sakkan's commerce. He glanced around until his eyes landed on a clothing merchant as he completed the sale of a robe. As in Endego, the merchant brought forth a small scale onto which the customer measured out her currency, pouring her grains from a small leather bag with care.

Grains! He surmised. *Thank the Lord Elyon, they use grains for currency here as well!*

Dempsey reached for his purse, and found it rather light, containing only enough for perhaps some food. *Oh well. I reckon I could eat.*

Following the savory aroma drifting from some stall in the vicinity, Dempsey soon located a vendor selling kebabs of strange-looking, unidentifiable meat.

Though he eyed the food dubiously, his stomach growled with appreciation.

It must be the seasonings, Dempsey postulated, approaching the vendor, a young etém barely an adult with skin the pastel orange of cantaloupe.

"Excuse me. How much for one, please?" Dempsey asked, pointing at the row of appetizing kebabs.

The merchant looked up, his smirking face incredulous as he offered Dempsey a gentle, rueful shake of the head.

With a charming smile, Dempsey brought his purse up to his face.

"I can pay," he said, and shook the bag, the meager grains rasping abrasively against its leather interior.

"Come on," Dempsey persisted. "How much for just one? I'm in off the road, and very hungry, and . . ." He looked around with mock secrecy as he whispered, "And truth is, you're about the friendliest face I've seen in this place. What do you say?"

The vendor's grin widened as he relented, shaking his head once more, though this time with disbelief that he'd chosen to serve the foreigner. Wrapping the wooden end of a generous portion in a napkin, the vendor rolled it in the slurry over which it rested, tapping the skewer once against the edge of the dish to knock off any messy excess.

Handing over the questionable kebab, the merchant held up five greasy fingers, "The cost is fifty grains, stranger," then gestured to his scale, already set to the requisite weight. "Enjoy."

Dempsey, hoping to earn himself some goodwill with the kebab peddler, upended his purse over the scale, emptying it with flourish, "Thank you. Keep the change. In honor of your hospitality."

If Dempsey was attempting to impress, the result was quite underwhelming, and for a moment, it seemed he might be short. In the end, the scale tipped in his favor with perhaps three or four grains to spare, eliciting an eye-rolling scoff from the vendor, who turned his head aside as he tried to suppress a laugh. Indeed, it seemed Dempsey's absurd minimal gesture had won him more favor than a grander one may have.

"OK," the vendor said, beckoning Dempsey closer with a finger, "What is it you want, eh?"

Dempsey leaned in conspiratorially, and spoke, "Why, friend, I'm just a lone traveler in from–"

"Ah ah ah," the merchant tutted, "My first piece of advice around here is to keep your business your own. It's better for us both that way, understand? Just tell me what you need and spare me the details."

An honest man, Dempsey was pleased there'd be no need to dissemble, and began again, "Well, that simplifies things, and I appreciate it. I just need medical assistance. Might you please direct me to the doctor in this village?"

His new acquaintance's face fell at hearing Dempsey sought the doctor in Sakkan. He looked around nervously, sighing heavily before he continued, "My second piece of advice is that you forget about seeing the doctor in Sakkan. If you thought you had a hard time here in the market, there's no way you'll get anywhere near Scarsburrow."

Undeterred, Dempsey retorted, "Listen, I am grateful for everything you're doing here, my being an outsider here and all, but I must insist." He looked intently at the etém, pleading, "Please. It's urgent."

The vendor through pursed lips squeaked out his heaviest sigh yet, and looked upward at the sky, prayerfully putting his hands together while his eyes quested back and forth as if seeking escape from this moral quandary.

At last, with lips still pursed he dipped his head, waving it to one side as he looked at Dempsey, "Sure. Why not? What have I got to lose? I'll take you there myself. That's the only way you'll get to see him anyway."

He untied his apron with frenetic, jerky movements, wadded it up, and threw it with force into the serving tray, clearly conflicted over the course of action he'd chosen. Whatever his new guide's reasons for helping him, Dempsey's primary concern was that his resolve prevailed until they'd secured some help for Rae.

Coming out from behind the counter of the stall, his benefactor offered Dempsey a hand in greeting, "I figure if I'm going to be helping you, we might as well introduce ourselves. I'm Frenlee."

"Clearly," Dempsey replied, taking the proffered hand. "I'm Dempsey. What's your name?"

"Nah. Nope," his companion said, shaking his head in frustration. Bracketing the air with his hands, he moved them in cadence with each spoken word, "My. name. is. Frenlee."

Spotting Dempsey's smirk, Frenlee's eyes and mouth aligned in perfect, parallel level to indicate his lack of amusement.

"What?" Frenlee asked in counterfeit confrontation. "You don't think I've heard it all? What do you want from me? It's a family name."

"I'm sorry, Frenlee. I really am," Dempsey apologized soberly. "I haven't had a good laugh in a long time. I couldn't help it. I really *do* need your help, though."

"OK. OK. You don't have to beg," Frenlee responded in magnanimity. "We're good. Just stop apologizing already."

Calling over to a shriveled jeweler nearby, "Hey Galtish, if Barkway drops by you want to let him know I'll be gone the rest of the day? If he still wants me to work for him, he knows where to find me."

Galtish just gave him a sour look and went back to his work, muttering something unsavory about helping strangers.

Without looking back, Frenlee waved at Dempsey to follow as he called, "Come on, then!" and strode out of the market.

Frenlee led Dempsey through Sakkan, disregarding the open contempt of the many villagers who disapproved of him helping an interloper. They journeyed to the heart of the grove, to a towering oak at its center, beneath which stood an imposing cylindrical structure crafted from obsidian. Standing perhaps three storeys high, the glassy black building glistened wetly in the dampened sunlight as they approached it on a forking path that curved around the tree, its many tributaries leading up the homes planted there. When they were about a dozen steps from the edifice, a pair of fearsome Etom guards intercepted them.

"What do you want, Frenlee?" the goon on the left demanded.

Frenlee's orange hands flew up, each a flag of surrender, as he responded, "We just want to see Scarsburrow." Jerking a thumb at Dempsey, he confided, "My friend here has a medical problem, alright?"

The goon examined them both, then waved them on. Instead of heading into the obsidian tower, they continued on the path, Frenlee cutting left on a narrow path that ran alongside the tower. Behind the tower loomed the tree, and the path they walked on led right up to its trunk. Arriving at the tree's trunk, Frenlee approached a large, discolored patch of bark before them. He kicked the lower right corner of the patch once and pounded the upper left twice. With a click, the patch swung open, revealing itself as a door into an unlit tunnel bored into the oaken trunk.

"Close quarters for a minute here, mate," Frenlee forewarned as he closed the door behind them, sealing out the sunlight. "And dark, too."

In the darkness, Frenlee pressed past Dempsey, to tap a rhythmic pattern against the wall. They waited several minutes there in the stifling darkness before Frenlee tried again, more assertively this time. Long seconds ticked off into the void, and Dempsey sensed his guide's impatience in the rapid tip-tap of Frenlee's foot.

"Forget this," Frenlee griped, turning to fumble past Dempsey for the outer door. A narrow sliver of light gaped before them, interrupting his departure, and growing wider as the inner door opened without a sound.

Frenlee spun around and stalked through the doorway. Dempsey was just a step behind and blinked in the warm light of a homey great room, the ceilings of which arched high overhead. A switchback stair led up to a darkened corridor trailing further back into the tree, and through a doorway opposite the entrance, Dempsey spied a kitchen.

"You think that's funny, don't you, Scarsburrow? Were you watching us the whole time, you old crackpot?" Frenlee's shouts reverberated throughout the arboreal abode hewn into the oak.

From the dim corridor above, a demented chuckle preceded the wizened form of Doctor Scarsburrow, who shuffled into view to join them in the great room. Dempsey found Scarsburrow's appearance striking. For though he was bent with age, his skin was blood red.

Frenlee barked up at the doctor, who yet struggled down the stairs, "There you are, you old coot! Did you have a good laugh making us wait in the dark like that?"

Scarsburrow, having finally reached the lower floor, glared at Frenlee from beneath his arched brows, and responded with a wicked smile, "Oh, you *know* that I did, Frenlee."

He lightened the mood with a bright snicker before scolding Frenlee, "Now do be quiet while I greet my new guest."

Doctor Scarsburrow looked Dempsey up and down with cool scrutiny before asking, "So what brings someone here from Endego? It can't have been an easy journey. Not these days."

Caught off guard, Dempsey sputtered, uncertain if he should even attempt to deceive the doctor. Realizing his reaction had already confirmed much for the doctor, Dempsey made no effort to pretend, and spoke plainly his request, "Doctor Scarsburrow, I have an injured child with a head injury who needs your care. I am here to implore your assistance. Please. Will you look at her?"

Without answering Dempsey, Scarsburrow looked to Frenlee, cocking a brow, "Where did you find this one, eh? You bring me more strays than anyone else."

Frenlee laughed, and for the first time, Dempsey noticed the streak of Stain running down the etém's tongue.

Dempsey returned his attention to the conversation as Frenlee replied to the doctor, "Honestly, I was at the market just minding my own business, or rather Barkway's, and he came up to me. I guess I just attract people in need at this point."

Dempsey didn't quite enjoy the way they were carrying on as if he weren't present, and so interrupted, "Listen, doctor. I apologize if I've inconvenienced you, but if you're not going to help us, I should be on my–"

"No need for that," Scarsburrow cut him off. "I will see to the child. But not here. You recall the black structure you passed on the way in? It serves as my clinic. Bring her there as soon as you are able. A head injury could be serious. Very serious, indeed. I trust your camp is not far?"

Unwilling to reveal too much, Dempsey mumbled, "Er, no. Not far."

He still wasn't sure he could trust Doctor Scarsburrow. Or Frenlee, for that matter.

The doctor continued, "You will find your way back into the village is much easier if you enter from the south. Just take the main road and turn right at the third street. My clinic will be on the right. Now, I assume you'd prefer rather some privacy on your way out of Sakkan over an escort from Frenlee here?"

Feeling bare before Scarsburrow's insight, Dempsey answered, "Yes. You are correct. Quite right."

Dempsey thanked the doctor and went to shake his hand. Apparently put out by Dempsey's gesture, the doctor stared at Dempsey's hand a moment before limply offering his. For the rest of his life, Dempsey could not recall another handshake more disagreeable than Scarsburrow's grudging, clammy envelopment of his hand. It was difficult to say which party was more relieved when it was over, but it's certain Dempsey was pleased to trade the doctor's hand for Frenlee's. By comparison, Frenlee's grip was firm and warm, and Dempsey thanked him heartily for all his help before departing.

Dempsey took his leave, hurrying away in the opposite direction of the camp to throw off anyone who might follow. He was eager to be clear of the strange village, and back among familiar faces. He departed the northeast edge of the grove, and gave Sakkan a wide berth as, creeping through the natural camouflage of his surroundings, he circled back to where the others awaited his return.

It was not quite nightfall when Dempsey arrived back at camp and shared the good news that he'd located a doctor willing to treat Rae in Sakkan, and that they could take her first thing in the morning. Not wishing to quash the group's relief at the news, Dempsey chose not to share his misgivings with them.

After they'd all enjoyed dinner together, however, he joined Nida on watch to express his concerns, "I don't know how to explain it. The doctor, Scarsburrow, knew I had come from Endego."

Nida considered Dempsey's disclosure before answering, "Do you think it might be a trap?"

Dempsey exhaled loudly, "I don't know. My instincts tell me something isn't quite right, but Rae . . . We need to get her back on her feet. For her, and for the mission. I don't see any other way right now."

"You say this doctor, Scarsburrow? He told you to come from the south?" Nida asked.

"That's right. He could be setting us up for an ambush or could be he just wants to help. What do you think?"

Nida looked out into the sparkling sky, weighing the matter before answering, "I think we need to take Rae to see Scarsburrow. All of us. At first light. But we need to be ready for anything. Come on. Let's tell the others."

They returned together to the heat of the glowing embers around which the rest of their number reclined. As unlikely it might be the children could help in the event of treachery, Nida still involved them in the planning. She didn't want them unaware they could be walking into a trap.

Nat and Rae had matured a great deal over the months since they left Endego, and Nida recognized the need to entrust them with the shared responsibility for the group's survival. Nat was now physically tougher than many adults they had left in Endego, as would Rae have been, but for her current injury. Nevertheless, the young etma had successfully applied survival and scouting skills on par with the rest of the team, and her mind had sharpened somewhat since she had awoken. An extra pair of eyes could be the difference between freedom and capture, life and death.

In the end, the plan didn't leave much to discuss, given the unforeseeable nature of the threat. It was simple: Come armed. Be vigilant without seeming so. And be prepared to fight or to fly with every ounce of their strength if it came to it. Before long, Nida went to her watch, and the others to their rest until their turn. The village not far from their camp, Nida kept an eye toward it, noting the light in low windows, and the hooting of owls high in the trees over Sakkan.

Chapter Twenty-Seven

Intensive Care

Finishing the last watch of the night, it fell to Tram to wake the others before dawn as planned. The children stirred groggily while the adults busied themselves with breakfast and breaking camp. After a short stretch and a yawn, Nat hopped up from his bedroll, and set to work.

So practiced were they that it only took minutes for the company to pack the camp, and they enjoyed a warm breakfast in the morning chill. Within moments of completing their meal, they had put away the dishes, and had stashed most of their gear at the mouth of an abandoned rabbit warren. Unwilling to leave themselves altogether without equipment, Nida concealed a sword beneath her garments, while Nat and Kehren each tied a coil of rope to their belts. As the sun broke over the trees, they were on the move, circling southward to enter the village as Scarsburrow had directed.

If there were any clues to the doctor's treachery, they may well be on the road he'd laid before them, so it was with eyes wide and minds alert that they entered Sakkan. Tram and Dempsey again carried Rae's travois between them, as they had on the bridge, prepared to move at speed if the need arose. Though the sun had a while ago risen, they found the broad thoroughfare into the village eerily deserted. Not a soul swept a porch or ambled from the squat domiciles beneath the oaks lining the road.

The profound quiet of the neighborhood stirred within Dempsey a deep disquiet, recalling from the day prior the general bustle of the village.

Sauntering up alongside Nida, litter in tow, he whispered to her, "I don't like this. You saw the village from camp yesterday. It's too quiet."

She nodded, but urged, "Agreed, but we are already here, and Rae still needs help. We are as ready as we can be for trouble. Best stay the course."

They passed the first, and then the second road to their right without incident. The silent stillness persisted until they approached the turn to Doctor Scarsburrow's clinic. From just beyond the intersection, the company perceived the din of everyday activity, and observed several Etom traversing the boulevard.

Dempsey and Nida exchanged a knowing glance, and turned right, the ebony column now in view down the lane. As if following them, the quiet hung over the group, their eyes flashing left, right, up, and down in search of the lurking threat they sensed yet could not identify.

Without delay, they pushed forward to the obsidian structure to which the doctor had invited them for Rae's treatment. The goons posted at the entrance recognized Dempsey from the day before, and waved them inside without a word, opening the heavy double doors wide for the reluctant guests to enter.

The windowless interior was likewise constructed of the black stone, and the broad, dark corridor opened into a brightly-lit circular atrium, where Doctor Scarsburrow awaited them, carmine skin glistening, as crookedly he stood in his white coat before a strange dwarf tree planted in the center of the chamber. The tree stood maybe three times the height of an adult Etom and appeared quite healthy for being sequestered indoors.

Curious, Nida glanced up to discover the chamber was lit by the sunlight pouring through a large skylight, a rarity among Etom for the difficulty in procuring sufficient glass for such an extravagance. More than ever, the structure seemed out of place in an Etom village, further adding to the outsiders' sense of foreboding.

Not one to stand on social niceties, the doctor ignored everyone but Dempsey as he shambled to Rae's side.

"This must be my patient," he stated, then looked at Dempsey. "Has she taken any food or water since the injury?"

Kehren answered protectively, "Yes, doctor. Only a little, but she is eating and keeping it down."

"Very good. Very good," Scarsburrow muttered, as if to himself. "Please. Bring her back to my examination room so I can get a good look at her."

With that, the doctor shuffled around the atrium to open a door painted black to match the obsidian interior. Nida held the door for Dempsey and Tram to carry Rae in, the quartet seeming particularly haggard against the sterile white of the room.

It's metal! Nida thought as she leaned against the cool surface while the others slipped past. So much metal on hand they could expend it on doors? Another curiosity.

"Let's get her on this bed here," Scarsburrow directed, pointing to a high bed covered in a pristine white sheet.

"Now," he began, looking around at the three adults, "There's only room enough for a few. Who is going to stay with her during the examination?"

To this point, Kehren had been content to stand behind Nat in the doorway, hands on his shoulders, but now jumped to answer the doctor, "I will. I'm her mother."

Tram likewise answered, "I'm the father. I'll stay, too."

"Very well," Scarsburrow replied, "The rest need to step outside to wait. I will close the door for the sake of the patient's privacy, but I assure you it won't be long."

Nat, Nida, and Dempsey walked out into the atrium to wait, Nat gaping at the exotic surroundings while the adults examined them more critically.

"Have you ever seen anything like this?" Nida asked Dempsey, with a sweep of her arm.

Dempsey shook his head with dismay, "Never. This structure is unnatural. It doesn't belong in an Etom village, and I find it highly irregular that we didn't see a single Etom on our way in."

"I agree," Nida responded, "But if this place doesn't belong *here*, my question is 'Where *does* it belong?' We best stay alert."

Nat had wandered around the chamber, locating a climbing set of stairs off a shadowy corridor opposite the entryway.

He had his hand on the rail and a foot on the first step when Nida noticed his wandering, and shouted, "Nat! Get back over here!"

Besides the guards at the door, the doctor, and themselves, the place seemed deserted, but Nida didn't know *what* they might find within the alien structure. Calling her son over, the trio sat down on the stony benches around the tiny tree to wait.

Meanwhile, Doctor Scarsburrow had slipped on thin rubber gloves to examine Rae, who, out of dislike for the strange etém, involuntarily flinched from his touch as he reached for her. In another peculiarity, it seemed the doctor's distaste for the touch of another's skin had vanished, and his demeanor had grown more congenial as he began the examination.

When Rae recoiled, sitting up in the bed, Scarsburrow patiently and calmly clasped his hands behind his back and explained, "I am sorry, dear. We haven't even formally met. As you may have already overheard, I am Doctor Scarsburrow. May I ask your name, please?"

Kehren placed an arm around her daughter's shoulder while Tram patted Rae's leg to reassure her.

Timidly, Rae responded to Scarsburrow's much-improved bedside manner, "Rae. My name is Rae."

"Very nice to meet you, Rae," the doctor replied, and without any compunction, offered his hand in greeting.

Rae thought it strange to shake a gloved hand but was pleased to discover the doctor's grasp firm and convincing. He asked to proceed with the examination, and she relaxed, laying back in the bed while he checked her over and questioned them about Rae's injury and her condition since it had occurred.

Seeming satisfied, Scarsburrow put away his instruments as he finished.

Kehren, anxious to know the diagnosis, asked, "So? How is she? Will she recover?"

Chuckling with condescension, the doctor answered, "Yes. Yes, of course. She will be fine. Just a concussion after all. What she really needs is rest. Two or three days in one of our rooms upstairs should do it."

Tram, Kehren, and Rae were relieved to hear Rae would recover with such a simple treatment but were simultaneously alarmed at the prospect of remaining in Sakkan for such an extended period. Observing their apprehension, the doctor came close, Tram noting in his nearness the sickly creep of Blight beneath the doctor's crisp, white collar.

Scarsburrow asked them in a low voice, "Are you all quite safe? With the others outside, that is? It looks like you've been on the road quite a while. Are they forcing you along somehow?"

In imperfect concert the trio shook their heads, laughing in incredulity at the thought before Kehren responded, "No, doctor. They are about the closest friends we have outside of one another. They're family, even."

"Exactly," Tram agreed, reaching for the door. "We ought to tell the others Rae is going to be fine and discuss whether we can afford to stay and let her rest."

"Oh dear," the doctor interjected, his tone growing icy. "I'm afraid Rae's treatment is not optional. You see," Scarsburrow continued, peering at Tram through glowering brows, "I just couldn't live with myself if anything were to happen to her."

"Well, that's not *your* decision to make, is it?" Tram retorted defiantly. He opened the door, and called, "Dempsey, we need to get Rae out of here. Quick!"

Dempsey, Nida, and Nat had shot up from their seats the moment the door opened, eager to find out how Rae was. The urgency in Tram's voice quickened them further, and Dempsey was in the room helping Tram in a flash.

"What's going on?!?" Nida asked as they filed swiftly from the exam room on their way to the entrance.

Kehren cried, "He wants to keep Rae here!"

"He said we *must* leave her here," Tram continued. "For treatment, he says. But we don't get any say in it."

Doctor Scarsburrow meantime scuttled from the room to call after them, "You mightn't bother trying *that* way. You will discover it quite closed to you."

Nida confirmed Scarsburrow's declaration, crashing into the doors, and finding them locked. They, too, were metal, and they soon discovered them impossible to force. Their way was barred.

Panic threatened to scatter the company, but Nida, praying strength and wisdom, recalled the stairway, and urged the others across the atrium, the dear doctor snickering all the while in smug disdain. Nida hit the stairs first, running up them a few steps at a time, hoping to get far enough ahead of the others to forewarn them if she encountered resistance, or direct them if she found an escape route.

Tram and Dempsey did their best to keep up, but for Rae's safety, they could barely manage a jog up the stairs, slowing their overall pace as a group. Thankfully, Nat and Kehren at the rear detected no pursuit other than the doctor's cruel chuckles, which echoed throughout the chamber and up the stair.

At the front of their short column, Nida had arrived on the second storey at a long, broad walkway that curved around the chamber's perimeter. A rail ran alongside the side open to the atrium, and doors lined the other side every dozen steps or so. Nida bolted for the nearest door to try it, arriving to find it locked just as Tram and Dempsey reached the walkway behind her.

The locked door was the of the same black, metal as the exam room below, uniform in style but for a small window centered at eye level in the door.

More glass! she thought, shaking her head at the conspicuous opulence.

Curious, Nida shielded her eyes with cupped hands and peered through the window into the darkness beyond the door. So thick was the murk, she could distinguish neither form nor movement, and, sensing the approach of the others, was just turning away from the window when inches away from her face, something struck the glass with a muffled thud. Nida shrieked involuntarily with surprise as she fell back against the rail, yet recovered quickly, the greater horror now in identifying what she saw through the glass.

Pressed up against the pane was an etém's grimy face, contorted in anguish as he pounded on the door, his insulated shouts stifled against the impenetrable portal. Their whole company was stopped at the cell door now, each face a reflection of pity for the prisoner, and of repugnance at the doctor's cruelty.

Scarsburrow had followed their progress from below, and now taunted, "I see you've found another of my patients. They require *extensive* treatment, as do you all. No worries. I'll make certain you receive the highest level of care."

Nida's anger flared as she fired back, "We're not interested in your *care*. Now let us out of here, or we'll make you."

This last she said as she pressed past the others back toward the stairs, her hand on the hilt of her sword, and her intent to threaten the doctor's life if he would not release them.

Doctor Scarsburrow tutted gleefully, "Ah ah. You mustn't do *that*. It seems you'll need some persuasion to cooperate with your treatment."

The doctor stepped back toward the wall, and pounded it with a meaty, red fist. A panel hidden in the wall sprung open, revealing a lever, which he pulled. The ringing of bells erupted all around, freezing Nida in her tracks halfway down the stairs. Within seconds, several large etém dressed all in white burst into the chamber to flank the doctor.

Urgency became emergency as Nida reversed course up the stairs.

"Dempsey! Tram! Get moving!" she commanded. The pair instantly started around the walkway again, still carrying Rae.

"Check every door!" she barked at Nat and Kehren. "Maybe we'll find a way out!"

She joined her son and Kehren as they set to work, dashing door to door to test each handle.

"I assure you," the doctor called, "you will find no exit. Why don't you just come here for treatment? Why don't you just come take your medicine?"

Frustrated that his new patients ignored him, Scarsburrow waved his squad of orderlies after them, instructing them as they gave chase, "Please do not hurt them! Remember: 'First, do no harm!'"

Alone again in the sunlit atrium, the doctor approached the tree, reaching up to caress the leaves as he muttered, "Why don't they ever just accept my care? Why won't they just *take. their. medicine*?" He punctuated his last three words, stripping a healthy leaf with each word spoken. A bitter grimace twisted his face as he crumpled them in his hand, only to cast them fluttering to the ground.

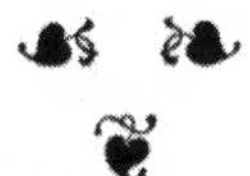

Finished searching the second floor, Nida, Nat and Kehren had yet to locate a single unlocked door and came flying up the stairs on Tram and Dempsey's heels. The etém yet bore Rae onward though they had reached the top storey of Scarsburrow's asylum, determined to stay as far ahead of the doctor's goons as they could. Dempsey carried the front of the litter and was first to see a ladder to the roof where stood flights of stairs on the lower floors.

"Tram, a ladder!" he shouted over his shoulder.

Within a few seconds, they were at the ladder. They set Rae down, then Dempsey was up it in a jiffy, pressing on the hatch he hoped would deliver them from this nightmare. Discovering the hatch would not budge, he looked for a latch, locating a short, thick lever to the side. Dempsey pulled on it fruitlessly until he noticed the small, round keyhole at the lever's base.

"Locked!" he shouted, as he pounded on it in frustration.

Tram looked up at his friend on the ladder, despair in his eyes. Nida, Nat, and Kehren soon joined them there, hunched over with hands on their knees as they puffed from exhaustion. Not one door had opened to them. Their pursuers were still a floor below, striding after at an unhurried pace, confident their quarry had no escape.

Out of ideas and with nowhere to run, they looked at one another forlornly as Nida walked over to the rail. They had reached the end of themselves, and it seemed no hope remained but for that they placed in Elyon. Taking her son's hand, she called them all together. Often had they gathered thus, hand in hand on their journey as they sought the way. Looking up into the light, Nida closed her eyes to offer up a desperate prayer, the others joining her to pursue the incomprehensible peace they'd come to know so well. Even with the sound of their would-be captors tramping up the stairs, their spirits touched the heavens in the knowledge of Him who would deliver them in the end.

Nida opened new eyes, the glare of the sun now difficult to bear as it glinted near the skylight's edge where it met stone overhead.

"What is that?" she wondered aloud, staring at the glowing thread.

Following her gaze, Dempsey almost whispered his response, "That, Nida, is a crack."

Sensing opportunity, Nida shouted orders to Nat and Kehren, "Your ropes! Tie them together! Now!"

Reaching inside her jacket, Nida produced her blade, calling for a loose end of the rope as she did. With practiced fluidity, she tied a knot around the hilt above the pommel and looked to see if Nat and Kehren had finished combining their lengths.

Satisfied that all was ready, she shouted, "Get back!"

The company hunkered against the wall as far from the rail as possible. Tram and Dempsey rolled Rae over facedown against the wall, and covered her backside with the overturned travois, while the rest shielded themselves as best they were able in anticipation of a piercing deluge. Nida flung the sword at the crack in the skylight overhead, holding the attached rope in the other hand, raising her other arm protectively and stepping back as the missile flew.

Flying true, the sword struck the gleaming seam with an anticlimactic "BONK!!!" that left the skylight overhead unscathed. Disappointed, yet undeterred, Nida began to reel the sword back up by the rope to try again. They were running out of time, and this was their last chance.

Their adversaries, meanwhile, had for the first time recognized the possibility of their prey escaping. Scarsburrow from where he stood below began shouting at his minions to hurry, his remonstrations futile and unheard in the continuous cacophony of the alarm bells. Goons though they were, the white-clad orderlies yet identified the need for urgency, and, already halfway around the chamber, increased their pace to a run.

Nida pulled up the sword, which, dangling, flashed in the rays shining overhead, and swung with greater frequency as she shortened its tether. Perhaps Nida was too forceful in pulling up the sword for another cast, perhaps not. What is certain, however, is that inexplicably, the knot around the sword's hilt–a knot she would have trusted her life to–slipped loose a mere arm's length below the walkway, just out of reach.

All eyes fixed on Nida's progress, Nat and her friends let out a collective groan from the rail where they stood while their antagonists cruelly cheered. Nida lunged past the lower rail to grasp the sword as it twisted down to stick in the loamy earth around the tiny tree below and might have fallen herself if Dempsey had not grabbed her jacket to pull her back up.

Together, Company Jasper looked up at the hairline seam in the skylight with disappointment, well aware they had nothing left equal to the task of shattering the glass ceiling. Their foes smiled smugly as they neared, and Dempsey prompted Tram to join him as he positioned himself between their assailants and the others. Everyone else was focused on the impending assault, and none but Nat took note of a flitting shadow that fell over them.

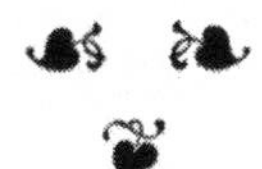

A small, blue butterfly alit on the crack in the skylight, and twitchingly fluttered its wings once or twice before departing as suddenly as it had come. No one else took notice of the creature, but Nat was grateful nonetheless, for in its parting, it left a gift: the crack, once almost imperceptible in its insignificance, now spread furtively, its web of ruin streaking forth in every direction.

Nat, a simultaneous desire to celebrate and warn the others at war within him, jerked Nida's sleeve with excitement as he jumped up and down, pointing toward their last hope, and exclaiming, "Mom! MOOOOOM!!! Look!"

So enthusiastic was Nat's gesticulation that every last Etom on the walkway looked, his mother and friends with joy, their pursuers with chagrin. Repeating their earlier drill from Nida's cast at the glass, Company Jasper ducked back, Rae pulling the litter over herself this time just in time for the entire skylight to explode in a shimmering cascade.

The moment Doctor Scarsburrow had seen the crack begin to radiate, proliferating throughout the skylight, he shuffled back toward his office, tucking himself in and closing the door just in time for the deafening crash of the glass, which was audible even over the persistent alarm. The orderlies on the walkway failed to react soon enough, and fared worse as they suffered in the stinging shower of ricocheting shards.

The way up and out now open, a refreshing breeze blew over the harried and hunted company, who, exulting in the triumph of the moment, nevertheless strove to escape. The edge of the now-bare stone lip on which the skylight had rested was directly over the walkway. Nida eyed the distance between the rail and lip, and determined a leap between them implausible, even for her. She looked around frantically for some means of achieving the escape that was now within grasp, her eyes landing on the travois that Rae had tossed aside after the skylight had fallen.

"Yes!" she exclaimed, then commanded Kehren, "Help me stand this up." The dustup had failed to take their pursuers entirely out of commission, and notwithstanding their numerous lacerations, the oafs collected themselves from the ground.

Dempsey and Tram yet stood in protective opposition to the brutes when Nida shouted to them, "Buy us as much time as you can!"

Miserable at feeling useless, Rae looked around for some way to help. Putting a hand down to prop herself up, she winced as sliver of the broken glass littering the ground cut her. Instead of self-pity, inspiration took hold, and she began to crawl around the walkway, carefully sweeping together the pointed shards around her into a pile.

"Dad!" she called, "Gather the glass so you can throw it! It will slow them down!"

Tram, recognizing the potential in Rae's idea, also crouched to collect the glass at his feet. Dempsey and Nat followed suit, and each soon had a respectable mound of irregular and razor-sharp transparent darts before them. Nat delivered his ammunition to the adults at the front line, then did the same for the hobbled Rae. As the goons came within range, Tram and Dempsey began pelting them with the sheer shuriken, discouraging their advance.

Nida and Kehren in the meantime stood the travois on end, its poles just shy of reaching the roof's edge. The litter's poles were sturdy, but Nida was uncertain if the knobby twigs would support an adult.

"Nat!" she called.

Her son reported instantly, "Yes, Mom?"

Taking him by the shoulders, she spoke quietly and deliberately, a tone reserved for only the most important of discussions, "Nat, I need you to climb up first and anchor the rope, so we can follow. Can you do that, son?"

"Of course, Mom," he responded, coming around to mount the rail for transfer onto the travois.

"Shall I?" he asked, pointing up with a carefree grin.

Nida nodded with pride. Nothing seemed to get her son down. She and Kehren supported the poles on either side as Nat clambered on with ease. Horrified, Nida imagined the travois losing balance and dropping Nat over the rail to plummet the three storeys to his death. She quelled the thought, concentrating on the task of stabilizing their makeshift pseudo-ladder while her son completed the climb.

The trickiest part proved to be right at the end, Nat maneuvering agilely to stand on top of the poles. His face serene, he balanced atop the crude stilts, took a breath, then leapt for the edge. His hands were iron claws grappling the lip, his legs dangling beneath him before he pulled them up, swinging both to one side to get a foot, then a knee and an elbow, then his whole body up over the edge.

Nida, Rae, and Kehren all watched in breathless anticipation until Nat summited the lip. Nida sprung into motion the instant he was up, however, grabbing the coiled rope from the walkway and tossing it up onto the roof. Her son's cheerful face poked out over the edge as he held up an end of the rope to demonstrate he'd gotten it.

"Good!" she shouted, relieved. "Now tie it off. Quick!"

"Nida?!?" Dempsey called. "We're running out of ammo here!"

He and Tram had depleted their stores, and Kehren had just brought them the meager last that she and Rae were able to collect. Scarsburrow's minions persisted in stalking them, advancing slowly, yet relentlessly through the shimmering hail Tram and Dempsey poured on. Holding meaty arms up before their faces, the brutes plodded forth, their heads down. Perhaps they grew numb to the piercing pain, but their shredded flesh told the tale of their determination. Whatever the reason, the orderlies pressed on, closing the gap.

On the roof, Nat quickly and calmly sought a substantial anchor for the climb out. On the outside cover of the nearby roof access hatch were two thick metal handles which would suffice. He walked to the handles, dropping to his knees and looping the rope through them. He tied a solid knot as quickly as he could, then speedily returned to the edge where his mother awaited him.

"Drop the rope to me, Nat," she called up.

Nat did as she asked, holding onto one end, just as their pursuers decided they had had enough. Dropping their arms, the foremost pair sprinted full-speed, crossing the span between the parties in a blink to tackle Tram and Dempsey. Both etém were tough and gangly from their months in the wild and put up a respectable fight. In the end, however, their adversaries were just too strong, too sizable, and too numerous to overcome. The second wave enveloped Rae and Kehren, leaving only Nida free.

Realizing there was no longer time for her own escape, she looked up at her darling son, and said, "I love you, Nat."

Then she threw the rope back up onto the roof, and in tears his lovely mother commanded, "Go!"

Then they were on her.

Nat cried out in his distress, "MOM!!!"

Brawny arms enveloped Nida from behind to pin her arms to her sides in vicelike constriction. Nida kicked back at her captor, flailing her feet viciously until another of the brutes caught hold of them.

Instinctively, Nat desired to protect his mother and friends, but stood powerless to aid in their escape. Without weapons and outnumbered, he foresaw any of his attempts to save them ending in failure. His valiant heart ached in helpless confusion while he tarried, unable to decide.

A meaty arm covered Nida's mouth as the goons dragged her away, until her teeth found bloody purchase in the available flesh, and her abductor pulled away from the bite with a holler.

Nida bucked against her captors and shouted to her son now her voice was free, "Go now, Nat! Hurry! FIND HIM!!!"

Nat, shocked at the sudden disaster that had overtaken them, stumbled back from the edge, the end of the rope still in hand. Stunned, he looked down at the rope in his grasp, then recalled his mother's final words to him. Though tears streamed down his face, he made not a sound as he obediently swept off the edge of the baneful tower, training taking over in the numb descent.

Instead of retracing their earlier steps in leaving Sakkan, Nat took the most direct route out of the accursed village to their broken camp, trampling through gardens and leaping fences in his reckless expedience.

No other hope remained but in completing the mission, and he intended to do just that. Once he'd located their gear, he haphazardly disassembled the packs to extract only the essentials for his journey, not forgetting to take a blade. Looking out on Sakkan with longing in his eyes, he vowed to free them all. Then he turned his back on the spited view to trek westward.

Chapter Twenty-Eight

Alone

Back on mission, Nat hiked straight through that first night alone, out of the oaken forest, over the river on the bridge of Men, stopping shortly after he'd scaling the rope they had left anchored at the precipice. Once he had surmounted the cliff, he left the hard, grey scrabble at the top, heading west into the underbrush as far as his legs would carry him before he collapsed, exhausted, in a heathy hollow. Thankfully, he slept a dreamless sleep, and no worry vexed his mind, a glow as of a firefly hovering dimly over his sleeping form.

Nat awoke to the noonday sun, the sticky heat of these higher climes intensifying his discomfort beyond his slumber's insulation. Finding appetite diminished in his unfeeling grief, he took little food, just a bite or two of hardtack, before continuing westward on his solitary quest.

He intercepted Company Jasper's old trail south of where they'd left it, laughing with wry humor as he considered the name: Company Jasper. It seemed *Company* Jasper was just him now, so it'd be up to *him* to keep himself company.

He laughed again, this time exclaiming, "That's funny!"

Speaking aloud to himself in the sylvan quiet echoed frightening apprehensions of madness, capture, and failure. No matter. He didn't need to speak loudly to hear himself, so he muttered a song, and whispered a tune, finding solace in his solitude until he came up a broken, blood-stained machete lying in the grass.

The sight of the blade brought bursting forth recollection of the past few days, culminating in the forceful abduction and imprisonment of those Nat held most dear. Overwhelmed in the overflow, his heart recalled its use. Falling on his face, he wept without control, convulsing in his sobs and drowning in his tears.

How long he lay, accompanied by a solitary ray of sunshine breaking through the canopy, is difficult to say. He arose late in the day, listless of spirit, yet resolved not to surrender in *this* place. This place whence misery had so much derived. Nat grit his teeth in determination to take *one. more. step*. Then another. And then another. Before he realized, he marched yet again, though twining, thorny thicket arose before him, desiring to entangle him.

Wielding his bantam blade, Nat struck out at the obstruction, cutting through to discover another. And another. And another, this time snagging limbs and blade in curling snarl. He struggled in futility, raging at his impotence, and losing his grip on the dagger, which slipped down into the inscrutable tangle, lost.

Nat hung there in the binding shade, whispering Lord Elyon send him just a ray of hope, or else deliverance from life. He closed his eyes in surrender, destitute of strength. And opening them, he saw shine clear a single, guiding ray. An opening now lay before him, once hidden from his sight. Relaxing, he felt his bonds grow slack as he ceased to fight. Crawling forth upon the ground, he passed beneath the hedge.

Arising now from prostrate stance, Nat beheld a Tree, impossibly ruined, yet strikingly vital, and emanating life to all conjoined. From the forking of its boughs gushed a sparkling stream, its gentle falls spreading to pool in reflective tranquility. The waters saturated the surrounding earth to form a shallow wetland, replete with bearded rushes sprouting up through glassy floor.

Struggling feebly to reach the gnarled and beautiful roots, he pressed on in the presence of a familiar, frightening goodness. He moaned, uttering unintelligibly his desperate cry for aid in grasping even a blade of the Tree's grassy hem. His feet tangled in wet, twining grasses, and he tripped into a puddle, short of his goal. He fell it seemed in slowing time, noting in horror his mirrored countenance in the water's surface. Two Stains, teary tracks, ran down his cheeks, a sign of the despairing, bitter grief that burdened him. The unfolding moment passed, and then he splashed headlong into the water.

A shivering spark passed through him as he crawled from the pristine pool. His weariness, departing heart and limb, drew together

Approaching the Kinsman's Tree

and poured out amidst fresh tears, crying forth in surrendered shudders the relief of an exonerated soul. A nearby frond, stirring gently in the breeze, dipped inevitably toward his hand, bowing graciously to graze his knuckles, once marred by passage through harsh underbrush.

Stretching forth his spotless hands, he viewed them with wonder, and turning back to the water, he met a face made immaculate in the reflection. Suddenly welcome in the presence of terrifying virtue, he gathered himself in new-found strength and charged full-speed with arms wide into the trunk, nearly knocking himself senseless. And there he collapsed, happy and sobbing against its bark as the wizened Tree bowed down over him in the wind, its branches curving toward him in seeming embrace.

Epilogue

He awoke in sheltered darkness, at first aware of his encapsulation, then of stifling warmth. The severity of his confinement became increasingly apparent to him as he discovered that he was unable to move any of his extremities but for limited movement of his hands.

Spurred by momentary panic, he felt around the inside of his enclosure, and, encountering a woody texture, struck out in an attempt to shatter his breathy prison. Curiously, he sensed his enclosure sway as he contemplated his failed attempt to break free.

With all the strength he could muster, he rocked back and forth, pressing his hands against the walls in concert with his efforts as his swings grew in length and intensity. He swayed violently to one side, then the other, noting that he did not tumble, his head apparently affixed to the inside of his mysterious pod, before hearing a sharp "snap!" at the apex of his swing. For an instant, he experienced floating, which quickly became falling, as he plummeted in darkness, eyes wide and hands pressed out, braced against the inevitable . . .

Look for
The Æglet's Answer*, Book 2 of *The Kinsman's Tree Series
Available Now

Endego

The Anvil

The Bunker

Nat & Nida's

Potter's Arch

The Temple

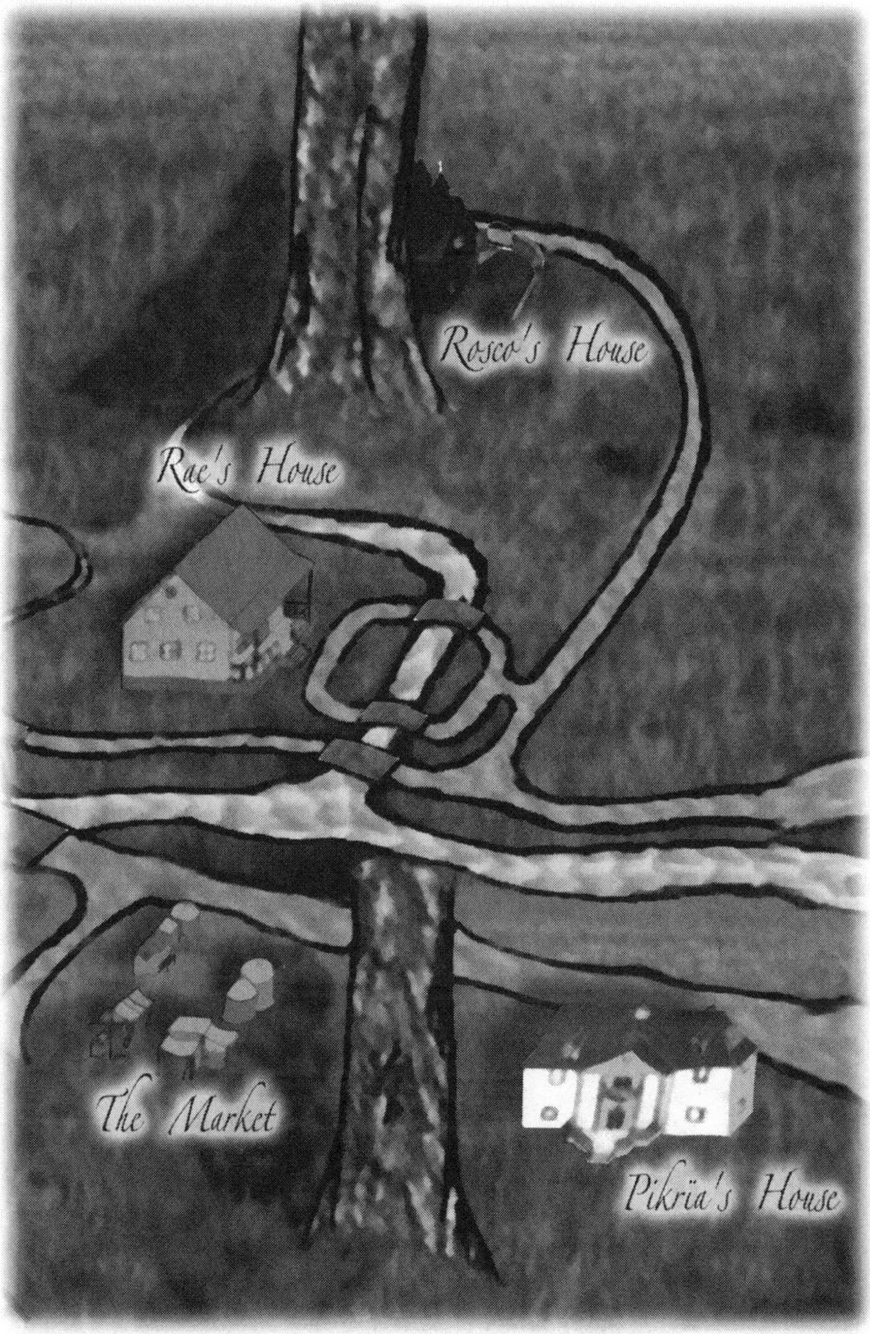

Rosco's House

Rae's House

The Market

Pikrïa's House

Author Biography

Timothy Michael Hurst continues to pursue God's call and is working hard to finish *The Kinsman's Tree* series by summer of 2019. He holds a bachelor's degree in Foreign Languages and Literature from the University of New Mexico, and currently resides in New Mexico with his wife and four children.

In the author's own words:

"I am a writer who believes that the life lived best is lived in service to God and that only under the guidance and power of the Holy Spirit one might produce a worthwhile work. I seek to craft entertaining, enriching, and inspiring tales that glorify the Lord in confidence that the Holy Spirit will use them to change lives and draw people closer to Jesus Christ.

In simply offering myself in surrender to the Spirit, I have discovered the satisfaction of worshiping the Lord as an instrument of the writing process. I believe my experience be confirmation of God's calling on my life and pray that each and every person is as deeply transformed in reading these stories as I was in writing them. To Him alone be the glory."

– Timothy Michael Hurst

Breadcrumbs

A Kinsman's Tree Vignette

TIMOTHY MICHAEL HURST

A Note from the Author

Welcome to "Breadcrumbs" a vignette from *The Kinsman's Tree* series! I hope you will enjoy this short work that I developed alongside my first novel in the series. However, after some intense review, it was decided this part of *The Kinsman's Tree* story didn't fit within framework of the novel.

Nevertheless, I determined that my hard work in developing the misfit chapter would not go to waste, and being something of an emotional packrat, I couldn't bear to part with it. So here we stand, at the junction of sentimentality and utility, to bring you what I believe is a delight, short jaunt through the past lives of several noteworthy Etom of Endego.

For those not yet familiar with the world of *The Kinsman's Tree*, you will see the introduction of these characters with eyes opening to survey for the first time the world of these wee and colorful beings. Etom are quite small, maybe three inches tall, and these live beneath the shelter of Endego's many willows.

For those already acquainted, I anticipate gasps of recognition and nods of comprehension as you view the Etom you know in new light. Each of them has grown quite dear to me, and I hope you feel the same.

Some of you may wonder, "Why the title 'Breadcrumbs?'" Well, drawing on many a fable, I saw this as an opportunity to lay many such "crumbs" in your path to lead you back to the greater story of *The Kinsman's Tree,* and answer some questions that might arise in reading the novel. Now, without further ado, I present to you, "Breadcrumbs!"

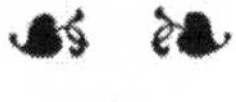

Breadcrumbs

Breadcrumbs:
A Kinsman's Tree Vignette

Pikrïa in the flower of her youth knew grace and beauty in the incomparable blessedness of the family wealth. In truth, a life more charmed was unknown within the borders of grove Endego. And thusly showered in the season of her life's spring, sprinkled with blessing, many good things sprung up from the soil of her heart: courtesy, dignity, courage, and influence, to name a few. However, as is often the case among those of substantial means, benefits unearned deposited alongside the favorable seed that of self-importance, albeit constrained to languish among the good that blossomed there.

When Pikrïa had reached the appropriate age, a steady flow of suitors sought her hand, and the competition among them grew fierce, for to claim as wife the solitary daughter and heir to the fortune was quite a prize indeed. While Pikrïa enjoyed the attentions of her numerous suitors, none of the well-to-do etém calling at the gate caught her eye. It instead would be an artisan's son who drew her attention.

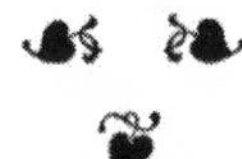

One spring morning, Pikrïa accompanied her father, Savaal, to the clockmaker's shop, which rested beneath the boughs of Endego's sole olive tree, where he hoped to commission a custom timepiece. The clockmaker had an impeccable reputation for second-to-none craftsmanship. His work was very much in demand, so it was with some trepidation that Savaal approached.

As a rather impatient etém used to getting his way, Savaal loathed a delay. He'd come anticipating one and was nonetheless prepared to offer a price well above fair to ensure his order was completed at once.

Savaal burst into the shop, the bell over the door complaining with a loud clank at his forceful entry. Pikrïa followed her father, crossing the threshold demurely. Her face, a deep amber color, was just visible as she peered from beneath the brim of her feathered hat. The shop was dimly-lit and depended almost altogether on the springtime sunlight pouring through its storefront windows for illumination.

The space was marked by a sense of busy, cluttered industry. It was nevertheless tidy in that the wood shelves and clock cases were dust-free and oiled to a muted shine. The glass display cases sparkled, and the floor was well-swept. To the left, several grandfather clocks huddled together, their pendulums swaying in solemn metronomy as they chimed in time. Hanging from and adjacent wall and stalwart post, a cluster of cuckoos crowed merrily in seeming protest of their neighbors' gravity.

Among the dissonance, Pikrïa yet discerned a deliberate synchronicity in the timepieces. As each second ticked and moment tocked, she heard their unified beat as of a heart. She listened hard to hear a hitch yet perceived no such arrhythmia. Instead she fell into a trance, her own heart's beating counting out in time with theirs.

Interruption caused her breath to catch, when from the doorway behind the counter a young voice called. "Be with you in a moment!"

"Please be quick about it!" Savaal responded curtly, "We'd prefer not to be kept waiting."

A young Etom of gray complexion came bounding from the back room, wiping his hands on a grimy rag as he approached.

With a humorous twinkle in his eye, he responded, "Certainly, sir! If we understand one thing here, it's the value of time!"

He wore a plain linen smock that at one time had been white, though now it bore a number of dark stains where his rough apron did not cover.

Having wiped hands clean to his satisfaction, he offered one in greeting, "My name is Shoym. At your service!"

For a moment, Savaal stared at Shoym's hand in open disdain. Then, reconsidering his chances of receiving his order speedily, he shook young Shoym's hand, a subtle and unconscious sneer contorting his mouth as he did.

Savaal abode the unsavory contact for a fleeting moment, then addressed the youth, "I am Master Savaal, young sir. I've come to commission a timepiece. One of those new pocket watches that are all the rage right now. I trust you're familiar?"

"Absolutely, Master Savaal!" Shoym responded with enthusiastic sarcasm. "I believe you'll find these samples of our work to your liking," he said, pointing to a row of pocket watches displayed behind a glass case in the counter.

A finery of gold and silver lay nestled in the shallow, plum velvet trench beneath the glass to display the clockmaker's obvious skill in filigree, engraving, and relief on the pocket watch encasements. Perhaps a dozen of the watches was present, and the clockmaker had selected a variety of case styles for to showcase the versatility of his craftsmanship.

Several of the more common open-face watches rested there, the stylish work on their bezels reflecting the artisan's creativity, while more ornate designs covered the lids on the hunter-case watches.

"Ah! Here's one in an older style, pair cased." Shoym lifted one especially weighty-looking watch off the end of the row to show them.

At first glance, it appeared a simple open-face watch, but thicker, until Shoym opened the outer case to remove a smaller case set within.

"The outer case protects the watch from dust and such, while the inner case contains the movement. You can see the small opening here on the back for the winding key."

Savaal responded, "These are all very nice, but I'm looking for something particular. In gold, of course. Like a hunter-case, though with a clever, circular 'window' in the case to show the movement of the hands beneath. I'd like to see the dial on the outside of the case, so I can read it without opening it."

"I know just the style, Master Savaal!" Shoym answered. "Demi-hunter it's called, and it's quite rare in these parts."

Frustration furrowing his brow, Savaal enquired, "Are you telling me you can't do it, then? I thought your shop was best in the grove!"

"Now just a moment, sir!" Shoym retorted, "I never said we couldn't manage it. Just that it was rare in Endego. It's not a matter of skill, but of supplies. If you want quality that will endure, we'll need specialty items for the outer dial. Give me a moment, please, and I'll check with my father in the back."

Savaal consented with a sneer, "Yes, of course. And please do be quick about it, youngster."

Shoym slipped from sight into the back room, and a few moments later, snippets of murmured conversation drifted their way.

Savaal turned to his daughter to offer with condescension, "It's exactly this manner of provincial nonsense that I cannot abide. You do well that not a one of your suitors is this kind of riff-raff."

Pikrïa nodded, uncertain. When her father was in such a mood, which was often, it was best just to agree with him.

"Merchants! Artisans!" he sniffed. "What would they do without the nobility?"

Savaal looked around the shop in contempt, and answered himself, "Languish in even greater squalor than this, I imagine."

Unbeknownst to her father, who was absorbed in his diatribe, Pikrïa cocked an eye in question, again noting the spotless state of the clockmaker's shop. Besides some disorder due to the lack of space in the very crowded showroom, she failed to see that which her father deemed tantamount to squalor. If anything, the quality of the goods spoke for themselves, and she admired the obvious care with which they were created. They doubtless manifested greater skill than she or her father possessed.

A strange thought occurred to her, *I wonder if that's why he hates them so? Jealousy?*

She dismissed the notion out of respect for her father. The passing hypothesis regardless clung to her mind thereafter, only to recur in instances of ever mounting evidence in the affirmative.

Shoym returned, and a proud grin upon his face revealed his expectation to please the grumpy new customer.

Pikrïa noted the enthusiasm with which he approached and felt sorry at his gleeful anticipation. *I wish you well, Shoym. My father is a difficult man to please.*

Savaal barked, "Well then? Can you do it, or do I need to take my business elsewhere?"

"Master Savaal, I have spoken with my father, our master clockmaker, and he assured me that we have the supplies on hand to complete your custom timepiece. We will be happy to add your order at the cost of 300 grains. Quite a bargain, I might add, and we'll have it ready for you within a fortnight!"

Pikrïa recognized her father's cold, still stare for the danger it was, and, light as a butterfly, placed a gloved hand on his arm in attempt to calm him.

"Now listen to me," Savaal seethed, his normal, clay-colored features heating to that of fresh-fired brick as he tossed his daughter's hand aside.

He paused to peer about with scorn, "We've come down to your...your shop at some inconvenience to myself and my daughter with the expectation we'd be served in a manner appropriate to our station. Do you know who we are? That we need even associate with rabble such as yourself in the conduct of our business is disgrace enough, and now you're telling me our order is dead last in the queue? A fortnight?"

Pointing over at the clocks on the wall, he shouted, "I care not if some common *bumpkin* receives their cuckoo on time! I could buy this shop and every other under this tree! Now go tell your father that I want my watch by the end of the week, and I won't pay over 200 grains for this quaint handicraft!"

Pikrïa hung her head, embarrassed at her father's outburst, and peered out from under her hat, anticipating Shoym's crestfallen shock.

To her surprise, the clockmaker's son maintained his grin, though acerbic amusement was now apparent in his tone as he answered, "My apologies, sir. I believe you misunderstand. It is our policy that orders placed first are those first completed, barring any delay we may experience while awaiting the arrival of supplies. We believe our policy is a fair one and know a great number of *bumpkins* who agree with us."

Shoym continued, "Just look around the shop, sir. The disarray is not for display purposes, however rustically charming it may seem to your nuanced sensibilities. *We. are. busy.*"

"And if you must know, I am my father's foremost apprentice. He plans to pass the entire enterprise on to me and has already given me discretion regarding which orders we take and at what price."

"Therefore, to prevent any further disappointment on your part, I have decided to refuse your order, and bid you a good day!"

As he finished, Shoym pointed at the door with an open hand to dismiss them from the shop, while in Pikrïa's direction he offered in gentler tones, "I must apologize, miss. I wish our meeting could have been more agreeable. Perhaps you might visit us another time? Alone?"

"How dare you speak to her!" Savaal snapped, appalled that this low-born filth would have the gall to refuse him and then make overtures toward his daughter.

Savaal stood trembling in mute rage before grabbing Pikrïa by the hand to storm out the door. He grumbled gratingly as they went, loud enough for Shoym to hear.

But the young etém responded with infuriating cheer, "Good day, sir!"

Forgetting in his provocation that the shop door opened inward, Savaal collided with it at full force when reaching to push it open. Pikrïa barely managed to stop in time to avoid a collision with her father. She was right on his heels, however, and reversed course to give her father space to pull open the door.

Shamefaced, she looked over her shoulder to back up, catching from the corner of her eye a wink from the still-smiling Shoym. In the relative quiet of the shop, she heard only their awkward scuffling and the singular, steady beat of the clocks. Tick. Tock. Tick. Tock.

Savaal yanked open the door, this time loosening the bell from its fixture to fall with a jangle to the wooden shop floor. His momentous exit a complete failure, Savaal departed with a baneful look, spitting some unintelligible curse over his shoulder on the way out.

Once more, Shoym called in chipper response, "And a fine evening to you, too, sir!"

Her embarrassment knowing no present bounds, Pikrïa hitched her skirts and minced over the threshold, eyes wide and wincing as she escaped further mortification.

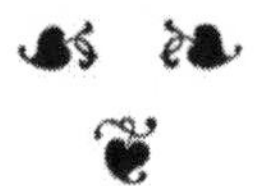

Savaal seethed in silence the entire journey home. Pikrïa knew better than to disturb him in the stifling silence, and thus held her tongue. A paradox, her father's explosive anger was most treacherous when the turbulent waves of agitation ceased. The surface calm signaled tranquility while in murky, crushing depths lurked a spiteful leviathan, eyes bright and open in the dark to await its opportunity to burst forth suddenly from its den.

His malice lashed round with grasping coils to seize captive its quarry, and heavy under animus, slip back beneath the languid sheen to plunge its prey in pulverizing, unrelenting fate.

Pikrïa retained the record of Savaal's varied contentions with rivals and antagonists alike. A witness she remained to the plots of their demise. Reminded of her father's goaded antipathy, she now, for Shoym and his enterprise, feared her father's calculated reprisal.

A word between them yet unspoken, Pikrïa and Savaal parted company at the stairs ascending from the foyer – he to his study on the main floor, and she to her bedchamber upstairs. Since the death of Pikrïa's mother several years past, a chill had come to occupy the home's vast and open spaces. A vigorous and sociable woman, Pikrïa's mother had once adorned the manor with life and warmth and had produced in Savaal a tenderness to combat his blunt abrasiveness. In matters of her daughter, she had ever stood an advocate, a bulwark to withstand Savaal's demanding rage.

Without her mother's love to shield her any longer, Pikrïa relied now on the safeguard of distance for protection. Until the door had latched behind her, her face remained an impassive mask, so afraid was she to reveal any reaction to the events of the day. She remained concerned for Shoym and his family, yet beneath anxiety another sentiment surfaced.

Humiliating as her father's behavior had been, she wished Shoym the best regardless of his response to Savaal. Upon reflection, Shoym's mirrored good-will toward her grew clearer. If anything, the pity he'd shown embarrassed all the more. For Savaal's daughter she was, and her pride abode no sympathy from inferiors such as he, yet absent from his gaze had been anticipated reproach. Just simple, honest kindness met her eyes when, in memory, she glanced once more over her shoulder before stepping out the door.

Within his tender eyes, her brittle ego broke, fragmented under the gentle blow that after caught each fragile piece. Collapsing headlong on her bed, she thrust her face into a pillow, resolved that above all else, her wailings remain unheard. It was on her bed of tears that regret first bloomed from seed sprouting among the thorns of her own foolish pride.

Over passing months, fondness for the young watchmaker grew within Pikrïa as sun-soaked memory shone upon his countenance. Her heart made arguments two-fold against Savaal's prohibitions: Shoym's courageous opposition to her father's bullying, and his kindness toward her amidst the rebuke. Oft-revisited in Pikrïa's recollection, Shoym's actions stood illumined as stained glass stationed over the chambers of her heart.

It was an autumn afternoon in Endego's bazaar, the sun lowering in the west to set the grove's leafy panoply of gold and orange aflame. When by sneaking, sudden chance, they crossed each other's paths, Pikrïa's amber visage glowed with favor under Shoym's cheerful, kindly smile.

"Good day," he spoke in gentle words, with no trace of irony.

"Good day," she managed.

Shoym shifted the bundle over his shoulder, glancing around before returning his focus to her. "I don't see your father about. Should I be concerned?"

Pikrïa snickered. "No. No. I am unaccompanied today. A relief for us all, I imagine."

In seeming impossibility, Shoym's smile broadened. "Then I'm glad to have you to myself for a moment."

His steely features fell serious and plaintive before he continued, "Mistress Pikrïa, I must apologize for causing you distress when last we met."

Shaking her head in disbelief, Pikrïa absolved him, "Master Shoym, my father's anger and impatience were the only cause for distress that day. Both mine and yours. I should beg instead your pardon. My father was altogether unreasonable, and I admire your courage..."

Pikrïa fell silent at the slip of her tongue, her cheeks blushing bourbon. She hadn't intended to gush so.

Shoym, recognizing her embarrassment at the revelation, with grace accepted her apology, and ignored the rest in his response, though he deemed it too crucial to forget.

Rather, he changed the subject, inquiring, "Do you visit here often in the afternoon?"

Pikrïa smiled knowingly as she answered, "Not often."

Shoym, somewhat disappointed at the news, nevertheless pressed on, "I should very much like to see you again, Miss Pikrïa. If you would like."

"Well, I was thinking I ought to exercise more regularly. Perhaps a walk this Friday afternoon would do me some good?"

"I, uh...I hear the weather will be unfavorable this Friday," Shoym hinted. "Maybe Saturday afternoon would be better for a stroll."

Pikrïa mulled the decision over before agreeing, "Saturday would be a fine day for a walk. I imagine I'll pass this very spot right after lunch."

Getting back underway, Shoym winked at her in play. He steadied his burden with a shrug and wished her a wonderful evening and a pleasant stroll on Saturday. Disappointed at his sudden departure, but pleased at his discretion, she offered half a wave as he disappeared into the market crowd.

They met as planned on Saturday by calculated happenstance, both pleased to amble about Endego's many paths among the underbrush. Shoym implicitly understood their need for secrecy, and their budding romance flourished even as Nature fell dormant. Beneath the grove's naked trees, they strode hand-in-hand through autumn, concealed among the mouldering mounds of fallen leaves.

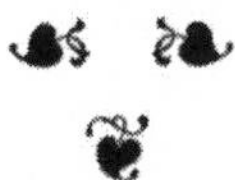

The winter struck with bitter fury, and scathing winds whistled between frequent flurries. The weather proved inhospitable to the blooming courtship, stripping it bare of stem and flower, though roots remained untouched beneath the hoary land.

Desperate to see his beloved, Shoym ventured across the winter waste during a lull in the storm, hoping that, through frosted pane, he might catch a glimpse of her. Skittering atop wind-glazed snow, he arrived at her home, surveying the substantial grounds in the blanketed silence. The tops of the skeletal hedges bordering the estate were just visible through the deep snow, and a heavy drift lay half-way up the mansion's eastern end, where a lazy curl of smoke drifted from a chimney.

There! he thought. *I might reach her from the drift.*

The expanse provided no cover for his approach, so Shoym doggedly advanced across the ice-encrusted snow, unconcerned with being spotted. Without event, he arrived at the base of the sloping drift, stopping to catch a foggy breath before attempting the slippery climb.

Having never visited Pikrïa at home, he was unfamiliar with its layout, and took his time at the bottom of the drift to assess his options. A nearby window on the second floor glowed with promise and offered a ledge broad and deep enough it might support him. He decided on the window as his destination, hopeful he'd find Pikrïa on its other side.

Shoym started his way up the side of the snowbank, sliding down the slick slope several times before developing an effective strategy to tackle the climb. With his sturdy boots, he kicked holes in the snowy crust to make footholds. Then, standing in the footholds, he balled his gloved fists up and punched handholds in the embankment. Using his hands and feet, Shoym crafted holds as he ascended the side of the icy drift, climbing until he had reached the level of the window he'd set as his goal.

Up close, the stretch from the snowbank to the window's ledge seemed greater than it had, and Shoym hesitated, uncertain he could reach it. Remembering their shared devotion, Shoym took heart, and leapt sideways along the wall, extending a leg and arm to catch the window's sill and jamb, respectively.

It was a narrow thing, and Shoym almost missed his footing on the icy windowsill, but he steadied himself with his hand, and, using his momentum, succeeded in pulling himself across. There he stood, nervous and spread-eagle across the window as he braced himself against its frame. A thin scrim of frost on the window obscured his view of the room beyond, though he concluded his silhouette would be visible to any who might glance his way.

In care and quiet, Shoym used the heat of his breath to melt a patch of the frost, then wiped it clear with a corner of his scarf. In the biting cold, his porthole soon began to frost over afresh, but through it he saw the blaze of a fireplace to his right and could make out a hazy figure seated before its hearth, across which lay an iron poker.

Repeating the melting procedure with greater vigour and ambition, Shoym cleared a larger patch. The seated figure grew more distinct, now identifiable as an Etom covered head to toe in a thick, burnt-orange blanket, and bent forward into the fire's heat. Shoym continued to wipe the frosting glass, looking for any sign that it was Pikrïa who warmed herself inside.

Shoym imagined her initial shock when he revealed himself with a tap at the window. In his daydream, Pikrïa approached with frigid caution, until she recognized him, and in her joy all inhibition melted away. He'd be with her again in a heartbeat.

A hand reached forth to grasp the poker, a bulbous ring standing forth pronouncedly from burly knuckle.

That's not Pikrïa! Shoym perceived with fear. *It's Savaal!*

The lovers' fate turned upon a tiny thing – a momentary, surprised slip as Shoym registered the figure's identity. He caught himself before he fell, his boot banging against the window. Startled, Savaal turned sharply toward the sound, his brow furrowed in indignation. An etém stood outside his window, in distinct outline against the pallid frame.

Savaal advanced, poker in hand, as he confronted the intruder. "Who is it?!? What are you doing here?!?"

Shoym sought escape, looking to the drift at his right in preparation to jump. *I can't let him see who I am!*

Shoym's feet slid on the icy windowsill as he tried to gain the purchase necessary for his leap away. Before he was able, Savaal swung the window wide, pushing Shoym back as he without success grasped for the open frame. Shoym plummeted to the ground, its level raised by the deep snowfall, and his backside punched a hole through the icy shell. Beneath its frozen top layer, the snow was powdery and readily surrendered beneath Shoym's weight, folding him in half with arms and legs pointed skyward. He was stuck.

Savaal glared down at him from the open window, poker yet in his furious grip, before he muttered as if to himself, a note of curiosity sounding over the symphony of rage swelling beneath, "You. I know you...don't I?"

With a shrug, Savaal tossed the shroud from his shoulders, and stalked away from the window. Shoym correctly deduced that he was on his way down and struggled to extract himself from his frosty predicament. Driving back toward the ground with his legs and heels, he lifted his hips from the hole, hoping to raise himself high enough to roll to one side or the other. His plan might have worked, but the brittle crust, weakened by his impact, yielded under the press of his legs. His body entire fell beneath the surface, and he landed again on his sore hindquarters with legs splayed before him.

The size of the hole he had created afforded now enough freedom of movement he was able to stand. Panicked that Savaal drew near, he propped his elbows on the edge, and began to wriggle out, cautiously spreading his weight as best he could to prevent another collapse. Shoym's back was to the door of the manor, but his ears detected the creak of its opening, and the crunch of rapid footfalls as doom drew near.

At last surmounting the hole's edge, Shoym rolled onto his back with hands up in defense as he pleaded for mercy, "I'm sorry! I'm sorry! Please don't hurt me!"

"Shoym!" Pikrïa exclaimed. "Why ever would I hurt you?"

Happy surprise replaced Shoym's distressed grimace, and he, in wonderment, replied, "Pikrïa?"

Looking up at the open window, and then down into the hole, she understood what had transpired.

Shoym sensed her concern, and sprang to his feet as he announced, "I'm alright. Not hurt a bit."

She ran to him and embraced him, sobbing, "I'm so happy to see you. I've missed you."

A whispered shuffle caught their attention, and both looked up to find Savaal standing, shaken, a few steps off. Still in his hand was the fireplace poker, and he wore a bathrobe over his pajamas and a pair of slippers upon his feet. Vexation and perplexity warred beneath his brow, before pitiably he asked, "Wha – What is this?"

"I love him, father," Pikrïa entreated from within Shoym's embrace, and from the sky, a snowflake fell to warn of the impending squall.

Savaal ignored his daughter, and instead pointed the iron prod as he leveled his accusation, "I know you. You're that clockmaker's son. And with my daughter!"

Shoym released Pikrïa and stepped away from her with hands held out before him as he appealed to the older Etém, "Please, sir. I truly care for your daughter. For Pikrïa. If you'll ju –"

"I knew it," Savaal interrupted, taking a step toward Shoym. "I knew you had eyes for her."

"Father," Pikrïa spoke, inserting herself between the two. "Please just let him leave. He's done no harm."

Snow, carried sideways on a blasting wind, stuck to their clothes as it began to fall in earnest.

"No harm!" Savaal scoffed, in pointed ire thrusting his club at Shoym as he continued, his voice rising. "You come here, skulking like a thief to break into my home, and hoping to plunder MY DAUGHTER!!!"

He lunged for Shoym, swinging his weapon wildly at the younger Etém. The hooked prong of the poker caught in Shoym's thick pant leg, tearing it and the flesh beneath as Savaal recoiled for another vicious stroke. Shoym fell back, and without delay rolled to one side as he scrambled to regain his footing. Pikrïa threw herself on her father's arm, determined to stop his assault. Glowering at Shoym, Savaal stood motionless while Pikrïa clung to him.

Though winded in his excited state, Savaal spoke in a low, measured voice, "It seems this time *I* have something *you* want. But you're not good enough for our kind, and you never will be. Begone! Before I slay you here, as is my right to do with thieves come to take my property."

With imploring eyes, Shoym looked to Pikrïa, who shook her head and silently mouthed one word, *GO!*

Shoym struck his thighs with his fists and gave a pained, primal cry before he fled. Only once did he look back at her, longing in his gaze. Then he was gone into the shifting white of the winter storm, leaving Pikrïa alone with her father, embroiled in a storm of their own.

In the prolonged and embattled negotiations between Savaal and Pikrïa that followed, he made two things clear. First, she was never to contact Shoym again, and second, he regardless intended to bring Shoym and his family in Endego to utter ruin.

To prevent Shoym's destruction, Pikrïa spent in the transaction the solitary coin available to her–if her father desired she stay away from Shoym, she would do so only under his solemn oath that he not harm Shoym or his family. Grudgingly, Savaal accepted her terms, preferring the indignity of thwarted revenge over that of intermingling with their house with the lower class, and Pikrïa bore her heartbreak with a dignity that bespoke her station.

In time, Pikrïa came to accept her loveless existence as a fact of noble life, as incontrovertible as the changing seasons and the march of time. And, indeed, time marched on, the many years leaving behind the young, well-bred Etma who had lost in a gamble on love in exchange for a lonely, aging heiress.

After her father died, Pikrïa's solitude intensified until her uncle returned from afar to settle back in Endego. He was a kinder man than Savaal, and younger by two decades. He brought home a wife and a daughter from distant northern climes. The Etom of Endego considered both mother and child exotic in appearance, for the mother was bright lavender accented with blushes of sunny yellow, and the child, Nida, was fuchsia with distinctive black markings.

Until she met the precocious lass, Pikrïa hadn't acknowledged her own deep longing for children. She delighted in Nida, who was a lovely child, brilliant in body, mind, and soul. In the knowledge that she'd never bear her own children, Pikrïa informally adopted Nida, requesting only that she call her "Great Aunt." Though they were in reality cousins, the title "Great Aunt" better suited the distant gap in their ages, and all accepted it without complaint.

It was well that Pikrïa took to Nida so, for in a tragedy of sweeping plague, Nida's mother and father both fell, as did countless others in the village, and Nida came to live with Pikrïa. For a season, warmth and joy returned to the massive home, for Nida inspired Pikrïa to revisit a life lived heretofore only in memories of her long-dead mother. Dances and promenades filled the parlours and salons with laughter, conversation, and society. And Nida received her share of suitors, all of whom Pikrïa approved, eager to enjoy the children befitting surrogate grandmotherhood.

In time, Pikrïa noticed the flood of Nida's courters slow to a trickle before stopping altogether. Nida was not forthcoming when questioned about the shortage of suitors, though her nervousness betrayed something distantly familiar to Pikrïa. Out of concern, Pikrïa inquired in her circles to see what she might find. With a little effort, she discovered Nida had turned down all her suitors, rendering herself an inviable prospect.

Her curiosity whetted, Pikrïa confronted Nida in the foyer of their home, "Nida, dear, what is going on? I've just come from high tea with the mothers of several of your suitors. They informed me that you had rebuffed every one of their sons."

Nida didn't dare an open lie and chose rather to remain silent.

"Answer me!" Pikrïa insisted. "What was wrong with them?"

Exasperated, Nida exclaimed, "Nothing! Nothing was wrong with *them*. They just weren't right for *me*."

"Well, who would be, then?" Pikrïa asked. "You've met every eligible bachelor in Endego."

"Not every bachelor," Nida muttered.

Only half-hearing Nida, Pikrïa cocked an inquisitive brow while she unraveled the enigma.

With a muted gasp, she understood, and nodded her head subtly before she spoke, "Who *are* you seeing then, dear Nida?"

Nida, having stepped onto the first step of the staircase to flee further inquiries, swung around, momentarily flabbergasted at the accuracy of Pikrïa's guess.

Discerning she had been found out, Nida divulged her secret, "Fine. If you must know, his name is Jaarl, and we are in love."

Cutting to the chase, Pikrïa inquired, "I've never heard of this Jaarl. Who are his father and mother?"

"No one you know, I'm sure," Nida replied. "His father is a carpenter, and he's teaching Jaarl the trade, too."

"And this, this carpenter's son is why you refused your other suitors?" Pikrïa asked incredulously.

"I am committed to Jaarl, and our courtship has become quite serious," Nida answered.

At first, Pikrïa was shocked, but remembered her own youth, and recovered in short order to discuss the matter practically, "You can't be serious, Nida."

Nida responded, "I honestly expect him to propose any day now."

Putting hand to head, Pikrïa turned away in weary, troubled thought. In the heartache following her coerced separation from Shoym, Pikrïa had abdicated her identity to the mores of upper society bit by bit.

Though social sensibilities might separate her from the one person in the world she truly cared for, Pikrïa couldn't bear to jettison the principles that had come to define her. If Nida chose Jaarl, then Pikrïa would no longer have anything to do with her.

Though now long-dead, Savaal's expectations yet echoed in his daughter's mind, prompting her to scoff at Nida's fanciful infatuation as she reminded Nida, "You represent a highborn house of Endego. Our house. As it was mine, your duty is to the family, regardless of your feelings."

"Our love is real," Nida protested adamantly. "It is not simply feelings."

Adopting anew the impassive mask behind which she'd so often hidden in her father's presence, Pikrïa attempted one final gambit, which, on its face, was meant to salvage Nida's social standing. In her most secret heart, however, Pikrïa wished desperately to prevent their estrangement.

She stated, matter-of-fact, "I will not support your decision, Nida. Jaarl cannot properly provide for you, nor will I give a penny toward establishing your home if you marry him."

With determined fire in her eyes, Nida answered, "When he proposes, I intend to say '*Yes*.'"

With confident strides, Nida ascended the stairs to her room, and Pikrïa recalled her many like journeys to escape her father in fear. She detected no such fear in Nida. She accepted Jaarl's relative poverty, and the improbability of upward social mobility if she married him yet persisted in her devotion to him. The youthful relationship bore all the hallmarks of "true love," a sentimental notion that Pikrïa's disappointed affair with Shoym had rendered absurd in her reckoning.

Pikrïa envisioned the remainder of her life, alone but for the company of crones likewise shackled in bitter obligation. An icy flurry, memories of that winter's day, flew into her mind, and long-restrained resentment broke forth as an avalanche, crushing what remained of her soul's hope.

Now moving to the darkened study, Pikrïa begrudged her father his brute temper, his heavy expectations under which her will had buckled to the detriment of love. Society, too, now vexed her, its every fawning flattery profaning authenticity. She despised herself for cowardice, the inability to choose boldly in the face of consequence. And last, she hated Nida for her uncompromising courage – for choosing what she hadn't dared. Though her face did not betray her rage, Pikrïa perceived the leviathan's creep within her own heart, and pleasured in it.

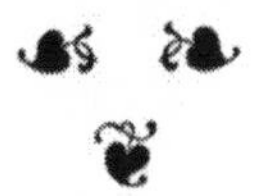

Made in the USA
San Bernardino, CA
26 November 2019